"If you're looking for a heroine who'll stand out from the rest, give this latest of Ms. Martin's books a try. Kathryn's dilemma will tug at your heart from the opening line, and just when you think you know what will happen next, you find out you're wrong. I loved every page! Never a dull moment, and a most entertaining read." —*Interludes*

NIGHT SECRETS

"A tender, emotional tale . . . Kat Martin combines salt spray with the ballrooms and bedrooms of Regency England to create the ideal atmosphere for her characters' adventures . . . NIGHT SECRETS incorporates sensuality and mystery with a strong love story and a colorful backdrop." —*Romantic Times*

"Lots of energy and adventure . . . The writing is crisp and clear, and the characters are larger than life." —*Booklist*

"A whirlwind that pulls the reader into a romance filled with heartache, deception, and passion. Kat Martin can always be depended upon to produce a story that is a 'can't-put-down.'" —*Rendezvous*

WICKED PROMISE

"Conflict dogs the steps of the protagonist while tension keeps the reader alert. Humor is like icing on a cake in this delightful tale." —*Rendezvous*

DEVIL'S PRIZE

"Tempting, alluring, sensual and irresistible—destined to be a soaring success." —*Romantic Times*

"Kat Martin is a premier historical romance author . . . and DEVIL'S PRIZE enhances her first-class reputation." —*Affaire de Coeur*

BOLD ANGEL

"This medieval romance is a real pleasure . . . the romance is paramount." —*Publishers Weekly*

"BOLD ANGEL moves quickly through a bold and exciting period of history. As usual, Kat has written an excellent and entertaining novel of days gone by."
—Heather Graham

"An excellent medieval romance . . . Readers will not only love this novel but clamor for a sequel."
—*Affaire de Coeur*

HEARTLESS

KAT MARTIN

St. Martin's Paperbacks

HEARTLESS

Copyright © 2001 by Kat Martin.

All rights reserved. No part of this book may be used or reproduced in any manner whatsoever without written permission except in the case of brief quotations embodied in critical articles or reviews. For information address St. Martin's Press, 175 Fifth Avenue, New York, NY 10010.

ISBN: 0-312-97944-4

Printed in the United States of America

St. Martin's Paperbacks edition / May 2001

St. Martin's Paperbacks are published by St. Martin's Press, 175 Fifth Avenue, New York, NY 10010.

10 9 8 7 6 5 4 3 2 1

To my editor, Jennifer Enderlin, who helped me so much on this book. Thanks for the input, support, and just plain fun.

CHAPTER ONE

Oh, if I could only be like you. Crouched behind the hedge-rows along the lane that led to magnificent Greville Hall, Ariel Summers watched the ornate black carriage roll past, the top down, the earl's gilded crest gleaming on the door. Seated on red velvet squabs, his daughter, Lady Barbara Ross, and her companions laughed as if they hadn't a care in the world.

Ariel stared at them with longing, imagining what it might be like to dress in such beautiful clothes, gowns fashioned of the finest silk, in shades of pink, lavender, and an almost iridescent green—each with a small matching parasol.

Someday, she thought wistfully.

If she closed her eyes, she could imagine herself in a gown of shimmering gold, her pale blond hair swept up in dazzling curls, her slender feet encased in matching kid slippers. *Someday I'll have a carriage of my own,* she vowed, *and a different gown for every single day of the week.*

But it wouldn't happen today, she knew, giving up a dispirited sigh, nor anytime in the foreseeable future.

Turning away from the disappearing carriage, she lifted her coarse brown skirts above her sturdy shoes and raced back toward the cottage. She should have been home an hour ago. Her father would be furious if he found out what she had been doing. She prayed he was out in the fields.

Instead, when she lifted the leather curtain that served as the door of the cottage, Whitby Summers was waiting. Ariel gasped as her father painfully gripped her arm and slammed her against the rough-textured wattle-and-daub wall. Forcing herself to look into his puffy, florid face, she flinched as his big hand cracked across her cheek.

"I told ye not to dawdle. I said for ye to deliver that mendin' and get back here as quick as ye could. What were ye doin'? Gawking at the ladies in their fancy carriage? Ye was daydreamin' like ye always do—wasn't ye? Wishin' for somethin' yer never gonna have. It's time ye faced the truth, gel. Yer nothin' but a cottager's daughter and that's all ye ever will be. Now get yerself out in those fields."

Ariel didn't argue, just ducked away from the fury she read in her father's flushed face. Outside the cottage, she dragged in a shaky breath and shoved her pale blond braid back over her shoulder. Her cheek still burned from her father's painful slap, but it had been worth it.

As she hurried across the dusty earth toward the vegetable garden, her apron flying up in the wind, Ariel stubbornly set her chin. No matter what her father said, someday she *would* be a lady. Whit Summers wasn't one of those fortune-tellers she had seen last year at the fair. He couldn't see into the future—especially not *her* future. She would make a better life for herself, escape the dreary existence she now lived. Her destiny was her own, and somewhere beyond her father's dismal patch of ground she would find it.

For now, with her mother long dead, Ariel worked from dusk till dawn. She swept the earthen floor of their two-room cottage and cooked the meager fare that was all the small rented plot of ground could provide, gathered potatoes, pulled turnips, worked at hoeing and weeding the vegetable garden, and helped her father in the wheat fields.

It was a dreary, backbreaking, endlessly dull existence that she intended to escape. Ariel vowed it with every ounce of her being.

And she had a plan.

As he did once each month, Edmund Ross, Fourth Earl of Greville, spent the day inspecting his fields and checking on his tenants. It was hotter than usual today, the sun a scorching white orb burning down across the earth and baking the rutted roads to the consistency of granite. He usually preferred riding one of his blooded stallions, but today, with the weather so warm, he took his light phaeton instead, hoping the top would provide a bit of shade.

He leaned back against the tufted leather seat, grateful for the slight breeze blowing in from the north. At forty-five, with his olive skin and silver-tinged wavy black hair, he was still an attractive man, especially popular with the ladies. In his youth, he'd had more than his share—as heir to an earldom he could pick and choose. But as he'd grown older, his tastes had subtly changed. Now, instead of the skills of a practiced lover, he preferred the tenderness and exuberance of youth.

Edmund thought of his current mistress, Delilah Cheek, the young woman he kept in London. Delilah was the daughter of an actress he'd once known in the biblical sense. He had been sleeping with Delilah for over a year, and her young, tender body still excited him. Just thinking of her small, firm breasts and long coppery hair made him hard. At sixteen, when he had first taken her, the girl had been a virgin. Since then, he had taught her well how to please him.

Still, she was reaching her maturity, her body ripening past the slender, almost boyish curves that enticed him, and soon he would grow tired of her. He would yearn for the youth and beauty of an innocent, the way he always did.

God's breath, it was a troublesome predilection.

His mind slipped backward to the days of his youth, and a foul word hovered on his breath. He'd been wed at nineteen, an arranged marriage that had produced only bitter memories of a cowering, frigid wife, long dead now, and a beautiful but worthless daughter, not the son and heir he needed.

Of course there was his bastard son, Justin, that spawn of the devil he had sired with Isobel Bedford, the daughter of a local squire. Isobel had been wild and beautiful, as reckless and hedonistic as he. He might not have believed the boy was his, but the physical resemblance—and the enmity between them—was irrefutable proof of the deed.

As the phaeton turned down the dirt lane that led to his tenant, Whitby Summers's, cottage, Edmund's thoughts swung briefly to Delilah and how he would use her young body when he returned to the city. But at the sight of Whit's fair-haired daughter, just turned fourteen, his interest focused in a different direction. Ariel was tall for her age, her body reed slender, not yet budding into womanhood. Still, the signs were all there. With her long flaxen curls, big china blue eyes, soft, bow-shaped mouth, and heart-shaped face, the girl was destined to be a beauty.

When he came to visit, he was unfailingly kind to her. She wasn't ripe enough to suit him yet, but Edmund always liked to keep the doors to opportunity open.

Ariel watched the earl's sleek black phaeton roll up in front of the house. She had known he was coming. The earl always came to visit on the same day of the month.

Checking her appearance, she smoothed her plain blue skirt and clean white blouse, freshly washed last night for the occasion. Unconsciously she rubbed the welt on her thigh where her father had taken a switch to her. She'd been flirting with Jack Dobbs, the cooper's youngest son, he had said. It wasn't the truth. Jack Dobbs was over-the-top for Betsy Sills, the butcher's daughter, Ariel's best friend, but when Whit Summers had been drinking, as he was last night, the truth didn't matter.

And in a strange way, Ariel was glad it had happened. It was the final nudge she needed to set her long-thought-out plan into motion.

The carriage rolled up in a swarm of dust. The earl set the brake and jumped down. He was handsome, she supposed, with the silver in his thick black hair and those odd gray eyes, at least for a man of his aging years.

"Mornin', milord," she said, making him a deep, respectful curtsy. She had been practicing for days and was pleased as she executed the difficult maneuver that she didn't lose her balance.

"Indeed it is a fine morning, Miss Summers." His eyes ran over her in that admiring way he had. It made her feel like a woman instead of just a girl. "Where is your father this fine day?"

"He had an errand to run in the village. He musta forgot you was comin'." And Ariel hadn't bothered to remind him. She had wanted him gone so she could talk to the earl alone.

"I'm sorry I missed him, but I suppose it doesn't matter." He glanced out across the fields, his expression warm with approval. "I can see the crop is faring well. If the weather stays good, you ought to bring in a very good harvest this year."

"I'm sure we will." The earl turned away from her, started back toward his carriage, but Ariel caught his arm. "Excuse me, milord, but there's somethin' I been wantin' to talk to you about."

He smiled as he turned to face her. "Of course, my dear. What is it?"

"Do you . . . do you think I'm pretty?" She thought that he did, since he always seemed to stare at her in that strange, assessing way, but still she held her breath. Her plan was doomed to fail if the answer was no.

A slow, appreciative smile curved his lips. He studied the shape of her mouth and the line of her jaw, let his eyes drift down to her breasts. She wished they were round and full like Betsy's.

"You're very pretty, Ariel."

"Do . . . do you think a man . . . someone like yerself . . . do you think—in a few years, I mean—that a man like you might be interested in a girl like me?"

Lord Greville frowned. "There are different kinds of interest, Ariel. You and I are not from the same social circles, but that doesn't mean I wouldn't find you attractive. I believe—in a few years' time—you'll grow into a beautiful young woman."

Her heart kicked up with hope. "If that is so, I was

wonderin' . . . I've heard stories, milord . . . about the ladies you keep in London."

The frown reappeared, mixed with a look she couldn't quite read. "Exactly what sort of stories have you heard, my dear?"

"Oh, nothin' bad, milord," she hastened to assure him. "Just about the girls . . . that you treat 'em real good and buy 'em pretty dresses and all."

He didn't ask where she'd heard the tales. It was common knowledge in the village that over the years the earl had kept a number of young women as his mistresses.

"What exactly are you asking me, Ariel?"

"I was hopin' maybe you and me could make some sorta bargain."

"What sort of bargain?"

It all rushed out in a single long breath, as if a dam had suddenly broken. "I wanna be a lady, milord—more than anything in the world. I want to learn to read and write. I wanna learn to speak right and wear pretty clothes—and put up me hair." She swept the long mass up on her head to demonstrate her words. When she released it, it tumbled back down past her waist. "If you would send me to school so's I could learn all those things . . . if I could go to one of those fancy finishin' schools where they teach you to be a lady, then I'd be willin' to be one of yer girls."

She watched the surprise in his eyes turn to speculation, rather an unholy gleam, she thought, and felt the first faint stirrings of trepidation.

"You want me to pay for your education—is that what you're saying?"

"Aye, milord."

"And in return, you would be willing to become my mistress."

She swallowed. "Aye."

"Do you understand what that word means?"

A beet red flush stole into her cheeks, as she knew it meant sleeping in the same bed with the man. What else it might entail she wasn't completely sure, but it didn't really matter. She was willing to pay whatever price it took to escape her father and her wretched life on the farm. "Mostly, milord."

He studied her again, his pale eyes raking her from head to foot. She felt as if he were stripping away her clothes piece by piece, felt the ridiculous urge to fling her arms up to cover herself. Instead, she endured his scrutiny and stoically lifted her chin.

"That's a very interesting proposal," he said. "There is your father to consider, of course, but knowing him as I do, perhaps something might be arranged that he would find satisfactory." He reached down and caught her chin, turned her face from side to side, studying the hollows beneath her cheekbones, the slight indentation in her chin. He traced a finger over the curve of her lips, then nodded as if in approval.

"Yes . . . an interesting proposal indeed. You shall hear from me soon, my dear Ariel. Until then, I suggest you keep this conversation between the two of us."

"Aye, milord. That I will." She watched him climb into his carriage, watched him slap the reins against the backs of his glossy black horses. Her heart was beating fiercely, her palms slightly damp.

Excitement pumped through her, the knowledge that her plan might actually succeed. Uncertainty followed close on its heels. Ariel couldn't help fearing that in return for the chance at a better life she might have just traded her soul.

CHAPTER TWO

"He is arrived, my lord. Shall I see him in?" Stoop-shouldered and gray-haired, the butler, Harold Perkins, stood just inside the door of the Earl of Greville's massive bedchamber in his country estate, Greville Hall.

"Yes, with all haste, if you please." Edmund struggled to sit up a little straighter in the bed, reached out a shaking hand to grip the glass of water sitting on the nightstand. Water slopped over the edge and onto his bed jacket as he worked to carry it to his lips, and a footman who stood nearby hurried over to help him.

He took a drink and waved man and glass away just as the door swung open and Justin Bedford Ross, his newly adopted son and heir, ducked his head beneath the jamb and stepped across the threshold of the room.

"You wished to see me?" The deep, penetrating voice had an eerily familiar ring. Justin didn't approach the bed, just stood at the foot looking tall and dark and completely forbidding. There was no doubt the man was his son. He had the same high cheekbones, the same lean, broad-shouldered build as Edmund's own, the same long-lashed, black-fringed eyes, though Justin's were a darker gray, without a hint of his mother's pale blue.

"The paperwork has been . . . completed," Edmund told him. "You are now legally . . . my son and heir. In a very short time . . . so the physicians tell me . . . you will become the next Earl of Greville."

The bitter thought sent a spasm of pain coursing through him. Edmund bent forward, coughing fiercely into the handkerchief he pressed against his trembling lips. He wiped away a trace of saliva mixed with a pink tinge of blood. By God, he never thought it would come to this, that he would be forced to pass his fortune, his legacy, to the man who hated him beyond all reason.

Then again, he hadn't expected to die for at least a dozen more years.

Justin said nothing, just stared at him from behind the blank, unreadable mask of his coldly handsome face.

Edmund drew in a shaky breath. "I called you here because there is some . . . unfinished business I wished to discuss. A personal matter. . . ."

A finely arched black brow went up. "Personal? Interesting. . . . I would presume, since we both know your penchant for the fairer sex, that you are speaking of a woman."

Edmund refused to look away from that penetrating stare. "Not exactly, though she will become one soon enough." He coughed again, a racking spasm that made the veins stand out on his forehead. Silently he damned the lung disease that was slowly but surely killing him. Recovering himself, he lay back against the pillows, his face the same white hue. "She is my . . . ward, of sorts."

Edmund motioned to the footman, who stepped forward to place a bundle of letters within his reach. Edmund rested the stack on his chest, lifted the one on top with an unsteady hand, and gave it over to Justin.

Long dark fingers opened the sheet of foolscap, and Justin scanned the letter, putting to use the expensive Oxford education Edmund had paid for. He might not have claimed the boy until he'd been forced to, hadn't given the lad the slightest thought over the years, but had never abandoned his financial obligations to the child or its mother.

Justin glanced up. "You are seeing to the girl's education?"

He nodded. "And anything else she needs."

Justin's smile was hard and mocking. "I never realized what a benevolent soul you were."

Edmund ignored the sarcasm. "We had a bargain of sorts." He went on to explain the pact the two of them had made, sparing no detail, forcing himself to meet the disdain in his son's iron gray eyes. "Ariel was fourteen when she went away to school. She is sixteen now. Her father was a tenant of mine. He drank himself to death last year." He sucked in a breath of air, let it wheeze out of his lungs. "I leave it to you . . . what to do with her."

Justin stared down at the letter, what appeared to be the first of a series the girl had written. The letterhead stated simply: "The Thornton School for Girls."

Lord Edmund Ross, Earl of Greville

Dear Lord Greville,

I send to you my good wishes. As this is my furst attempt at penning a letter, I hope that you will overlook any mistakes I make. I would have writtin sooner, but I have only just learnt enough to attempt the task. Still, from this day forward, at least once each week, I shall take pen in hand and do my best to relay my acheevements.

Justin read the balance of the letter and handed it back to him. Edmund studied his face but couldn't discern a single trace of what his son might be thinking. "What will you do?" he asked.

Justin gave a noncommittal shrug, lifting those broad shoulders so much like his own. He was dressed in a black coat and dark gray breeches, the white of his fine lawn shirt a stark contrast to the darkness of his skin. "You gave your word. If I am earl, I will respect your pledge."

Edmund just nodded. For some strange reason, a feeling of peace crept over him, and he settled more comfortably against the pillows. Unconsciously his hand came to rest on the stack of letters. He had read each one a half-dozen times.

He hadn't seen the girl in more than two years, had never really known her. And yet he felt close to her in a way he couldn't explain. When had Ariel Summer become so important to him? How had he grown so fond of her? It was the letters, he knew. Each week, he found himself looking forward to them. He had never answered even one of them, wouldn't have had the slightest notion what to say. Yet as he had fallen more and more gravely ill, they had brought a bit of sunshine into his fading world.

Perhaps making Justin his heir had been the right thing to do after all. At least his Ariel would be protected. His son might despise the father he had never known, but Justin was a man of his word. The lad had graduated from Oxford with the highest marks. Since he had reached his majority, he had prospered in the world of business, and though he had a reputation for being ruthless in his dealings, he never made a pledge he didn't keep.

"Will that be all?" Those cool dark eyes found his. Though Edmund lay dying, there wasn't a trace of pity in their chilling depths.

"Yes. . . . Thank you . . . for coming."

Justin made a slight bow of his head, turned, and started for the door, his elegant long-legged strides carrying him away without a moment's hesitation.

A shudder slid through the earl's pain-racked body. He might have made the girl his mistress, but he would never have mistreated her. He strained to listen to the hollow, echoing footsteps retreating down the hall.

For the first time, it occurred to him that the bargain he had made with Ariel Summers might also appeal to his coldhearted son.

CHAPTER THREE

Lord Edmund Ross, Earl of Greville

Dear Lord Greville,

It is a fine day here in the Sussex countryside. The trees have leafed out and the sky is the clearest, most startling color of blue. Unfortunately, by necessity, most of my time is spent indoors. The tutors you have arranged are very fine indeed, though they are difficult taskmasters. Still, I am determined. I study late into the evening, then rise several hours early to begin anew the following day. Reading has become my favorite pastime. In the beginning, it was difficult, but oh, what wonderful doors it has opened! There are novels and plays, incredible poems and sonnets.

I vow, such a gift is, in itself, worth the price of our bargain.

Justin Bedford Ross, Fifth Earl of Greville, read the letter he had pulled from the stack he kept locked in the bottom drawer of the desk in his study. He had read them all more than once, some with faint amusement, others with a trace of pity, an emotion he rarely felt.

After his father's death, from the day Justin had moved into the old stone mansion in Brook Street, he had been inexplicably drawn to the innocent ramblings of the young woman his lecherous father had intended to make his whore.

Justin's jaw tightened at the image of the earl that rose into his mind, a licentious, arrogant man who thought only of his own selfish needs. He couldn't help feeling a shot of satisfaction at the odd turn of fate that had made him his father's heir. For most of his twenty-eight years, his father had ignored him. As far as Edmund Ross was concerned, Justin Bedford was simply a costly mistake, a bastard spawned off one of his numerous whores.

Two years ago, gravely ill and dying, he had sent for Justin and offered him the single thing the earl could give him that he could not refuse.

The legitimacy of his name.

Even the lure of the Greville fortune and the power and prestige of an earldom would not have been enough to entice him. It was the name that he had wanted, the name he had yearned for since he was a boy. Justin had accepted his father's offer of adoption, becoming Justin Bedford Ross, because he would no longer be the bastard son who had been laughed at and scorned for as long as he could remember.

He leafed through the stack of letters, drew out another, and scanned the page:

My studies continue. By necessity, before I left my home in Ewhurst, I had learned to work a bit with numbers, enough to help my father sell his crops and livestock at market. Here I have studied at length the Young Ladies New Guide to Arithmetic *and have become quite accomplished at mathematics. History is another subject I enjoy, especially learning about the ancient Egyptians, Romans, and Greeks. I can't believe the women actually went about half-naked!*

His mouth edged up. Justin folded and replaced the letter in its proper order in the stack. As he had promised, he had kept his father's bargain, struck with Ariel Summers more than four years ago. The girl was now beyond eighteen and ready to leave Mrs. Penworthy's School of Feminine Deportment, the expensive finishing school he had arranged for her to attend.

A thousand times since he'd become earl, he had tried

to imagine what she looked like. Beautiful, he was sure. His father had always had exquisite taste in women. He wondered if she was dark or fair, tall or short. He hadn't the slightest notion about her appearance, and yet, through her letters, he felt he knew her better than anyone he had ever met.

He wasn't sure what he would do about her, now that her education was complete, but the girl was an innocent, someone his father had taken unfair advantage of, and he felt responsible for her in some way. She had no family, no one to see to her needs. Whatever decision he made, he wouldn't do as his father had done to him and abandon her.

Reaching out, he picked up the white-plumed pen on his desk, dipped it into the inkwell, and scratched out the first words he had ever written to her, instructions for her to follow when she departed the school.

He would send the Greville carriage to transport her to his house in London. He had business to attend to in Liverpool that could last as long as several weeks, but upon his return they would discuss the future. He signed it simply: *"Regards, the Earl of Greville."*

It occurred to him that it was scarcely proper for a young woman to be living in the residence of an unmarried male, but he cared nothing for the rules of convention and he wasn't about to put himself out any more than he already had. He would supply her with a lady's maid, one who knew, along with his other servants, the wrath they would suffer if they were anything less than discreet.

Justin reread the letter he had written, used a drop of wax to close it, and imprinted it with the Greville seal, the image of a hawk swooping down on a hare. He rang for a footman, who came on the run, gave him tuppence, and instructed him to post the letter.

Ariel left the bedchamber she had been given in the Earl of Greville's town mansion and hurried down the wide stone staircase. She had been living in the city for nearly two weeks, each day since her arrival more exciting than the next. She was in London! London! There was a time she never would have believed it.

It was still hard to accept the changes that had taken place in her life in four short years. She had a thorough education, could read both Latin and French, and speak as well as any member of the nobility. She dressed in fashionable clothes and traveled about in Lord Greville's expensive black carriage, though in truth, she hadn't yet ventured far. Of course, the house was nothing at all as she had imagined, nothing like the earl's magnificent country estate, Greville Hall.

Instead it was dank and dreary, built of thick gray stone and heavy timbered wood, a massive structure at least 200 years old, with smoke-blackened rafters and not enough windows. No wonder the earl had spent so much time in the country!

Still, she was in London, on the road to fulfilling her dreams. And though, deep down, there were times she still felt like the ragged cottager's daughter she truly was, there was no place on earth she would rather be.

Dressed in an apricot muslin day dress sprigged with white roses, a narrow frilled underskirt, showing merrily beneath the hem, she tucked a strand of pale blond hair into the ringlets swept up on her head and walked through the door of the Red Room.

She grinned when she saw her best friend, Kassandra Wentworth, seated on a burgundy velvet sofa. "You came! Oh, Kitt, I wasn't sure you would." Her friend stood up, and the two girls hugged.

"You really didn't think I would come? Don't be silly— I could hardly wait to see you. It took a bit of doing, I'll admit. My stepmother would scarcely approve of my visiting you in the home of an unmarried man."

"I suppose not."

"Your note said the earl hadn't yet returned from his business trip."

"Not yet."

"What will you do when he does?"

Ariel worried her bottom lip and sank down on the edge of the sofa. "Talk to him. Try to make him understand. I realize he has spent a goodly sum of money in the past four years, but surely I can find a way to repay him."

Sitting beside her, Kitt rolled eyes a brighter shade of green than the gown she was wearing. "You can repay him, all right—in about a hundred years." Kitt was shorter than Ariel and less slenderly built, with fiery red hair and an irreverent, saucy smile. She was the youngest daughter of the Viscount Stockton, a widower in his fifties who had married a woman just a few years older than his daughter.

Ariel fidgeted, plucked at the folds of her gown. "Perhaps the money won't matter. Once I explain that at the time we agreed to the bargain I didn't really understand exactly what it entailed, I don't think he'll be unreasonable. He's an earl, after all, and extremely wealthy. If he wants a mistress, he can have any woman he pleases."

"He wants you, Ariel. That's why he agreed to your insane proposal in the first place."

Ariel's gaze shot to Kitt's face. "But the man hasn't seen me since I was a child. He doesn't even know what I look like."

Kitt pointedly studied Ariel's blemish-free complexion, fine features, and silver-blond hair. "Well, he won't be disappointed, rest assured."

Ariel stared down at her lap, her chest feeling suddenly tight. "I gave him my word. Whatever happens, I am bound by it. I shan't break the vow I made unless he releases me from it."

Kitt sighed, knowing that when Ariel made up her mind there was little chance of changing it. "You said in your letter you had met someone. Maybe he can help."

Ariel smiled brightly, her glum thoughts instantly fading. "Oh, Kitt—I can hardly believe it. It was an accident, pure and simple, a miracle—or destiny, perhaps—that we chanced upon each other the way we did. It was a lovely day and the house is not far from the park. I decided to go for a walk and there he was."

"There who was?"

Ariel grinned. "My prince charming, of course. He is blond and fair, quite possibly the handsomest man I've ever seen. His name is Phillip Marlin. He's the second son of the Earl of Wilton."

Kassandra tried to recall Marlin's face, whether she had met him somewhere in the past, finally gave up, and shook her head. "The name sounds familiar, but I don't think I know him. Perhaps my father does."

"For heaven's sakes, you mustn't mention him to your father—at least not until I've worked things out. Phillip doesn't know anything about my past or why I am here. He thinks the earl is a distant cousin."

Kitt scoffed, "From what you've told me, Greville plans to know you far better than that."

Ariel ignored her. "Phillip and I have been meeting in the park each morning. Yesterday he took me for a ride in his carriage."

A frown creased Kitt's brow. "Do you think that's a good idea? You don't really know anything about him."

"I know all I need to know. Oh, Kitt—I think I'm falling in love with him."

"In little more than a week?"

"You've heard of love at first sight, haven't you?"

"Yes, and I'm not convinced there is any such thing."

"Well, I believe there is and I'm certain that Phillip does, too."

Kitt reached over and caught her hand. "You may have learned a lot of things in Mrs. Penworthy's school, my dear, but you don't know tuppence about men. They'll say anything—do anything—to get you into their bed."

Ariel felt a slow burn creeping into her cheeks. "Phillip isn't like that."

"Just be careful," Kitt warned. "I'm far more worldly than you. I know from experience how deceitful a man can be."

There was something in her friend's voice that said more than her words. Ariel wasn't sure what had happened to

Kitt, but it was obvious she hadn't completely got over it. Ariel wanted to ask what it was, but she wasn't sure her friend would tell her.

"When are you leaving for the Continent?" Ariel asked instead, opting for a change of subject.

"The end of next week. First they send me to a boarding school miles away from home. Now they're shipping me off to a cousin in Italy." She sighed and shook her head. "My father's only doing it to please his wife. He knows Judith and I don't get along."

"I wish you didn't have to go." Ariel would miss her, the single friend who knew the truth of her past and never made her feel the least bit self-conscious about it.

"I'm scarcely eager to leave." Kitt squeezed Ariel's hand. "Just remember what I said about men. And that applies to the earl as well as Phillip Marlin."

Justin Ross, Earl of Greville, leaned back against the tufted leather seat of his carriage and picked up the several-days-old copy of the *London Chronicle* he had retrieved that morning at the inn. He had concluded his business in Liverpool several days early, a financial matter that involved the building and financing of a new fleet of ships, and, of course, there was the small matter of the bankrupt textile factory he had purchased for a fraction of what it was worth.

He had resolved his business exactly in the manner he had wished and was now on his way back to London. As he thought of the houseguest who would be waiting, it surprised him to discover how much he looked forward to the meeting.

In the past few years, aside from the challenge of increasing the Greville fortune, which he had substantially managed to augment in the two years since he'd become earl, there was little out of the norm that happened in his well-ordered existence. Perhaps that was the reason he had become so intrigued by Ariel's letters. Each week, when one of them arrived at the house, for a brief instant in time a faint ray of light crept into his dark, cynical world.

He had read every letter she had ever written and looked forward each week to the next. Now, before the day was through, he'd be arriving at his house in Brook Street and their long-anticipated meeting would finally commence.

He tried to imagine her face, but no suitable image arose. The vibrant young woman in the letters seemed nothing at all like the other women he had known: hedonistic, self-centered creatures like his mother or the featherbrained females of the *ton* who wanted nothing from a man but the coin in his purse and the power of his name.

Ariel was different. She was the embodiment of honesty, purity, and innocence. She was—

Justin frowned, wondering where his ridiculous notions about the girl had come from. He was no longer the lost little boy who cried in the night for the mother who had abandoned him or the naive young fool who'd been crushed by his sweetheart's betrayal with another man. That person no longer existed, hadn't for a good many years.

The man who returned this day to London knew from brutal experience that honesty, purity, and innocence were qualities that simply did not exist.

CHAPTER FOUR

Laughter drifted up from the open black carriage as it rolled through Hyde Park. A man's deep voice joined with the lighter, crystalline tones of a woman. The ground still shimmered with the last of an early-morning mist, and though the breeze blew steadily, a warm sun beat down through a scattering of clouds, brightening Ariel's apricot parasol and Phillip Marlin's tall beaver hat.

"My dearest Ariel." He captured a white-gloved hand and brought it to his lips. "With the wind in your hair and the blush in your cheeks, you look like a princess."

Ariel flushed and lowered her lashes, hoping to shield the effect of his words. As she had done each day, she had met Phillip that morning in the park. He was tall and fair, his hair a shiny golden blond, the image of a London aristocrat. Though he wore his clothes with a casual air, they were cut of the finest cloth and perfectly tailored to fit his square-shouldered frame.

"You flatter me, sir." Ariel toyed with a strand of long blond hair that had escaped from beneath her bonnet. "The wind is blowing. I probably look a fright. You are simply too gallant to say so."

" 'The southern wind doth play the trumpet to his purposes, and by his hollow whistling in the leaves foretells a tempest and a blustering day.' "

Ariel laughed at the quote she recognized as being from Shakespeare's *Henry IV*. " 'We shall be winnowed with so rough a wind that even our corn shall seem as light as chaff, and good from bad find no partition.' "

Phillip smiled with pleasure at the sally. "You are a delight, my sweet Ariel. I am a fortunate man to have found you."

Ariel said nothing, just allowed herself to bask in the rays of Phillip's adoration and listen to the sound of his matched bay horses clopping along the lane. But the clouds overhead began to thicken and grow dark, and the breeze kicked up even more. When thunder rumbled in the distance, Phillip turned the horses toward her home.

"We'd better hurry," he said. "It's going to start raining any minute."

The wind blew leaves around their feet as Ariel took his hand and they rushed up the steps of the big stone mansion in Brook Street. She wasn't exactly certain how it had happened, whether it was his idea or hers, but a few seconds later Phillip stood beside her in the entry and it seemed he would be staying to tea. She remembered he had asked if her cousin was yet returned and she had told him with a shake of her head that he was not due for another two days.

She flashed a brief smile at the butler, a man named Knowles, whose expression remained as blank as a clean sheet of paper.

"Mr. Marlin will be joining me for tea in the Red Room," Ariel informed him airily, having discovered that all you had to do to gain a servant's obedience was pretend that you deserved it. "Will you see to it, Knowles?"

Scarecrow thin and balding, the man gazed from Ariel to Phillip and back again. This time, there was no mistaking the disapproval on his face. He merely lifted his bushy eyebrows and said, "As you wish."

Working to suppress a smile, Ariel took Phillip's hand, led him down the hall and into the Red Room, guiding him over to a sofa in front of the fire.

The tea arrived a few minutes later, and Ariel poured, saying a silent prayer of thanks that she had learned the social graces necessary to move in Phillip's world.

He took a sip from the gold-rimmed cup she handed him, his eyes, the blue of pretty Delft china, moving slowly over her face. "I cannot begin to tell you how much I have enjoyed these days we've spent together."

Ariel rested her cup and saucer back down on the table. "I've enjoyed them as well." It *had* been fun, being wooed by a handsome man, the son of an earl, no less, trying out her feminine wiles for the very first time. In the beginning, she had been self-conscious—Phillip was, after all, a member of the aristocracy and socially miles above her—but his ready smiles and easy charm had quickly put her worries to rest.

"You've been wonderful, Phillip. If it hadn't been for you, my days in this house would surely have been dismal."

He smiled. "The pleasure was mine, I assure you. 'Your fair discourse has been as sugar, making the hard way sweet and delectable.' "

She felt herself blushing. He was forever spouting poetry. It was so romantic, so courtly. "Shakespeare?" She knew how fond he was of the Bard, but this time she wasn't really sure.

He nodded. *"Richard II."*

Ariel sipped her tea, then carefully set the cup back down in its saucer. "I should love to see it performed sometime."

"Then I shall make it a point to take you." He reached out and caught both of her hands. "My dearest Ariel. You must know the way I feel."

She glanced down at the hands holding hers, soft, pale hands, the hands of a gentleman. Her heart beat almost painfully. Surely it was too soon for him to speak of marriage.

"I don't . . . don't know what to say."

Phillip glanced to the door, which Ariel hadn't realized was closed, eased her nearer, then pulled her into his arms. "I realize we haven't known each other long, but sometimes, when two people share such a strong attraction, time isn't important. I must kiss you, my darling Ariel. I have thought of nothing else since the moment I first saw you. I've gone half-mad thinking about it."

Ariel felt suddenly uneasy. As Phillip had said, they'd been seeing each other for little more than a week. "Phillip, I don't think—"

His lips cut off her words. She had never been kissed before, but she had dreamed about it often. Though the sensation was pleasant, there was none of the fire she had imagined, none of the glorious passion. She gasped as she felt Phillip's hand on the underside of her breast, and he took full advantage, sliding his tongue inside her mouth.

Shock jolted through her. What was he thinking of to take such liberties? Did he believe she was the sort of woman who would allow a man she barely knew to touch her so intimately? Determined to end the kiss, she tried to twist free, shoving her hands against his chest just as Phillip abruptly jerked away, surging to his feet so fast he nearly knocked her off the sofa.

He was breathing hard, his hands tightly clenched. "Greville . . ." was all he said.

She hadn't heard the door swing open. Now, as she struggled to comprehend what was happening, she saw that a man stood just inside the drawing room. He was several inches taller than Phillip, with a dark complexion and jet-black hair. His mouth was set, his jaw clenched so hard it appeared cast in stone. Eyes the color of pewter sliced into her like a knife blade.

"Who . . . who are you?" she asked, the icy chill of his gaze making it difficult to force out the words.

"I believe your . . . companion . . . knows well enough who I am."

Phillip turned confused blue eyes in her direction. "I thought you said Greville was your cousin."

"I said that, but this isn't—"

The tall man made a stiff, formal bow of his head. "Justin Ross, Fifth Earl of Greville, at your service, madam." Rage, barely controlled, dripped from every word. When he turned those fierce gray eyes on Phillip, she could have sworn he flinched. "Miss Summers and I have business to discuss," the earl said curtly. "I believe, Mr. Marlin, it is in your best interest to leave."

Wordlessly Phillip rose from the sofa, his pale hands still clenched into fists. A blast of cold seemed to pervade the room as the two men stared at each other. Phillip clamped his jaw, turned, and walked toward the door.

"Phillip . . . wait!" But he only kept on walking, out of the room and down the hall, his footsteps a chilling, hollow echo as they receded.

Ariel fixed her attention on the man beside the door. "I don't . . . don't understand what is happening."

His smile could have frozen steel. "What is happening, my dear, is that my father, the fourth Earl of Greville, was good enough to die some two years past, leaving his title to me."

Ariel nervously wet her lips. "The earl . . . the earl is dead?" She was having trouble grasping what he said. Everything seemed to be spinning around just outside her reach.

"The former earl is dead. I'm Justin Ross, the fifth and current Lord Greville, the man who has been paying for your finery, for your room, board, and education. As you might imagine, it comes to a very tidy sum."

"Yes, I-I'm sure it does. That is one of the things I wished to speak to the earl—I mean you—about." Dear God, the earl was dead. She didn't really know him, hadn't seen him in more than four years, but she had been certain that he was the one who'd been helping her.

"I believe you spoke to the earl about those things some time back. I believe the two of you came to an arrangement more than four years ago."

She swallowed, forced a little courage into her spine. "I suppose at the time we did."

"As I understand it, in exchange for your education and expenses, you agreed, upon reaching your maturity, to become the earl's mistress."

Bluntly spoken, but true. "Yes, but I . . . I was younger then. I didn't exactly realize—"

"You're some years older now, nearly nineteen, if I recall, no longer an innocent young girl—as evidenced by your conduct with Mr. Marlin." Ariel blanched. "You've received an extensive, extremely costly education. I would imagine during that time you came to understand exactly the bargain you made—is that not so?"

Misery washed over her. Her stomach rolled with nausea. "Yes."

"Still, you accepted the money I sent you, let me pay your tuition."

"Yes."

"You allowed me to purchase your clothing—that gown, for instance, that you are wearing."

Unconsciously she smoothed the lovely apricot silk, her fingers brushing a row of delicately embroidered roses. A painful knot rose in her throat. "Yes."

"Since that is the case, the bargain must remain."

Tears burned behind her eyes. She blinked several times, refusing to let them fall. "Yes. . . ." Her throat ached. Dear God, she had never believed it would actually come to this.

The earl turned and started walking, making his way the several short paces into the hall outside the carved double doors. He was tall and lean and dark, and the powerful presence he exuded seemed to remain in the room even as he walked away. Pausing, he turned once more to face her.

"I require your presence upstairs, Miss Summers." He didn't bother to wait, simply started walking again, certain she would follow. Sick with dread, she did, letting him move ahead of her as if he were the master and she the slave, ignoring the insult, continuing up the wide stone staircase, along the sconce-lined hall, and into the master suite.

She had never been inside the rooms before. Now she noticed in some vague corner of her mind the dull blue Turkish carpet, the faded velvet draperies that thinned the weak sun trying to press through the mullioned windows. Not surprisingly, the huge suite of rooms was as dark and dreary as the rest of the house.

Lightning cracked outside. Gray, angry clouds blotted the sun, the storm now a full-fledged gale. With an eerie hiss, the wind thrust its way beneath the windowsill. Ariel's footsteps slowed as the earl passed the marble-topped furniture in the sitting room and continued on into his bedchamber. He didn't stop until he reached the foot of his massive four-poster bed.

For a moment she paused, her heart pounding raggedly. She could feel his eyes on her, wintry gray, cold as the north wind blowing outside the house. He stood there waiting, his expression glacial as she slowly, tentatively, made her way toward him, stopping just inside the bedchamber door.

"Close it," he commanded. Icicles dripped from his voice. Instead of the hot rage her father had unleashed on her as a child, the earl's chilling fury slid toward her in frozen sheets that were far more terrifying.

She bit down on her trembling lip and did as he said, quietly setting the latch into place with a shaking hand.

"Come here . . . Ariel."

She didn't want to. Dear God, she wanted to turn and run. Still, she wasn't a coward, had never been a coward. She had survived her father's beatings. Somehow she would get through this.

Pride stiffened her spine. She walked toward him on legs that felt wooden, praying they would continue to hold her up.

"A bargain was made," he said. "I have fulfilled my part. Now it is your turn to do so. You will remove your clothes. I wish to see what I have purchased with my hard-earned money."

For several long seconds she simply stared at him in horrified disbelief. "I couldn't . . . couldn't possibly—"

"If I hadn't arrived when I did, you would have removed them for Marlin. You will do so now for me."

A shudder of fear slid down her spine and she bit back a sob that tried to escape from her throat. Dear God, this couldn't be happening! Of all the scenarios she had envisioned, none of them were as terrible as this. Her eyes were burning, threatening to fill with tears. She forced them away, determined not to cry in front of the coldhearted beast who was now the earl.

Instead she lifted her chin. "You're mistaken, my lord.

I would not have let Phillip take . . . take liberties with my person."

A fine black brow arched up. "No?" His lips twisted into a bitter, mocking smile. "And that little scene I witnessed in the Red Room? Are you going to stand there and tell me I imagined the two of you entwined in a lovers' embrace?"

Ariel bit down on her lip. It was only a kiss and yet, from the start, something about it had felt wrong. "What . . . what you saw was a mistake. Neither of us intended for that to happen."

His brows pulled together in a dark angry line and his mouth flattened out. He strode toward her, his expression thunderous, and unconsciously she took a step away. "If you believe Phillip Marlin did not plan your seduction then you are a bigger fool than I am. Now remove your clothes—or I shall remove them for you."

Tears filled her eyes. She blinked furiously, trying to stop them, finally succeeding. Courage came from somewhere deep inside her, a place scourged into her by the cruelties her father had inflicted. He could beat her, but he could never break her.

Neither would the earl.

Turning, she presented her back to him, standing ramrod straight though her legs were shaking. "You will have to help me with the buttons."

The earl moved forward. She could hear his shiny black shoes making a muffled sound on the carpet. He ignored the buttons and instead she felt the heat of his fingers at the nape of her neck as he took hold of the gown and ripped it open to the waist.

The sob in her throat tore free, but when she turned to face him, those flat gray eyes held not a single trace of pity.

"Now, do as I said. Take off the dress." He took a few steps backward, as if he wished to view her distress from a more casual distance.

Her hands were trembling. She gripped the delicate apricot silk and slid the ruined dress off her shoulders. *Such a beautiful gown,* she thought fleetingly, each one so precious to her, a woman who had never owned such lovely things. She tried to think of something she might say, some way to make him understand what had happened between her and Phillip, but one look at his face told her the effort would be futile.

She stood in front of him in only her slippers, white silk stockings, satin garters, and fine lawn chemise, the fabric so transparent it revealed the faint pink circles of her nipples, the pale hair between her legs. Her face turned scarlet as those cold silver-gray eyes moved slowly over her breasts. They traveled past her waist, down her legs, to her ankles, then returned to her face.

"Remove the pins from your hair. I wish to see how it looks around your shoulders."

Ariel bit the inside of her cheek, not sure she had the courage to continue. A shiver rippled through her, then another. She couldn't bear to think what the dark, forbidding earl intended to do. The thought returned that she should run, make at least some effort to save herself. But she didn't believe for a moment the angry, predatory man who stood across from her would ever let her escape.

Instead, she steeled herself and did as he said, praying God would intercede and some miracle would occur, hoping she could think of a way to save herself. Her fingers were shaking so badly she couldn't hold onto the pins. They made soft pinging sounds when they hit the wooden floor at the edge of the carpet. When the last pin was removed, her pale hair tumbled down past her shoulders.

"Now the shift."

Oh, dear God. Fresh tears sprang into her eyes and this time she could not stop them. They brimmed over and slid down her cheeks. "Please . . ." she whispered. "I'm sorry about what happened. I know I shouldn't have let him come in, but I had no idea he was going to kiss me."

His jaw clenched. She closed her eyes against the sight of his tall, hard frame bearing down like a vision from hell.

He stopped directly in front of her, his hands reaching out to grip her shoulders.

"I'm not a fool, Ariel. It's obvious Phillip Marlin is your lover. Since that is the case, from this day forward, you will simply warm my bed instead of his."

Her lover? Misery crashed over her in great numbing waves. She only shook her head. "Phillip isn't . . . my lover. I've never . . . No one has ever . . . That was the first time anyone has ever kissed me."

His fingers tightened on her shoulders almost painfully. "You're lying."

"I'm telling you the truth." She stared into the stark planes of his face. "We only just met last week. I was walking in the park and he . . . he simply appeared. Today we went for a ride in his carriage. It was starting to rain, so I . . . I asked him in to tea. Then he kissed me."

Thunder crashed outside, shaking the windows. Another bolt of lightning stabbed into the overcast sky, illuminating the shadowy angles of his face. Ariel caught a flash of something in his eyes she hadn't expected. Something stark and filled with pain. Something he hadn't meant for her to see.

His long dark fingers dropped away. For the first time, he appeared uncertain. "You're not saying . . . You're not telling me that you are still a virgin?"

Ariel's face went warm. She stared down at the carpet, studied the faded blues and reds in the intricate patterns. "I would never let a man . . . I wouldn't . . . Yes. . . ."

Greville caught her chin, forcing her gaze back to his face. It was there again, deep in his eyes, the pain, the bitterness, the hurt, like a man betrayed by his closest friend. She didn't understand it, yet it touched her in some way.

His gaze held hers for long silent moments. He stood so close she could feel the warmth of his body, the brush of his clothes. The color of his eyes began to change, shifting from a frosty gray to a crystalline silver, the rage still there but changing, beginning to shimmer with heat.

Then without warning, his mouth crushed down over hers.

There was nothing of tenderness in the kiss. It was hard, brutal, savage, a punishing kiss meant to repay her for the betrayal he must have felt. For the second time that day she suffered the will of a man she barely knew, yet each man's attentions were totally different. The earl's brutal kiss ravished her mouth in retribution, yet as the seconds passed, it softened, heated, changed.

Ariel swayed as his lips moved over hers, beginning to coax, starting to seduce, becoming something she hadn't expected, something that pulled at her from dark, secret places.

Something far more disturbing than the kiss she had shared with Phillip Marlin.

The contact ended as abruptly as it had started and Greville turned away, pacing toward the small mullioned window, looking nearly as shaken as she. He raked a hand through the wavy black hair that edged over his collar. It gleamed blue-black in a jagged fork of lightning.

"Perhaps you're telling the truth. It doesn't really matter."

But a chink had appeared in the armor he had been wearing, and for the first time since this nightmare began, Ariel felt a ray of hope. She gathered what little courage she had left and drew in a steadying breath.

"I can't begin to know what you are thinking. What you must surely think of me. Whatever it is, I am truly sorry for what has occurred."

He turned, casting the full measure of that hard gray gaze in her direcion. "Are you, indeed?"

She moistened her lips, noticed that they still tingled from his kiss. "I made a bargain. As you said, you fulfilled your part. It was never my intention not to live up to mine. I only hoped—prayed—that whatever happened between us would be agreeable to both parties."

The earl said nothing.

"What I mean to say is, I had hoped we might be able

to work things out in an amiable manner. I thought we would have time to discuss it. I didn't realize you would expect me to . . . to fulfill our bargain the first time we met."

He actually looked a little embarrassed. "It was not my original intention."

Her pulse speeded up as hope continued to build. "If that is the case, there is a favor I would ask."

A thick black brow arched up. "A favor? I believe you have received more than enough favors from me already."

For an instant she glanced away, her own cheeks warming with embarrassment. He had given her more already than she could ever have asked. "It is merely the favor of time, my lord. As I said, when I came here, I assumed we would have a chance to become acquainted. I hoped that we might develop a . . . a friendship of sorts before our relationship progressed any further."

The earl came away from the window. Now that his anger had lessened, some of the harshness had seeped from his features. For the first time she realized that in a different, more brutally masculine way, the earl was every bit as handsome as Phillip.

"Friends?" he repeated with a slightly mocking air. "That is a novel concept, Miss Summers—having a woman for a friend. I find it almost amusing."

Ariel lifted her chin, wishing she wasn't forced to have this conversation in a state of near-undress. On the other hand, that they were talking at all was a miracle for which she was sorely grateful.

"There is nothing amusing about friendship, my lord. And no reason at all that a man and woman could not share such a bond."

His eyes raked over her thin chemise, fixed pointedly on her breasts, and hot color burned into her face. In the wake of such scrutiny, it took sheer force of will to remain where she stood.

"There are any number of reasons, my dear Miss Summers, that friendship between the sexes rarely occurs. The fact that you don't seem to know what they are makes me believe you might actually be the innocent you claim." He moved closer, until he stood merely inches away. Though Ariel was taller than the average woman, she had to tip her head back to look at him.

He lifted a lock of her pale blond hair and smoothed it between his fingers. Ariel felt an odd tingling in the pit of her stomach.

"Just how would you suggest we go about building this ...*friendship?*" he asked softly. His hand brushed her shoulder as he let the curl drop back into place and the tingling turned to gooseflesh that slowly edged down her arm.

Surely it was hope, she thought, that set her heart to pounding. If he agreed to wait before demanding she come to his bed, she might have time to convince him to reconsider their bargain.

"I've never been to London," she said, dredging up a wobbly smile. "Since my arrival, I've seen little of the city. Perhaps you could show me some of the sights."

"Sights? What sort of sights?"

Ariel's mind worked frantically, struggling to come up with an answer that might prove her salvation. "The opera, perhaps. Or a play! I-I should love to attend the theater. Shakespeare perhaps. I've always wanted to see *King Lear.* You live here in the city. Surely you know places that might be of interest. I would be happy to go wherever you suggest."

He seemed to ponder that. He turned his back to her and resumed his scrutiny of the branches scraping against the windowpanes. "All right, Miss Summers." His attention swung back to her. "For the present, we shall set aside your ... obligations. I would rather have a willing woman in my bed than one who is there merely at my command."

Ariel swayed on her feet, fighting a wave of relief so powerful it made her dizzy.

"Since that is the case, you may put your dress back on."

She didn't hesitate, just snatched the gown up off the

floor and struggled into it, jamming her arms into the small puffed sleeves, pulling it up over her shoulders, releasing an inward sigh of relief when she was decently covered again.

The earl said nothing more and Ariel took his silence to mean she was dismissed. Ignoring the missing buttons at the back of the dress and the fact that her hair was a wind-blown mess, she whirled toward the door, certain that even if any of the servants saw her, they would say nothing. From the day she had arrived at the house, she had noticed their somber, businesslike manner. Little laughter was heard in the mansion. After meeting their coldhearted employer, she understood why.

Struggling to keep the torn gown in place, she silently fled the bedchamber. She was nearly running by the time she reached her room. Once inside, she hurriedly turned the brass key, locking the door, and leaned against it. She was safe for the present. But how long would that safety last?

She wished she had the answer, wished there was a way out of the situation she had got herself into. In truth, her options were limited. She had no money, no job, and no place else to go.

And she had given her word.

Ariel squeezed her eyes shut and tried not to weep.

CHAPTER FIVE

I am excited to be here at Mrs. Penworthy's School of Feminine Deportment, finishing school being the next step in accomplishing my dream, that of becoming a lady. Still, I worry I shall never quite fit in. The other girls are all so refined and sure of themselves while I am constantly in peril of saying or doing the wrong thing. I have heard them making fun of me behind my back, but mostly they simply ignore me. In a way I am grateful. I fear, should the secret of my low birth be known, I would be ostracized completely.

A memory of the letter slowly faded. Justin restlessly paced in front of the slow-burning fire in his bedchamber. Though the rain had stopped and the storm had moved on, the August evening was chill, the leaves on the trees still dripping wetly onto the muddy earth.

He was tired tonight, bone-weary in a way that had nothing to do with his long journey home and everything to do with disillusionment and utter disappointment. They were rare emotions, since he had long ago accepted that life was little more than a series of disappointments. It was strictly the way things were.

He reached for the poker beside the hearth, then knelt to stir the red-orange flames, his mind replaying the scene he had come upon in the Red Room. Anger rose up as it had before, making his fingers tighten around the heavy length of iron.

His long-awaited meeting with Ariel Summers was nothing at all what he had imagined. Never once in his musings had he expected to find the sweet young woman in the letters wrapped in the arms of the most notorious rake in London—his most bitter enemy, Phillip Marlin. Justin damned the girl to hell for the betrayal he felt and silently congratulated himself on not losing his temper far worse than he had.

Setting the poker aside, he walked to a carved wooden sideboard and poured himself a brandy, his thoughts on his longtime rival. He and Phillip had been classmates at Oxford. With his golden good looks and powerful family name, Phillip was spoiled and arrogant, willing to use his sizable allowance to cultivate a circle of sycophantic friends. He was the sort who drew pleasure from ridiculing others, who preyed on other people's weaknesses.

As a youth, Justin had battled the boys who taunted him about his bastardy, using his fists to repay them for their cruelty, being caned more than once for fighting in the school yard. Eventually, he simply withdrew, keeping more and more to himself. He learned to control his anger, his pain, replacing it with a cynicism that kept people at a distance and shielded him from the world.

He kept himself well away from Phillip Marlin and his spiteful, taunting words—until the night Justin happened upon him with Molly McCarthy in an Oxford tavern. Molly was a saucy, irreverent bit of baggage who earned a few extra coins seeing to the needs of the local males. She made no secret of it, but Phillip's ego was so large he mistakenly believed her favors were reserved just for him. The night he caught her in bed with one of his friends he went insane, tearing the room apart, then unleashing his wrath on Molly, breaking her arm and beating her until Justin, who happened to be passing down the hall, had no other choice but to stop him.

The battle had been brief and painful for Phillip. Brawling with a man who had learned to defend himself with his fists had left Marlin with two black eyes, a broken nose, and a bloody lip.

It left Justin with a powerful enemy.

His jaw clenched at the memory. He took a sip of the brandy he rarely drank, then grimaced as the fiery liquid burned down his throat. In a bedchamber down the hall, Ariel would be sleeping, her flaxen hair spread out across the pillow, her pretty pink lips softened in slumber. It had never been his intention to demand she fulfill his father's loathsome bargain, but when he had seen her with Marlin—wearing the expensive clothes *he* had paid for—something inside him had snapped.

He'd wanted to kill Phillip Marlin.

Justin took another sip of brandy, then set the snifter down on the hearth. What should he do? Did he really mean to make the girl his mistress?

Unwillingly his mind conjured shadowy impressions of pale pink nipples, long, shapely legs, small stocking-clad ankles, and the downy silver-gold triangle that marked her womanhood. With her flawless skin and fine features, Ariel Summers had surpassed his father's highest expectations.

Edmund Ross wouldn't have had the slightest qualms in demanding she warm his bed, especially after he had caught her in the arms of another man.

But Justin was nothing like his father. At least he hadn't thought so until today. The truth was he wanted Ariel Summers. Had wanted her, perhaps, even before he met her. He closed his eyes against the sudden wave of desire that washed over him, making him go hard inside his breeches.

Perhaps he should pay a visit to Madame Charbonnet's House of Pleasure. Celeste Charbonnet prided herself on providing beautiful women skilled in the art of pleasing a man. He hadn't been there for quite some time, too long, it would seem, by the painful ache he now suffered.

Justin sighed into the silence. He didn't want one of Celeste's trained courtesans. He wanted Ariel Summers. He had bought and paid for her—why shouldn't he have her? By damn, the girl belonged to him.

Whether or not she was Phillip Marlin's lover no longer mattered.

Justin intended to have her.

Ariel awakened covered in a fine sheen of perspiration, the sheets kicked down to her knees, her nightgown bunched up around her hips. She had suffered a nightmare, she knew, and though she couldn't recall what it was, she had a strong suspicion it had something to do with the earl.

Ariel shivered, gooseflesh rising against the cold that pervaded the room. She slipped from the bed and drew on her quilted silk wrapper, fastening the buttons up the front.

A light knock sounded and the lady's maid the earl had provided walked in, Silvie Thomas, a dark-haired girl in her twenties with round hazel eyes and an equally round, slightly pudgy face. "You're up early, miss. You should have stayed in bed till I came to add coal to the fire."

"Yes, well, there are matters I need to attend to this morning." That was a half-truth. What she intended was to head for the park, hoping she might see Phillip. She needed to speak to him, try to straighten things out between them, but mostly she wanted to escape the house before she encountered the earl.

"Well, if you're heading off, then we had better be getting you dressed."

Ariel let Silvie fuss over her, thankful to have something to do to occupy her thoughts. In a gown of pale blue muslin, her hair pinned up in curls, she grabbed a fringed India shawl and headed down the stairs and out the door, grateful to escape without being noticed. It was early. If Phillip appeared at their usual meeting place—which she very much doubted he would—it would yet be some hours away. She wandered about for a while, strolled into a bakery and bought a sweet cake and a cup of cocoa.

As she pulled a coin from her reticule to pay for the items, she suffered an unexpected pang of guilt. As the earl had so harshly pointed out, she was gowned in clothes *he* had paid for, enjoying food purchased with the allowance *he* had sent. When she was a child, desperate to escape her miserable, battered existence, it hadn't mattered what she did to get away. Now it bothered her to think of the false promises she had made.

Greville is right, she thought. *I owe him.* Everything she had learned, everything she had become, was a direct result of the earl's generosity. She owed him an insurmountable debt, but surely there was another way to repay him, aside from the use of her body.

With a sigh, Ariel made her way to the plane tree she came to each morning. The grass was moist with dew, the morning chill still in the air. She pulled her shawl more tightly around her shoulders and waited, praying that her golden-haired prince would arrive.

Relief filtered through her when he did, since she had been more than half-certain she would never see him again.

"Ariel, my darling girl."

"Phillip . . . I didn't think you would come."

He reached out and captured her hands, his eyes taking in her pale face and obvious distress. "A dozen Grevilles couldn't have kept me away. I've been so worried. I shouldn't have left you . . . not knowing the earl as I do. I was angry and confused."

Ariel summoned a smile, though it wasn't all that easy. "It's all right. I am just so glad you are here. I have so much to explain, so much to tell you. I should have done it sooner, but I . . . I was afraid."

Phillip pulled his handkerchief from the pocket of his coat and dabbed at the tears she hadn't known were spilling from her eyes. "Come. Sit down over here." He used the handkerchief to wipe the dew from a bench beneath the tree, and they sat down holding hands. Phillip listened with a growing frown as Ariel told him the truth of her low birth, having to force each painful sentence past her lips.

". . . So you see, Phillip, I am not the person you believed. I am not . . . not truly worthy of your attentions."

He gently squeezed her hand. "Don't be foolish. Your past is unimportant. It's the woman you are now that matters."

Ariel glanced away. How fortunate she was to have met a man like Phillip.

"You say your father was the old earl's tenant?"

"Yes."

"Is that the reason Greville decided to help you?"

Ariel bit down on her lip. When she had come to the park, she'd intended to tell Phillip everything, admitting her low birth and that she had sold her body to the earl in exchange for fancy clothes and an expensive education. She had told him the truth of her past, but there was something different about him today, an almost fanatical gleam in his eyes when he looked at her. She remembered the enmity that had burned like fire between Phillip and Greville, and the memory kept her from revealing the rest of the story.

"My father drank too much. When he did, he could be cruel. I asked the earl to help me and he agreed." It was the truth—not all of it but all she had the courage to divulge. "I didn't realize the first Lord Greville had died and that my . . . gratitude . . . now belonged to his son."

"His bastard son." Phillip nearly spat the words. "He never would have become the earl if his father hadn't fallen ill. Justin was the only male child he had sired and he was desperate for an heir, even if his son was the by-blow of a whore."

Ariel blanched at the term, disturbed more than a little by the hatred in Phillip's voice, knowing if she was forced to fulfill her bargain, he would be using the same word for her.

His fingers tightened over hers, a little too warm and slightly moist. "I'm sorry. You're a lady. I shouldn't have spoken to you in so coarse a manner."

"How . . . how do you know so much about him?"

"We were classmates together at Oxford."

"Will you tell me about him?"

Phillip stared off toward the stream that meandered through the park. He was heart-stoppingly handsome, every woman's dream, and yet she couldn't help comparing his fine blond features to the seething dark beauty of Greville.

When he returned his attention to her, there was a different, unreadable look in his eyes. "He's a cruel man, Ariel, a dangerous man. You're not safe in that house with him."

A little shiver ran through her. She remembered the cold,

remorseless way he had demanded that she remove her clothes and tried not to think what might happen to her in his bed.

"In school he stayed mostly to himself," Phillip continued. "His father stood by his obligations and supported him and his mother, but I doubt the earl saw him more than a couple of times over the years. His mother was the daughter of one of the local squires. She ran off with some married European noble when Justin was still a boy. His grandmother raised him for a couple of years, until he was shipped off to boarding school."

It sounded like a dreadful existence to Ariel, nearly as painful as her own. "Perhaps that is the reason he seems so hard and uncaring."

"Don't make excuses for him, Ariel. He doesn't deserve it."

"Lord Greville has been extremely generous. I owe him a very great debt."

His mouth tightened. "A debt he surely means to collect. Justin Ross doesn't do anything unless there is something in it for him."

She thought of the bargain she had made and suppressed a second shiver.

"There was a woman when we were away at university," Phillip said. "A tavern maid named Molly McCarthy who worked in the village. One night I accidentally chanced upon the two of them together. Justin was angry at something poor Molly had done. He beat her savagely. I don't know what would have happened if I hadn't forced him to stop."

Ariel bit hard on the inside of her cheek, fighting against the brutal image. A memory of the terrible scene in the earl's bedchamber rose up. If she hadn't obeyed his commands, would he have beaten her? She tried to imagine him raising those hard, dark fists against her, but somehow she could not.

"I have to go," she said, suddenly weary as she came to her feet. "They'll be looking for me if I don't return soon."

"When will I see you again?"

"Are you certain you want to?"

He cupped her chin with his hand, stroked a finger down her cheek. "How could you doubt it?"

"I know where you live. You drove me by your town house the day we rode in your carriage. I'll send word as soon as I am able to get away."

He looked into her face, raised her hand to his lips. "You know the way I feel. Don't make me wait too long."

Ariel didn't answer. She had no idea what her future held, no idea if she even had a future. Perhaps she should have told Phillip the truth of her situation, begged him to help her.

Next time she would, she vowed. If he cared for her as he seemed to, he would help her find a way to repay the earl.

Justin paced the floor of his study, one ear cocked toward the entry. Where the devil was she? Had she run away with her lover? Was she lying in his bed even now, her slender arms wrapped around his neck as she lay naked and writhing beneath him? *Innocence and purity, bah!* He knew better. He couldn't believe he had been such a fool.

He heard a noise and stopped his pacing, listened to the light sound of footsteps in the entry, knew that Ariel had returned, and strode toward the door.

Gowned in pale blue muslin, her face flushed prettily from her time out-of-doors, she lifted her skirt and started up the wide stone stairs.

"So . . . you have decided to grace us once more with your presence." His deep voice halted her midway to the top.

She slowly turned to face him. "My lord?"

"I'd like a word with you, please—in my study."

Some of the color bled from her cheeks. Her shoulders straightened a bit as she resolutely descended the stairs. Justin led the way down the hall, waited until she swept past him into the room, then quietly closed the door.

He pinned her with a glare. "I was looking for you earlier. Where have you been?" He tried to keep his tone even, but it was impossible to disguise the slight thread of anger in his voice.

Ariel lifted her chin. Her eyes met his and did not look away. "I went to the park, as I have done each morning since my arrival. I won't lie to you, my lord. If we are to form a friendship, it must start with the truth. I went to see Phillip Marlin." He stiffened. "I felt he deserved an explanation for the scene he witnessed here yesterday. And the truth about my past."

Anger made his jaw feel tight, though he couldn't help admiring her candor. He had once believed in her honesty. He wanted to do so again. "And what did Mr. Marlin have to say?"

A look of unease stole over her features, and he knew in that moment that Marlin had relayed the sordid truth of his birth.

"He said . . . he said that he knew you at Oxford."

"He told you that I was a bastard."

Her eyes flew to his face. He wondered if there was something in his tone that betrayed how much the notion pained him.

"Phillip told me a number of things. Perhaps he shouldn't have, but I gave him little choice."

"Why?"

"Because whatever happens between us, I would like to know the man you are, the man who has helped me become the woman that I am."

"And I suppose, with Marlin's help, you now believe that you do."

"I believe your past was as troubled as mine. Do you think I am proud of being the daughter of a drunkard? A man who beat me whenever he felt the slightest urge and without the least remorse? Do you think I enjoyed telling Phillip I was an illiterate peasant until you and your father sent me away to school?"

There was so much pain in her face Justin could feel it

like a tangible force. His eyes moved off toward the window. It was gray and overcast outside, a weak sun hidden behind a wall of clouds. "Perhaps we are alike in some ways."

"Yes . . . I believe we are. Your mother abandoned you. Mine died when I was so small I can't even remember her. Your father, in his own way, was every bit as cruel as mine. If an unpleasant past is all we have on which to build a friendship, it is more than most people have."

He moved away from the window, walked over to where she stood. Such a lovely face, so full of innocence. Or was it all a sham?

He reached out and caught her chin. "You must not see Marlin again. When it comes to women, he's a very dangerous man."

"That is exactly what he said about you."

And after the things he'd done yesterday, why shouldn't she believe it?

"Phillip told me about a woman you were seeing," she went on, "a tavern maid named Molly McCarthy. He said that you beat her."

Astonishment shot through him. "Marlin beat her! He might have killed her if I hadn't stumbled across them when I did."

She let the denial pass. "What of yesterday? Upstairs in your room . . . if I hadn't done exactly as you commanded, what . . . what would you have done?"

A muscle bunched in his cheek. "I don't beat defenseless women, if that is what you are asking."

Her gaze remained steady and he was amazed at the will it must have taken to press him as she was. "If you hadn't believed I was a virgin, would you have taken what you wanted by force?"

Would he have done such a thing? Watching her disrobe, seeing her lovely, slender body, he had wanted her more than any other woman he could remember. Would he have raped her? Pressed her down on the mattress and savagely thrust his hardness inside her? He closed his eyes against the brutal image and slowly shook his head.

"I would not have forced you." When he looked at her, he saw that she studied his face. She didn't believe he had told her the truth about Marlin, but he could tell by the slight relaxation of her shoulders the exact moment when she decided that she was safe with him.

"Then there is hope for us, my lord."

Hope. It was a word that was dead to him. As cold as the unfeeling heart that beat inside his chest. "I meant what I said. I don't want you going near Marlin again. I forbid you ever to see him."

Something flickered in the blue of her eyes; then it was gone. That faint spark of hope he had witnessed seemed to slowly fade away. "As you wish, my lord."

He wondered if he could believe her.

Then he wondered if she truly believed him.

Justin sat at the wide mahogany desk in his study three days later, his jacket off, his shirtsleeves rolled up. Unconsciously he rubbed his weary eyes, then returned his attention to the ledgers he had been studying, but his mind wasn't on profit margins or money lending. It was on the girl upstairs, Ariel Summers, the woman he meant to make his mistress.

Images of the pale, slender body beneath her thin chemise rose into his mind and his loins quickened. He could still feel the softness of her lips when he had kissed her, taste the sweetness of her mouth. Only one other woman in his life had tortured his senses as Ariel did—Margaret Simmons, the woman who had betrayed him.

A light knock sounded at the door, two quick raps, then a third, and his painful recollections slowly faded. The silver knob turned. He smiled as his best friend, Clayton Harcourt, walked in. Clay, an acquaintance he had made in school, was the illegitimate son of the Duke of Rathmore. It was their bastardy that had drawn them together. At the time, it was the only thing the two of them had in common.

"I figured I'd find you here," Clay said, "poring over the books. Do you never do anything but work, old man?" He was nearly as tall as Justin, slightly heavier in the chest and shoulders, with dark brown hair and brown eyes. Where Justin was remote and too often brooding, Clay was outgoing, casually arrogant, and, when it came to women, a completely conscienceless rogue.

"Actually, I haven't got much of anything done—not for the past few days, at least." Justin rose from his desk, strode toward Clay, and the two of them shook hands.

"I suppose I should be grateful you're such a dedicated sod, considering the money you've made me over the years." In the days since they'd finished their schooling, Clay had wisely entrusted Justin with the management of the small inheritance he had received from his mother, as well as any monies the duke doled out and whatever he managed to scrape together himself. As Clay had hoped, Justin's knack for investing had turned the sum into a tidy little fortune that no one but the two of them knew about.

"So . . . shall I guess what is keeping you from your labors?" Clay asked. "She *has* arrived, hasn't she?"

His friend knew about Ariel, her letters, and the bargain she had made with his father. "She's here. As we speak, she is fast asleep upstairs."

"Not in your bed, I take it."

His mouth curved faintly. He would hardly be down here if she were. "Unfortunately, no."

"Is that a note of regret I hear in your voice? I thought you said you had no interest in making the girl your mistress."

Justin didn't answer. Perhaps he hadn't, not at first. Now he had every intention of doing just that. Unfortunately, after their last conversation and the forthright way she had spoken, some of his original beliefs about her had begun to surface again. He wanted Ariel more than ever. But he wanted her willingly in his bed.

"There is no point in lying. I want her, Clay. I have since the moment I met her." He told his friend everything that had happened since her arrival, including Ariel's involvement with Phillip Marlin.

"Marlin—how did that bastard manage to get his hooks into her so quickly?"

"By chance, I gather. She claims she hasn't slept with him. There is no way to know for sure."

"Oh, there's a way. Once you bed her, you'll discover whether or not she's the innocent she claims."

His jaw tightened at the thought. "Yes, I suppose I will."

Clay threw himself down on the brown leather sofa and lounged back against the arm. "So . . . how do you plan to seduce her? Forcing a woman isn't your usual approach."

"You're the expert on women. What would you suggest?"

Clay uncurled his big body and sat up straighter. "I'd probably buy her something—flowers, candy, some pretty little trinkets. I might try taking her out, showing her around the city."

"She is living in my house. Should the fact be known, she would be considered a fallen woman, whether I am bedding her or not. I could hardly take her out among the *ton*."

Clay pondered that. "True enough, but hardly a problem. I could make a list for you, places I take Teresa." Clay's current mistress. "There's a little out-of-the-way theater called the Harmony in Covent Gardens. Or perhaps she'd enjoy gaming at one of the Jermyn Street hells. In truth, there are far more interesting places to take a whore than there are to take a lady."

Justin frowned at the use of the word. He didn't like to think of Ariel in that way. "Unfortunately, I don't have time. Day after the morrow, I leave for Birmingham to check on the progress of my new factory. After that—"

"Take her with you. Women are hardly immune to you, Justin—even if the ones you usually bed are far less naive. Give her a chance to get to know you—the real you, I mean. Not the man you show the rest of the world."

Justin's glance strayed upward as if he could see through

the plaster ceiling into her room. "I'll give it some thought. Aside from my problems, there must have been some reason for your late-night call. What is it?"

Clay grinned. "Actually, I saw your lamp through the window. I knew you'd be working. I thought maybe I could convince you to join me at Madame Charbonnet's."

It was an idea Justin had considered himself, in light of his current situation and the ache he suffered every time he thought of the girl upstairs. "All right. Give me a minute to get my coat and I'll be right with you."

"Saints be praised! How long has it been?"

"Too long," Justin grumbled. "Too damned bloody long."

CHAPTER SIX

The days slid past. Ariel dreamed again that night, and in her dream she was kissing her handsome, golden-haired prince, Phillip Marlin. Her arms slid around his neck and he lightly pulled her against him. It was a sweet, tender kiss, little more than a faint brushing of lips, a gentle show of affection.

Then the dream began to fade, to blur and dim at the edges, to thicken into a bleak, dense fog that shrouded the recesses of her mind, and her handsome prince disappeared. In his place stood the fierce, dark earl, holding her imprisoned in his unforgiving arms, pressing her indecently against his long, lean body.

"No . . ." she whispered, beginning to struggle, trying to break free. The earl held her easily, drawing her even more firmly against him. Bending his head, he took her mouth with such savage force her legs nearly buckled beneath her. The kiss went on, hot, harsh, demanding, penetrating her senses until she felt consumed by him, absorbed by his powerful presence, unable to tear herself free.

And no longer certain that she wanted to.

She awakened shivering all over, trembling with fear and uncertainty, her skin hot and clammy, tingling in that unfamiliar way it had before.

Silvie arrived moments later, bearing a summons from the very man who haunted her, even in sleep. She was to join the earl in the breakfast room overlooking the garden at the rear of the house.

Ariel's heartbeat kicked up, anxiety making her legs a little unsteady. Crossing to her rosewood armoire, she chose a simple tunic dress fashioned of soft mauve silk embroidered with dark pink roses. Dressing hurriedly, she fidgeted while Silvie finished pinning up her hair, then left the room and headed downstairs, her mind alternating between the violent dream she'd had and the earl's softly spoken denial that he would have forced her into his bed.

He had never beaten the tavern maid, Molly McCarthy, he'd said. In fact, he had accused Phillip Marlin of the crime.

Surely it was the earl who lied. Phillip was a gentleman. He was her handsome prince. He would never invent such a tale.

But something gnawed at her. Something in the earl's voice, or perhaps it was the horror in his expression when she had accused him of the deed. Whatever it was, it made her wonder. . . .

He was waiting when she walked through the door. He stood at her approach and pulled out the ornately carved high-backed chair on one side of him. Dressed in a dove gray tailcoat and snug black breeches, he seemed a little less formidable today. Even his eyes seemed different, less fierce, more assessing.

Ariel studied him more closely, appraising him as she hadn't really done before. Now that he was no longer angry, he looked even more handsome than he had before, lines of his harshly beautiful face as if sculpted in marble. With his straight nose, high, carved cheekbones, and slashing black brows, he had the look of the predator he had seemed, yet those hard, bold features were compelling in a way she had refused to acknowledge until now.

He settled himself in a chair at the head of the table and unconsciously her thoughts returned to the savage kiss she had suffered in her dream, or perhaps it was the one he had claimed upstairs in his bedchamber. Whatever it was, she forced the memory away and hoped he wouldn't notice the faint edge of color that crept into her cheeks.

"You look fetching this morning, Miss Summers. I trust you slept well."

Except for her disturbing dreams. Her cheeks grew noticeably warmer. "Well enough, my lord."

"I've been thinking about our conversation—more particularly the suggestion you made."

Her heart took a leap. The suggestion that they become friends before becoming lovers? She prayed for the reprieve it would mean. "Yes, my lord?"

"Inasmuch as I know, through your letters, a great deal about you, but you have but recently met me, it seems only fair that we do as you suggest and spend a little time getting to know each other."

Ariel's pulse took another jump. Spending time in company with the earl was a highly disturbing thought, never mind that it was her idea and the answer to her prayers.

"Since my schedule demands a brief trip out of the city, I thought that perhaps you would join me."

"Out of the city?" It came out with a noticeable squeak.

"The small town of Cadamon, some thirty miles southeast of Birmingham, to be precise. I recently purchased a textile factory there."

A dozen thoughts passed through Ariel's head. At the forefront was the knowledge that she would be a number of nights with the earl. "Birmingham is a goodly distance away."

He nodded. "More than a day's journey each way. We'll be five or six days gone, I should imagine."

Ariel blanched. Five or six days! Dear Lord, who would protect her from him for nearly a week? She nervously moistened her lips. "Perhaps it would be better if we began our acquaintance upon your return."

Those straight black brows slammed together and his mouth flattened into the thin, disapproving line that she had seen before. "I'm afraid that isn't an option. We leave first thing in the morning. I'll expect to depart no later than nine o'clock."

She forced herself to nod. "As you wish, my lord."

"In the meantime, I think today would be well spent doing a bit of shopping."

"Shopping, my lord?"

"I wish to purchase a few new gowns for you to wear and whatever you might need to go with them."

Ariel shook her head. "You have already paid for a number of very lovely gowns. I have scarcely worn them. I hardly need more." More of a debt she would owe him. More she would have to repay. Inwardly, she groaned.

"For the occasions I have in mind, I would like to see you in something a bit less . . . conservative. Your gowns are fine for day wear, but for evening, they make you look as though you are fresh from the schoolroom."

Ariel glanced down at the cup of cocoa a footman had just set in front of her. "That is exactly what I am," she said softly.

The muscles tightened across his shoulders. "You're no longer a child, Ariel. I don't intend to treat you as one."

Ariel said nothing more. She knew he was thinking of the kiss they had shared and the debt he intended to collect. Turning toward the footman who stood near the door, he signaled for the man to serve the balance of the light morning meal, then leaned back and took a sip of his coffee, those cool gray eyes once more on her face.

Beneath the table, Ariel clenched her white linen napkin into a knot that matched the one in her stomach. The footman set a delicate, sugary cake on the plate in front of her along with a spoonful of ripe red berries, but Ariel was no longer hungry.

They finished their breakfast in silence. As soon as the plates were removed, Justin rose and approached where Ariel sat shoving the food around on her plate. He said nothing as he led her to his waiting carriage, just motioned to the driver, who climbed into his seat on top. A soft slap of reins against the rumps of the four matched grays, and they were off, the iron wheels rolling over the cobblestone streets.

The sights of the city moved by outside the window, taverns and coffeehouses, butcher shops and rug merchants. Ariel's gaze slowly turned in that direction, and he couldn't miss the glow of fascination that slowly brightened her face. It didn't take long to reach St. James's, an area of elegant shops and stores that catered to wealthy members of the *ton*. Justin ordered his coachman to stop in front of a narrow establishment wedged between a dealer in spiritous liquors and a chairmaker's shop. There was only a single window and a small, obscure wooden sign that read: "MADAME DUPREE, Couture."

"Shall we?" He offered his arm and Ariel took it, letting him lead her inside.

In the small, well-appointed room, several women worked over bolts of colorful fabric, busily applying needle and thread to complete the garments they fashioned. One of them, a wide-hipped, beefy woman, rose at Ariel and Justin's approach and scuttled toward the rear of the shop, disappearing behind a velvet curtain in search of the proprietor.

"How did you know about . . . ?" Ariel looked up at him, the question trailing away. He knew she was thinking that he must have been there before, buying gowns for other of his mistresses.

"How did I know about the shop?" he finished for her.

"I suppose I am not the first woman you've brought here," she said a bit tartly, staring at him down her small, straight nose.

Amusement lifted the corner of his mouth. "Actually, you are the first. I know about the place because my father made a number of purchases here. I paid the bills after he died. Since I could never fault his taste, I figured it would accomplish our purpose."

She cocked a blond eyebrow. "And what, exactly, might that purpose be?"

"You said you wished to see the city, perhaps attend a play or an opera. You will need the sort of gowns Madame Dupree can provide you."

She said nothing to that. How could she? It was her idea, after all. He settled a hand at her waist, noticing how incredibly small it was, guiding her farther inside. The curtain rustled. The owner stepped into the salon with a smile and began walking toward them.

"May I be of help, my lord?" She was gray-haired and slightly wrinkled, her cheeks heavily rouged. She had large, pendulous breasts, the cleavage modestly hidden beneath a lace fichu at the neck of her fashionably cut silk gown.

"I would like to purchase some evening gowns for the lady."

She smiled. "You're Greville, are you not?"

He wasn't surprised that she knew him. Though it galled him to admit it, he knew how much he looked like his father. He made a slight inclination of his head. "I'm Greville."

"The late earl, your father, was a very good customer. You look remarkably like him." She turned her attention to Ariel. "And you, my dear, must be a . . . friend . . . of his lordship's."

Color washed into Ariel's face. Her head barely moved in a nod.

"Come now; there's no reason to be shy. In the past, I dealt with a number of the late earl's . . . friends. I'll have you properly fitted out in no time."

Justin watched the two women leave and found himself frowning. He didn't like the smug way Madame Dupree had smiled at Ariel or the wash of humiliation that had tinged her pale cheeks.

Justin silently cursed, wishing he had never brought her to the shop. He had always loathed his father's constant need for fresh, innocent young women. Justin looked very much like him. Was he more like his father than he cared to admit?

He shuddered to think of it, then blocked the painful notion as he had taught himself to do, shutting it completely out of his head. He didn't want a string of young women. He wanted Ariel Summers, and in time, he vowed, he would make her want him.

The women returned. Madame Dupree placed Ariel atop a low, round dais in front of a brocaded sofa and began to swathe her in bolt after bolt of fabric. At first she was reticent and he knew she was pondering the reason he was buying the dresses. He had made no secret of his intentions.

He wanted her in his bed and he would do whatever it took to make that happen.

She stood stiffly on the dais, embarrassed to be wearing little more than a shift, and he suppressed a sudden, violent urge to sweep her into his arms and carry her away from the woman's sly looks and knowing glances. Ariel said nothing at all and only replied to questions that were directly asked.

Still, she had been born into poverty, and eventually the beautiful fabrics—the lush velvets in ruby and sapphire, the sumptuous satins in cream and rose, the shimmering silks in emerald and gold—had her smiling.

It pleased him, that smile, warmed him in some way. He helped her choose the fabric and style for five new gowns, two more than he had intended, just to see the glow of pleasure on her face. They agreed on each one, both surprised to discover their tastes were so much the same.

Though the dresses were cut far lower than any she had worn before, the daring style was the height of fashion, and seeing her in them would help ease his conscience. Ariel was a woman, not a girl. A beautiful, desirable woman— one entirely capable of fulfilling the bargain she had made. Exposing so much of her lovely breasts would prove it.

They left the store loaded down with boxes and, after a stop at the shoemaker's shop around the corner to order matching slippers for each of the gowns, headed back to his waiting carriage.

They had almost reached it when he spotted a tall blond figure stepping out of the haberdasher's shop up ahead. Phillip Marlin strode along the paving stones, carrying an armload of boxes. He didn't see them and simply kept on walking away, but the moment Ariel saw who it was, she stopped dead in her tracks.

As Justin caught her reaction, a spark of anger burned through him. He clenched his jaw to tamp the feeling down. Ariel's gaze followed Phillip's progress across the street to where his carriage waited. She frowned as she noticed the small black child, perhaps six years old, who hurried to open the door.

"Is the child . . . is the little boy a servant?" she asked, her eyes still fixed on the child who was decked out garishly in full-legged purple satin trousers banded at the ankles and a matching purple vest. He wore a rhinestone-encrusted gold-and-purple turban on his small, dark head, making him look top-heavy, like a flower wilting from too much time in the sun. Little gold slippers curled into points on the toes.

"The child is a blackamoor," Justin told her. "One of Marlin's more recent acquisitions. He keeps the boy around as a conversation piece . . . rather a pet of sorts. It amuses him to watch people's reaction to the color of the boy's skin and the way he is clothed."

Ariel couldn't seem to stop staring. She continued to watch as Marlin thrust the stack of boxes into the boy's small, pink-palmed hands, then climbed inside the carriage and slammed the door. The child struggled with the boxes for a moment, handed them to a footman, then fought to climb up beside the driver, teetering near the top so precariously Justin heard Ariel gasp in a worried breath. Eventually, the little boy made it, and Phillip ordered the coachy to make way.

"I can't believe he would treat a child that way," Ariel said softly.

"There are a number of things about Phillip Marlin you couldn't begin to imagine," Justin said dryly, knowing she wouldn't believe him if he told her. Taking a firm grip on her arm, wishing Marlin to perdition, he led her on down the street.

No matter how she tried to will it not to, the next day arrived and with it their departure for Birmingham. Ariel had spent a restless night thinking of the earl and Phillip Marlin, remembering the concern for her, the unexpected sympathy, she had seen in Lord Greville's eyes at the dressmaker's shop. He had sensed her embarrassment, her utter humiliation. There was a moment she thought he might sweep her up and whisk her out of there, so dark was the look on his face.

And then there was Phillip. Surely Greville was wrong about Phillip's association with the boy. Perhaps he was helping the child in some way. Perhaps the lad was an orphan. Still, it bothered her the way he had treated the boy, like some sort of prize to be displayed. She tried to imagine Lord Greville treating a small child that way, but the image refused to surface.

The coach was waiting out in front when Ariel descended the stairs. She was packed and ready well before time to depart, her little maid, Silvie, standing nervously beside her, a small traveling valise clutched in the girl's pudgy hand.

Lord Greville appeared in the entry a few minutes later, sweeping in with the power of a storm.

Ariel forced herself to smile. "We're ready, my lord."

He gave her a cursory glance and frowned. "I thought you understood. I've a good deal of work to do. I'll need my privacy. As we are taking only one carriage, your maid will not be coming along."

Ariel blinked in surprise. "But you must let her come. It is unseemly for a lady—" She caught his scowl, started over again. "How could I possibly manage without her? Who would help me undress?"

"You managed for a good many years without a servant; I imagine you can survive for a few days more."

It was highly unseemly, yet Ariel didn't argue, knowing it would do not the least amount of good. Instead she stood rigidly aside as her little maid climbed back up the stairs. Greville took her arm and guided her out the door and down the front steps of the old stone mansion. He helped her climb into the carriage, then took a seat across from her. His shoulders looked even wider in such close quarters, and though his clothes were simply cut, he wore them with an air of authority. In truth, it was hard to imagine him ever being anything other than an earl.

They spoke little on the way out of the city, and eventually she lapsed into enjoying the sights. Unfamiliar with London, she had stayed fairly close to the house, and Phillip had driven her mostly in the park. Even the earl's recent shopping excursion hadn't carried her all that far away.

Now, as they headed into the burgeoning traffic, she watched with growing fascination the hordes of people who filled the narrow streets to overflowing: inksellers, ballad singers, a man selling secondhand clothes.

A ragged little boy with a grimy face and small fingers poking through the ends of his gloves sold apples on a corner. Conveyances of every size and shape converged in the bustling cobbled lanes, creating a cacophony of shouting drivers and neighing horses.

The incredible sights and sounds enthralled her, making her forget her nebulous circumstances, at least for a while.

Then the earl's deep voice broke into her thoughts, a jarring reminder that she was alone with him and about to leave the somewhat questionable protection of the city.

"I've a stop to make before we leave town. It shouldn't take all that long."

They rounded a corner a few minutes later and the carriage pulled up in front of a three-story brick building in Threadneedle Street. "I need to speak to my solicitor. You may come in if you like."

She was surprised by the offer. She started to decline, then thought, *Why not?* She was traveling with the man, though certainly not by choice. Any information she might garner could prove useful. "Thank you. I believe I shall."

He caught her hand to help her descend the iron steps, and they made their way inside the building. A young clerk with sandy brown hair and a studious expression greeted the earl, then led them down the hall into a well-appointed wood-paneled office.

"My solicitor, Jonathan Whipple." The earl tipped his head, indicating the gray-haired man who rose from behind his desk and started toward them. A slender man in his fifties, he wore wire-rimmed spectacles that perched on a long, crooked nose. "Jonathan . . . may I present Miss Ariel Summers. She is newly arrived in the city."

"A pleasure, Miss Summers." He smiled, made a politely formal bow, then returned his attention to the earl. "I have those figures you requested, my lord. I was just in the process of making the final additions before you arrived." The two men moved toward the desk, leaving Ariel to survey Mr. Whipple's domain.

It was cozy and warm, with a fire blazing in a small oak-manteled hearth and bookshelves along one wall. A pile of aging newspapers sat beside a brown leather chair, but aside from that the room was rather Spartan and scrupulously clean. It occurred to her that the earl was much the same, neatly ordered and pristine. It appeared he also demanded those qualities in the people who worked for him.

Ariel wandered along the bookshelf, drifting closer to the big mahogany desk in the center of the room, perusing the numerous leather-bound volumes, most of which were financial in nature. From the corner of her eye, she caught sight of the earl, seated in the chair behind the desk, his dark head bent over a stack of open ledgers.

Arithmetic had been her best subject in school. Watching as he studied the numbers on the page in front of him, she began to add the columns in her head, as she had learned to do.

Ariel frowned. "Excuse me, my lord, but there is an error in the column on the right."

He cocked a brow in her direction. "It comforts me to know that among your newly acquired talents you are also an expert in accounting."

She flushed at the sarcasm in his voice but refused to back down. "I know little of accounting. I do know those numbers do not add up. The total should be two thousand, six hundred, and seventy-six, not three thousand, one hundred, and forty-eight."

Greville frowned. The gray-haired man beside him

looked suddenly worried and quickly set to work, adding
once more the numbers on the page.

"Oh, dear. I'm afraid Miss Summers is correct, my lord.
I can't imagine how I could have made such an error." He
sighed. "Now I shall have to refigure all of the other columns based on the adjusted figure. It will take a bit of
time."

"I can do it for you," Ariel offered. "It turns out I have
rather a knack for numbers." She glanced down and silently
set to work. "The total in the first column should be forty-
two hundred fourteen. The second column is . . . thirty-
three hundred eighty-seven, and the third should be—" She
stopped, glanced over at Jonathan Whipple. "You didn't
write that down," she said to him, but he simply continued
his furious addition, trying to come up with an answer of
his own.

"Forty-two hundred fourteen pounds," he confirmed,
glancing at the earl over the rims of his glasses. "The lady
is quite correct."

Greville's astonished gaze swung to her face. "How the
devil did you do that so quickly?"

Ariel smiled, more pleased than she should have been
that she had impressed him. "It's a trick I learned. You
simply group the numbers in combinations of ten whenever
you can, or add them slightly out of sequence, or see two
or three numbers as a single larger number—eight, twelve,
and ten equal thirty, for example."

"Very impressive."

"I had an excellent mathematics teacher, thanks to you,
my lord. I can also do rapid multiplication and division—
if you should ever find the need."

The edge of his mouth quirked up. "I shall keep that in
mind."

The earl finished his meeting and the two of them returned to the carriage. He said little as the conveyance
rolled off toward the outskirts of the city, though she
thought that perhaps he studied her from beneath his lowered lids. His lashes, she noticed were even blacker than

his hair and thicker than any man's she had ever seen.

An hour passed. The sun broke through the clouds and slanted in through the isinglass windows, casting shadows beneath Greville's high cheekbones.

The rumble of his voice broke into the quiet: "I suppose, after spending time in London, the country will seem dull and boring."

She looked out at the rolling green hills, the small flock of black-faced sheep grazing on the knoll, a sky that was a clear, crystalline blue, as it never was in the city.

"On the contrary, my lord. I've no desire to return to the dirt-floored hovel where I was born, but I shall always be partial to the sweet clean air and green grasses of the country. London teems with all sorts of life, but in a different way, so does it here. There are colorful insects, an endless array of beautiful birds, and interesting four-legged creatures, both wild and domestic. As a child, I yearned to leave it. Now I see that it was the poverty and ignorance I wanted to leave, not the land itself."

The earl said nothing, but she thought she caught a hint of approval in his expression.

"And you, my lord? Do you find country life 'dull and boring'?"

His glance strayed toward the window. "To be truthful, I find most of life dull and boring. The country, however, can, on occasion, bring one a certain degree of pleasure."

"Then why do you not spend more time at Greville Hall? Especially since it is so much more . . ." She let the words trail away, realizing she had nearly paid him a very grave insult.

One of his straight black brows arched up. "So much more what, Miss Summers? Elegant? Or perhaps *palatial* is the word you are looking for."

There was no choice now but to finish the thought, whether he liked it or not. "*Cheerful* is the word I would have chosen, my lord. Greville Hall is the most beautiful place I've ever seen. It is light and gay, with dozens of windows to let in the sun and air. The gardens seem always to be in bloom and even the furniture and draperies are sunny and warm."

"How is it you are such an expert on Greville Hall?" he asked dryly. "I don't imagine my father ever invited you over for supper."

She cast him a sideways glance. "I don't imagine you received an invitation, either."

"Touché, Miss Summers."

"I know what the house looks like because I used to climb over the fence behind the garden, sneak in behind the bushes, and peer inside through the rear windows. Sometimes, when I saw candles burning late at night, I would sneak over to watch the ladies dancing. They looked so beautiful and they seemed to be having so much fun. I vowed one day I would become a lady, too."

"And so you have."

But she hadn't, not really. A lady didn't journey across the country with a man she barely knew. A lady didn't become a man's mistress.

The earl turned away from her to stare back out the window. "I was only at Greville Hall on one occasion and that was just before my father died. My half sister, Barbara, lives there now, with her small son, Thomas. We do not get along."

"Why not?" It was an impertinent question and she knew it. Still, she hoped that he would answer.

The earl looked down his nose at her, an intimidating stare that made her wish she hadn't asked, which was exactly what he intended.

The question lingered and finally he sighed in defeat. "Barbara is a widow. If my father had not made me his heir, the Greville title and fortune would have gone to her son."

Ariel remembered the beautiful black-haired girl who had lived in the house when Ariel was a child, remembered watching her and her friends that day in her father's open carriage. She hadn't even known Lady Barbara Ross had been married. It seemed a good deal had happened since she'd struck her devil's bargain and been shipped off to school.

"She is terribly young to be a widow," she said. "Just a few years older than I, if memory serves. It must have been terribly hard on her, losing her husband so soon after they were wed."

The earl merely scoffed. "Barbara is six and twenty, and I believe my sister was relieved when her husband died. The Earl of Haywood was some forty years her senior, a crotchety old fool with more money than sense. I think Barbara married him in the very hope he wouldn't live a great many years and she would be left with the majority of his fortune. Unfortunately, she was Haywood's second wife. The earl already had two grown sons, which meant there wasn't much chance of Thomas becoming his heir."

"Even so, surely he provided for her and the boy after his death."

"I'm sure he intended to—in the beginning. Then he caught her in bed with his estate manager. There were questions about missing household funds, and soon after he changed his will. My father managed to smooth things over. Still, when Haywood died, he left her nearly penniless."

"Are you saying she now survives solely by your charity?"

"More or less. She could remarry, of course, and I'm certain in time she will."

"But if she is the sort of person you describe, why are you helping her?"

He shrugged the wide shoulders beneath his perfectly tailored black coat. "What choice do I have? She is my half sister, after all. I can hardly toss her and the boy out in the street. Society might not view me in the most desirable light, but I do not wish to be ostracized completely. It would hardly be good for my business dealings."

Ariel said nothing to that. He provided for his sister not out of affection but simply to protect his social status. He didn't want to lose the financial benefits inherent in being a member of the *ton*. Still, if what Greville said was true, he had painted a very grim picture of his sibling. With a father who had ignored him, a mother who had abandoned him, and a ruthless, money-hungry sister who took advantage of his fortune, how could he be other than the cold, unfeeling man he seemed?

Ariel felt an unexpected twinge of pity.

Conversation faded. They traveled most of the day in silence. Ariel read or embroidered while the earl pored over volumes on textile manufacturing or the numerous investment portfolios he had brought along. The ride was lengthy and she was exhausted by the time he signaled his coachman to stop for the night at an inn called the King's Way.

Apparently, the earl had sent word ahead, as two private bedchambers were waiting. The knowledge that she would have her own separate sleeping quarters should have put her at ease. Instead, as she wearily entered the front door of the ivy-covered inn her nervousness returned full measure.

The earl stood at the foot of the stairs, his cool gaze shuttered, yet she sensed a faint tension in the muscles of his long, lean frame. "Will you join me in the taproom for supper or would you prefer to have something sent up to your room?"

Relief coursed through her that she could escape to the sanctity of her bedchamber. "I discover I'm quite fatigued, my lord. Something in my room would be preferable, if you don't mind."

His mouth edged up as if he knew her thoughts. "Very well, I shall bring it myself."

Ariel stiffened, worry slamming into her again. "Thank you," she whispered, barely able to force out the words.

When she heard his light knock at the door she was still fully dressed, having been unwilling—not to mention unable—to remove her clothing with the earl yet to arrive with her supper.

He frowned as he stepped inside the room, strode over, and set the tray down on the plain wooden dresser against the wall. "I thought you said you were tired. Why is it you are still dressed? Ah, but how could I forget? You haven't a lady's maid, have you? I suppose I shall have to do the honors myself. . . . Come here, Ariel."

There was something in the soft way he said her name that sent little shivers running through her. She made no move to obey him. Dear God, she could still remember the way he had ordered her to undress for him in his bedchamber.

"You aren't afraid of me, are you? I thought you understood that I am not going to hurt you."

"I'm not . . . not afraid, my lord." So what exactly was it that kept her rooted to the floor? She wasn't really certain.

"I know you're tired. I only wish to help you. Let me loosen your gown so you can undress and prepare for bed."

She moved toward him on legs that felt stiff and unresponsive, stopping just in front of him. She felt his hands on her shoulders, gently turning her around; then he started unfastening the buttons at the back of her traveling gown one by one. It was the oddest sensation, far too intimate by half, yet not entirely unpleasant.

If the man had been Phillip . . . if he had been her husband, she might even have enjoyed it. But the Earl of Greville wasn't Phillip Marlin, and instead of a comfortable, faintly pleasant stirring, she felt the brush of his fingers like a hot brand burning into her skin.

The gown finally loosened and she held it modestly over her breasts. He still stood behind her, the firelight casting his long shadow across the room. The fabric of his tailcoat brushed against her back as he pulled the pins from her hair one by one, then spread the pale blond strands around her shoulders.

"Like sunlight in winter," he murmured, his long fingers gently combing out the tangles. "Shall I plait it for you?"

An image arose of those elegant dark hands working to accomplish the task, and her stomach did a soft little curl. When she turned to face him, she saw that his eyes had turned a deep silver gray, the centers so black they glinted like obsidian in the firelight.

Her heart was beating too fast, her mouth suddenly dry. "Thank you . . . my lord," she said softly. "You needn't trouble yourself. I'll be able to manage the rest by myself."

He made a slight, stiff nod of his head, as if he were regretful of her decision. "As you wish. Good night, Miss Summers."

Ariel counted the long, graceful strides that carried him out of her bedchamber. It wasn't until the door closed firmly behind him that she released the breath that she had been holding.

CHAPTER SEVEN

The following day they reached their destination, the small town of Cadamon in a narrow river valley southeast of Birmingham. It was growing late by the time they got there. Instead of heading for the factory, the earl checked in to a nearby inn, the Wayward Sparrow, not nearly as well appointed as the King's Way had been.

The earl sniffed his disapproval as he carried Ariel's tapestry traveling valise into the small, airless room above the kitchen that she would be using and set it on the lumpy feather mattress. His own quarters were a few doors down the hall and presumably no better than hers.

"I apologize for the accommodations. I had hoped they would be more suitable. Apparently when the mill fell upon hard times, so did the town."

"The room will be fine, my lord." She had certainly lived in far worse. The cottage she had shared with her father had been meager at best, though she had done what she could to make it comfortable.

"I'll have a bath sent up," he said. "You can rid yourself of the road dust, then rest for a while. We'll sup in an hour. I'll call for you then."

He gave her no chance to decline, just walked out the door and strode down the hall to his room. An hour later, he returned, his hair still damp from his own ablutions and shining like polished jet against the white stock around his neck. His eyes swept over her, taking in the plain blue muslin gown she had changed into, lingering for a moment on her breasts. An odd little quivering started in her belly and spread out through her limbs. Her breath seemed to catch in her chest.

"Hungry?" he asked, returning his gaze to her face.

Ariel forced herself to smile. "Actually, I am. Perhaps the food will be better than the rooms."

He nodded. "Let us hope so."

Fortunately, that was the case. They dined on flaky pigeon pie and Cheshire cheese and enjoyed a bottle of rich red Portuguese wine. The earl made pleasant conversation, first speaking of the weather, which lately heralded the coming of fall, then talking about what he might find when he got to the mill.

"I realize the place is in disrepair, but that is exactly what gives it such potential."

"Do you own other factories as well?"

"Not yet, but I may be interested in acquiring more. First I want to see what I can do with this one. Tomorrow should be quite telling."

"I imagine so."

"The day starts early—half past five. I want to be there when they begin. I'm not certain how long I'll be gone. Will you be all right here until my return?"

Ariel swallowed the bite of cheese she had been chewing. "Why don't I go with you?" The words sprang out of nowhere. She hadn't even known she was going to say them. "I've never seen a mill. I think I should find it interesting."

The earl looked dubious. He took a sip of wine, then set the pewter goblet back down on the table. "Business matters are hardly among a lady's usual pursuits."

"True enough. But we both know I am a peasant, not a lady, and I find the prospect of learning about investments intriguing."

"Five-thirty comes early."

She smiled. "Until I arrived in the city, I always awakened well before dawn. It gave me extra time for my studies."

He hesitated a moment more, then nodded. "All right, then. I shall call for you at five. That should give us ample time to get there."

Ariel nodded with a degree of enthusiasm she hadn't expected to feel; then the old fears crept in and her smile slowly faded. What on earth had possessed her? She hardly needed to spend more time in company with the earl. Still, she wanted to go. She loved to learn about anything new, and this was another chance to do so.

They continued with the meal. She could feel his eyes on her, and in the light of the flickering candle some mysterious swirling current seemed to settle around them. He was incredibly handsome, she now saw, his dark beauty magnified by the power of his silvery gaze and the unsettling way he looked at her, as if no one else existed in the private world he had created.

By the time dessert, a warm apple tart sweetened with clotted cream, was finished, her palms were damp and their conversation had dwindled to a few brief words. Uncertainty rose up, began to gnaw at her. She knew what he wanted, why he had brought her along. His nearness stirred a strange mix of emotions, most of which she didn't recognize, but a growing one was fear.

So far he had played the gentleman, but would he continue to do so? Should he decide that he wanted her, there would be no one to help her, no one to stop him from having his way.

She shivered as she climbed the stairs in front of him, feeling his presence like a cool, dark shadow behind her. She stood by nervously as he opened the door to her room, then shoved it open.

"Will you need help with your gown?"

She shook her head. "This one is easier to unbutton. I believe I can manage on my own." She steeled herself for whatever might come next and pasted on a smile. "Good night, my lord."

He didn't move. Instead, a long dark finger stroked gently along her jaw. Very slowly he lowered his head and settled his mouth over hers. It was a soft kiss, little more than a brushing of lips, but for an instant their mouths met and clung, and a jolt of heat shot through her. Her hands crept up, trembled where they pressed against his chest. It was hard as granite, the long bands of muscle beneath his coat stretched taut.

When he straightened, ending the kiss, his eyes were the color of steel. "Good night, Ariel. Sleep well."

Her legs felt oddly disjointed as she walked past him into the room, certain she wouldn't sleep at all. She would toss and turn and remember the earl's soft kiss—a touch so light it shouldn't have affected her and instead left her shaking and barely able to breathe.

A kiss that was far more terrifying than the savage kiss he had claimed that night in his room.

As the earl had planned, they left the inn at dawn, driving into a grayish, faintly purple horizon. A dense, still air settled over them, smelling of dust and smoke. Apparently the townspeople were used to it, for they didn't seem to notice, just poured out of their run-down houses, filling the cobbled streets on the way to their jobs at the mill.

It took a moment for Ariel, leaning back against the carriage seat, to identify the odd clicking sound that mushroomed around them, increasing in volume until it reached a clattering din.

"Good heavens, it's their shoes!" she exclaimed in amazement, and the earl actually smiled.

"Wooden clogs," he said, the hard planes of his face softening in a way she had never noticed before. It was an amazing transformation, Ariel thought, making him look young and incredibly attractive. "The workers all wear them. They make quite a racket, don't they?"

"Yes. . . ." But the shoes were no longer of interest. It was the smile that lingered on the earl's handsome face, and she couldn't seem to stop staring. What if he smiled like that all the time? What if he even laughed on occasion? The effect would be devastating. She jerked her gaze away, wishing her heart would stop that ridiculous too-fast clattering that was nearly as loud as the noise of the heavy wooden shoes.

The carriage continued on to the factory, a huge brick building on the south side of town built on a rise above the Cadamon River.

The manager, Wilbur Clayburn, a short, stocky man with fat, veined cheeks and a bulbous nose, was waiting in his office when they arrived. "A pleasure, milord. All of us here at the Cadamon Mill have been looking forward to your visit."

His words, though spoken with a smile, seemed to drip with insincerity. It was obvious the earl's inspection was the last thing he wanted.

"Are you indeed?" Greville glanced around the small, cluttered office and frowned. Unlike Jonathan Whipple's tidy work space, Clayburn's quarters looked every bit as disheveled as the man himself. Papers were strewn across his battered desk, and the floor was littered with enough bits of woolen fuzz and dirt to keep an ambitious housekeeper busy for a week. His rumpled clothes looked as if they had been worn for at least a fortnight, and Ariel took an instant dislike to him.

Greville's frown deepened and she inwardly applauded the disapproving look, certain she knew what the earl was thinking.

"I believe in keeping things in order, Mr. Clayburn. That applies in particular to people in positions of authority. If that is a problem for you, I suggest you find a way to solve it or you will soon be looking for another job."

The color drained from the man's fleshy cheeks, making the end of his nose look red and swollen. Ariel's father's nose had looked much the same, and she wondered if perhaps Wilbur Clayburn was also a heavy drinker.

The rotund man worked to collect himself. "I guess you'll be wantin' a look at the place," he said a bit sullenly.

"That is the reason I am here." Greville turned his attention to her. "Would you prefer to await me here or in the carriage?"

She was there. She might as well see it. "I would prefer to join you, my lord, if you don't mind. As I said, I have never been to a textile factory. I should like to discover how it works."

After only a momentary pause, he nodded. "As you

wish. But I warn you, you may get your very pretty dress soiled in the process."

The compliment surprised her, since it was the same blue gown she had worn to supper the night before. She wondered if his words were a subtle reminder that he was the one who had paid for it. "I'll try to be careful."

"I'm afraid I gotta warn you," Clayburn put in, "the place ain't what it used to be. As you know, profits have been down. The owner lost interest and the mill has fallen into a pretty sorry state."

The earl merely shrugged. "One man's albatross is another man's opportunity. Shall we go?"

Clayburn led the way, eyeing Ariel with a hint of speculation as he passed into the hall. She knew he was wondering exactly what her relationship was to the earl.

Since Ariel wasn't sure herself, it was difficult to fault him.

The place was grim, Justin thought. Everywhere he looked there were little hills of litter and piles of dust that floated in the air and made it difficult to breathe.

The ground floor of the long, narrow three-story building was dominated by the giant wheel that provided power for the mill. It was turned by water from the pond above the dam, creating energy for the upper floors. The wheel made an annoying racket, and the floor around it needed a good scrubbing.

Climbing rickety wooden stairs, they made their way up to the second floor. When they reached their destination, the scene was the same, dust and litter, compounded by row upon row of mechanical spinning machines—spinning jennys—crowded next to one another, along with the workers necessary to run them.

Clenching his jaw against the overcrowded working conditions in the mill, Justin turned his attention to Ariel, who stood far too quietly beside him. "Perhaps it would be better if you returned to the carriage," he said gently, reading the concern in her face.

"I want to see the rest," she said with a stubborn shake of her head.

"Are you certain?"

"Yes."

Justin didn't argue. If she wanted to come, the decision was hers. Still, he could see how the plight of the workers was affecting her. Determined to focus his attention on the purpose of his visit, he forced his attention back to his surroundings, directing question after question to Wilbur Clayburn, his mood growing blacker at the answer to each one.

They climbed another set of stairs, arriving on the third floor of the mill, where the rough plank floors seemed to overflow with humanity. Men and women crowded onto this floor fashioned the yarn fabricated on the floor below into various types of woolen cloth.

Justin rubbed his eyes, wishing for a moment he had never gotten involved with the mill in the first place. In every available space around him, workers bent to their tasks, breathing in the smoky air, each face lined with a hint of despair.

"It's so dark in here," Ariel said, her voice little more than a whisper. "Couldn't they have built it with more windows?"

Inwardly he cursed himself for letting her come along. This was hardly the place for a lady, and no matter Ariel's status at birth, she had made herself one. Still, she had asked to see the place and he admired her continued determination to learn.

"The mill was constructed in this manner out of necessity," he told her. "If the machinery isn't close to the power wheel, problems occur." He studied the tall paned windows designed to let in the sun. "The lighting, however, could be vastly improved simply by getting those windows properly cleaned."

He turned a hard look on Wilbur Clayburn. "Once we're finished, I'll draw up a list of things for you to do. Foremost among them will be cleaning this place from top to bottom—including those damnable windows."

"But that'll take days, milord. The mill's already in financial straits. We can't afford to take that much time away from production."

"Since the mill now belongs to me, I'll decide what we can and cannot afford. You, Mr. Clayburn, will simply obey my dictates."

Clayburn looked chagrined. "Yes, milord."

Justin returned his attention once more to his bleak surroundings. "How many people does the mill employ?"

"Two hundred, milord, counting millwrights, mechanics, overseers, and operators."

"I noticed a number of children working here as well."

"About thirty of 'em, milord. We use 'em to piece up broken strands or doff the wound yarn packages and set in the empty cores. They're the only ones small enough to fit in such tight spaces."

"How many hours a day do they work?"

Clayburn frowned. "How many hours? Why, they work just like everyone else—'bout ten hours a day. Keeps 'em outta trouble."

Justin glanced at Ariel, whose eyes looked suspiciously bright. "I believe I've seen enough for today, Mr. Clayburn. I'll be back later on this afternoon with that list we discussed. In the meantime, I should like to go over the company's ledgers. Have one of your men load them into the back of my carriage."

Clayburn nodded. "Aye, milord."

Ariel stood staring at the dozens of people laboring over the looms. Her head snapped up as he took her arm and guided her back down the stairs. The moment they stepped out into the sunlight, she dragged in a deep breath of air.

Justin frowned. "I shouldn't have let you come." He stopped beside the carriage to await the arrival of the ledgers. "The place is a disgrace."

She only shook her head. "I'm not sorry I came. I used to think my life in the fields was a terrible existence. Now

I can see there are far worse lots than the one I suffered."

Justin raked a hand through his hair, still unsettled by the dismal conditions he had seen. "I purchased this property because I felt very strongly that industry is the way of the future. I believed, with a few strategic changes, the profits from the mill could be enormous. But I never . . ." He straightened, refusing to allow his emotions to wander in that direction. "Something must be done. People cannot work efficiently in such surroundings."

Ariel tipped her head back and looked into his face. "Perhaps it's good that you bought it. Perhaps you can make things better."

He couldn't miss the plea in her voice. He gruffly cleared his throat and glanced away. "Yes, well, whatever improvements are made will only add to the profits in the long run."

Ariel gazed back toward the mill, her eyes on the smoke rolling out of the chimneys. "What will you do?"

He waited while a third heavy ledger was loaded into the boot of the carriage, then helped Ariel climb in and climbed aboard himself. "As I said, first I intend to have the place cleaned from top to bottom. People perform far better when they have a decent place in which to work."

"And?" she pressed.

"And I don't see any reason for the children to labor such long hours. If their help is truly needed, we'll make certain they work shorter shifts."

Her thoughtful glance held approval. "Their parents need the money the children earn. I think that's a very good solution."

"In the future, I intend to mill cotton as well as wool. That means we'll need more hand loom weavers. The job is paid by the piece, so some of them can work at home— that is, they could if their housing were suitable, which, from what I've seen thus far, it is not."

Ariel's eyes brightened even more. "But you could make it so, could you not?"

"Yes. With some sort of inexpensive housing."

"I should think, my lord, that both morale and productivity could be improved by instigating such a plan."

Justin studied the shabby, dilapidated buildings that housed the workers' families. "I believe you may be right."

Ariel gave him such a bright smile it seemed a ray of sunlight had burst through the window of the carriage.

Unconsciously Justin found himself smiling back, the action so rare the muscles around his mouth felt stiff. Then the smile slowly faded. He wanted her in his bed, but he didn't want to give her any false impressions. He was the man he was, not some bleeding-heart do-gooder. She would have to learn to accept that.

"You realize these changes are strictly good business."

"Of course." But she continued to smile as if it was far more than that.

"I'm not doing this out of any sense of charity. I'm doing it because I believe I'll make more money."

"Yes, my lord," she said, the smile slowly slipping away.

"I just wanted to be certain you understood."

Ariel merely nodded. She made no further comment and returned her gaze to the window.

Justin leaned his head back against the leather squabs and closed his eyes, trying not to recall that bright, sunny smile that had so warmed him.

The one she had given him when she believed that he actually deserved it.

The earl went back to the mill that afternoon and didn't return until late in the evening. The following day they left Cadamon and set off on the journey home. For much of the trip, Lord Greville was silent and remote. He had been working over the ledgers, Ariel presumed, late into the night. Faint smudges darkened the skin beneath his eyes, and his expression looked vaguely fatigued.

For several hours he was so deep in thought she wondered if he remembered she was there. "What are you thinking?" she finally asked, unable to stand the silence a moment more.

Greville glanced up, blinking as if he was trying to get his bearings. "To be honest, I was thinking of those blasted mill accounts. I was hoping to finish them once we reach the inn, but if I do, I'll be up again half the night."

"What exactly are you doing?"

"Checking the figures. Making projections based on the changes I'm planning, that sort of thing."

Ariel brightened. "If that is the case, why don't you let me help you?"

He shook his head. "I hardly think—"

"Why not? You know how good I am with numbers. I could save you immeasurable time."

He studied her so thoroughly she fought not to squirm on the seat. Perhaps she shouldn't have offered. She would wind up working late with him, just the two of them, alone in his room. Considering what the earl had in mind for her, it was a dangerous situation.

"You said you could do rapid multiplication and division," he said, leaving her question unanswered. "How do you do it?"

Ariel smiled. "There isn't any single formula. It's a combination of different tricks. Each one depends on the number. To multiply by twenty-five, for example, you divide whatever number you want by four, then add the proper amount of zeros."

"For example?"

"Take twenty-eight times twenty-five. You would simply divide the number twenty-eight by four—that's seven—then add enough zeros. Seventy is obviously not enough. The answer is seven hundred."

He made a similar mental calculation himself, and his mouth curved up. "That's quite a trick."

"Do you know the quickest way to multiply any two-digit number by eleven?"

"No, but I imagine you're going to tell me."

"If we were to take twenty-four times eleven, we would

make a hole between the two and the four, add the two numbers together—that's six—then stick that number in the middle. The answer is two sixty-four. Of course if the number in the middle adds up to more than one digit you have to carry. Thirty-eight times eleven, for example, would become four eighteen."

The earl sat forward in his seat. "Good God—you'd be a terror at cards."

She gave him a wicked grin. "Perhaps we could play sometime."

"Surely they didn't teach to you to play cards in school?"

"My best friend, Kassandra Wentworth, taught me. I favor loo, but I also play whist, rouge et noir, and Macao. If we played a bit, it would certainly make the trip go faster."

He chuckled softly. "Did your friend Kassandra also teach you to gamble?"

"Of course. Kitt loves gaming. It's something her stepmother abhors, which means Kitt does it every chance she gets."

"According to your letters, you didn't like her much at first."

Ariel smiled. "Not in the beginning. But Kitt is nothing at all as she first appears. Her parents ignore her. She behaves badly simply to gain their attention." She glanced out at the passing landscape, not really seeing it. "She is my only real friend and I miss her dearly."

The earl made no reply, but his look turned slightly brooding. Perhaps it was the fact that Kassandra Wentworth was a well-bred lady. As such, she and Ariel could no longer remain companions once Ariel became his mistress.

Ariel lapsed into silence, her bright mood suddenly gone. She had offered to help him tonight, and though he hadn't yet accepted, there was every chance he would.

What would Phillip say if he knew she would be alone with the earl in his bedchamber? So far Phillip had overlooked the fact that she was staying in Lord Greville's house without a chaperone. What if he somehow discovered she had traveled to Cadamon with him?

It was hardly her idea, Ariel consoled herself. As long as she remained in his debt, she was his to command. Besides, she had no family, no money, and nowhere else to go.

Oh, Phillip, what should I do?

But no answer came and Phillip's handsome blond image slowly faded. Instead her thoughts returned to the tall, forbidding man seated across from her. She remembered the soft way he had kissed her at the door to her room, and an odd little flutter began in her stomach. If they were alone together, what would he do?

She glanced at his hard, chiseled profile, and her stomach fluttered again. She wasn't sure if it was fear or if it was anticipation.

CHAPTER EIGHT

The afternoon lengthened. They played gin rummy, and though the earl wasn't easy to beat, Ariel accounted herself well and Greville seemed to actually enjoy himself. Ariel studied his face and thought again, in a far different way from Phillip, how very handsome he was.

"When we get back, would you mind if I did a profile miniature of you, my lord?"

He cocked a brow. "A silhouette?"

"I learned to do them in school. I've become quite good at them."

His mouth edged up at the corner. He was so tall that every time he straightened, his head nearly brushed the roof of the carriage. "I begin to believe you are good at any number of things, Miss Summers."

"Then you'll let me do it?"

"I must say it's an odd request. I can't remember anyone ever asking for my likeness before."

"No? But surely there is someone who would cherish such a picture."

His gaze sliced toward the window, and it bothered her to notice how desolate he suddenly appeared. "I'm afraid not."

"You lived with your grandmother for a time. Is she not still living?"

His features slightly softened. "Yes, she is alive, though I haven't seen her in years. I take care of her financial needs, of course, and we correspond on occasion."

"Then when it is finished, we will send it to her."

He studied her in that intense way that seemed a habit of his. "If that is your wish."

Ariel smiled. "As soon as we get back, then. In the light of the fire, perhaps."

Something moved in those fierce gray eyes. They slid

down the column of her throat and across her shoulders, lingered for a moment on her breasts. Her nipples grew tight and hard, rasping in an odd, tingling manner against the fabric of her dress.

Ariel thought of her offer to help him, imagined being alone with him, imagined those piercing gray eyes moving over her body as they did now, and knew with a bone-deep certainty she had made a very grave mistake.

Justin held the door, waiting as Ariel brushed past him, entering the room he had taken at the King's Way Inn, where they had stayed before, the halfway point on their return trip to London. Deciding to accept her offer of assistance with the ledgers, he had ordered a second table set up in the room. One of the mill ledgers sat open on the top, next to pen and ink, lit by a glowing whale oil lamp.

"I appreciate your assistance," he said. "With both of us working and any luck at all, we'll be done in just a few hours."

"I'm happy to help, my lord." He watched her cross the room to the table, careful not to look at him, trying valiantly to hide her nervousness. Her efforts didn't fool him. The moment she had stepped into the room, her glance had strayed toward the bed and worry had risen in her features.

Justin's gaze drifted in that direction, to the clean sheets and soft feather mattress, and his body tightened with need. In the days since they had journeyed from London, his desire for Ariel had mushroomed tenfold. Every simple glance, every accidental touch, inflamed his blood. His want of her bordered on obsession.

And yet he was no closer to achieving his goal than he had been before.

Standing at the table a few feet away, Justin sighed as he stared down at the column of numbers on the page. Forcing her into his bed was out of the question. He wouldn't do that to any woman and especially not to this one. His respect for her had returned in the days that they had spent together. She was sweet and caring, intelligent and forthright—qualities he had sensed when he had read her letters.

Qualities he had rarely known in a woman.

She was also wary and distant, determined to remain at arm's length.

And yet, she couldn't completely ignore him. As his friend Clayton Harcourt had said, there was something about him women seemed to find attractive. Perhaps it was the darkness inside him or his hard, predatory nature.

And there was the bargain Ariel had made. He had noticed a deep sense of honor where she was concerned. She would stand by her promise, he believed, and though he preferred she come to him out of feelings of desire, he wasn't above holding her to her word.

Quietly he moved up behind where she worked, her fair head bent over the open ledger, her slim fingers sliding across the rows of blue-inked numbers, lips moving as she added, multiplied, and subtracted with such amazing skill. Her hair was as pale as the flax they wove into the wool at the mill, the skin at the nape of her neck as smooth as the petals of a rose. He knew a desperate urge to press his lips against the spot, to slide his fingers into her shiny silver-gold curls and scatter the pins that held them in place.

It was foolish, ridiculous, to be moved in such a way, yet he couldn't deny the feeling. He could smell her soft perfume, almost taste the silkiness of her skin. The image sent a jolt of heat spearing through him, so fierce he went instantly hard. Cursing himself, grateful for the coat that hid the uncomfortable ridge in his breeches, he took a step away.

He cleared his throat and she jumped at the unexpected sound of his voice: "I've written down changes I wish to make." Her eyes struggled upward. For a moment she looked off balance, so deeply was she immersed in her work. He handed her the paper he had written the numbers on, and she set it in front of her on the desk. "Do you know how to calculate the projections?"

"I believe so. I multiply the existing numbers by the new

numbers in the column on the left. It shouldn't take all that long."

She returned to her work and he returned to his. Unfortunately, with Ariel in the room, he found it difficult to concentrate. A task that should have taken minutes took nearly half an hour. Ariel finished more quickly, and he handed her another batch of numbers.

They finished their tasks at about the same time, Justin setting his quill pen aside and rubbing the back of his neck.

Ariel looked over at him and smiled. "That wasn't so bad. In fact, I rather enjoyed it."

His mouth curved faintly. "Did you? I find the task loathsome, myself, but once it's finished, it gives me the information I need to go forward. My joy comes in watching a project like this one progress. That's what makes business so interesting." Rising from the chair, he made his way toward Ariel, who stood at his approach.

"Thank you for helping me." He tried not to notice the way the lamplight shadowed her delicate features, the cleft in her chin, the curve of her cheek.

"As I said, I enjoyed it."

He was standing closer than he intended. His hand came up of its own accord. He traced a finger along her jaw. "Perhaps I should put you on a permanent retainer," he said.

Ariel looked at him and nervously moistened her lips. "Yes . . ." she said, a slight catch in her voice. "Perhaps you should." She was taller than most of the women he knew. He liked that about her, that they fit so well together, liked the slenderness of her build. Without thinking, he caught a loose strand of hair and smoothed it back from her temple. "On second thought, there are other, more interesting things I should like for you to do. Far more pleasurable things than work."

She blinked but made no move to escape. Justin thought he had never seen eyes so blue or lips such a lovely shade of pink. He had to kiss her. He couldn't have stopped himself if he had wanted to. Gently he tilted her chin and, with exquisite care, settled his mouth over hers. Ariel stiffened, but only for an instant; then her eyelids fluttered closed and her lips turned pliant under his.

He groaned as he deepened the kiss, tracing her lips with his tongue, tasting the corners, coaxing her to open for him. Her fingers curled into the lapels of his coat, and he felt her tremble. Her lips molded perfectly to his, and Justin fought an urge to crush her against him. Instead, he eased her into his arms and tasted her more fully, coaxing her to surrender.

She did so slowly, reluctantly, allowing his tongue to slide in, making a soft little whimpering sound in her throat. Inside his breeches, he was hard and aching for her, wanting her more than he could have imagined. His hand found her breast and he cupped it, teased the nipple with his thumb, felt it tighten. He plucked at it gently, and a shudder rippled through her. He turned his attention to the other breast, stroking it lightly, determinedly. Ariel stiffened for a moment and started to move away.

"Easy, love." Justin kissed her again, gentling her, urging her to trust him. He massaged the fullness beneath his fingers, tested the weight, admired the apple-round shape, wished the gown was gone and he was caressing her firm, warm skin.

She trembled as he cupped her bottom and pulled her more snugly against him, her soft heat pressing into the hardness of his sex. Ariel must have felt it, must have realized where all of this was leading, for her whole body went rigid.

"It's all right, love," he said softly, gently. "I'm not going to hurt you."

But her tension didn't lessen and her hands flattened against his chest, shoving him away, determined to break free. Slowly, regretfully, he let her go.

Ariel backed away like a frightened deer.

"There is nothing to be afraid of," he said calmly, though that wasn't the least how he was feeling. "What happened between us is the natural course of events between a man and woman. In time you'll learn to enjoy the pleasure we can share."

She made a little sound of denial. "I won't do it," she whispered, firmly shaking her head. "I'll find another way to repay you."

"It's you I want, Ariel. You may not be ready to accept it, but I think you want me, too."

"No! I don't—" She moistened her lips. "I don't want you. I won't be your mistress. I . . . I'll go to Phillip, tell him the truth. Phillip will help me—I know he will."

The sound of Marlin's name sent a wave of fury shooting through him, smothering his desire. It left a bitter taste in his mouth. "Marlin will help you? That is what you believe? Marlin will bed you without the slightest qualm, then cast you out into the street."

Her chin angled up, casting a shadow on the tiny cleft in the middle. "Phillip cares about me!"

"Marlin cares about no one but himself."

"He has been kind to me. He has been my friend."

"He wants you in his bed. He'll do whatever it takes to get you there."

Her slender hands clenched into pale, shaking fists. "If that is the case, the two of you are exactly the same. You want to make me your mistress. If that is what he wants as well, what is the difference?"

Unconsciously he stepped toward her. Ariel took a step away. "I won't abandon you, Ariel. Once our relationship comes to its natural conclusion, I'll set you up in a small house in town—or the country, if you prefer. I'll settle a sum of money on you, enough to provide for your needs over the years. Marlin would never do that."

The idea hadn't occurred to him, but now that he had said it aloud, it seemed the logical solution. "Your choices are limited, Ariel. Surely you can see that. You could have stayed on the farm, married some nice young peasant boy, but you didn't want that."

"I wanted to be a lady."

"You wanted to wear expensive clothes and lavish jewels, drive around in a fancy carriage. I can give you those things and more."

Ariel said nothing, but her pretty blue eyes filled with tears. "I'll find another way," she whispered. "I'll repay my debt somehow."

The anger returned, deadening the hurt he didn't want to feel. It changed into something cold and bleak that penetrated his insides. She wanted Marlin, a man who would use her, then treat her with contempt. She would choose Marlin over him, just as Margaret had done.

The cold increased, chilling him to the bone. He pinned her with an icy glare. "You liked kissing me, Ariel. You liked it when I touched you." A flush rose into her cheeks. "Your body says yes, sweeting. Even if your mind says no."

"You're a devil, Justin Ross. A devil in the guise of a man."

The words stung. He was amazed that he could feel it. He had thought even that small flicker of emotion long dead. He blocked the sensation with a frigid calm, the protective armor he wore like a shield. "Perhaps you're right," he agreed. "It really doesn't matter. Sooner or later, I'll have you. You may count on it, my dear."

Ariel pressed her lips together. He noticed that they trembled. Whirling away from him, her back ramrod straight, she marched to the door, yanked it open, and stepped out into the hall. Cursing, Justin followed, remaining in the opening until he was certain she was safely inside her bedchamber.

Bloody hell! Striding back into his room, he slammed the door behind him. He hadn't mean to say those things, hadn't really meant for any of this to happen. What was there about her? How could she so easily make him lose control?

He had only meant to kiss her, nothing more. But the moment he had pulled her into his arms, he was lost.

Not that he hadn't enjoyed their passionate encounter. If he closed his eyes, he could still feel the softness of her lips, hear her faint sigh of pleasure when he had cupped her breast.

"You're a devil, Justin Ross." His eyes squeezed shut, the cruel words surprisingly painful, perhaps because they'd come from her. They dredged up hurtful memories that he had thought long dead. Memories of his father, of a seven-year-old boy who had looked up to him as if he were a god.

"You're the devil's own spawn," his father had said. "Isobel should have drowned you in the river like the unwanted pup you are." Earlier, his mother and father had been fighting, his mother pleading with the earl to give her more money. Isobel always wanted more money.

Justin had stared at his father, seen the loathing he felt for his son that he made no effort to hide, and had simply turned and run, his small heart breaking in two. He'd said nothing then, and over the years he had learned to rein in his emotions until he didn't feel them at all. It was easier without them. Easier and safer. After a while, he couldn't even remember what it had been like to have them.

Justin sighed into the silence. It wasn't like him to lose his temper. Years of practice usually kept him in careful control. He didn't like the notion that Ariel had somehow broken through the protective wall he had built so solidly around him.

He began to pace the floor, his long-legged strides carrying him from one end of the carpet to the other. Tomorrow they would arrive in London. They would return to his dark, dreary house in Brook Street and the separate lives they led. He had hoped this trip would help to breach the distance between them, yet his goal seemed even further away.

Patience, he told himself. The patience he had shown thus far had won him a very great deal. Tonight he had destroyed some of the progress he had made, but what he'd said was the truth—Ariel *had* enjoyed his kiss, his touch. Her body responded to him, whether she wished it or not, and he meant for that to continue.

Time was all he needed.

When the prize was worth it, Justin could be a very patient man.

Ariel struggled to awareness, the early-morning light shining in through the windows, rousing her from a troubled sleep. For a moment, she simply lay there, remembering the night before, wishing she could forget. With a groan, she struggled to her feet.

It didn't take long to make ready. Ariel bucked up her courage and prepared to face the earl, determined to pretend nothing had happened between them. To pretend he hadn't kissed her, hadn't caressed her breasts. That she hadn't melted against him, hadn't returned those heated kisses with astonishing abandon.

The truth was, all of those things had happened and more. She had responded to him like the harlot he intended to make her. Justin Ross had made her feel things she hadn't known a man could make a woman feel. She'd been out of her depths, angry at herself, and guilty for betraying Phillip. It was a humiliating experience, and perhaps the reason she had lashed out at him so cruelly.

A shadowy memory arose of warm male lips and deep, drugging kisses. It was overridden by the sound of her own voice taunting him with Phillip's name. She had known he would be angry, known it would end the encounter, exactly as she had wanted. What she hadn't expected was the brief flash of pain she had seen on his face.

She had hurt him, she knew, though it was nearly impossible to believe. It made her wonder if the man he appeared to be was the man he really was. Was he truly the cold, heartless man he seemed or perhaps something . . . something altogether different.

The thought intrigued her, made her want to know more about him, to discover what thoughts might lie behind the cool gray of his eyes.

Ariel took a fortifying breath, steeled herself, and made her way to the door, prepared to face the same angry man she had encountered the night before. Instead, when she lifted the latch, the man who stood in the hall wore a cool, emotionless mask that was far more disturbing than his rage.

"Before we begin our journey, there is something I wish to say."

Her heart began thudding, knocking uncomfortably against her ribs. How could he do that so easily? "Yes, my lord?"

"I owe you an apology."

The unexpected words struck with so much force an odd swell of emotion rose inside her. The arrogant Earl of Greville was apologizing to her? It was impossible and yet it appeared to be true.

"Last night I took advantage of your generous offer of assistance. I didn't set out to. It simply happened, and I am sorry."

Ariel stared at him as if he were a stranger. She had always been good at reading people. Until she'd met Greville. More and more he intrigued her. "Perhaps we should both apologize. I said a number of things I didn't mean. I was angry, perhaps more at myself than at you. I'm sorry I said what I did."

Something shifted in his features. He made a slight inclination of his head. "Then last night is behind us."

"Yes. . . ." But it wasn't, not really, not when a single twist of those sensuous lips made her remember the heat of them moving over hers. Not when she knew her dark attraction to the earl could lead to her ruination.

And there was Phillip to consider. She might be intrigued by the earl, but Phillip was the man who held her heart. Or was he? She shoved aside the image of the small black boy Phillip dressed up to amuse his friends and treated like a pet. He was helping the boy, she told herself again, giving the child a home when he would otherwise have been orphaned. Phillip simply didn't realize how that kind of treatment must make the boy feel.

Phillip was kind and caring. He was a gentleman. He

was nothing at all like the cold, brooding earl. And unlike Greville, his intentions were honorable. Ariel was certain of it, no matter what Lord Greville said.

She needed to speak to Phillip, tell him about the terrible bargain she had made and ask for his help. She would send him a note as soon as she dared, asking him to meet her. That she had promised the earl she wouldn't see him no longer mattered. Not when her happiness, her entire future, was at stake.

Greville took her arm as they descended the stairs, and a trickle of heat radiated into her stomach. When those long, dark fingers settled at her waist to guide her toward the door, a melting sensation curled out through her limbs.

"There is one more thing," he said, returning her attention to his face. "A favor I would ask."

"Yes, my lord?"

"Do you think, at least when we are alone, perhaps you might call me Justin?"

She swallowed, unable to tear her gaze away. "Justin . . ." she repeated, thinking it didn't come out sounding harsh or cold, as she had imagined it would, noticing the way his features softened when she said it.

They settled themselves inside the carriage and those intense gray eyes moved over her, the long black lashes sweeping slowly downward. She could feel the power of that sensual, heavy-lidded gaze almost as if he touched her.

Ariel's pulse kicked up. A soft, buttery sensation sank low in her belly.

Sweet God, she would be glad when they got home.

"Welcome back, my lord." That from Knowles, who stood in the entry of Justin's dreary stone mansion in Brook Street, greeting them on their return. "I hope your journey was a pleasant one." The butler's gaze sliced toward Ariel, but only for an instant.

"Yes, thank you, quite pleasant," Justin said, "though I am grateful to be home."

"Yes, well, perhaps that will change when you learn that you have guests."

"Guests? What guests?"

"Your sister, my lord. Lady Haywood and her son, Thomas, arrived at the house the day before yesterday."

Justin swore softly. "Where is she?"

"In the Red Room, my lord. She is expecting the arrival of friends."

Friends? Was that what she called them? Her bevy of admirers, the cloying milksops who hung on her every word?

For the first time he remembered that Ariel still stood beside him. "My sister is here," he said flatly. "She doesn't come often to the city, but apparently we're to have the pleasure of her company for a while."

Ariel merely nodded. He noticed that her face had turned a little bit pale. There was something in her features, a look of uncertainty, of vulnerability, perhaps, that he had never seen before. It reminded him that she was a lady, not by birth, but only out of sheer determination. On the surface, she looked as polished as any other woman of the *ton*. She was a lady, but she hadn't been born one. A fact she obviously knew far better than he.

"If you are worried about my sister, don't be. Her opinion matters not in the least."

"It matters to me," she said softly.

"Nevertheless, you will have to meet her sooner or later. It might as well be now." Justin offered his arm, and Ariel took it, letting him guide her down the hall and into the Red Room, where Barbara sat on a nest of cushions like a queen preparing to hold court.

"Well, if it isn't my beloved brother."

"I would say welcome to my humble abode, but I see you have already made yourself at home." With her glossy black hair, pale gray eyes, and faultless complexion, she was beautiful—he couldn't deny the fact. Why she had ever married a man as old as Nigel Townsend when she could have had her pick of the *ton* he couldn't imagine. Then again, Barbara had always valued her independence. Except for losing control of her husband's fortune, perhaps things had turned out exactly as she had planned.

She arched a fine black brow at Ariel, who still clung to his arm. When she realized what she was doing, her cheeks grew flushed. She eased her hold and took a step away.

"Lady Haywood, may I present to you Miss Ariel Summers." He graced his sister with a mocking half-smile. "Ariel was our late dear father's . . . ward."

"Father had a ward?" She laughed, a deep, throaty sound. "I thought the only young women he was interested in were his whores."

Ariel's color deepened.

"Miss Summers is currently in residence here at the house. I trust you will make her feel welcome."

Barbara's keen gray eyes swung to Ariel's face, taking in the pure lines and delicate curves, the glorious crown of flaxen hair. "You're staying here?"

"That's right," Justin answered before Ariel had the chance.

"But how can she? Who is acting as her chaperone?"

He gave her a malicious smile. "If you are concerned about propriety, you may play the part yourself while you are in residence."

Barbara came to her feet, her eyes narrowed in sudden understanding, a cold smile curving over her features. "She was with you in Cadamon, wasn't she? The girl isn't Father's ward and never was. You bring your mistress into the house and have the nerve to ask me to play the part of chaperone?"

"What you do or do not do is of little consequence."

"I'm not his mistress," Ariel put in defensively, finding her voice at last.

"You're lying," Barbara said.

"I'm telling you the truth."

"Then what in God's name are you doing here?"

"I'm . . . I'm . . . I'm helping Lord Greville with his

books. He . . . he needed someone to help him calculate the figures and I have a talent for numbers."

Barbara cast a disbelieving look in his direction.

"Ask her to multiply eleven times thirty-six."

"It's three hundred ninety-six," Ariel hastily replied before Barbara could open her mouth.

"There, you see? Miss Summers's help has been invaluable."

Clearly his sister had her doubts, but Justin was rapidly growing bored with trying to placate her. "How long will you be staying?" he asked, simply to change the subject.

Barbara cast a brittle look his way. "Less than a week, I'm certain you'll be happy to know. I'm here for the occasion of Lord Mountmain's wedding. Afterward, Thomas and I will be returning to Greville Hall."

A week of his sister was more than enough. He prayed she would keep her vicious tongue away from Ariel. "Since that is the case, enjoy your stay."

She might, he thought, but he certainly wouldn't. He wouldn't have a moment's peace until his sister was gone.

CHAPTER NINE

Ariel turned away from the venomous gray eyes of Lord Greville's sister and accepted the arm the earl offered, grateful for the chance to escape.

They had only taken a few steps toward the door when the sound of small running feet filled the corridor. The child, perhaps six or seven, slid to a halt in front of them, his eyes shooting upward. When he recognized the earl, his narrow face split into a grin.

"Uncle Justin!" The child launched himself into Lord Greville's arms, laughing joyously as the earl lifted him into the air, then settled him against a broad shoulder.

"I believe you've grown, young Thomas."

"I have?"

"Without a doubt." Justin turned to Ariel. "This is my nephew, Thomas. Thomas, this is Miss Summers." There was a softness in the earl's stern features she hadn't seen before, a look of affection Ariel wouldn't have believed him capable of. It was obvious he cared for the boy. Perhaps even he didn't realize how much.

Ariel smiled. "Hello, Thomas."

The child turned suddenly shy, his long black lashes sweeping down over Greville gray eyes. Justin set the boy back on his feet and the child eased a little behind him.

"It's nice to meet you," Thomas finally said, giving her a small, sweet smile.

His mother's voice rang out just then, approaching from down the hall: "Thomas! I thought I told you to go upstairs and play." His shy smile faded. "You know I'm expecting visitors. What on earth are you doing down here?"

He looked up at her with beseeching eyes. "Cook made the best gingerbread cookies. I thought you might want one." Reaching down the front of his shirt, he pulled out a still-warm, slightly mashed gingerbread cookie, offering it to his mother in a small, grubby hand.

Barbara frowned and took a step away. "Good heavens, get that thing away from me—it looks as if it's been stepped on. If you're not careful, you're going to dirty my gown."

Thomas's thin shoulders sagged. The hand that held the cookie drooped as if it suddenly weighed a hundred pounds.

"Come on, Thomas." Justin hoisted the boy back up on his shoulder. "Miss Summers and I would both like a cookie. Perhaps you could show us where to find them."

He grinned, exposing a missing front tooth. "They're really good, Uncle Justin."

"I'll bet they are."

The boy turned to wave good-bye to his mother, but she had already disappeared back inside the Red Room. Greville's jaw tightened. It was obvious he was protective of the child.

Ariel suddenly wondered if the real reason he provided so well for his sister wasn't the financial considerations he'd expressed but because he was concerned for his nephew.

The earl lowered Thomas to his feet in front of the door to the kitchen and the child raced inside.

"He's a darling little boy," Ariel said, remembering the sweet smile he had given her.

Greville dismissed the statement with a shrug. "All children are darling at that age."

"I quite agree, but I'm surprised you think so. I imagined you would consider a child a burden."

Something flickered in his eyes. She had the ridiculous notion it was hurt. "On the contrary," he said. "I think children are a very precious gift."

A gift? The answer was hardly what she would have expected. Dear Lord, would she ever understand this man, even a little? "Then you intend to have children of your own?" She shook her head at the absurdity of the question. "But of course you will. You'll need an heir, after all."

Justin scoffed at the assumption. "I don't give a damn what happens to my father's bloody title. As for having children of my own . . . I am scarcely the sort for father-hood."

"Why not?"

"I wouldn't know the first thing about raising a child. I would probably do a worse job than my sister."

Ariel didn't believe that for a moment, not after seeing him with the boy. She thought of Phillip and the little black boy and tried to convince herself it wasn't the same. If the child were his own, Phillip would be a wonderful father. But she couldn't really convince herself, and failing so miserably to do so, she opted for a change of subject.

"Is your sister always so . . . ?"

"Self-centered and uncaring? Usually. If I didn't know better, I would think she was my mother's daughter, instead of Mary Ross's."

Ariel didn't miss the implications of that. His mother and Barbara Townsend were a great deal alike, which meant his mother had also been selfish and uncaring. Since the woman had abandoned him, that was undoubtedly true.

"Your sister doesn't like me."

"Barbara doesn't like anyone, especially me."

"She doesn't like being in your debt. But then, neither do I."

The earl cast her a sideways glance but made no reply. "Thomas is waiting," he said instead. "Shall we go in?" He shoved open the swinging door that led into the warm, steamy interior of the kitchen, but Ariel shook her head.

"I think I'll forgo the cookie, if you don't mind." Too much was happening. She didn't want any more glimpses of this new, even more disturbing side of the earl. "The trip was rather tiring. Perhaps I'll lie down for a while."

He made a slight bow of his head. "As you wish."

Ariel turned away and started for the stairs, seeking the safety of her bedchamber, determined to forget Justin Ross, at least for a while. But again and again, her mind returned to the tenderness in the earl's expression when he had held the child.

Phillip Marlin reread the note he'd received that morning and a satisfied smile lit his face. Damn. The chit had led him a merry chase, but it looked like that chase was about to end.

Dearest Phillip—

I must see you. Please meet me at the Pig and Rooster at ten o'clock tonight.

Your friend,
Ariel Summers

It wasn't exactly a romantic entreaty, but what the hell? The girl was sneaking out on Greville, risking the man's formidable wrath in order to see him. Once he got her alone upstairs at the inn, she would give him what she had been giving Greville, and he'd make sure she kept her mouth shut about it. He smirked to think what Justin would say when he found out Phillip had been tupping his little blond whore.

And sooner or later, Phillip would make sure he did.

The day seemed to drag. He was eager for the night ahead, eager to have Ariel naked beneath him. He grew hard just thinking about it. The girl was softly feminine, unconsciously seductive, and even Greville's lovemaking hadn't been able to erase the air of innocence Phillip found so attractive. He could hardly wait to spread her legs and plunge himself inside her.

He would leave the house at half past nine, giving himself plenty of time to spare. He needed to make arrangements for a room for the night and order a light supper for them to enjoy upstairs, along with a goodly amount of wine. He didn't intend to leave anything to chance—not this time.

Now that he knew the truth of Ariel's low birth and that she was undoubtedly Greville's whore, Phillip intended to have her. Tonight would be the first time, but it wouldn't be the last.

"So . . . how goes the hunt?" That from Clayton Harcourt, who lounged in the doorway of the dark, wood-paneled study of the Brook Street mansion.

Seated behind his wide mahogany desk, Justin merely grunted. "Not well, I'm afraid."

Harcourt strolled over to the sideboard, poured himself a snifter of brandy, then flung himself casually down on the sofa in front of the hearth. "Are you telling me she isn't attracted to you?"

Justin sighed, shook his head, thinking of the last time they had been together. "I wouldn't exactly say that." No, he would say what had happened between them was like tasting sweet fire. "Unfortunately, she is smart enough to realize that once she comes to my bed, her chances for any sort of respectable future are slim."

Clay propped his shoulders on the end of the sofa, lazily swirling the liquid in the snifter. "If she wants a husband, after you grow tired of her you can always find her one."

Justin hadn't thought of that. With his wealth, he could accomplish that end quite easily, simply by providing her with a large-enough dowry. It wasn't a bad idea and yet he found himself disturbed by the notion. "I'll give it some thought."

"In the meantime, why don't the two of you join Teresa and me for the evening? We're going to Madison's. It's a gaming hell in Jermyn Street, very discreet. Teresa always enjoys it. Perhaps your Ariel will, too."

He looked down at the pile of papers he had been studying. Some of them pertained to the textile industry; some involved shipping or other of his business interests. "I've a great deal yet to do."

"You've got plenty of time. The evening doesn't begin

until latc. Besides, you can't woo the girl if you're never with her."

"True." Actually, he wasn't making much progress when he *was* with her. "All right, if Ariel agrees, we'll join you." Clay gave him the address, which Justin scratched down on a piece of paper. As soon as his friend left the house, he sent for Ariel, who appeared in the doorway a few minutes later.

"You wished to see me, my lord?" She wore a rose silk day dress with bands of moss green velvet beneath the bosom and around the hem.

"You look very fetching in pink, Miss Summers."

Her face flushed nearly that same soft shade. "Thank you, my lord."

"A friend of mine, Clayton Harcourt, has invited us to join him and a friend for some gaming tonight. I thought you might enjoy it."

For an instant, her face lit up. Then she blinked and her joyful expression disappeared. "I should like that, my lord, but I'm afraid I have a previous engagement." Her eyes slid away from his, and there was something in her face that made him suddenly wary.

"And might I ask what it is?"

She moistened her lips, stared down at her feet, looked anyplace but directly at him. "I'm going to visit a friend, a . . . a classmate from school. She's an acquaintance of Kassandra's."

"I see." She was lying. She was particularly poor at doing so, a fact that made him a little less angry than he might have been.

"I'm sorry I won't be able to join you," she said, for the first time sounding sincere. "I imagine it would have been fun."

"Yes. . . . Indeed, I'm sure it will be. Which is why, the more I think on it, the more certain I am that you should go. Send your friend a note. Tell her your plans have changed."

"But I couldn't possibly—"

"Oh, but you can." He clenched his jaw. "May I remind you, until your part of our bargain is fulfilled—in whatever manner—you will do as I say. Now, you will send your regrets to your *friend,* and we will spend the evening together at Madison's."

Ariel's lips thinned into an angry line. "As you wish, my lord." She said nothing more, just turned and walked out of the room.

Justin clenched his fist where it lay on top of the papers on his desk. She had been lying—but why? Surely she wasn't meeting Marlin. Surely she wouldn't be that foolish. The second son of the Earl of Wilton was a dangerous man when it came to women, particularly those not under the protection of an aristocratic name. Justin had told Ariel as much, but he was afraid she hadn't believed him. There was every chance she would risk herself for Marlin, a fact that sent a violent stab of jealousy spearing through him.

It was an emotion so foreign that for a moment he didn't realize what it was. He hadn't been jealous since the days when he had been so foolishly infatuated with Margaret. He had never imagined experiencing the feeling again.

Justin set his jaw, working to rein in his temper. Whatever Ariel intended, she wouldn't be meeting Marlin tonight, nor any night in the foreseeable future. Beginning on the morrow, he would keep a tighter leash on her or, at the very least, instruct one of the footmen to keep watch over her to be certain that she was safe.

Justin thought of Ariel with Marlin, and a soft ache throbbed in his chest. He tried to convince himself she was smart enough to see the man for what he really was, that she would never be foolish enough to fall in love with him, but the ache in his chest refused to go away.

CHAPTER TEN

*How the years have passed. It is difficult to believe that
in a few short weeks I shall be graduating and leaving
school, a place that now seems more a home to me than
any I have ever known. I shall desperately miss it, and
the friends I have made, yet I am eager to enter this
new world you have opened to me, to take my place as
the person into whom I am reborn.*

The letter faded from his thoughts as Justin helped Ariel
cross the paving stones toward the entrance to Madison's
Gaming Parlor, a nondescript two-story brick building in
Jermyn Street. Settling a hand at her waist, he led her
through a door guarded by a heavyset man in a frayed burgundy tailcoat into the dimly lit, slightly smoky interior.

Beneath his fingers, he could feel her stiffness, the faint
rigidity in her slender frame. All evening and particularly
at supper, which, fortunately, his sister had been too busy
to attend, Ariel had been cool to him, carefully keeping her
distance.

Now, as she looked at her surroundings, her calm reserve began to disappear, replaced by the natural curiosity
that was so much a part of her, the desire to experience life
that had led her down the path to his father and finally to
him.

They passed through the main salon, which was done in
shades of murky red and brassy gold, with fringed draperies
and faded Turkish carpets. The decor was garish, the heavy
flocked wallpaper lifting in several places, the furniture a
little worn. The room, which led into several smaller parlors, was crowded with people, most of them well dressed,
some more modestly garbed, a few looking as if they had
just staggered in off the street.

It was obvious that Madison's catered to a wide range

of customers, a number of them there to avoid being scrutinized by the ever-watchful gossipmongers of the *ton*.

As Justin led Ariel deeper into the interior, he could feel her excitement build. That she found nothing wrong with the vaguely shabby establishment, noticed nothing amiss in the over-rouged women and slightly drunken men, only made him dislike it more.

"I never knew there were places like this," she said with a hint of awe, staring at the patrons seated at the green baize tables or bent over the hazard tables trying their luck with the dice. She flashed him a bright, unexpected smile. "I'm glad you made me come."

But Justin wasn't glad. Ariel didn't belong in a place like this and he wished he'd never listened to Clayton Harcourt. Turning in search of him, Justin spotted the object of his disgruntlement lounging against the wall. Dressed in a brown tailcoat and buff breeches, he stood next to a woman in a low-cut emerald-and-black silk gown, a petite, dark-haired female who laughed a little too loudly at whatever it was Clay whispered in her ear.

"Over there." Justin urged Ariel in their direction. He noticed a momentary flash of uncertainty; then it was gone, masked behind a sunny smile. Clay waved when he saw them and maneuvered Teresa in their direction.

"You made it." Reaching out, Clay shook Justin's hand. "I wasn't really sure you would."

"Clay, this is Miss Summers. You've heard me speak of her."

"Indeed I have, on a number of occasions." His assessing brown eyes traveled the length of Ariel's tall-for-a-woman frame and warmed with approval, but there was nothing seductive in the appreciative look he gave her. "A pleasure, Miss Summers." Somehow Clay had surmised that Ariel meant more to Justin than simply a woman to fill his bed. She was safe with Clay. Justin thought how fortunate he was to have made Clayton Harcourt his friend.

The balance of the introductions were made. Teresa Nightingale was an attractive woman, perhaps one and twenty, the daughter of an actress, Clay had told him. Any trace of uncertainty Ariel might have felt in meeting her faded in the wake of Teresa's warm greeting.

Still, it bothered him to see Ariel in a place like this. Since the gowns he had purchased were not yet ready, she was dressed tonight in a demure pale blue silk, her silver-gold hair swept on her head. With her slender stature and innocent blue eyes, she stood out like an angel in the devil's parlor.

Justin inwardly winced at the image.

"Where shall we begin?" Clay asked, a slight drawl in his voice. "We've been playing hazard for the last few hours, but they nicked us pretty good."

"Miss Summers enjoys playing loo," Justin said, remembering what she'd said on their trip to the country. "Why don't we start there?"

Ariel grinned, her earlier pique long faded. He liked that about her, that her anger rarely lasted. He thought that perhaps she simply didn't have time for it, not when there were so many things she wanted to do.

The four of them approached a table, but there was only room for two more players. Ariel sat down beside Teresa, and Justin placed a stack of chips in front of her. She was very good at cards, he knew from their games in the carriage. It amused him to think she might actually win.

Ariel fingered the growing stack of chips in front of her. Teresa, who had been steadily losing, had finally tossed in her hand and excused herself to join Clay. The two men had disappeared into another gaming room while Ariel continued her game.

The dealer shuffled the deck, preparing for the next round of play, and her glance strayed to the ornate clock on the mantel above the fireplace at the end of the parlor. Ten o'clock.

She should be meeting Phillip at this very hour, explaining the bargain she had made with the earl and beseeching him to help her. Instead she had been forced to send him a second message, canceling the appointment she so desperately needed.

You wouldn't need Phillip if you simply ignored the debt, her mind suggested as it had a dozen times. *Lord Greville said he wouldn't force you.* But it wasn't her way to make promises she didn't keep, especially not one that underlay everything she was, everything she had worked so hard to accomplish.

She owed Justin Ross. Somehow she intended to repay him. Phillip would help her. If she had the courage to approach him.

Her stack of chips slowly grew and with it a triumphant smile. She could hardly wait to show the earl her winnings. She could almost see the look of approval she knew would appear on his face.

Her stack of chips grew even more impressive, eliciting comments from other players: a skinny bald-headed man in a frayed blue tailcoat, a buxom blonde with long-lobed ears, an attractive brown-haired girl in a low-cut red silk gown who appeared to be of an age with Ariel. The diamond-and-sapphire necklace that graced her ample bosom was expensive, but the way she was flirting with the man who stood behind her, Ariel wondered if perhaps she had sold her favors for the jewels.

It was a disturbing notion that hit a little too close to home. Ariel forced the thought away, along with the woman's suggestion that she should double her bet. There was always the chance she would lose, and she meant to keep her winnings. With that goal in mind and pleased by the considerable amount she had already won, she excused herself and left the table, her hands overflowing with chips.

Making her way to the cashier's window, she collected her winnings and stuffed the money into her reticule. She was just crossing the room in search of the earl when her gaze lit on a tall blond man escorting two women through the mirrored front doors. At the sight of Phillip Marlin with a brassy blonde on one arm and a toothy redhead on the other, Ariel came to a jarring halt.

Good heavens, it couldn't be!

But of course it was.

Phillip stopped dead in his tracks when he saw her, momentarily looking for all the world like a little boy caught with his hand in the cookie jar. His hair was slightly mussed, his posture a little too relaxed, and she realized that he had been drinking. With a brief word to his companions, he left them at one of the tables and started toward her, stopping right in front of her. He spoke so softly that only she could hear.

"Ariel . . . forgodsake, what are you doing here? And why did you cancel our meeting?"

She glanced around, hoping the earl wouldn't see them, knowing how furious he would be. "It's a long story, Phillip, and now is not a good time." Her gaze returned to the overblown women. "Besides, it's obvious you have far more important matters to attend."

Phillip's face turned red. "What did you expect me to do? I've been waiting to hear from you for weeks. When you finally do find time for me, at the very last minute you change your mind."

"I couldn't get away. I thought I could make it tonight, but—"

"But Greville had other plans."

"Yes." Another glance at the women. "Apparently, you did, too."

He tossed a look at his companions, who were dressed in bright satin and feathers and looking like a pair of strumpets, which, Ariel guessed, was exactly what they were.

"A man has needs, Ariel. Surely you can understand that."

Perhaps she could. Perhaps not. For the first time, she wondered what his true feelings were for her.

"Those women mean nothing," he went on as if he had read her thoughts. "It's you I care about. I want to see you. We can meet tomorrow afternoon at the Pig and Rooster, just as you suggested."

But suddenly Ariel felt uneasy. "I don't know. . . . I . . . I'm not certain I can get away."

"Three o'clock," he said. "I'll arrange for a private dining room. Just tell the owner you're there to see me and he'll take care of the rest."

"But I'm not sure—"

"You must come, Ariel darling. Please don't disappoint me again."

From the corner of her eye she caught the blur of movement, and Ariel sucked in a breath. Neither of them had heard the earl's quiet approach, but she knew with certain dread he had heard at least part of the conversation.

Hard gray eyes sliced into Phillip Marlin. "Miss Summers will be busy on the morrow. And every day after that. She won't be there, Marlin. Not tomorrow or any other day in the future."

The muscles in Phillip's face went taut. "You don't own her, Greville."

The earl didn't bother to reply. "I believe your . . . ladies . . . are waiting." He cast a mocking glance toward the two gaudily dressed women Phillip had come in with. "You wouldn't want to disappoint them."

Phillip ground his jaw. His face was flushed with anger. A rapid pulse beat at the side of his neck. For a moment, she thought he meant to continue the confrontation, and she stood there holding her breath. Instead, he made a rigid bow to Ariel, tossed a hateful glance at the earl, turned, and walked stiffly away. When he reached the women, he didn't even look at them, just stalked on by as if they weren't there. One of them screeched for him to wait, but he just kept walking. They both hurried after him and disappeared out the door.

"So . . . it was Marlin you were to meet tonight after all." The noisy hum of the people in the room made them an island where their words could not be heard.

"I don't . . . I don't know what you're talking about."

"I knew you were lying. I just wasn't sure why."

Ariel lifted her chin. "All right, then. I wanted to speak to him. I wanted to ask for his help."

"Are you in love with him?"

The question, coming so unexpectedly, took her by surprise. Was she in love with Phillip? There was a time she had thought so. It seemed an eternity since then. "I don't . . . I don't know."

Taking a firm grip on her arm, Justin urged her toward the door. He paused only long enough to tell his friend Clayton Harcourt they were leaving, then started walking again.

The carriage appeared out in front, the matched gray horses dancing beneath their silver-studded harnesses, silver lanterns lit beside each of the doors. They climbed in and settled against the tufted leather seats, Justin on one side, Ariel on the other. No one spoke. The coach jerked into motion, the silence inside the carriage thicker than the smoky interior of the gaming hell.

"I didn't mean to lie to you," Ariel said softly. "I just didn't know what else to do."

Greville said nothing, but a glacial chill seemed to pervade the coach.

"I thought he might loan me the money to repay you. I hoped he would help me find employment; then, in time, I'd be able to pay him back." His sharp gaze swung to her face, watching as she dug frantically into her reticule and drew out her night's winnings. "This is the money you loaned me to play." She took his hand, pried open his stiff fingers, and counted the money into his palm. "This is what I won." She pressed the rest into his hand. "I know it's only a start, but—"

He crumpled the money into a fist, the bank notes and coins, all smashed together. The turbulence in his gaze made something tighten in her chest. The earl rapped hard on the top of the carriage.

"Pull over!" he commanded the coachman. "Now!" He swung the door open even before the conveyance rolled to a halt at the side of the street and climbed out, slamming the door closed behind him. "Take Miss Summers back to the house. See that she gets there safely."

"Aye, milord. But how will you be gettin' home?"

"I'll find my own way back." And then he was gone, striding away on those long legs of his, eating up the ground at an amazing pace. Ariel stared after him out the window, watching him leave, feeling oddly shaken. He was angry, furious, in fact. But it was the flash of pain she had seen in his eyes that made her ache inside.

She had hurt him. It seemed impossible, but she wasn't mistaken. He believed she was rejecting him for Phillip, but it wasn't the truth. She no longer trusted Phillip Marlin as she once had. Not when she remembered the little black boy he kept as a pet. Not after she had seen him with the women.

Still, she wasn't about to become the earl's mistress. She dreamed of being a lady. She wanted a better life for herself, a better life for the children she someday hoped to raise. In the years since she'd left home, she had learned that becoming a man's kept woman was the least likely means of accomplishing that. She wanted a husband and family, she now knew. Wanted to lead a respectable life, to be accepted by friends like Kassandra Wentworth.

She wanted to live up to the image of the person she had worked so hard to become.

And yet when she thought of the earl . . .

As the carriage rolled toward the house, her gaze returned to the window. She tried to ignore the worry for him that throbbed like a splinter in her heart.

Justin sat in the smoky taproom of the tavern—was it the Hare and Garter or the Garter and Hare? Perhaps it was the Hairy Garter—he didn't know and he didn't really care. Whatever the place was, it was cold, or at least Justin felt a noticeable chill, a creeping, icy numbness that made his joints stiff and his blood pump sluggishly. But a fire blazed in the hearth and no one else in the room seemed aware of the chill.

He had a strange suspicion the cold was coming from inside him.

He glanced around the tavern, a low-ceilinged establishment with heavy wooden beams and wide-planked floors, a place he had once been in with Clay. Fortunately, it wasn't far from the gaming hell and not in too seedy a part of town.

He swayed a little on the scarred wooden bench he sat on, leaned against the rough wall behind him, and shot back the last of another tankard of ale.

He rarely drank. He was already drunker than seven lords, but he didn't give a damn about that, either. He wanted to deaden his mind, blot out the scene with Ariel in the carriage. He glanced at the dwindling stack of money on the table he had been slowly drinking up—Ariel's meager winnings, money she had given him as payment on her debt.

Justin swore softly, foully. Did she really think he cared about the damnable money? He had more than he could spend in a lifetime, and his investment earnings mushroomed every day.

He didn't want her money. He wanted her. Wanted her in his bed. Wanted to be inside her. Wanted to absorb the sunny warmth that seemed to emanate from her like heat from a fire. He wanted to brighten, if only for a while, his otherwise dreary world.

It was the letters, he knew. The letters that had endeared her to him in a way that nothing else could have. He had come to admire her determination, the iron will it had taken to escape her life of poverty and make something of herself. He even admired the means she had employed, the courage and shrewdness of a fourteen-year-old girl to come up with a bargain that would appeal to a man like his father.

He admired Ariel Summers, though he still wasn't sure he could trust her, and he had come to loathe himself for the conscienceless way he had treated her. God's blood, he had never meant to make her go through with his father's lecherous bargain. Before he had met her, he had planned to help her get started in the new life she had earned by grit and perseverance.

Then he'd walked in and seen her with his most hated enemy, Phillip Marlin. The old animosity had slammed into him with the force of a hammer, driving him to lengths he hadn't believed himself capable of.

In an instant he'd been back in time, seeing Margaret's face instead of Ariel's, remembering her lying naked in Phillip Marlin's arms. Margaret Simmons, the daughter of a viscount, was beautiful and fiery. Justin had been drawn to her from the moment he had met her, at a party at her father's country estate not far from Oxford, where he was attending school. Clay had introduced them, and for months they met in secret, Margaret unwilling to tell her father she was seeing the Earl of Greville's bastard son.

With the education he was receiving, Justin believed he could comfortably take care of her. He was insane enough to think she would actually marry him.

Then one morning, he had received an anonymous note.

Come to the Cock's Crow at 3 o'clock tomorrow. Your beloved will be waiting.

It wasn't Margaret's delicately feminine scroll, yet there was something in the words that drew him. He arrived at the small, out-of-the-way inn promptly at three, and the innkeeper, obviously in someone's pay, led him to an upstairs room. He opened the door to see the feather bed rumpled, the sheets carelessly tumbled onto the floor— Margaret and Phillip lying naked in each other's arms.

Cold rage set in.

Margaret screamed, but Phillip merely laughed.

Justin wanted to kill them.

Instead, he made a slight bow of his head. "I apologize for the intrusion," he said. "I can see the two of you are busy." Margaret trembled, a terrified light in her eyes. Justin ignored her. "You'll find the lady quite talented," he said to Marlin. "A little overzealous on occasion, but gifted just the same." To Margaret he said, "I believe, my dear, you have found your perfect mate." Turning, he walked out of the room, his heart irreparably broken.

Justin scoffed to remember it. Those were the days when he actually believed he had a heart.

He took another slug of his ale, wiped the foam from his mouth with the back of a hand. He glanced toward the fire, thought of moving closer. Even the tips of his fingers felt numb.

The tavern maid walked up just then, a short, big-breasted redhead in a low-cut blouse that displayed magnificent cleavage. "Ye want another, 'andsome?"

His head was spinning. The liquor had dulled his senses until it was hard to think, which was exactly what he wanted. "I'll be needing a room. Do you have one available?"

"We got a couple a nice ones right up there." She pointed toward the wooden stairs at the end of the taproom.

Justin shoved the rest of the money on the table in her direction, more than enough to pay for the lodging and plenty more ale. "That ought to cover it, as well as the drinks I'll be wanting."

She swept up the money, saw it was more than enough, and flashed him a seductive smile. "For that much blunt, ye can 'ave a little bonus, if ye like." She cupped a weighty breast and squeezed it meaningfully, making the nipple peak under her blouse.

Justin shook his head. "Some other time, perhaps."

The redhead merely shrugged. "Suit yerself." She returned with another pewter tankard and set it in front of him. Justin quaffed a mouthful of the bitter brew and leaned back against the wall, letting the liquor seep into him, wondering if it would lessen the chill, wishing he were drunk enough to sleep without dreaming of Ariel, certain he was not.

It was lust, he knew, that had driven him to such extravagant measures. Any other sort of emotion had long since been exorcized from his being. He did, however have a conscience, and when it came to Ariel, it pricked him sorely.

His conscience vying with his lust.

Justin took a sip of his ale and wondered, in the long run, which of them would win.

Two days passed.

Another autumn night settled in, windy and cold, shrouding the house in the gray mist of solitude. Alone in her room, Ariel tossed and turned but couldn't fall asleep. In the eerie silence of the house, she strained to hear some sound in the darkness, some indication that the earl had returned. As yet there was no sign of him.

Barbara was out for the evening. She rarely came in before dawn. Young Thomas was safely tucked in bed, having convinced Ariel to read him a bedtime story. But Justin had still not come home.

No one else seemed concerned. "He is the earl," the butler simply said. "He will return when he is ready." But what if something had happened? It was late at night when he'd left the carriage, and he was alone. The London streets were dangerous. What if he had been injured? What if he needed help? Was there no one at all who cared for the Earl of Greville?

It occurred to her, with Justin away, she could have gone to Phillip. It was the chance she had been seeking. But after their last few encounters, she no longer trusted Phillip, and even if she had, knowing the way the earl felt about him, it would have been a betrayal of the very worst sort.

A noise pricked her ears. Ariel's senses went on alert. Unsteady footfalls thundered in the entry. Something crashed to the floor and she heard a softly muttered curse. She listened as footsteps thudded up the stairs, wandered down the hall in an odd, unsteady manner, then disappeared inside the room at the end of the hall.

Justin's room.

At last he was home.

A feeling of relief washed over her, so strong her body

went limp. Ariel's head fell back against the pillow. She released a pent-up breath and said a tiny prayer of thanks that at last he was safely returned. Grogginess set in. Her eyelids slowly closed over tired, burning eyes. For the first time in three long nights, she drifted into a deep, peaceful sleep and didn't wake up until late the following morning.

Chapter Eleven

Ariel didn't see Justin all of that day or the next. She knew he was avoiding her, but after what had last transpired between them, she was afraid to seek him out. Time and again, she wondered where he had been during the days he had been gone, and an image of the two garish women kept creeping into her mind.

"A man has needs," Phillip had said. If that were so, the earl must have needs as well. Ariel remembered the night they had worked together in his room at the King's Way Inn. A tremor ran through her at the memory of his kiss, a mixture of hunger and longing that had drawn her to him and frightened her at the same time.

She closed her eyes against a vision of Justin lying next to the brassy blonde. She tried to imagine him kissing the toothy redhead and knew instinctively that whatever woman the earl took to his bed would be unlike either one of those women. Whoever it was would be beautiful and desirable, and certain it was so, nausea rolled in the pit of her stomach.

She didn't want to think of the earl with another woman. She didn't want to imagine him kissing her, making love to her. And being the forthright person she was, she had to ask herself why.

She tried to tell herself it was simply a matter of pride. He had told her that she was the woman he wanted, as if no other woman would do. If he truly meant what he'd said—

If he truly meant what he'd said, would it mean that he cared for her in some way? Would it mean that she was special, different from the other women he had known?

And even if that was so, what did it matter?

But deep in her heart where she didn't want to look, she knew that it did matter. It mattered very much.

Ariel sighed as she finished dressing, then fled Silvie's morning chatter and started down the stairs, heading for the breakfast parlor. She wasn't really hungry, but she knew she should eat. She had barely touched food since the night she had last seen the earl.

Halfway down the wide stone staircase, she paused. Barbara Townsend waited at the bottom, wearing her usual condescending expression. Ariel's stomach rolled and any thought of food instantly fled. She forced herself to continue, then stopped at the foot of the stairs.

"Lady Haywood." Sinking into a very proper curtsy, she lowered her lashes to cover her turbulent thoughts.

"It appears my brother wishes to see you. I told him I would give you the message."

Ariel hesitantly lifted her gaze. "D-do you know what he wants?" The minute the words left her mouth, she wished she hadn't said them. It was a stupid question. Justin never told his sister anything, and he certainly wouldn't discuss anything pertaining to her.

Barbara flashed a vicious smile. "If my brother is anything like our dear departed father, he has probably grown tired of your somewhat dubious charms by now." The ruby lips curled. "Never fear, however. I'm sure he'll be generous in his settlement. It isn't in the Greville tradition to leave a city full of disgruntled whores."

"I told you—I'm not his whore."

Barbara arched a perfect black eyebrow. "No? Well, then perhaps that is what he wishes to discuss. If he hasn't already had you, he must be quite determined to do so. Whatever it is, you will find him in his study." Barbara left with a swish of her aqua silk skirts, continuing her journey down the hall.

Ariel drew in a shaky breath, preparing herself to face the man who had, little by little, become so much a part of her life. She didn't know exactly how or when it had happened, didn't realize it actually had until the night he didn't come home. She hadn't been able to sleep, hadn't been able to eat. Worry for him had been a gnawing ache in her heart.

Ariel shivered as she moved down the hall. He'd been angry when he left the carriage. Was he mad enough to demand she fulfill her bargain? Part of her dreaded the upcoming encounter, yet another, secret part of her longed to see him, no matter what he wanted.

She knocked briefly on the door, and he gave her permission to enter. She walked into the study to find him standing behind his desk facing away from her, his hands clasped behind his back, staring at the rows of books but not really seeing them. He turned at her approach, and her heart squeezed hard at the weariness in his face.

He looked drawn and tired, and defeated in a way she had never seen him. Ariel started forward, a painful ache throbbing in her chest.

"Thank you for coming," he said formally, indicating that she should take a seat in the chair across from him. She did so slowly, purposefully arranging her skirts around her, using the time to compose herself. As the seconds slipped past, she studied his expression, searching in vain for a clue to his thoughts.

Searching for something to say.

"I was . . . We were all of us concerned for you. I'm glad you got home safely."

He looked up at her, those penetrating gray eyes dark and intense, the skin beneath them faintly smudged from lack of sleep. "Are you?"

"I . . ." She looked him straight in the face. "Yes. Very glad."

He said nothing to that, but a flicker of some indefinable emotion appeared for an instant in his gaze. He seated himself behind the desk and leaned forward, resting his elbows on the top. "I imagine you can guess why it is I wished to see you."

She smoothed a fold of her skirt. "Actually, I'm not completely certain."

"The days are slipping past. It is time we discussed our bargain."

Her stomach clenched. Dear God, she was afraid of this.

Ariel moistened her lips, remembering his sister's words. *"If he hasn't already had you, he must be quite determined to do so."* "What . . . What about it?"

He straightened a bit, fixed his gaze on a spot on the wall above her head, studying it as if it were the most interesting object in the room. "It is obvious I was mistaken in believing that, in time, you might return the . . . affection . . . I feel for you. Since the notion of becoming my mistress is so repugnant—"

"That's not so!" she broke in, appalled at the words he had chosen. "You mustn't think it is you, my lord."

"No? What is it, then?"

Ariel searched for the words, knowing how important this was. "It isn't you," she repeated. "Well, perhaps it was in the beginning. I didn't know you then, and in truth, you can be quite intimidating."

His mouth edged up, a rather fine mouth, she thought, remembering how much softer it felt than it looked.

"Yes . . . I'm certain I can be."

"Now that I know you, I find you . . . Well, I think you are a very attractive man and any woman who wished to become your mistress would undoubtedly be pleased to be chosen."

"But you are not that woman," he said dryly.

"No. That is, I don't wish to become any man's mistress."

"Not even Phillip Marlin's?"

She flushed. Did he really think she would prefer Phillip to him? Because suddenly and very clearly she realized, if she were forced to choose, she would far rather be involved with the earl.

"What I am trying to say is that becoming a man's mistress is something far different than I first understood. And in truth, when I made my bargain, I never really believed I would have to go through with it. I always thought . . . when the time actually came . . . I'd find another way to repay the money. Now that I'm older, I realize the sort of future a woman like that has. And I . . . Well, I despise the notion of selling my body like the lowliest strumpet."

A muscle bunched in the earl's lean cheek. "I never would have thought of you that way," he said softly. When Ariel made no reply, he released a long, weary breath and came to his feet. "Whatever the case, it is no longer important. I told you once I wouldn't force you into my bed. The other night I realized that by holding the cost of your education over your head, that is exactly what I was doing. As of this moment, Ariel Summers, your debt is completely and fully repaid."

Her heart jerked. Surely she hadn't heard him correctly. But her pulse was racing even faster and her mind was saying it was true. *It's over! I'm free!* shouted a little voice inside her. As she had hoped from the beginning, the earl had released her from their bargain. She sat there shaking, heady with relief, wondering why she wasn't smiling. Why she wasn't laughing with joyous abandon.

"I'll find a place for you to live," he was saying. "Arrange for a monthly stipend to be paid—"

"No." The word came out of its own accord, but once it was said, she recognized the rightness of it.

The earl's head came up. "What?"

"I said no. I won't accept any more of your charity."

One of those slashing black brows arched up. "You won't accept my charity? You have no family, no money, no one else to turn to. What in God's name are you talking about?"

"I'm telling you I won't take another farthing of your money—I've already taken more than enough. And I still wish to repay you." She glanced at the stack of paperwork that habitually sat on his desk, ledgers and portfolios, some of them dog-eared from hours of use, all of them filled with endless pages of numbers. "I wish to work for you as I did before."

For a moment he stood there utterly speechless. "That's impossible," he finally said.

"Why is it impossible? Between your duties as earl and keeping up with your investments, you work from dusk till dawn. You said yourself you hated doing the numbers. Let me do them for you."

"Respectable women don't do that sort of work."

"Respectable women don't make the sort of bargain I made."

He sank heavily down in his chair. "Where would you live?"

"Here, of course. There is plenty of room and I can pay my debt off faster if I don't have to worry about spending money for rent and food. You have dozens of servants in the house. I could live on the third floor with them."

Justin raked a hand through his hair, dislodging a few of the thick black strands. "This is insane."

At last she felt like smiling. "You've given me innumerable gifts—my education, my speech, even the clothes I am wearing. I intend to repay you with the gift of my labor. What is insane about that?"

He glanced up, pinned her with his steady gaze. It occurred to her that tired or not, angry or not, he was still one of the handsomest men she had ever seen.

"There is still the problem of the lust I feel for you," he said. "I want you, Ariel. That isn't going to lessen as long as you remain here."

Some little demon inside her reared its ugly head. "You can always go back to the woman you stayed with while you were away."

"I wasn't with a woman."

"Of course it's really none of my concern, but—"

"If you must know, I got reeling drunk and stayed that way for two straight days. I was drunk when I came home. Believe me, I paid for my folly."

She had the good grace to flush. "I'm sorry. As I said, it is none of my concern." But the demon was gleefully grinning, and Ariel was far more pleased than she should have been.

Justin rounded the desk and walked toward her, and Ariel stood up, too.

He stopped right in front of her. "All right . . . we'll do it your way—on three conditions."

She eyed him with a hint of suspicion. "What are they?"

"First, you remain in the bedchamber you currently occupy. We've both invested a great deal in turning you into a lady. I intend to see that you continue being treated as one."

"I can hardly protest living well. What are the other two conditions?"

"While you're here, we decide what to do about your future."

"And?"

"And you stay away from Phillip Marlin."

She couldn't see Phillip for as long as she remained with the earl. Funny, giving him up wasn't nearly so hard this time.

Ariel slowly smiled, feeling free for the first time in years. Free and in charge of her life. Whatever happened now, whatever future was in store for her, would be of her own choosing. "Agreed," she said firmly. Then she grinned. "When do we start?"

In the smoking room of Brook's Club, St. James's, Clay Harcourt lounged in a comfortable brown leather chair across from his friend Justin Ross. In the past, Justin rarely came to the club. For the past two weeks, he had been there nearly every evening.

Clay took a slow draw on his cigar, tilted his head back, and allowed the smoke to float upward in lazy blue rings. "So . . . how're things going with your newest employee?"

Justin glanced toward him, seemed to drag himself out of a fog. "I'm sorry. What did you say? My mind must have wandered."

"So I see. I don't suppose you were thinking about a woman? Perhaps a saucy little baggage with the smile of a saint and face of a silver-haired angel?"

Justin made a sound of disgust in his throat. "Unfortunately, she rarely leaves my thoughts these days. I almost wish my sister was still in residence. Barbara was a thorn in all of our sides, but at least she served as a sort of buffer. Without her and Thomas to intercede, it's been bloody hell."

Clay chuckled softly. Justin was often brooding and distant, but Clay had never seen him quite like this, not even in the days when he thought he was in love with Margaret Simmons. "Take heart, my friend. Her debt will be repaid in what . . . maybe another ten years?"

Justin cast a dark look his way. "I'm paying her a king's ransom for the work she is doing, and I find your attempt at humor in light of the situation more than a little annoying."

Clay bit back a smile. "Sorry," he said, though he wasn't the least bit repentant. Justin needed his usually unflappable demeanor ruffled once in a while. And Clay was happy to be the man to do it.

He swirled the brandy in his snifter, inhaled the vaguely sweet scent. "Ariel was living in the house with you before your sister's arrival. Why is it so much more difficult now?"

"Because ever since I told her she was free of her debt, she is different. Before she was always wary, afraid of what I might do. Now that I've released her from her pledge, she seems to feel differently about me."

"Perhaps she trusts you. You could have demanded she fulfill the promise she made, but you didn't. You did what you thought was right. That would surely inspire a certain amount of trust."

"I suppose it would . . . if that had been the case. In truth, I was acting selfishly, merely salving my conscience. It was hardly a noble thing to do."

Clay said nothing to that. Justin always rationalized his behavior in the harshest, most unpleasant terms, casting himself in the worst possible light. Clay knew exactly why his friend had done what he did—because he cared for the girl, because he admired and respected her—and there wasn't a damned thing selfish about it.

Justin sighed. "The worst part is, the more she trusts me, the more open and guileless she is, the more I want her. My noble image is wearing extremely thin, I can tell you. Every time she smiles at me, I want to tear off her clothes, drag her down on the carpet, and ravish her sweet little body. I don't know how much longer I can stand it."

Clay took a sip of his brandy. "If you want her so badly, you could always marry her."

Beneath his dark skin, Justin actually blanched. "Marry her?"

"Why not? You're a bachelor. Ariel's of an age to wed. Of course there is always the chance, much as I hate to suggest it, that she has been scheming to leg-shackle you from the start."

"That's ridiculous. I'm hardly in the marriage mart. Ariel is aware of that."

"Well, you did say how clever she was. Your father was scarcely an easy mark, yet he managed to succumb to her wiles." He grinned. "And she was only fourteen years old."

Justin merely grunted. "Marriage is not a possibility."

"Why not?"

"Because that kind of commitment ought to involve at least some measure of emotional attachment. All I feel for Ariel is a healthy dose of lust."

Clay took a draw on his cigar, let the smoke drift up. He wasn't about to argue, since it wouldn't do a shilling's worth of good. As far as Clay was concerned, his friend felt a good deal more than lust for Ariel Summers. Justin would never admit it, of course—not even to himself.

"Perhaps another trip to Madame Charbonnet's," Clay suggested, merely to test his theory. "The women there are beautiful and we both know how talented they are."

Justin looked mildly repulsed. "I don't think so. At least not at present."

He didn't want another woman. He wanted the willowy blonde. That he denied his feelings for Ariel came as no surprise to Clay. Between his father's lack of attention, his mother's abandonment, and Margaret Simmons's betrayal,

Justin had buried his feelings so deep even he couldn't find them. On the rare occasion they surfaced, he convinced himself it was something different, something far more pragmatic than simple human emotion.

Clay took a sip of his brandy, not sure whether to feel sorry for his friend or amused. "Give it some time," he said. "Things usually have a way of working out."

Justin didn't answer. Clay wondered how much longer his friend could go on like this before he snapped. It was only a matter of time, he guessed, before Justin's sweet, trusting little angel found herself flat on her back in the Earl of Greville's feather bed.

Then again, as Clay had said, perhaps that was exactly what the little schemer wanted.

October had arrived. Fall had descended, but Ariel scarcely noticed. This morning she hummed as she walked down the hall to the study, returning one of the ledgers she had carried up to her room last night. She was working hard every day and sometimes well into the evening, but she was amazed to discover she was actually enjoying herself.

It felt good to be doing something productive, using the knowledge she had studied so hard to gain. She wondered why other women hadn't yet figured out that working didn't have to be the drudgery men made it seem. If you were doing something you liked, it could actually be fun.

She came to the door of the study, turned the silver knob, and walked in without knocking. She shared the office with the earl now, he at his big desk, Ariel at a smaller desk on the opposite side of the room. Work came first for both of them; they were long past the formal stage.

Greville glanced up, muttered something to himself, then bent his dark head and went back to studying the portfolio that lay open in front of him.

Ariel paused for a moment just to look at him. He was dressed in a white lawn shirt and dark gray breeches, his burgundy tailcoat draped over the back of a nearby chair.

His sleeves were rolled up above nicely muscled forearms darkened by a sprinkle of coarse black hair.

It was overcast outside, the weather damp and chilly, a thick layer of clouds blocking most of the sun. A lamp burned on his desk, casting shadows across his face, shading the hollows beneath his high cheekbones. His black hair, usually perfectly trimmed, had grown a little longer, curled against his snowy stock.

She wondered if it was as soft and silky as it looked, wondered if his neck was as muscular as his forearms, and a funny little flutter whirred in the pit of her stomach. Aghast at her train of thought, she tightened her hold on the heavy ledger and walked to the shelf behind his desk to put it away, careful to keep her eyes straight ahead and her thoughts on the work ahead.

Propping the book on the top shelf where it belonged, she tried to shove it into place, but as tall as she was, she couldn't quite reach it. She heard his chair scraping back, felt him come to his feet right behind her.

"Here, let me help you." He stood so close her back brushed his chest. She could feel the muscles bunching beneath his shirt as he slid the heavy volume back in place. The task was completed, but neither of them moved. A warm thread of heat spun through her. The clock on the mantel ticked steadily, matching the heavy thudding of her heart.

Slowly, as if he feared she might bolt, he lowered his hands and his long, elegant fingers settled lightly on her shoulders. He smelled faintly of ink and some subtle male scent that belonged solely to him. She could feel the rise and fall of his chest, feel his warm breath on her cheek, moving tendrils of her hair.

"Ariel . . ." he whispered, his voice low and rough. The sound was a plea that went straight to her heart. She didn't question what she should do, simply turned and looked up at him, the answer to his plea in her eyes.

He lightly touched her cheek. His thumb moved across her bottom lip and little shivers raced over her skin.

"Justin . . ." she whispered, just for the pleasure of saying his name.

His eyes held hers, penetrating eyes, eyes that held a thousand unspoken thoughts. "Ariel . . . sweet God, what you do to me." He drew in a deep, shuddering breath, framed her face between his hands. With a groan of defeat, he covered her mouth with his. The kiss was soft and deep. A saturating, alluring, penetrating kiss. A moist, drugging kiss that made her senses reel and seemed to have no end.

"I've tried," he whispered softly, kissing the corners of her mouth, then brushing her lips again. "You'll never know how hard I've tried." Turning her head, he kissed her one way and then another, pressing deeper and deeper into her mouth, tasting her bottom lip, coaxing her to open for him. His tongue slid in like hot, wet silk, taking her deeply, claiming her in some way.

Ariel moaned and clung to him, her arms sliding up around his neck, her body swaying toward him. Liquid heat slid into her stomach. Her legs felt rubbery and numb. He had never made her feel like this—never. But she had been afraid of him before. She wasn't afraid of him now.

Justin kissed her again. He shifted a little, and she felt his hands on the underside of her breasts, making the nipples grow hard. Over the fabric of her gown, those long, dark fingers curled around the fullness, gently cupping her, and a low sound came from his throat.

"Ariel . . ." he whispered, kneading the softness, teasing her nipples, sending little tongues of fire shooting out through her limbs. Ariel clung to him, warm shivers running across her flesh, the bottom dropping out of her stomach. She knew she had to stop him, but dear God, the pleasure was so sweet, the sensations so wondrous, her traitorous body refused to listen.

Instead, she found herself pressing closer against his chest, leaning into the thick, unmistakable ridge of his manhood. Justin kissed the side of her neck, took her mouth again, and Ariel whimpered. She was trembling now, her heart pounding raggedly. She felt him reach for the buttons at the back of her gown, pop the first one open, reach for the second.

"Justin . . . ?" She barely whispered his name, yet the desperation was clear in her voice. If she didn't stop him now, she would no longer want to.

A heavy shudder passed through him. For several long seconds, he stood immobile, his beautiful hands dormant as he fought to regain control. For an instant, she wished that she had kept silent, let him work his magic, seen how brightly the fires could burn. Ariel knew beyond doubt that disaster lay along that course.

He dragged in a shaky breath of air, his posture straightening, becoming almost rigid. Turning her gently, he fastened the buttons at the back of her gown.

"I'm sorry," he said gruffly. "I didn't mean for that to happen."

An apology was hardly needed. She had wanted him to kiss her. She had wanted far more than that. But she could hardly say that to him.

"It wasn't your fault. It just sort of . . . happened."

Those intense gray eyes, usually so unreadable, flashed with some turbulent emotion. Then his mask fell back into place. "Considering what the consequences might have been, it had better not happen again. In fact, it would be wiser if we didn't see each other for a while." He moved away from her, carefully rolled down the sleeves of his shirt, and buttoned the cuffs. "In that regard, I have some business to attend to out of town. I'll be gone for several weeks."

Her heart slammed. "Several weeks?" She tried not to think how dismal the big, empty house would be without him. How badly she would miss him. "But you never said anything about leaving the city."

Justin looked uncomfortable and she realized he had only just made the decision. He was leaving because of her, because of what had happened between them, a happenstance that was her fault perhaps more than his.

"I need to check on the progress they're making on the

textile mill. I'll leave a list of things you can do while I'm away. I imagine you'll get a good deal of work done with no one around to bother you."

"Yes . . . I imagine I will." But he was hardly a bother. In fact, she looked forward to their lively discussions. She enjoyed working with him, she had discovered, enjoyed learning things about business, about what made a good investment and what made a poor one, about which banks paid the highest interest and what sort of person made a good candidate for a loan.

She liked talking to him, liked just knowing he was somewhere in the house.

He strode over and snatched his coat up off the back of the chair, shrugged it onto his wide shoulders. "I'm going out for a while. I won't be home until late."

Ariel said nothing, just watched his long, graceful strides carry him out of the room. Lately he'd made a point of staying out late most evenings. He was trying to protect her, and perhaps himself, trying to keep her safe from the desire he felt for her.

For the first time since her arrival at his Brook Street mansion, Ariel realized that being protected from the earl was no longer what she wanted.

CHAPTER TWELVE

Clayton Harcourt rapped on the door to Justin's house, then waited impatiently for the butler to let him in.

"Good afternoon, Mr. Harcourt." Knowles dragged open the heavy wooden door with his usual lack of enthusiasm. "I'm terribly sorry. I'm afraid Lord Greville isn't in at the moment. You may leave him a message if you like."

Clay frowned. He had business to discuss and he didn't have all that much time. "Yes, I'd appreciate that. I have some paperwork I'd like him to look at. I'll leave it in his study, if I may." He stepped into the entry, which was dark and always a little dreary, his flat leather satchel tucked under one arm. He removed his kidskin gloves, tossed them into his beaver hat, and handed them to the butler, who led him down the hall to Justin's study.

Knowles swung open the door, then came up short. "Excuse me, Miss Summers. I didn't realize you were still in here working. Mr. Harcourt has some papers for Lord Greville. He wishes to pen him a message."

"Of course. Please come in." She stood up behind the desk, a vision in navy blue and white, her pale blond hair swept up as she usually wore it. Smiling, she turned the crystal pen-and-ink set on the top of the desk in his direction.

"Thank you. I won't be a minute." She was even prettier than he remembered, so blond and fair, all lightness and sunshine to Justin's brooding darkness. Clay could see in an instant why his friend was so drawn to her.

And yet it worried him. He trusted very few women. He had known too many who would cut off a man's cods just to watch him squirm.

Knowles returned to his duties and Clay turned his attention to Ariel. Perhaps a word with her would set his mind to rest.

"I was hoping Lord Greville would be home," he said, easing into the conversation. "I stumbled upon a business proposition I thought he might find interesting. I rarely involve myself in financial matters, but this little deal looked so sweet, I couldn't resist."

"I'm afraid he won't be home until late. And on the morrow he plans to leave for Cadamon. Apparently, he'll be gone for several weeks." A fact she didn't look the least bit happy about.

"As I understand it, you accompanied him the last time he went."

"That was different."

"How so?"

Her chin inched up. "He intended to make me his mistress, as I believe you are aware."

He smothered a hint of amusement. "I gather that's changed."

"Yes." But she didn't look completely pleased about that, either.

He opened his satchel and pulled out the business proposal he had brought, set the papers on top of a stack on the corner of the desk.

"He would have treated you well, you know. Justin is nothing at all like his father. He doesn't make a habit of keeping women. In fact, he has never taken a mistress before—which is not to say he has been living the life of a monk."

"I'm sure he hasn't. In fact, I imagine there are any number of women who would gratefully accept the position he has offered."

"If he wanted them, yes. What I'm telling you is that you mean more to him than simply a casual affair."

Ariel made no reply. She wasn't making this easy.

"I don't know how well you've come to know him. Perhaps by now you realize he isn't the coldhearted man he appears."

Interest flickered in the delicate lines of her face. "Will you tell me about him?"

Clay smiled. "What exactly would you like to know?"

"He seems so terribly remote. Has there never been anyone he was close to, anyone who cared about him? I know his mother abandoned him and his father was never around. It's obvious his sister cares only about herself. He mentioned a grandmother once, but he never seems to see her, and young Thomas stays mostly in the country."

"I care about him," Clay said softly.

Ariel's blue eyes swung to his face, beautiful eyes, guileless eyes . . . or at least so they appeared. "So do I," she said.

Clay mulled that over, wondering if she were sincere, wondering if she were wise enough to see through Justin's hard, cynical exterior to the man he was inside. "From what I understand, you don't have anyone who cares about you, either. I suppose that gives the two of you something in common."

Her mouth curved into a soft, wistful smile. "In a way. But unlike Justin, I was loved very dearly as a child. I had the most wonderful mother a daughter could ever have and two very dear grandparents. It was only after they died and I was left in the care of my father that I suffered any sort of mistreatment. I understand how important love is. I don't think Justin has even the faintest idea."

"Perhaps you could teach him."

"Teach him?"

"I should think a person would have to know how it feels to *be* loved before he could give love in return. But surely that is something a man could learn."

"Perhaps it is. Perhaps if I were brave enough, I might try. Unfortunately, the risk is simply too great. As soon as my debt is repaid, I'm leaving. Lord Greville is paying me a ridiculously high wage, but I can hardly argue with that." She smiled impishly. "Besides, I am probably worth it."

Clay laughed, liking her confidence, the sense of self-worth that was so opposite Justin's own dark opinion of himself.

"Once I've completed my obligation, Justin has agreed

to secure some sort of position for me. I trust his judgment in that regard, and I believe I'll be happy in whatever job he finds me."

"I imagine you will be . . . at least for a while."

"What do you mean?"

He shrugged, hoping he looked nonchalant. "You're young and extremely attractive. It's only natural that someday you'll wish to marry."

"I'm a woman, Mr. Harcourt, no different from the rest. Someday I'd like very much to have a family of my own."

Clay just nodded. On the surface, she seemed everything that Justin had said she was—forthright and determined, sweetly sincere. "I wish you well, then, Miss Summers. Ask Justin to take a look at the proposal I left on his desk, will you? Tell him I'd like him to stop by my place before he leaves the city. We'll need to act swiftly if we're going to sew up this deal."

"I'll write him a note," Ariel said. "In case he leaves before I see him in the morning."

"Thank you." Clay made polite farewells, retrieved his hat and gloves, then left the house, his mind on the conversation he'd just had. When he'd spoken to Justin about Ariel at the club, he'd been more than half-convinced she was the conniving little saucebox she was at fourteen.

After their conversation, he was beginning to think he might be mistaken. If he was and Justin wanted her as badly as it appeared he did, perhaps marriage wasn't such a bad solution.

Clay tucked his hat beneath his arm and pulled on his kidskin gloves. Surely being married wouldn't be all that bad. A lot of people did it. In truth, he wouldn't mind having a wife and children of his own someday. Of course, he was hardly a one-woman man, but that was scarcely important—neither were most of his friends. It would probably be good for Justin—a couple of kids running around the house, a wife who could give him the affection he never had as a boy. Maybe she could help him dissolve that blasted irritating calm he wore like a heavy iron cloak.

Then again, perhaps the girl was nothing at all the innocent she appeared. Perhaps she was now simply far more sophisticated at achieving her goals than she had been at fourteen. He hoped Justin was wise enough to discern the truth.

And damned glad he wasn't in his friend's position.

Ariel stared up at the faded blue velvet canopy above her four-poster bed. Outside the window, a storm had set in, obscuring the moon and stars. A fierce wind howled and lightning cracked in great yellow spikes against an ominous black sky. It was well past midnight, yet she couldn't fall asleep.

She kept thinking about Justin, about what had happened between them in his study. If she closed her eyes, she could still feel the heat of his long, hard body, the hot, sweet sensations that speared like lightning through her blood. Just thinking about it made her tremble as she had in his arms.

The experience had been intoxicating, so heady she hadn't wanted it to end. Neither had Justin, she knew. In truth, she was amazed he had stopped when he did. *Why did he?* she wondered. But in her heart she knew.

For years he had been reading her letters. He knew her innermost thoughts and dreams, knew her better, perhaps, than anyone else in the world. He wanted to make love to her, but he knew that in doing so he would be crushing her dreams.

Ariel sighed. Justin pretended to be hard and uncaring. She no longer believed that was so. Working so closely with him, she was privy to the changes he was making in Cadamon—to increase profits, he had said. Undoubtedly a successful operation would be the end result, yet she found it hard to believe the lovely little four-room stone cottages he was constructing for the workers were being done strictly for money.

And there was the child, little Thomas Townsend, Justin's nephew. It was obvious the boy deeply loved his uncle, and the feeling was definitely returned. Justin was wildly protective of the boy. If he thought his sister would agree, Ariel believed Justin would keep the child there with him in London. But giving up her child would hardly be good for Barbara's reputation, and to the Countess of Haywood one's status among the *ton* was all-important. So the boy remained with his mother and Justin paid the bills, telling himself it was only a matter of financial practicality.

And there was the bargain Ariel had made. With the earl's generosity, she had received the education that she had so desperately wanted. Instead of collecting his debt, Justin had released her from her pledge and, if she had allowed it, would have continued seeing to her welfare.

"I don't know how well you've come to know him," Clayton Harcourt had said. *"Perhaps by now you realize he isn't the coldhearted man he appears."*

Justin wasn't the heartless villain she had first believed. Just desperately, achingly lonely.

A gust of wind rattled the shutters outside the window, drawing her attention. Rain fell in great gray sheets against the rough stone walls of the mansion. Justin was out there in the storm because of her, because he couldn't trust what might happen if he stayed in the house. He was out there, and she was worried about him.

Worried about him and a great deal more. Ariel fought down a painful swell of emotion, for the first time allowing herself to admit the truth.

Dear God, I'm in love with him.

The previously unimaginable thought brought a thick lump to her throat. How had it happened? *When* had it happened? Was it a certain moment in time, a special minute, a certain day, or did it overtake her little by little, like sand beneath an encroaching surf? Perhaps it was the first time she had looked past the bland reserve in those cool gray eyes to the turbulent emotions they so neatly disguised. Perhaps it was the moment she had realized his harsh facade was only a cover for the loneliness and despair that had haunted him for so long.

Tears stung the backs of her eyes. Tears for Justin and the empty life he led. Tears for herself for loving a man who would never love her in return. How could she have allowed herself to fall in love with a man who didn't know the meaning of the word?

"Perhaps you could teach him."

Harcourt's casual statement had haunted her since the moment he had said it. Was it possible for a man like Justin to learn to love?

And if it was, was she woman enough to teach him?

More important, did she have the courage to try?

She heard him just then, downstairs in the entry. A moment later, his weary footfalls started up the stairs. He rarely drank and she knew he wasn't drunk now. Just tired and wet and lonely.

On the morrow he would be leaving. She wasn't sure when he would return. For weeks she had avoided him. Now it suddenly seemed imperative that she see him—tonight, this very minute. Ariel's hands shook as she slid from the wide feather bed and drew on her quilted blue satin wrapper. She tugged her loosely plaited braid out from beneath the collar, letting it fall down her back, and started across the room, her heart thumping, her mouth suddenly dry.

Moving quietly, checking to be certain none of the servants were about, she opened the door and slipped out into the hallway. A silver lamp flickered on a table at the end of the passage, casting eerie shadows against the walls. She shivered from the chill in the drafty corridor and hurried toward the master suite, pausing for a moment when she reached it.

On the opposite side of the heavy wooden door she could hear him moving about. She took a breath for courage, grasped the silver knob before she lost her nerve, turned the handle, and stepped into the dimly lit room. Standing in the sitting room, she could see through the open door leading into his bedchamber. Firelight flickered in the hearth and an oil light burned on the marble-topped dresser.

Justin stood in front of it, preparing himself for bed.

For an instant Ariel couldn't breathe. He had stripped away his tailcoat, waistcoat, and white lawn shirt. Wet black breeches clung to his narrow hips like a layer of paint, outlining long, hard-muscled legs encased in tall black boots. His hair was wet with rain and clinging to the nape of his neck, while a thick lock hung over his forehead. His chest was bare, wide and dark and covered with a fine thatch of curly black hair that arrowed past a flat stomach heavily ridged with muscle.

Unconsciously Ariel moistened her lips, her gaze still riveted on the beautiful maleness of his body. She didn't realize she was moving, silently walking toward him, until he looked up and saw her and went completely still. Concern replaced surprise, and those slashing black brows slammed nearly together.

"Ariel? What's happened? What's wrong?" He started toward her, reached her in three long strides, worriedly grasped her shoulders. "Are you all right?"

She moistened her trembling lips. "I had to come. I had to see you."

"Ariel . . . love . . . tell me what's happened."

"Everything is fine. I just . . . I don't want you to go."

He said nothing for the longest time. "I don't understand."

"In a way I don't, either. I only know I don't want you to leave on the morrow. I want you to stay here with me."

His expression changed, hardened. A muscle leaped in his cheek. "You know why I'm going. Even you aren't that naive."

She flushed a little but didn't look away. "I know why you're going. You're trying to keep your distance, trying to protect me. You don't want to hurt me."

Turbulence rose in those incredible gray eyes; then it was gone. "I'm going because I lust for you. If I stay here, sooner or later, I'll take you."

Would he? Not unless she wanted him to. She knew that about him now, knew that she could trust him.

"Do you want me that badly, Justin?"

His jaw tightened. Something hot and hungry moved over his features. "You know I do."

"Then make love to me. Now. Tonight."

For an instant the pupils of his eyes flared; then he slowly shook his head. "You don't know what you're saying."

She reached toward him, rested a hand on his chest. "You're wrong, Justin. I know exactly what I'm saying." And she did. For the first time since she'd stepped into the hall, she understood what had compelled her to come to his room, understood exactly the risk she was taking, knew that she'd had to take it. "When you canceled my debt, you gave me back my freedom. You allowed me to make my own choices, my own decisions. I'm choosing what both of us want."

Justin stared at her as if she were another, different woman, his dark gaze troubled and intense. "You can't mean that. You've fought against this since the day we met."

"I mean it more than I've ever meant anything in my life. Make love to me, Justin . . . please." Long, disturbing seconds passed; then a shudder rippled the length of his body. His hands reached out, circling her waist, and he hauled her into his arms.

His chest was still damp with rain. She could feel his rapidly beating heart. His wet breeches soaked her robe, but Ariel didn't care. Sometime during the long hours of the evening, everything had become crystal clear. From this moment forward, she would do what her heart demanded, no matter the outcome, no matter the cost.

Justin's gaze moved over her face, studying each of her features, looking into her eyes as if he searched her soul. Then he lowered his head and kissed her, the fiercest, most achingly tender kiss she had ever known. A kiss that said all of the things she yearned to hear him say and probably never would. Ariel kissed him back with all the love she had just discovered, and dear God, it felt so right, so good.

She pressed soft kisses against the side of his mouth, against his throat, against his bare shoulder. She felt him tremble.

Justin dragged in a shuddering breath and gently caught her chin with his hand, forcing her to look at him. "Ariel, are you certain?"

Very certain, she thought. *I love you.* But she didn't say the words. He wouldn't know how to cope with those sorts of emotions—not yet. She had only just learned to accept them herself. "I'm sure, Justin."

Sliding her arms around his neck, she tangled her fingers in his damp black hair and drew his mouth down to hers, kissing his hard mouth to softness, inhaling the musky, masculine scent of him. Justin kissed her deeply, erotically, as if he couldn't get enough, his warm breath flowing into hers, their lips moist and clinging. Ariel swayed against him, marveling at how perfectly their bodies fit together, enraptured by the solid, protective feel of his chest.

Then he was lifting her up, striding through the doorway back into his bedchamber, laying her down on the big tester bed and stripping away her satin wrapper. He tugged the ribbon at the neck of her cotton night rail, then drew it off over her head. Embarrassment warmed her cheeks, but she didn't try to cover herself. Not when she saw the glow of approval that gleamed like silver fire in his eyes. He pulled the ribbon that held her loosely plaited hair and raked his fingers through it, spreading it around her shoulders.

"You're beautiful," he said, his voice low and husky. "Even lovelier than I imagined." He traced a finger along her jaw, trailed it down her neck and over her shoulder, let it drift lower, over the peak of a nipple, and a soft warmth shimmered through her. Justin bent his head and kissed her, long and thoroughly, cupping a breast, teasing the end, making it ache and tingle.

He left her only long enough to blow out the lamp on the dresser and remove his wet breeches and boots; then he joined her on the bed, his body still moist and slightly chilled as he came up over her, his gray eyes dark and intense.

"I know I should send you away. If I wasn't such a heartless bastard, I would." He brushed a strand of long blond hair back from her cheek. "But I won't let you go. I can't. I want you too damned badly."

"Justin . . ." She reached up to him, cupped his hard jaw in the palm of her hand. There was something in his eyes. She looked past the hunger, glimpsed the aching need, the raw, pain-filled yearning; then his mouth crushed down over hers. His tongue swept in, stroking deeply, possessively; and hot, sweet fire spilled into her belly. The kiss went on and on, wet and hungry, long and seeking, a kiss that made her nipples stiff and her heart beat like a drum.

Outside, the storm continued to build, a tempest that matched the raging in her blood. Justin's mouth moved along her throat and down her shoulder; then he captured a nipple between his teeth. He sucked the fullness into his mouth, and lightning spread out through the tiny blue veins beneath her skin. Ariel moaned. She was trembling now, her breasts tingling beneath the skillful stroking of his tongue, aching almost painfully. His hand smoothed over her rib cage, past her navel, moving lower, sifting through the pale blond hair at the juncture of her legs.

Ariel tensed. She didn't know much about making love, only what Kitt had told her, and she wasn't sure exactly what to do.

"I won't hurt you, Ariel," he said softly. "Do you believe that?"

She swallowed. Nodded. "Yes. . . ." She sighed as he kissed her again, let the warm sensations wash through her, and allowed her tense muscles to relax. A long dark finger probed gently between her legs, urging them to part for him, then slid deep inside her. A wave of heat washed over her, swelling like a tide. Justin began to stroke her, setting up a rhythm that matched the deep probing of his tongue and pleasure, sweet and fierce, tightened low in her belly. She caught her breath as he stroked her more deeply, gliding easily into the slippery dampness at her core.

Ariel shook with the onslaught of sensation that rolled over her, made a soft, whimpering sound in her throat.

Justin kissed her softly. "Your body is ready for me, Ariel. You're hot and wet, waiting for me to join with you."

She moistened her lips, knew that they trembled. "What . . . What should I do?"

He gave her one of his rare, sweet smiles, and her heart nearly melted with love for him. "Just trust me. I'll take care of the rest."

She smiled at him in return and caught the flash of tenderness in his eyes before he settled himself between her legs. She felt the hard, probing length of him as he carefully eased himself inside. Reaching her maidenhead, he paused. When he looked down at her, she saw a mixture of relief and something more, something so tender and sweet it made her heart turn over.

"It will only hurt for an instant," he said. "I'll try to be as gentle as I can."

She hadn't known it would hurt and unconsciously she stiffened. Then he started kissing her again. Outside the window, the storm crackled loudly. Lightning flashed and thunder rumbled. Justin was equally relentless. He filled her mouth with his tongue, filled her heart with love, filled her mind with thoughts only of him. Then he pressed home.

Her sharp intake of breath was muffled by his kiss as he slid into her completely, impaling his hardness full-length. Ariel clung to him, trembling, trying to adjust to the strange sensation. Holding himself in check, Justin braced himself on his elbows above her, his concentration so fierce that beads of moisture broke out on his forehead.

"Are you all right?"

"I . . . yes. It wasn't . . . wasn't all that bad."

Relief made his beautiful mouth curve up. He kissed her very slowly, very thoroughly; then he began to move. Ariel sucked in a breath at the pulsing sensations that began to pour through her. The rigid blade of his shaft slowly drove into her, filling her in a way that made shivers rush over her skin. Heat exploded inside her, burned like a wildfire through her blood. Ariel clutched his neck, her nails digging into the muscles across his shoulders, her body arching upward of its own accord. Harder, deeper, faster, the rhythm seductive, absorbing her mind and body, promising . . . promising . . .

Her body tensed, tightened around his hardened length. A jolt of heat roared through her, as white-hot as the lightning outside the window, and she shattered, bursting like the raindrops that splintered against the panes.

"Justin . . . !" Ariel clung to him with all her strength, afraid to let go, certain if she did she would be swept away. She felt his body stiffen, felt something hot and wet spilling in her womb. With a groan he slumped forward into her arms.

For long moments they lay there, listening to the sounds of the storm and the rhythmical beating of their hearts.

I was right to go to him, she thought. *Nothing wrong could ever feel so perfect.*

Justin softly kissed her. Easing himself away, he stretched out at her side and drew her into the circle of his arms. "I didn't hurt you too badly?"

Ariel smiled into the darkness. "I loved it."

She saw the edges of his mouth curve up. "So did I."

"As much as you imagined?"

"More. A thousand times more."

She relaxed against the pillows, agreeing with him completely. She thought that they would sleep now, but lying beside him as she was, tucked beneath his shoulder and against his side, her hand resting lightly on his chest, she could feel his muscles expanding as he breathed, feel the slight indentation of his ribs. She traced a path there, outlined each one, and felt an inward ripple of the same tingly heat she had felt before.

"You're playing with fire, little girl."

There was mischief in his voice, something she had never heard, and that small achievement thrilled her. She brazenly ringed his nipple with the tip of her finger. "Am I?"

Justin caught her wrist, dragged it down his stomach, and wrapped her fingers around his arousal, which was hard again and pulsing into her hand.

"Oh, my."

She heard him chuckle and liked the sound. She began to test the size, discover the length, which was every bit as big and hard as it had felt when it was inside her.

"I warned you," he said, his voice a little gruffer than before.

"So you did," she said, but she didn't stop touching him. She was feeling that same hot restlessness she had felt when they were making love. Now she knew it meant she wanted to feel him inside her.

Ariel gasped as he came up over her, parted her legs with his knee, and slid himself in with a single smooth stroke. "You shouldn't have done that," he teased. "Now you're going to get burned." Lowering his head, he kissed her.

Ariel kissed him back and inwardly she smiled. Tomorrow would be her nineteenth birthday. As a child, she'd been taught to stay away from fire. Not tonight. Tonight, she wasn't going to mind getting burned.

CHAPTER THIRTEEN

*Tomorrow is my birthday. I shall be sixteen years old,
though in some ways I feel much older. The other girls'
parents send them gifts to celebrate, but if I were to
choose, I would rather have a picnic, or perhaps take a
lovely trip somewhere. I have always loved visiting new
places, though I've rarely had the chance. I can hardly
wait to see London. I just know that I shall love it. It
must be quite wonderful indeed.*

As Justin continued down the stairs, his mouth curved
faintly at the memory of Ariel's letter. The date she referred
to was October 27. He distinctly recalled the day, having
made certain thereafter that she had received a gift on that
day each year, a pretty blue fringed cashmere shawl the
first year, a pair of expensive kid gloves the next. He
couldn't take her on the outing she had wanted back then,
but today he meant to remedy that situation.

The amusement he was feeling changed to something
else as he thought of the night he had spent making love
to her. She had been all that he had imagined and more,
her innocent passion more alluring than the skills of the
most practiced courtesan. They had made love twice during
the night and again just before dawn. Afterward he had
carried her sleeping form back to her bedchamber to protect
her from embarrassment when the servants arrived in the
morning.

Warmed by the memory, he reached the bottom of the
stairs to see Knowles hurrying forward. The tall, bone-thin
butler made a slight bow of his shiny bald head. "Good
morning, my lord."

"Good morning, Knowles."

"Your carriage is ready and waiting to depart for Cadamon, my lord, as per the instructions you left yesterday."

"Yes, well, there has been a change of plans."

"My lord?"

"I'll be traveling to Tunbridge Wells instead of Cadamon, and Miss Summers is going to accompany me."

If Knowles was surprised he didn't show it. "Yes, my lord."

"Have Miss Summers's maid pack a trunk for her. She'll need several evening gowns along with her other garments. And have one of the footmen bring down my traveling valise. He'll find it packed and sitting at the foot of my bed." He didn't have a valet, had never gotten used to another man performing such intimate duties.

"As you wish, my lord." Knowles hurried away on his scrawny bird legs, not the most attractive of butlers but certainly one of the most efficient. Justin made a mental note to give the man a raise on his return from Tunbridge Wells.

He headed into the breakfast parlor, his mind on the upcoming journey, sat down in his usual place at the head of the table, and motioned for the footman to pour him a cup of coffee. He was eager to see what Ariel thought of his plans. After what had happened between them last night, the notion of a trip out of London had descended upon him like a revelation from the gods. He wanted to spend time with her, wanted her to have a chance to get used to his lovemaking and accept the future he had planned for her.

Tunbridge Wells seemed exactly the place to begin. It was close to London yet far enough away that they could be private, and there were a number of entertaining things to do. Tunbridge had a number of fine restaurants, shops, and theaters, and there were lovely out-of-the-way cottages to rent. This time of year it wouldn't be difficult to find one.

The thought of being alone with Ariel, of making love to her without the restraint he had shown last night, made him go instantly hard. Sweet God, taking her three times hadn't begun to satisfy his appetite for her. He wanted to make love to her in a hundred different ways, and he wasn't sure even that would be enough.

Wishing he could simply return upstairs and climb back into bed with her, he gave up a sigh of resignation and contented himself with visions of the passion they would share in Tunbridge Wells.

Ariel stretched lazily beneath the sheets, winced at the stiffness in her muscles, the aches in places that had never ached before, and her eyes popped open. Frantically she glanced around the bedchamber, then relaxed when she discovered she was back in her own room and Justin was nowhere around.

Justin. Dear God, it was impossible to believe she had gone to him last night, that she had asked him to make love to her. It was incredible to imagine the intimate things they had done. And yet she was glad it had happened. She wouldn't have missed those hours in his arms, in his bed, for anything in the world.

Not even if it meant an end to her dreams.

The notion made her uneasy. She buried the thought beneath sweet memories of Justin. Later she would think about the future. Not today.

She stretched again, covered her mouth to stifle a yawn. She glanced at the clock on the mantel, saw it was nearly eleven o'clock in the morning, and, with only a minor wince, swung her legs to the side of the bed. Hearing Silvie's familiar knock, she called for the girl to come in, hoping her little maid wouldn't notice her slightly kiss-swollen lips or the pink, roughened skin on the side of her neck left by Justin's late-night trace of beard.

"Good morning, miss." Silvie bustled into the room with her usual hum of energy. "His lordship's asked me to pack you a trunk." She smiled. "Apparently you'll be taking another trip."

"A trip?" Ariel's head snapped up in surprise. "But where are we going?"

"His lordship didn't say. It's hardly likely he would tell his business to me."

Ariel sat down on the slightly worn blue tapestry stool in front of the mirror and began to pull the brush through the tangles in her pale blond hair. Cadamon, of course. Justin was supposed to leave today. A slow, secret smile played over her lips that he had decided to take her along.

"Oh!" Silvie hurried toward her. "Bless me, I nearly forgot. A servant came to the back door this morning looking for you." She dug into the pocket of her skirt and dragged out a folded piece of paper. "He left this message. Said no one was to get it but you."

Ariel frowned at the expensive white stationery sealed with a drop of red wax. Then she smiled. Perhaps Kitt had returned. If ever Ariel needed to see her dearest friend it was now. Hurriedly she tore the message open.

It wasn't from Kitt, and reading the name scrawled in blue ink at the bottom of the page made her hand shake so badly she nearly dropped the paper. *Phillip.* Dear Lord in heaven, Phillip Marlin was the very last person she wanted to hear from. She began to scan the message:

My darling Ariel,

You cannot imagine how worried I have been. I pray that whoreson Greville has not harmed you in some way. I must see you. I must know for certain you are safe. There is a small hotel in Albermarle Street, the Quintain. Meet me in the café at three o'clock this afternoon. If you value our friendship, if you care for me at all, I beseech you not to disappoint me.

Yours ever faithfully,
Phillip

Ariel crumpled the message in her palm, grateful Justin hadn't seen it. As she thought of Phillip, a sliver of guilt ran through her. She had never meant to hurt him. She was actually a little surprised that she seemed so important to him. She had made no promises, never pledged herself to him in any way, though there was a time she'd believed that was exactly what she wanted.

Ariel sighed. She couldn't meet Phillip this afternoon— she would soon be leaving town—and yet it wasn't fair that he should worry.

It wasn't right that she continue to lead him on, to let him believe she still had feelings for him when she knew her own heart so clearly now and, in truth, felt nothing more for him than friendship.

"I'll need pen and paper, Silvie. I should like you to deliver my reply to the gentleman yourself. Make certain it gets directly to Mr. Marlin and no one else."

"Yes, miss." Silvie fetched the small portable writing desk from its place on a shelf in the armoire, and Ariel penned her reply. When she finished, she folded it, sealed it, and handed it to Silvie with instructions as to where Phillip lived.

"Wait until we've gone. Then see that it's properly delivered. And keep this to yourself. There is no reason to upset Lord Greville."

"You needn't worry about me, miss," Silvie said.

Ariel hoped not. She knew the way Justin felt about Phillip Marlin, though she didn't believe Phillip was as bad as Justin made him seem. It was merely the fierce animosity between the two men that colored Justin's perception of the man Phillip really was.

She wondered what had happened between the pair to create such a strong dislike. Perhaps on the journey she could convince Justin to tell her.

"Shall we braid your hair today, miss? It would probably hold up better on the trip."

"Yes, thank you, that's a very good idea." And so she sat fidgeting while Silvie plaited her hair, pinned it in a coronet on top of her head, then settled her plum silk bonnet in place and tied it beneath her chin. All the while, her mind kept returning to Justin and their passionate lovemaking last night.

In the mirror, spots of color appeared in her cheeks as she thought of him naked, his beautiful body moving over hers, his hardness buried deep inside her.

Knowing he meant for that to happen again tonight.

Then she thought of Phillip, thought of Justin's fury at the mention of his name, worried what might happen should the earl discover Phillip's continuing pursuit, and a niggling premonition of trouble began to gnaw at the back of her mind.

Justin lounged against the seat of the carriage, watching Ariel from beneath half-lowered lids. She frowned as the conveyance reached the outskirts of London and turned south instead of continuing northeast on the road to Cadamon.

"Isn't this the wrong direction? If I remember correctly, Cadamon is the opposite way."

A corner of his mouth inched up. "We're going to Tunbridge Wells. It's a charming little town, very quiet, very pretty. I thought you might like to see it." She looked lovely today, in a plum silk traveling dress trimmed with ecru lace. The color was high in her cheeks, and her lips still looked a little kiss-swollen. He had done that to her, he knew. And it was only the beginning.

She gave him a brilliant smile that made his body tighten and sent a rush of pressure to his groin.

"Oh, yes. I've read about Tunbridge. I should very much love to go there."

"Happy birthday, Ariel."

Surprise widened her china blue eyes. "This trip is my birthday present? I didn't think you knew when it was."

"You didn't? You received the gifts I sent you. You thanked me in your letters."

She flushed prettily, and her gaze swung away. "Yes, I did. But I thought you paid someone at the school to buy the presents in your name."

Justin didn't answer. Of course she would think that. He had written no personal message, just left it up to the head-mistress to tell her that they were from him. "So . . . how does it feel to be all of nineteen?"

She smiled. "Not much different than being eighteen, except for—" The color deepened in her cheeks and he knew she was thinking of last night. His arousal throbbed almost painfully. He thought of pulling the curtains and taking her there in the carriage, but this was all very new to her and perhaps a little frightening. He didn't want to scare her with the true extent of his passion.

"You're a woman now," he said mildly, fighting images of her naked, of the newly awakened passion that he had so easily aroused. "I suppose that changes a number of things."

"Yes, I suppose it does."

"When we return, I shall find you a place of your own. A small town house not far from Brook Street. You'll be more comfortable there and we won't have to deal with gossiping servants."

Ariel studied him from beneath her lashes. "I would rather we didn't discuss the future until our return, if you don't mind. Today is my birthday and I shouldn't like any sort of disagreement to spoil it."

Disagreement? What could they possibly have to disa-gree about? She had come to him, made love to him as he had wanted for so long. Now it was time he made arrange-ments for her future. But he didn't say that. As Ariel had said, today was her birthday. Practical matters could wait until their return.

"How old are you, Justin?" Her question caught him off guard.

"Twenty-eight." But there were times he felt the weight of a hundred years pressing down on him. "You look sur-prised. Did you imagine that I was older?"

"At times I did. But there were other times when I looked at you and thought you weren't much older than I."

He scoffed at that. He had left his youth behind years ago . . . if he had ever had one.

"You look younger when you smile. Did you know that? You don't do it nearly enough."

Justin didn't answer. What could he say? That he used to smile all the time, but it was so long ago he could scarcely remember?

"What makes you happy, Justin? What things give you joy?"

He frowned at the absurdity of the question. "I don't have time to worry about that sort of nonsense," he grumbled, but it occurred to him that *she* brought him joy. Even now as he looked at her, wreathed in a beam of sunlight slanting in through the window, tendrils of silver-blond hair escaping from her bonnet, something sweet blossomed inside him. It warmed his cold heart, made him feel an odd, inexplicable yearning. For what he couldn't say. He had thought that once he'd had her, this yearning would go away. Instead, each time he looked at her, each time she smiled at him in that soft, sweet way, it seemed to light up the darkness inside him and the yearning grew more fierce. He wondered what would make it fade.

"When I was younger, I used to love storms," she said. "I used to climb up on the roof of our cottage and watch the heavy black clouds rolling in. I loved to watch the lightning, to listen to the thunder rumbling all around me. It was dangerous, I know, and yet it drew me, that turbulence, that encroaching darkness. I wanted to reach up and touch those clouds, find out what they were made of."

Perhaps she still did, he thought, thinking of his own personal darkness and the way she seemed able to reach inside him.

Ariel fell silent when he made no reply. Her attention turned to the window, and Justin was content just to watch her. The yearning rose up again, along with the aching lust for her that had become all too familiar since her arrival in London.

He wanted her, wanted to lose himself inside her.

Wanted to feel that moment of brilliant burning sunlight that he had glimpsed before. It was a hunger that rarely left him. It rose now with maddening force, making him hard inside his breeches. As soon as he reached Tunbridge Wells, he would rent a cozy little cottage, carry Ariel off to bed, and make love to her until his body was sated with her warmth. Until the darkness was eased from his heart and, for a while at least, he felt the glow of sunshine coming from deep inside him.

It wouldn't last, of course. Nothing could erase his true nature for long. The darkness would find him, descend again like a monster from the deep, dragging him down, wrapping him in its shadowy tentacles.

It would happen again as it always did, but not now. For now there was Ariel and she was a beacon in the darkness. For a while, at least, he intended to bask in the warmth.

The journey passed swiftly. Justin worked to make polite conversation and even smiled on occasion, but beneath his casual demeanor Ariel couldn't miss the hot, seething hunger in his eyes. He didn't try to disguise it as perhaps he might have but allowed her to glimpse the powerful effect she had on him. Seeing his blatant desire for her, feeling his barely leashed restraint, made her stomach muscles tighten, set off a warm little trembling in her limbs.

It was late afternoon by the time they reached Tunbridge Wells, Justin's mood growing steadily darker, becoming an urgent restlessness that Ariel was feeling as well. He stopped at the office of one Harry Higginbottom, Estate Manager, whose name Justin had acquired in London, a man who handled the rental of properties in the area. Arrangements were made to rent a cottage that was actually a fairly large house with servants' quarters and a stable in the rear. It sat at the end of a tree-covered lane at the outskirts of town, the two-story structure enveloped by a curtain of ivy. It overlooked a lovely little meadow ringed by trees decked out in bright fall colors.

"It's charming," Ariel said as he led her into the parquet-floored entry, then took her on a quick tour of the ground floor while the footmen carried their trunks upstairs. Though fashioned of stone, the house was nothing at all like the mansion in Brook Street. With its small, well-appointed parlors, colorful rugs, and dozens of sparkling mullioned windows, the house exuded warmth and charm.

They returned to the entry, Justin holding her hand. He glanced toward the curving staircase. "Shall we see what's up there?" There was a husky edge to his voice that hadn't been there before. When she looked up at him, she saw that his eyes had grown dark. There was heat there, and so much hunger that an answering warmth curled in her stomach.

"Upstairs? Yes, I . . . I think that's a very good notion."

They hurried up the stairs to the second floor hand in hand, both of them laughing like playful children by the time they had reached the heavy wooden door that marked the master suite. She had never heard him laugh so freely. She wouldn't have believed the sound could be so rich and warm. They stared at the door and slowly, their laughter faded.

"Do you have any idea how badly I want you?"

Ariel wet her lips, her eyes clinging to his, unable to look away. "Why don't you show me?"

A muscle leaped in his cheek and his jaw flexed. Then he was lifting her up, opening the door, and striding in, kicking it closed with his foot. He set her on her feet, framed her face between his hands, and took her mouth in a ravenous kiss. It was deep and thorough, turning her stomach to liquid, sending a soft melting heat out through her limbs.

She wanted to touch him. She had to. With hands that suddenly trembled, Ariel shoved his jacket off his shoulders, dragged his shirt from the waistband of his breeches. His skin felt like soft, warm glass as her palms slid over the ridges of muscle across his back.

Justin worked the buttons at the back of her gown, and in minutes he had stripped her naked. His mouth found hers. His tongue slid over her bottom lip, and she opened to him, welcoming an even deeper kiss. He found her feminine softness, palmed it, stroked over the tiny nub in the middle. Ariel moaned and hurriedly began to unfasten the buttons closing the front of his breeches. He paused only long enough to tear away the balance of his clothes; then he carried her over to the bed, which was big and soft, and she sank into it beneath his weight.

"Ariel . . ." There was a note of reverence in his voice. His hands moved over her breasts—skillful, relentless, determined—wrenching a soft moan from her throat. He found the entrance to her passage, settled his hard length at her core, and drove himself deep inside.

A great shudder rippled through him and for a moment he went still.

Then slowly he started to move.

She whispered his name as he eased himself out and drove into her again, beginning to move faster, setting up a rhythm, making her own need soar. He gave her no quarter, just took what he wanted, and she discovered that she wanted it, too. Giving in to the deep, pounding force, she let the sensuous pleasure sweep over her, and in minutes she had reached her peak, swirls of sensation rushing over her in waves. Justin came with thundering urgency a few moments behind her, making her peak again.

Ariel clutched his neck as she spiraled down, smiling faintly, thinking how much she loved him. Knowing no matter how old she got, this would be the birthday she would always remember.

Tunbridge Wells, Ariel discovered, was a charming little resort set around the chalybeate springs that had been discovered there in 1609. Medicinal waters from the springs were sold in flasks to travelers, who came to the wells to escape the frantic bustle of London and enjoy the assembly rooms, elegant shops, and theaters that had been built around the wells.

Leaving the house after a night of exquisite lovemaking,

Ariel accompanied Justin to town in his carriage. They luncheoned at a tiny restaurant that opened onto the tree-shaded Pantiles walk, then wandered among the shops and stores. They stopped for a while to listen to a concert in the park, then along the promenade watched a group of tumblers, tossing coins to a darling little monkey who scampered among the audience doffing his hat in thanks to the generous crowd.

As the afternoon wore on, Justin took her hand and led her into a shop that handled finely crafted jewelry. A small man, rather nondescript, wearing gold wire-rimmed spectacles beamed at them as they perused the expensive items in the glass case; then Justin asked to see a beautiful diamond-and-pearl necklace.

"Exquisite, isn't it?" the clerk said, handing the expensive jewelry over.

Justin merely smiled. Stepping behind her, he draped the fabulous necklace around her throat. "For your birthday," he said, surprising her. She had thought they were merely having fun—it never occurred to her he actually meant to buy it for her.

He motioned toward the clerk, whose smile turned smug and knowing as he glanced down at her hand and saw no sign of a wedding ring. Ariel felt a tightening in her stomach, and the smile she had been wearing slowly faded. Justin seemed not to notice, simply continued the transaction, making ready to purchase the extravagant gift as if it were no more than a trinket.

Ariel looked up at him and nervously shook her head. "No, please, my lord, I couldn't possibly. . . ." Reaching behind her neck, she unfastened the diamond clasp, and the necklace dropped into her trembling hands. It was the sort of gift a man might purchase for his mistress, as the clerk had apparently guessed, and though they had made passionate love only hours ago, Ariel refused to think of herself that way.

"It's lovely—truly it is—but I . . ." She glanced from the clerk's smug face to Justin's questioning dark expression, her heart beating painfully, praying he wouldn't be offended. "It's kind of you, but I don't . . . I don't wish for you to buy me such a gift." His gaze traveled past her, lit on the clerk, then returned to her colorless face. His eyes remained there, knowing eyes, eyes that held a wealth of understanding.

He didn't protest, just set the jewels back in the red velvet box on the counter and returned to studying the contents inside the glass case.

"I'd like to see that one if you please." He pointed toward a simple gold locket, which the clerk far less excitedly handed over. It was oval, beautifully etched, and a single small diamond glittered in the center.

"Perhaps this is more to your liking." He settled the locket around her throat and it felt cool and smooth against her skin. "Simple, yet as bright and sparkling as the lady who will wear it."

Blinking back a sudden well of tears, she flashed him a heartfelt smile. Her trembling fingers lightly brushed the locket. "I adore it," she said. "I shall treasure it always. Thank you, Justin."

Something moved across his features. He took her gloved hand in his, turned it over, and pressed a kiss into the palm. Ariel felt that warm touch like wings against her heart.

"The afternoon is waning," he said. "You must be getting tired. Perhaps we should return to the house." The heat had returned to his eyes, and it was obvious what would happen when they got there.

Ariel smiled brightly, relaxed once more and definitely liking the notion. "That's a very good idea, my lord."

Justin returned the smile, and it occurred to her that there seemed to be more of them lately. Perhaps Clayton Harcourt had been right. Perhaps she *could* teach Justin to love.

Ariel fervently hoped so.

She loved him a little more each day. The thought of failing to win his love in return made a painful band tighten around her heart.

CHAPTER FOURTEEN

All in all, it was a memorable birthday. Aside from an embarrassing encounter with the Earl of Foxmoor, one of Justin's business acquaintances who was there with his wife and daughter, Ariel loved the charming little town and the wonderful hours she spent with Justin. She found herself hating to leave, knowing the problems she would face once they returned to London.

Unfortunately, the trouble surfaced even sooner than that, in the carriage on the way, the moment they reached the outskirts of the city. Sitting on the seat across from her, the closer they got to home, the more Justin's manner had subtly shifted, changing from the easy, relaxed person he had become in Tunbridge Wells to the darker, more brooding man he had been before they'd left London.

"We'll be home soon," he said, breaking into her thoughts. "Tomorrow I shall contact my solicitor and have him begin a search for properties that might provide a suitable place for you to live. It may take a while, but eventually I'm sure we can find something of which you'll approve."

The breath refused to leave Ariel's chest. She had dreaded this moment. While they were away, she'd been able to forget it. Now it was here and she could no longer avoid the confrontation.

"I realize . . . after what has transpired between us, it is no longer suitable for me to remain in your house. But I . . . I was hoping you would help me find a place that I can afford on my own. It wouldn't have to be anything fancy. A small flat would suffice. Since my debt to you is not yet wholly repaid, I could work in my spare time for you and the rest of the time in whatever position you are able to secure for me."

Justin's hard gaze fixed on her face and a muscle ticked in his cheek. "What are you talking about?"

"I'm talking about finding employment. We are both agreed that our . . . relationship has made it impossible for me to stay in your home. Since that is the case, I'll need some sort of income. You promised to help me in that regard. All I'm asking is that you do as you've agreed."

"What you're proposing makes no sense. I'm the man who has taken your innocence. That makes you my responsibility. Since I have more than enough money to provide for you, there is no need for you to labor like a common peasant."

"I am a common peasant," she said softly.

Justin made a rude sound in his throat. "You're a lady. You've made yourself one by hard work and perseverance. I won't let you throw that away."

Ariel shook her head, fighting the sudden burn of tears. "You don't understand."

"You're young yet. You haven't any experience with this sort of thing. Perhaps it is you who doesn't understand."

She bit down on her bottom lip, trying to stop it from trembling. "You saw the way they looked at me; I know you did. You pretended not to, but you did. Lord Foxmoor's wife barely spoke and wouldn't have done so at all if her husband hadn't forced her. I know what she was thinking—what all of them were thinking. I could see it in their eyes. They were calling me your whore."

"Ariel . . . love—"

"It's true and you know it. If I let you pay my rent, if I let you buy me jewelry and continue to keep me in expensive clothes, I'll deserve the names they call me."

He straightened on the seat, his head nearly touching the roof of the carriage. "You knew, the night you came to my room, what you were choosing."

Ariel blinked back tears and glanced away. "I was choosing you, Justin. I wanted you to make love to me, but I thought my life would still be my own."

The stiffness went out of his shoulders. Justin moved to sit beside her and gathered her into his arms. "You have always been a practical young woman, Ariel, have you not?"

"I suppose I have."

"When you were fourteen, you knew you wanted more from life than what you would find on your father's small farm. You found a way to make that happen."

"It was the only choice I had."

"You were being practical, finding a solution to your problem. Be practical now. Let me take care of you."

It sounded so simple, so easy. Just let him look after her as he had done before. It bothered her to imagine becoming even more dependent upon him, but perhaps it would give her the time she needed. She wanted the chance to teach him to love. The more she was with him, the more of a chance she had.

"I realize this isn't turning out exactly the way you planned," he said gently, "but have you considered what would happen if there were a child?"

Her wandering thoughts slammed sharply into focus. "A child?"

"You know there is that possibility."

"Well, yes, of course . . . I know what we did could . . . could result in a child, but surely it takes longer than just a few days."

"It can happen in only a few minutes." He reached up and touched her cheek. "There is, in fact, the possibility even now that you carry my babe."

Unconsciously her hand came to rest on her stomach. It was flat and firm beneath her russet traveling dress, but according to Justin that could change. Would it be so terrible if it did? She thought of little Thomas with his dark complexion and big gray eyes. Such a darling little boy. Justin's son would surely look much the same.

She turned to look up at him. "I wouldn't mind having your child, Justin. In fact, I think I would like that very much."

His expression slowly altered and something turbulent flashed in his eyes. His gaze turned dark and enigmatic as he studied her face; then he looked away, focusing his attention on the landscape outside the window. Several seconds passed. When he looked at her again, his expression was as inscrutable as it usually was.

"At any rate," he said, "as I said before, it will take a while to find something suitable. Perhaps by then, you will have grown more comfortable with the notion."

"Perhaps," Ariel said noncommittally, resting her head against his shoulder.

She didn't want to be Justin's kept woman, but she loved him, and perhaps, as he had said, she had made that choice when she asked him to make love to her. Would being his mistress really be so terrible? At least they would be together. She wouldn't have to worry about money or finding suitable employment. And there was Justin himself to consider. She loved him. She wanted to make him happy. She wanted to help him banish the darkness that seemed to surround him like a heavy black cloak. Loving him was the answer. And teaching him to love her in return.

She would do it, she vowed. Her decision was made. In time, things would all work out.

She ignored the soft pang of loss she felt in the area around her heart.

Justin paced in front of the fire in his hearth. It was dark outside. Soon the servants would retire and he would go to her. They would make love in her deep feather bed and he would sleep with her nestled beside him until dawn threatened and he was forced to return to his empty room.

He should be happy with the way things had worked out, delirious that his seduction had been accomplished so well. Though Ariel hadn't yet accepted his protection in so many words, her protests had gradually faded. It was only a matter of time before she acquiesced to his wishes and he had exactly what he wanted.

What he had been after from the start.

Justin swore softly. He could still see her face as she had left the carriage, a little paler than it should have been, no longer radiant as it was before but filled with uncertainty and a hint of resignation. He hadn't missed the faint shimmer of tears.

What sort of woman would cry because a man wished to provide for her? Because he wanted to take care of her, to protect her and see she had some measure of security for the future?

God's blood, didn't she understand he was trying to do what was best for her? He had to admit, being the selfish bastard he was, he was also doing what was best for him.

Justin raked a hand through his hair, shoving it back from his forehead. Dammit, he wanted to be with her. He wanted to make love to her, wanted to laugh with her as he had done in Tunbridge Wells.

"God spare me the unfathomable mind of a woman," he grumbled, wishing there was another way to handle the situation, one that would erase the haunted look from her eyes.

As Ariel had guessed, he hadn't missed the smug, knowing smiles in Tunbridge Wells, the disdainful glances, the whispered words. It was simply to be expected, he'd told himself, but it bothered him just the same. Apparently, Ariel hadn't been ignorant of the snide innuendos any more than he was.

He sighed as he knelt to freshen the fire, wanting her already, wishing the hours would pass so that he could be with her. Wishing things could remain as they had been in the cozy house in Tunbridge Wells.

Knowing, as long as he was the man he was, they never could be.

A week passed, slid into the next. Ariel studied numbers in the column on the page in front of her, information on the project Clayton Harcourt had left for Justin before they had gone to Tunbridge Wells, a proposal to purchase the controlling interest in a Northumberland coal mine.

From the figures she studied, it appeared Clay had been right. The profits, should the mine live up to projections, would be enormous. Justin had gone along with his friend's proposal, putting in an offer, though he had refused to close the transaction as quickly as Clay had wished. Justin was far more patient than his impulsive friend, and he'd wanted to wait until Ariel had completed her own projections and confirmed that the numbers Clay had received were correct.

As far as she could discern, the investment would be a good one.

Ariel set the quill pen back in its holder and leaned back in the oak chair she sat in behind her desk in the study. She was proud of the work she had done and pleased to know how much Justin had come to rely on her.

She stretched a little on the hard wooden chair; then a knock at the door interrupted her. Ariel looked up to see Silvie hurrying toward her. She seemed nervous, her eyes darting around, and the feeling instantly transmitted itself to Ariel.

"What is it, Silvie?" Sliding back her chair, Ariel came to her feet and rounded the desk.

Silvie glanced over her shoulder as if she feared someone might see them, then stuck out her hand. "Another message came for you through the servants' entrance. Mrs. Willis, the cook, brought it to me straightaway."

Ariel accepted the wax-sealed message, uneasy with the thought that it had surely come from Phillip. "Thank you, Silvie." Turning away, she unfolded the paper and scanned the contents, a sinking feeling in the pit of her stomach.

My darling Ariel,

The days pass, but my worry for you will not end. You have told me you feel only friendship for me, yet my heart refuses to believe it. I must see you. As you undoubtedly know, tonight is Greville's weekly business meeting with his friend, Clayton Harcourt. Since you have refused to come to me, I shall come to you. Meet

*me in the stable behind the house at ten o'clock. Please,
I beg you, for your sake as well as my own, do not
disappoint me.*

> *Ever your friend,*
> *Phillip*

Dear God in heaven, Phillip sounded almost desperate,
and it was all her fault. She should have been more candid,
should have come right out and told him she had fallen in
love with the earl. Instead, she had tried to spare his feelings and in doing so only made matters worse.

She wasn't sure how Phillip knew about Justin's weekly
meeting with Harcourt, but it was a ritual he rarely missed.
They usually met at their club in St. James's, and Justin
never returned until well after midnight.

Justin would be gone, and perhaps it was for the best.
She could set matters to rest with Phillip once and for all.

"Do you wish me to carry a reply?" Silvie asked, jerking
Ariel's gaze in the dark-haired girl's direction. Lost in
thought, she had completely forgotten her maid was still in
the room.

"Yes, all right. Perhaps that would be best." Sitting back
down at the desk, she quickly penned a reply, telling Phillip
she would meet him as he wished. She sealed it with a drop
of wax and handed it to her maid.

"I'll see he gets it straightaway."

"Thank you, Silvie." She watched the girl disappear out
into the hall and wondered what she was thinking. Ariel
hoped she didn't believe there was any sort of illicit relationship going on between her and Phillip. She'd considered simply explaining, but it wasn't really any of Silvie's
business, and she wasn't sure exactly what to say. Hopefully, after tonight, the problem would be solved and it
would no longer matter.

Ariel sighed, wishing she didn't have to hurt Phillip
again, trying not to worry about what she should say. De-

termined to put their upcoming encounter out of her mind, she sat back down at the desk and continued with her work.

A warm early-morning sun cast rosy light through the stained-glass windows in Clayton Harcourt's town house. He kissed the voluptuous young woman he had escorted downstairs and now stood ready to depart.

Reaching down, he lightly patted her bottom. "Be a good girl now, Lizzy, and go home. You damned near killed me last night. Another few rounds like that and I might not recover."

Elizabeth Watkins, recently widowed Countess of May, laughed delightedly. "You've the stamina of a bull, Clayton Harcourt. I believe you've simply grown tired of me."

"Who could ever grow tired of you, sweeting? You've breasts like ripe melons, a mouth like a velvet glove, and a—" A knock at the door ended the rest of his ribald remark. Since he had dismissed his butler and most of the other servants to ensure a night of privacy, he gazed through the peephole himself. To his surprise, he saw his friend Justin Ross standing next to the lion's head statue on his porch.

A thread of worry filtered through him. It was far too early for a simple social call. Their business meeting wasn't scheduled until tonight. Whatever Justin wanted had to be a matter of importance.

Clay turned to Elizabeth, whose hair was a tangle of thick dark curls, her clothes, the same ones she had worn last night, rumpled from a night left lying on the floor, and smiled. "Unless you wish to encounter my friend Lord Greville, I suggest you hie out the back way instead of the front. I'll tell the coachy to pick you up in the alley."

Not that Justin would say a word even if he found her in Clay's early-morning company. It wasn't his friend's discretion he was worried about; it was the lady's sensibilities.

"Perhaps I'll see you later on in the week," Elizabeth suggested, giving him a last quick kiss on the cheek. When Clay remained noncommittal and instead simply nodded, she hurried off toward the rear of the house, a slight pout turning her pretty lips down at the corners.

Justin rapped again and Clay opened the door. "Sorry to keep you waiting," he said. "I was saying farewell to a . . . friend."

Justin cocked a brow as Clay strode past him down the front steps, gave his driver instructions to pick the lady up behind the house, then returned inside and closed the door.

"I thought we were meeting tonight," he said to Justin, motioning for his friend to follow him down the hall. He wasn't exactly dressed for company, having dragged on the breeches he'd carelessly discarded beside the bed, his feet still bare, his wrinkled white shirt hanging open. But then Justin didn't look as if he noticed.

"Our meeting's still on," Greville confirmed, looking a bit uncomfortable and even a little embarrassed. "This isn't business; it's personal. I was hoping for a bit of advice."

"Ah, then it must have something to do with a woman."

For the first time Justin noticed Clay's rumpled clothes. "One thing's for sure—you're an expert in that department. I hope this one was older than the last."

Clay looked aghast. "I had no idea the girl was only sixteen. She looked more like five and twenty. Besides, she was hardly a virgin." He grinned and pulled open the door to the breakfast parlor. "This one's a widow, if that eases your mind. A very lovely, very accommodating widow, if I may say so."

Justin's mouth edged up. He followed Clay inside the sunny little room that looked over the garden behind the house, and they sat down at the polished oak table. The cook, a portly gray-haired woman who had worked for him for the last four years, appeared a few minutes later to prepare his morning meal. Since the footman had not yet returned, she poured them each a cup of coffee, then scuttled back inside the kitchen.

Clay tilted his chair back until it rested against the wall and casually sipped his coffee. "All right, what's so important it couldn't wait until tonight?"

"I'm thinking of getting married," Justin blurted out, and Clay's chair slammed back to the floor.

"Married? You? I thought you'd sworn off marriage for life."

"I had. Have." He sighed. "I had until last night. But I've been thinking about it lately. Do you think it's possible for a man like me to marry and be happy?"

Clay studied him over the rim of his cup. " 'Happy' rarely enters into the married state," he said, thinking of his poor dead mother and her unrequited love for his already-married father. "Mostly it's done for money or position. But if you're speaking of Ariel, perhaps it's possible. Why would you want to? Surely it's too soon for the girl to be *enceinte*. Is she playing the injured virgin? Demanding you do the right thing?"

"To tell you the truth, I don't think the notion of marriage has even occurred to her. I'm an earl, you see. Ariel is the daughter of a poor tenant farmer. On the surface, she plays the role of lady quite flawlessly, but inside, she still thinks of herself as the lowly peasant she was born."

"She's become your mistress. That's what you wanted. Why not just go on as you are?"

Justin shook his head. "Because I find it isn't enough. I can't explain it, exactly. It's just that every time I look at her, I see the goodness inside her and I don't want to soil it. I want the light inside her to go on burning as brightly as it does right now."

Justin's long fingers curled around the handle of his coffee cup, but he didn't take a drink. "I know the risk she'll be taking. God knows I'll probably make a terrible husband. But at least she'd be able to hold her head up when she walks down the street. I can't love her as another man might—I wouldn't have the slightest notion how—but I can give her something else. Something far more practical. Marriage to me would bring her respectability. I can make her the lady she has always wanted to be."

Clay said nothing to that. Would marrying Ariel Summers be the right thing for his friend to do? Justin might not think he would be able to love her, but Clay believed he was more than half in love with the girl already.

"If we continue as we are," Justin went on, "there's every chance, sooner or later, there's going to be children. They'll be bastards, Clay. I don't think Ariel has any idea what that means, but I do." His gaze fixed on Clay. "We both know only too well."

That was the truth. And it occurred to Clay, if Justin cared for the woman half as much as he seemed to, sparing her and his children the pain he and Justin had suffered would be reason enough for him to marry her.

"I don't think you need my advice," Clay finally said. "I think you've already decided." He smiled and stretched out a hand. "Congratulations, my friend."

Justin accepted the handshake and flashed him the bright sort of smile Clay had rarely seen. It was filled with relief and what looked to Clay a good deal like joy.

Justin shoved to his feet. "I'd better go. I've got a number of things to do. I want everything to be perfect when I ask her."

"I'll see you tonight at the club," Clay said, waving as Justin strode to the door.

"I'll be there," Justin called back to him. There was a lightness in his voice that hadn't been there when he had come in, and Clay smiled. Justin deserved a little happiness. God knew he hadn't had much of it in his life so far. Clay just hoped Ariel Summers was the woman Justin believed she was.

He clenched his jaw hard. God help her if she wasn't.

The clerk at Sanborn and Sons, Purveyor of Fine Custom Jewelry, in Ludgate Hill, stood behind the counter, surveying the well-dressed gentleman who had just walked in, a wealthy nob of the very first water, by the look of his expensive dove gray tailcoat and the ruby ring glinting on his finger. Quite likely, a member of the nobility.

The clerk, a man in his forties with a broad nose and

receding chin, hurried forward. "Good afternoon, my lord. Might I be of help with something?"

"A friend recommended your shop. He said you had a reputation for honesty and that you sold gems of the highest quality."

He smiled, pleased at the words, which were undoubtedly true. "My family's been in business for over fifty years."

"I'm looking for a ring," the man said. He bent to study the contents in the case, his straight black brows drawing together. "Sapphires would be best, I think, to match the lady's eyes, and diamonds of course. Something elegant but not garish. Something appropriate for a wedding ring."

The clerk fairly beamed. Most of the *ton* were content to gift their brides with an ancestral ring, perhaps one worn by their mothers. This man apparently wanted something personal, a ring of his own choosing.

"We can design whatever you wish, of course, but if you'll give me just a moment, I have several rings in the back. One of them might do very nicely." The ring he had in mind was fashioned of perfectly cut sapphires surrounded by flawless diamonds. Large enough to please the most discriminating lady, yet subtle, not the least bit garish.

He hurried to the rear of the shop and returned with three of the shop's most expensive pieces, setting them down on a black velvet cloth beneath an overhanging lamp that showed off their brilliance to the best advantage.

As the gentleman lifted and examined each one, the clerk studied his face. He was a handsome man, tall and broad-shouldered, yet somehow forbidding. The jewelry in the shop was fashioned of the highest quality, and the clerk was glad. It was clear the man had a very discerning eye, and it was equally clear that it would not be wise to displease him.

He picked up the last ring on the cloth and examined it closely, an array of emotions swirling in his cool gray eyes, each one more difficult to read than the last. Nervousness, love, desire? There was one thing that couldn't be mistaken. It was hope, and it made the clerk smile.

Once in a while, the job he did with such care and dedication was rewarded by a man who was so inspired.

"I'll take this one." He held up the exquisite circle of perfectly faceted stones.

"Excellent choice, my lord. It is exactly the ring I would have chosen." He carried the other rings back to the rear of the shop and returned with a small velvet box lined with white satin. When the payment was settled, he placed the ring in the box and handed it over. "I wish you felicitations on your upcoming nuptials, my lord."

"Thank you." The tall man smiled as he slipped the box into the inside pocket of his perfectly tailored coat, turned, and strode out of the shop.

The clerk watched him leave, thinking that his steps seemed lighter than they had been when he'd entered the store.

Then again, perhaps it was only his imagination.

CHAPTER FIFTEEN

Darkness fell. A mist rolled in from the north, shrouding the city in a ghostly blanket of gray. Standing in the Red Room, Ariel stared out the window into the thickening blackness, her mind on her upcoming meeting with Phillip.

"Ariel?" Justin's voice, coming from a few feet away, snapped her attention in his direction.

"Yes, my lord?"

He was preparing to leave for his meeting with Clayton Harcourt, giving her the chance to clear things up with Phillip as she should have done before.

"You seem distracted this evening. Is something wrong?"

Her heart lurched. "N-no, my lord, of course not." She forced herself to smile. "I've a bit of a headache is all. I think I shall go to bed early."

"Perhaps if you are ill, I should cancel my meeting and stay home with you."

"No! I mean, don't be silly. I'll be fine by the time you get back."

He studied her face a moment, and she prayed he wouldn't notice how nervous she was. Finally, he nodded. "All right, then. I suppose it's time I was off."

Ariel kissed him dutifully, followed him into the entry where Knowles draped a cloak over his shoulders, watched him go out through the heavy oak door, and gave up a sigh of relief.

Then she glanced at the ornate grandfather clock, thought of her meeting with Phillip, and her nervousness returned full measure. With a sigh, she made her way upstairs. Time seemed to drag and she found herself pacing in front of the window, waiting for the hour of her scheduled assignation. She wasn't looking forward to it, and yet in a way she was.

Her life was moving forward. Justin's solicitor, Mr. Whipple, still hadn't discovered exactly the right property for her to move into, but she was certain he would very soon. In the meantime, Justin came to her bed each night and they made wild, passionate love. He stayed till nearly dawn, Ariel curled peacefully in his arms, and left with what seemed a great deal of reluctance.

He was coming to care for her more each day, she believed. She didn't want problems with Phillip to come between them.

Standing at the bedchamber window, Ariel stared into the darkness, watching the swirling gray mist settle over the narrow walkways, weighing the words she would say. She would tell Phillip very plainly that she wasn't in love with him. In truth, she now knew, she never had been. Whatever feelings Phillip might hold for her, they were simply not returned.

She wanted him out of her life, wanted the threat he posed to her happiness over and done.

She glanced at the clock on the mantel. Five minutes to ten. Time for her to leave. Grabbing her warm blue woolen shawl off the bed, she wrapped it around her shoulders, headed out the door and down the servants' stairs. Most of the staff had retired to their quarters. Ariel quietly made her way outside and hurried along the stone walkway to the stable at the rear of the house.

It was shadowy and dim inside, lit by the glow of a single lantern. The place smelled of liniment and manure, freshly oiled leather, and newly cut hay. She made her way deeper into the interior, heard the soft luffing of the horses, the sound of hooves clicking lightly against the stone floor. She checked to be sure none of the grooms were about and continued searching the shadows for Phillip.

"Ariel . . ." He called her name softly, stepping out of the darkness of an empty stall. "I'm glad you came. I was afraid you'd disappoint me again."

She approached where he stood, stopped a few feet

away. "I never meant to disappoint you, Phillip. Sometimes things just happen."

He moved closer. She could smell his fragrant cologne, see the golden glint of his hair. He reached out to her, cupped her cheek in his hand. "Do you know how much I've missed you? How badly I've wanted to see you?"

Ariel turned away from him, feeling a thread of guilt. "I need to tell you something. I thought . . . hoped when you read my note, you'd understand."

In the light of the lantern, she saw the muscles in his jaw go hard. "Understand what? That Greville has seduced you? That he has deceived you and tricked you into his bed? Do you think I'm a fool, Ariel? Did you think I wouldn't guess?"

Ariel opened her mouth to argue, but the words got stuck in her throat, and only a little mew of denial escaped.

"You don't know him the way I do," Phillip said. "You don't realize what the man is capable of. I tried to tell you. I tried to warn you, but you wouldn't listen."

Ariel shook her head. "He isn't like that. He's good and decent. He just doesn't know it."

"He's a villain, Ariel. He has stolen your innocence—do you deny it?"

She glanced away, the pink rushing into her cheeks confirming the truth of his words. "I love him."

Phillip gripped her shoulders. "He's using you, can't you see? As soon as he tires of you, he'll cast you aside like so much flotsam."

Tears burned her eyes. "You're wrong. Justin would never do that."

"Ariel, you mustn't trust him. You must leave this place, now, tonight. Come away with me, darling. What's happened is past. I'll take care of you from now on, protect you from Greville."

She shook her head, lifted her chin. "I've told you the way I feel. Please, Phillip, I'm asking you to leave. It's dangerous for you to be here. If Lord Greville knew you had come—" She gasped as he hauled her against him, gripped the back of her head, and covered her mouth in a punishing kiss. He thrust his tongue between her teeth and down her throat so deep Ariel nearly choked.

Shoving against his chest, she tried to turn her head away, tried to break free, then stiffened at the feel of Phillip's hand sliding into the bodice of her gown. He grasped her breast, squeezed it ruthlessly.

"You're mine," he whispered. "I found you first." The gown tore, then her chemise as he harshly abraded her nipple. Ariel choked back a sob and tried to kick him, but he was stronger than he looked and she only succeeded in ripping her skirt and knocking the pins from her hair. She fought him harder, for the first time truly afraid. Her foot slipped, caught in the hem of her dress, and both of them tumbled into the straw on the floor of the stall.

"Get off of me!" she demanded, struggling beneath his heavy weight.

"I'll have you—I swear it. You're used to the smells of the barn—you were born to it. I should have taken you this way from the start."

Ariel tried to scream, but one hand clamped over her mouth and the other feverishly worked to bunch up her skirts. She tried to bite him, tried to twist free, felt him groping to unfasten his breeches; then his heavy weight flew off her as if it were lifted by some superhuman force. Phillip whirled to defend himself and a meaty fist connected with his chin, slamming him backward into the wall, dislodging a heavy leather harness that crashed down on top of his head.

Ariel jerked her gaze to the big, beefy red-haired man who stood with his fists bunched and his legs splayed—Cyrus McCullough, Justin's head groom. She started to tremble, could barely force her lips to move. "Mr. McCullough . . . th-thank God you came."

Phillip groaned, and his eyelids fluttered open. His chest rose and fell in a harsh, unnatural rhythm, and a trickle of blood seeped from the corner of his mouth. He wiped it away with the side of his hand. "What the hell do you think you're doing?"

"Where I come from, laddie," Cyrus said, "we dinna take kindly to a mon havin' his way with an unwillin' lass."

Phillip clenched his jaw, shoved the harness off onto the floor, and staggered to his feet. Ariel dragged her disheveled hair back over her shoulder, tried to brush the straw from her skirts, but her hands were shaking too badly. "H-how did you know we were in here?"

"I heard the noise from my room upstairs. Thought I'd best come down and see what was causin' the ruckus."

"Thank you. I don't know what would have happened if you hadn't come along when you did."

A few feet away, Phillip's pale hands fisted. He fixed a murderous glare on Cyrus McCullough. "I'm the son of an earl. Do you know what that means, old man? You'll spend the next twenty years in Newgate for what you've done."

"No, he won't," Ariel said firmly, flashing Phillip an equally nasty glare. "You say one word about this to anyone and I'll go to Greville. I'll tell him you tried to rape me." Even in the darkness, she could see Phillip blanch. "I don't want trouble and neither should you. None of us will say a word about what happened here tonight. Do you hear me, Phillip?"

He spat a curse, then raked his hands through his hair, combing it back into place. Grudgingly he nodded.

"Ye'd best be gettin' back, lassie. Before someone discovers ye've gone."

Ariel nodded and flashed a grateful smile at Cyrus McCullough. "Thank you again." With a last glance at Phillip, she turned and hurried away. The door closing behind her muffled the sound of the beefy Scotsman's fist connecting one last time with Phillip Marlin's chin.

Justin stood at the window of his darkened bedchamber watching Ariel leave the stable. In the light of the quarter moon forking down between the clouds, he could see a rip in the bodice of her gown, a tear along the side. Long

strands of pale blond hair floated around her, loose from
the pins that had held it in place. The shawl she had been
wearing had gone missing, and as she disappeared through
the back door of the house he noticed straw and dirt on the
back of her wrinkled skirt.

Justin closed his eyes, fighting a wave of nausea and the
heavy weight pressing down on his chest that made it impossible to breathe.

He had returned to the house just minutes after he had
left, quietly entering through a side door and making his
way upstairs. All evening he had watched her, seen her
growing more and more tense.

He had known she was lying, of course. And he had
been determined to find out why.

Now he knew.

Anger mixed with bitter despair, and a shudder went
through him. It had been mere chance that he had spotted
Phillip Marlin in the alley behind the house and seen him
go into the stable. Before that, he'd been listening for the
sound of Ariel's departure from her room, certain she intended to leave, wondering where she could be going and
why she hadn't wanted him to know.

The moment he'd seen Marlin go into the stable, the
truth had hit him like a blow, though at first he had refused
to believe it. He had waited, watching and hoping he was
wrong, praying that Ariel wouldn't go to him, that there
was some other explanation. He'd considered confronting
them, but he had humiliated himself in front of Marlin once
before; he wasn't about to do it again.

Instead he stood there watching, his stomach churning,
his hands sweating, praying he was wrong.

Then Ariel had finally come out of the stable, her clothes
covered with dirt and straw and her hair in tangles. It was
obvious she had been trysting with Marlin, and the torment
that had been building inside him burst open like a festering
sore. He ached with it, felt sick with it, wanted to die of it.

He hadn't believed he was capable of suffering such an
agony of raw, unbearable pain. Ariel had done that to him,

destroyed the protective wall he had so carefully built around him, left him open and vulnerable, broken and bleeding, the shell of the hard, perfectly contained man he had been before.

He hated her for it. Hated her even more for making him weak than he hated her for betraying him with Marlin. Woodenly he moved around the darkened room, guided only by the pale rays of moonlight filtering in through the mullioned windows. In the darkness, he sank down on a wooden chair in front of the hearth, staring at the cold, unlit fire, feeling the chill sweep through him.

Inside his chest, his heart beat dully, a dead, frozen lump that should have been numb and instead pulsed with a throbbing ache. How had he let it happen? How had he allowed himself to be taken in so completely?

Ariel. Just the sound of her name whispered from the recesses of his mind made a bitter ache well up inside him. With her false brightness and calculated warmth, she had melted the wintry shield that had been his only protection. She had charmed him, deceived him, practically unmanned him.

Justin stared at the cold, spent ashes in the hearth and thought that they mirrored the years of his life. Cold and spent at twenty-eight years old, with a frozen heart and a glacial, arctic soul.

The thought drew harsh, chilling laughter from deep in his throat. He ran a shaking hand over his face, surprised the tears in his eyes didn't turn to ice as they slid down his cheeks.

Justin sent for Ariel late the following morning. He hadn't slept at all, and though the mirror had reflected eyes that looked sunken and bleak, no other emotion showed on his face. He wouldn't allow it. Not today. Not ever again.

Waiting for her to appear in his study, he plucked a piece of lint from the sleeve of his immaculate black coat, carefully straightened the cuffs of his white lawn shirt. He had dressed with care this morning, choosing somber clothes, perhaps as a sign of the end of this particular phase of his life.

Ariel knocked only briefly, then stepped in and closed the door. She gave him a soft, welcoming smile, though a faint edge of uneasiness marked her approach. He hadn't come to her bed last night. Perhaps she wondered why.

"Good morning, my lord."

"Good morning, Ariel. I trust you slept well."

Her cheeks colored a bit. "Not as well as I have been."

The reference to his absence would have pleased him in the past. Now it only made his jaw harden.

"I missed you, my lord. I thought . . . hoped you would come to my room when you got in."

How did she do that? How was it possible to be such a poor liar at times and at others accomplish the task like a master?

"Our meeting ran late. Afterward, Clayton and I got . . . distracted."

Her pretty face fell. "Oh." She was dressed in soft yellow wool, her silver-blond hair pulled back on the sides with small mother-of-pearl combs he had bought her in Tunbridge Wells.

God, she was lovely. The smoothest skin and bluest eyes he had ever seen. Amazing that as much as he despised her, he could still want her. His groin tightened at the thought and he began to grow hard. It hadn't occurred to him to have her before he sent her away, but why not? He and Marlin had shared women before. Somehow the notion seemed fitting.

"Come here, Ariel."

She looked up at him and smiled, but the warmth in her eyes could no longer reach him. A layer of frost protected his heart, and he would never allow her to thaw it again. She came toward where he lounged against the bookshelves, his shoulders propped against the gilt-edged leather volumes.

"I got a great deal of work done yesterday," she said,

stopping just in front of him. "I have all those new figures you wanted and—"

He silenced her with a rough, demanding kiss, taking her a little by surprise. For a moment she tensed; then she relaxed against him and her mouth went soft and pliant. Justin gentled the kiss. He wanted to remember this last coupling. On the rare occasion he might allow himself to think of her, he wanted to remember the sweet victory of taking her so thoroughly, so utterly completely, just before he sent her off to Marlin.

He kissed her again, his tongue stroking deeply, his hands moving over her breasts, coaxing her nipples into stiff little buds, making them pulse with need. She made a soft sound in her throat and her hands slid up around his neck. Justin turned, easing her backward till her shoulders came up against the bookshelves. He settled his thigh between her legs, nudging her mound and lifting her a little. He heard her swift intake of breath, felt her fingers digging into his shoulders.

Reaching down, he began to slide up her skirt, running his hand along her leg and up her thigh as he bunched the bright yellow fabric around her waist. He deepened the kiss, his hand replacing his knee, slipping between her legs, probing her softness, stroking her until she was wet and ready.

He kissed her deeply, worked the buttons at the front of his breeches, and his shaft sprang free. He was hard as a stone, throbbing with heat and need.

"Part your legs for me, Ariel."

She swayed a little, her pulse beating rapidly, but did as he commanded, opening herself to him, trusting him as he had once trusted her. He parted the folds of her sex and drove himself inside her with a single determined stroke, impaling himself completely.

Ariel moaned as he began to move, thrusting into her hard and deep, lifting her a little off the floor. Her body trembled and her head fell back. Justin kissed her throat, gently bit the side of her neck, and she pressed herself against him. Long penetrating strokes had her clinging to his neck, arching upward, whimpering his name.

Inwardly he smiled as her body tightened around him, milking him sweetly as she reached a powerful release. Still, he drove on, plunging into her until she peaked again. Only then did he allow his own release, pounding into her ruthlessly, taking what he needed, hotly expelling his seed.

Seconds later, he turned away, keeping his back to her, waiting for his heartbeat to slow, casually refastening the buttons at the front of his breeches. There must have been something in his expression—or more likely it was the lack of anything at all—that alerted her.

"Justin . . . ?"

He turned with a calm that made her pretty face pale. "I summoned you here for a purpose," he said matter-of-factly. "I suppose it's time we got on with it."

"What . . . what purpose? What's happened, Justin?"

His expression remained bland. "Last night Clayton and I . . . well, we stumbled across some rather entertaining companions." It was a lie, of course, he had never left his bedchamber, but he owed her nothing of the truth anymore.

"Entertaining companions? You aren't talking about . . . about women?"

"I'm sorry, my dear, but you knew sooner or later it would happen. You were quite good, really, better than I had expected, but a man's tastes change. Since that is the case, I believe it would be best if you left the house."

"You're . . . you're sending me away?"

"Think of it more as putting an end to your employment."

She looked stricken. "But what about . . . what we just did?"

"I didn't summon you here for the purpose of fornication, but it does make a rather nice parting memory, don't you think?"

A strangled sound came from her throat. Ariel's face went paper white and she gripped the edge of the table to steady herself. "You're telling me it is over between us.

You're saying that you no longer . . . no longer want me."

He shrugged. "You're a fetching little piece. Bedding you is hardly a burden. There is simply someone else I want more."

Her eyes filled with tears. Big shiny drops began to slide down her cheeks. In the past, he would have ached at the sight of them. Not anymore.

Ariel brushed at the wetness with a trembling hand and lifted her chin. "I'll need to find lodging. Give me a day or two—"

"It would be better if you left today." He reached into the pocket of his waistcoat, plucked out a single gold guinea, caught her wrist, and pressed it into her palm. "That ought to keep you for a while, long enough to find a new protector." With Marlin waiting in the wings, it wouldn't take any time at all.

The thought of them together made the bile rise in his throat. Justin clenched his jaw so hard a muscle spasmed in his cheek.

Ariel's fingers tightened around the coin and she lifted her eyes to his face. "I was right about you in the first place," she said softly. "You're vicious and cruel. You're the most heartless man I've ever met. How could I have been such a fool?"

Justin said nothing to that, just watched as she raised her chin, squared her shoulders, and walked with quiet dignity across the room.

If anyone was a fool, it was he. But he wouldn't be one again. He thought of the beautiful ring he had purchased, the life he had envisioned with Ariel, and a sharp, squeezing pain stabbed into his chest. It hardened into a thick wall of ice that blocked all other sensation as she walked out of the room and closed the door.

Fighting back tears, numb with shock and pain, Ariel closed the door to the armoire in her bedchamber, leaving the expensive clothes Greville had bought her inside. Instead, she gathered those few possessions she would need, said good-bye to a teary-eyed Silvie, picked up her small tapestry satchel, and left the house.

Once she reached the street, the tears she'd been fighting came with a vengeance, blurring her vision until she could barely see.

Oh, God, oh, God, how could he? A bitter sob slipped from her throat. She had thought she knew him. She had trusted him. She had fallen in love with him.

But she didn't know the cold, detached, ruthless man she had encountered in the study. A man who had made love to her to satisfy his momentary lust, then cast her aside like a worn-out shoe.

Oh, dear God. Ariel wrapped her arms around her waist and doubled over, a soft moan seeping past her lips. In all the years of her father's abuse she had never hurt like this, never felt such agony, such unbearable pain. She had never been so totally and completely lost, felt so utterly without direction. She had nowhere to go, only the small bit of money he had given her, and not the vaguest notion what to do. The only friend she could go to for help was Kassandra Wentworth, and Kitt was somewhere in Italy, hundreds of miles away. In the past, she might have gone to Phillip, but after what he had done, she knew better.

Phillip was just like Justin. Callous and unfeeling. Lying and deceitful. Perhaps the two men's hatred had risen from the fact they were so much the same.

Swaying unsteadily along the paving stones, her heart aching, her eyes full of tears, Ariel stumbled and nearly fell. She caught herself and leaned against a wrought-iron fence to catch her breath, trying to think what to do, where she should go, but her mind was fuzzy and numb, and as the hours passed, her legs simply carried her aimlessly from one street to the next.

The day was slipping away. Soon it would be dark and she would need shelter. She looked down at one of her hands, feeling as if it were detached from her body, saw that she still carried her small tapestry satchel, remembered that it contained her belongings and the coin the earl had given her. If she was careful, perhaps there would be enough to survive until she could find some sort of employment.

She took a steadying breath and glanced around her. She had wandered farther than she'd realized. The buildings in this section were slightly run-down, some of the windows cracked, shutters hanging loose on their hinges. She had no idea where she was, and the neighborhood was far shabbier than the one she'd left behind, but there was a small hotel in the middle of the block up ahead. Perhaps she could find inexpensive lodging.

She walked into the dingy lobby, set her satchel down on the threadbare carpet. "Sir? Could you be so good as to help me, please?"

The ruddy-faced clerk looked up from his paperwork and scowled, peering at her from beneath a brown leather visor that partially covered his thin fringe of hair. "You want a room?"

"That's right. Nothing expensive, just something simple."

He glanced around, saw no one else. "A room just for you?"

Ariel nodded. "Yes, please."

He studied her clothes, a simple brown wool day dress with a white muslin fichu at the neck and a plain brown bonnet she wore tied beneath her chin. "Where's your husband? You run away from him?"

"No! I'm not . . . I'm not married."

The clerk's scowl deepened and he shook his head. "Sorry. Your kind's nothing but trouble. We don't want no trouble round here."

Ariel's face burned crimson. Dear God, he thought she was a lady of the evening! "I assure you, sir, I am not . . . not that sort. I was . . . I was just . . ." Frantically she searched her muzzy brain for a plausible story, anything that would account for a young woman being alone in the city. "I was supposed to meet my cousin here today. Something must have happened. She must have been delayed. I'll just need a room until she gets here."

He only shook his head. "Try someplace else."

She could see it would do no good to argue. Ariel stumbled back out on the street, blinking against a fresh wash of tears. Justin must have known what would happen when he sent her away. Everything she'd believed about him was wrong. He'd never cared about her. She meant less than nothing to him. Her heart ached unbearably.

She tried two more hotels without success and finally wound up in a stuffy attic room above an inn in the Strand. A taproom sat directly beneath. Ribald laughter drifted up the stairwell, but at least the room was clean and there was a lock on the door.

Ariel sank down on the narrow bed shoved against one wall. She thought of Justin and tried to imagine how she could have made such a terrible mistake. Why hadn't she seen the man he really was? How could she have been so wrong about him? But no answers came, and as the hours slipped past and darkness settled in, she curled up on the mattress still wearing her clothes and tried to fall asleep.

She was still lying there, still awake, still numb with pain and grief, when the sun came up the following morning. She tried not to think of the tender, caring man Justin had pretended to be, but again and again, the memory reappeared. They were laughing together in Tunbridge Wells. She was helping him with his ledgers, making plans to build stone cottages for the workers in Cadamon. Making tender love in the cozy house he had rented.

The morning grew later, slipped into afternoon. She tried to convince herself to leave, but she was so exhausted, so completely drained, she couldn't think what to do, and even if she knew, she didn't have the will to do it. Instead, she sat there unmoving, her hands and feet numb with cold, feeling the sluggish beat of a heart that was broken in two.

Another day passed. Thoughts of Justin grew fuzzy; the torment of her hopes and dreams began to fade. It was all a lie, she knew. His rare, beautiful laughter, his gentle care of her, his concern, none of those things had been real. Little by little, she banished the memories of them, shoved them to the back of her mind, buried them deep inside her heart.

By the time she came out of her room the following morning, weak from not eating, her eyes swollen and red from the tears she had shed, Ariel had accepted that Justin Ross was exactly the cold, heartless man he had been in his study the day he had sent her away.

And she hated him for it.

She hated herself, as well, for being so easily taken in. She vowed she would never again be so naive, so utterly trusting of another human being. She had learned a painful lesson, but she was young yet, and life went on. She would find a way to survive, just as she had done when she was fourteen.

Only this time, she would do it on her own. She would owe no one. She would make her own way, no matter what it took. No matter how hard she had to work, no matter the sacrifice she would have to make.

Whenever she despaired of failing, she would think of the cold, unfeeling man she had once thought she loved. And she would simply be grateful that at last she was free of him.

Chapter Sixteen

Clayton Harcourt walked into the study of Justin's house in Brook Street. He hadn't seen his friend in over a week. Justin had never arrived at their scheduled meeting at the club, had only sent word of his regrets the following day. Clay still hadn't heard from him, and frankly, he was worried.

If nothing else, it simply wasn't like Justin to let his business interests go by the wayside.

Clay found him working behind his desk. He rose at Clay's approach and Clay's feet stopped moving at the sight of him. Thin and sallow, his cheeks slightly sunken in, he had the look of a man who had recently fallen ill. But it was his eyes that made Clay's chest go suddenly tight. They looked empty, completely without emotion, and Clay knew in an instant whatever had happened had something to do with Ariel Summers.

"It's good to see you," Justin said, coming from behind the desk with an outstretched hand. Clay returned the handshake. "I'm sorry about our meeting. . . . Something unexpected came up."

"I thought I had better check on you. It isn't like you to put off pressing matters of business."

"Yes, well, I'm sorry about that, too. I've signed the necessary papers. We can close the deal on the mine anytime you wish."

Clay just nodded. He couldn't take his gaze off the hollow-eyed man in front of him. "It's obvious something has happened," he said gently. "Whatever it is, it has to have something to do with the girl."

Justin turned away. "I'd rather not talk about it, if you don't mind. Suffice it to say, the wedding is off."

"Just like that?"

Justin shrugged his shoulders. "It is probably for the

best. I was hardly cut out for the role of husband."

"Where is she?"

Justin reached toward the stack of papers perched on the corner of his desk, began to sift through it. "I imagine by now she has found another protector."

He said the words with a casual air, but when he glanced up, there was so much pain in his face Clay felt it like a blow. He wanted to ask again what had happened, but pressing Justin for answers wouldn't do the least amount of good. His housekeeper, Mrs. Daniels, had friends among the servants in the house. He would ask her if she could discover what had occurred.

"Are you certain you're all right?" Clay asked. "You don't look very well." Only one other time in his life had he seen his friend so remote, so painfully withdrawn—after he'd discovered Margaret Simmons in bed with Phillip Marlin.

Marlin? Surely not. God wouldn't be so cruel. But Ariel had been involved with Marlin when Justin first met her, and Phillip had always had a way with women.

"I'm fine," Justin said. "Just a little tired is all."

From the look of him, that was the understatement of the year. Clay forced himself to smile. "Since you are once again unattached, why don't we make a visit to Madame Charbonnet's?" He only asked to test the waters and watch his friend's reaction.

Justin's lips curved up in the coldest smile Clay had ever seen. "That sounds like a very good idea. I've a brief trip to make out of town, but as soon as I return, I'll hold you to it. After all, one woman is as good as another, once they are flat on their backs beneath you."

The bitter words, harsh even for Justin, sent a shiver down Clay's spine. If Justin had been cold and wary before, he was a man of ice now.

Clay thought of Ariel Summers and wished he could wrap his hands around her slender neck and squeeze the life out of her.

Just as she had done to his friend.

*   *   *

The biting fall winds whistled through the cracks in the
walls of the small attic room above the Golden Partridge
Inn. Ariel shivered and tried to keep warm. Her money had
run out long ago, but the owner had agreed to let her work
in the kitchen, filling in for Daisy Gibbons, who was ailing
in her last weeks of pregnancy. But money was tight and
he had enough help already. Once the baby was born, Daisy
would return to work and Ariel would have to leave.

"What am I going to do?" she said more to herself than
to Agnes Bimms, the cook at the inn, as she scoured the
burnt bottom of a huge iron kettle in the kitchen. "Mr.
Drummond has done his best to help me, but Daisy's baby
is due any day now. She needs the money. She'll be returning to her job as soon as she can. I've answered ads in
the paper, knocked on doors, tried to find work through an
employment agency. I've done everything I can think of.
Without references, no one will hire me."

"And a cryin' shame it is, too, what with your fancy
schoolin' an' all. Ye'd make a fine governess, ye would,
fer one of them rich nabobs in the West End. A shame is
what it is."

"I have to do something. It doesn't matter what sort of
work it is—I'll take anything I can get."

Agnes cocked a woolly gray eyebrow. She was a short,
stout woman with a tuft of whiskers on her chin and kindly
blue eyes. "There is one thing ye might wanna try."

Ariel's head came up. "What is it, Aggie?"

"They's a mop fair this Saturday, down to the park near
the corner. Ye might give that a try."

"A mop fair? I'm afraid I don't have the faintest idea
what that is."

" 'Tis a hirin' fair, don't ye see? Ye go there and whoever's in need of a servant or worker takes a look at ye. If
they like what they see, they'll hire ye for a year. Then
permanent, if ye do a good job."

Ariel smiled, feeling a shot of hope. "Oh, Aggie—that's

a wonderful idea. Surely there'll be someone there in need of a good worker."

"I'm sure there will be, dearie." Agnes handed her another heavy pot to scrub, but the hard work couldn't wipe the smile off Ariel's face. This time she would find work; she was sure of it.

On Friday, Daisy Gibbons returned to her job in the kitchen, and on Saturday, Ariel packed her satchel, left her drafty attic room, and headed for the mop fair. Dressed in a simple brown skirt and white blouse and wearing her sturdiest shoes, she was among the first to arrive. She had considered wearing something a little nicer, perhaps the soft gray wool, one of the two fashionable gowns she had allowed herself to keep, in the hope of finding a position as governess, where she could at least use her painfully acquired education, but something told her that without references her chances would be slim and she would be far more likely to find work if she dressed more simply.

The mop fair was in full swing by midmorning. At one end of the grass a platform had been built, and a crowd of people gathered around it, some of them well dressed, obviously there to hire, the rest attired more simply. On the platform itself, job seekers climbed the stairs to allow potential employers to get a better look at them.

It was a little like purchasing a cow or hog at the farmers' market, Ariel thought, suppressing a shiver at the notion. It was a humiliation she would rather not have to endure, but she didn't have any other choice. For a while she simply watched, noticing that certain workers wore distinctive articles of clothing or carried a symbol that identified the sort of labor they performed. Freight haulers tied a piece of whipcord around their hats; roof thatchers carried a fragment of woven straw.

She wasn't sure what symbol represented ordinary household servants, so she waited a little while longer. She searched the crowd, hoping she might find someone who needed a governess, but no such person appeared. She went up on the platform with a group of young women applying

for the position of lady's maid, but they all had experience
or references, and she wasn't chosen. She went up twice
more, for a job as a cook's helper and later as a housekeeper, but the same thing happened each time. Finally a
man came forward looking to hire a chambermaid. Determined not to be disheartened, Ariel climbed up on the platform again.

A well-dressed man with thinning brown hair stood on
the ground in front of them, carefully surveying each young
woman in need of a job. Ariel had been passed over so
many times that she blinked and simply stood there when
the man pointed at her and motioned for her to come forward.

She did so hopefully, trying to control her pounding
heart. She thought for sure he would ask how long she had
worked as a chambermaid, but this time her lack of experience didn't seem to matter.

"How old are you?" he asked instead.

"Nineteen."

"Where are you from?"

Ariel nervously moistened her lips. She had nowhere to
spend the night and no money. She said a silent prayer that
he would give her the job. "I was born on a cottager's farm
near the hamlet of Greville."

"Any family here in London?"

Ariel shook her head.

"Then you'll be wanting room and board as part of your
employment?"

"Yes, sir."

He nodded, seemed satisfied. "Get your things," he said
curtly.

"You're giving me the job?" Hardly able to believe her
good fortune, she hurried toward the stairs leading down
from the platform, her pulse leaping with excitement.

"Lord Horwick is giving you a job. I'm his steward,
Martin Holmes." When she reached his side, he turned and
pointed to an open carriage. "Wait for me there. When I'm

finished, I'll take you to the house and you can get settled in."

"Yes, sir." She made a brief curtsy. "Thank you, sir." Relief filtered through her. At least she would have a roof over her head and food in her belly. And perhaps Lord Horwick had children or knew of someone who did. In time, if she proved herself, she might still get that job as a governess.

Her spirits were high on the way to the carriage until she heard two women speaking in whispers as she walked past: "Poor gel. She don't know about old Horwick. That old lecher will have her skirts up over her head and a bun in the oven afore she's been there two months."

Ariel flushed crimson and kept on walking. Whatever sort of man Lord Horwick was, she needed this job. If a problem arose, she would simply make it clear to him that she was a chambermaid, not a strumpet.

A memory of her near-rape by Phillip Marlin arose, followed by a painful image of Greville. She had dealt with far worse than a lecherous, aging aristocrat. If Horwick had anything other than employment in mind, it wouldn't take her long to disavow him of the notion.

Justin leaned against the back of a gold brocade settee in Madame Charbonnet's House of Pleasure. Clay sat in a chair beside him, one leg casually crossed over the other as they watched a parade of beautiful, nearly naked women walk past. Clay had chosen a tall redhead with a slight French accent. She stood behind him, lightly massaging the back of his neck while Clay finished his glass of brandy and waited for Justin to choose.

"How about the brunette?" Celeste Charbonnet suggested. Celeste was a tall woman in her thirties, dark-haired and elegant, with excellent taste in everything from clothes to fine French wines. She had made a fortune out of understanding the likes and dislikes of men, and the women she employed were the most beautiful—and talented—in London.

"Gabrielle has skin as smooth and soft as a baby's, and hands . . . Such beautiful hands could please the most discriminating of men." The chestnut-haired woman parading past them was lovely in the extreme, but Justin shook his head.

"Blond, I think, for this evening."

Gabrielle took the rebuff with a smile. There were a number of patrons in rooms throughout the house. She would have no trouble finding a man to entertain for the night.

His attention turned toward the gold velvet curtains. They parted to reveal a young blond woman, petite but full-figured, smiling seductively, walking toward him in nothing but a nearly transparent swath of lilac silk that fell from her shoulders to the curve of her bottom.

Justin frowned. "Too short. I'm in the mood for someone taller."

Two blondes came out this time, Norwegian twins. They were beautiful, strong-boned, and elegantly built.

"Two is certain to double the pleasure," Celeste said. But something wasn't right. The color of the eyes, perhaps. He couldn't quite put his finger on it. He simply knew they weren't the ones to satisfy his needs for the night.

"I want someone more slender, blue-eyed, and more . . ." Justin stopped midsentence, the words trailing away as he realized with dawning horror exactly what he was doing. He chanced a look at Clay and saw that his friend was frowning.

Justin closed his eyes as Celeste snapped her fingers and another blond woman walked into the room, a lovely little English rose, naked to the waist, wearing white silk stockings and blue satin garters. She was perfect in every way, but he knew she wouldn't do.

She wasn't Ariel Summers.

Justin rose from the settee, cursing himself, cursing Ariel for what she had done to him. "Perhaps this wasn't such a good idea after all," he said to Clay, who was watching him with a worried expression, ignoring the redhead who now sat on his lap, her naked breasts pressing into his chest.

"Perhaps it wasn't," Clay said, setting the girl back on her feet and standing up as well.

"Don't let me spoil your evening. There's no reason for you to leave."

"It's all right. I wasn't really in the mood, either." He smiled at Madame Charbonnet. "Another time, perhaps." He dropped a heavy pouch of coins into her long, slim fingers. "So the girls won't forget us."

"Do not worry, m'sieur. They do not forget either of you. That you need not fear."

Barely conscious of the lady's words, Justin reached the door and pulled it open. He paused outside to drag in a lungful of air. "Sorry," he said to Clay. "I didn't mean to disappoint you. I don't know exactly what happened in there."

"I do," Clay said gently. "It doesn't matter. We'll come back again some other time."

Justin just nodded. He had tried to block Ariel from his mind and most of the time he succeeded. Once in a while, like tonight, he remembered the woman he had foolishly believed she was, remembered her gentle laughter, her intelligence, remembered the sweet, innocent girl of her letters. He remembered the woman he had made love to, had trusted as he never had another woman, and pain unlike anything he had ever known knifed viciously into his heart.

His jaw clenched. He took a deep breath and slowly released it. "I'm a bit more tired than I thought. I believe I'll go on home, if you don't mind."

"No . . ." Clay said. "I don't mind. Take care of yourself, my friend."

Justin nodded and turned away, wishing he hadn't come, wishing he hadn't seen the pretty little blonde who reminded him of Ariel—reminded him that she was just as much a whore as the girls at Madame Charbonnet's.

Working for the Earl of Horwick proved to be a difficult job. The house itself was huge and the staff kept at a minimum. The place was old and drafty, always full of dust, and difficult to keep clean. Not only was Horwick a demanding employer, working his servants from dawn till dark, serving them meals that were scarcely fit to eat, but he was also every bit as lecherous as the woman at the mop fair had said.

A disgusting little man, slightly obese, thick-lipped, and smelling of liquor and cigars, twice he had come upon Ariel in the hallway, pressed her up against the wall, and tried to steal a kiss. Each time, she had avoided his unwanted advances and escaped down the passage.

She hated working for a man like him, and over the weeks avoided him as much as she could. She needed to find another job, but she had heard what he had done to other girls who had left him, refusing to give them references and spreading lies about them, making it nearly impossible for them to find other employment. She would have to continue to save her money and bide her time, keep searching for a job on her one day off. Once she found something suitable, she would be able to quit.

"We'll be needin' the beddin' changed in the last four guest rooms in the east wing." Mrs. O'Grady, the housekeeper, passed by her in the hall. "Lady Horwick will be arrivin' from the country on the morrow. She's plannin' her usual round a' parties and a special ball for her niece's birthday. There'll be relatives arrivin' in droves."

"I'll see to it immediately, Mrs. O'Grady." She made a curtsy to the portly gray-haired Irishwoman who ran the earl's house on the skimpy budget he allotted. Ariel liked the stout little woman she had come to think of almost as a friend. She grabbed up the broom she carried and headed upstairs, hoping old Horwick was nowhere around and grateful that Lady Horwick was about to arrive. Surely the fat old lecher wouldn't try any of his tricks with his wife in the house.

Ariel worked all morning and into the afternoon. Unlike much of the house, a number of guest chambers and all of the main-floor salons were lavishly appointed and showed none of the wear evident in the rest of the aging mansion. She had just about finished with the last guest room when the door opened and a short, barrel-shaped man walked in.

"Hello, my dear," Horwick said. "I've been looking for you. I hoped I would find you in here."

Ariel's heart sank. "Looking for me? What do you want?"

Horwick frowned. "You're not frightened? If you are, there is certainly no need. Surely by now you must realize how attractive I find you."

"I have work to do," Ariel said, carefully backing away from him as he strolled toward her.

"Yes, I imagine you do. I could help in that regard, you know. If you would be a bit more cooperative, your work load could be lightened quite dramatically."

"I don't mind the work." Her back came up against a rosewood dresser. Horwick stood a little to the right, so she skirted to the left, hoping to duck around him. "I do the job I was hired for."

"Yes, you do, and quite admirably, I might add. Perhaps a bit of a raise in your salary would make you a bit more . . . amiable."

He moved to block her way again and Ariel stiffened. "I'm a chambermaid, my lord. It would be unseemly for me to become . . . amiable . . . with a man of your social status. Now, if you'll excuse me . . ." She darted to the left, but as rotund as he was, he could move quite quickly, dodging in front of her, spreading his short, thick arms, and catching her like a fly in his web. Ariel shrieked as a blunt-fingered hand grabbed hold of her bottom and he gave it a punishing squeeze.

He chuckled as she tore herself free and bolted for the door, escaping the room as if the hounds of hell were nipping at her heels, her face flaming scarlet. She rubbed the bruise on her bottom. Damn the old bastard to perdition! The next time he tried that she would . . . she would . . . What could she do? She needed this job, at least for a little while longer. She would have to find a way to stay out of his clutches.

Ariel sighed and headed off down the hall, her mind still shouting angry epithets at Horwick. She worked the rest of that day and late into the evening. The following day Lady Horwick arrived.

Ariel was more than grateful. At least for a while, she'd be safe from the woman's lecherous husband. Unfortunately, with the festivities her ladyship had planned, Ariel's work load nearly doubled.

She was exhausted by the time the house was ready for Lady Horwick's first affair, a small soiree for an intimate group of her husband's friends and business acquaintances. Even after the grueling day she'd put in, the woman expected her to help serve the refreshments. Ariel stuffed a strand of loose hair up beneath her mobcap and gave up a weary sigh. She could hear the strains of a small string orchestra playing in the music room. Guests were still arriving. By the time the entertainment—one of old Horwick's relatives performing on the pianoforte—was over, the late buffet was supposed to be on the table in the adjoining salon.

Carrying a silver platter heavy with assorted cold meats, Ariel started out of kitchen and headed down the hall. She had almost reached the door to the salon when she heard the butler's voice and realized another of Lord Horwick's guests had arrived.

"If I may please have your hat and coat, my lord, I shall be happy to announce your arrival."

"Of course. Thank you." With those few words, Ariel froze midway down the hall, her head snapping toward the sound of the familiar deep voice. She saw the tall, imposing figure dressed mostly in black, and a weight crushed down on her heart. She wanted to flee, but her feet wouldn't move. She wanted to disappear, wanted to vanish like a puff of smoke, never to be seen again in her simple black skirt and white cotton blouse, the silly little mobcap that sat askew on her head.

By sheer force of will, she summoned the wit to flee. She started back down the hall, nearly ran into a footman hurrying in the opposite direction, pressed the tray into his hands, and kept on going. She had almost reached the safety of the kitchen when she heard the sound of a man's heavy footfalls behind her.

"Ariel! Ariel, is that you?"

She kept on going, past the kitchen and out the back door, into the moonlit night, hoping to escape him completely. She heard the door slam open behind her, heard his shoes crunching on gravel, felt his long fingers closing around her arm, stopping her mad flight and forcing her to face him. When she did, one of his slashing black brows arched up as if he couldn't quite believe his eyes.

"So it is you," he said darkly. "What are you doing here?" His eyes ran over her from top to bottom, taking in her simple clothes. Then he frowned. "And why are you dressed in the garments of a servant?"

She wanted to laugh in his face. She wanted to weep. Instead she simply lifted her chin and forced herself to look at him. "I'm here because this is where I work. I'm dressed in the clothing of a servant because that is exactly what I am."

His frown grew deeper. "What about Marlin? I assumed—"

"You assumed what?" She couldn't keep the anger from her voice. She didn't even try. "Pray tell, your lordship. I should like very much to know what you assumed."

"Let's not play games, Ariel, shall we? I saw you and Marlin together. The night you met him in the stable. I was watching from an upstairs window."

For a moment, it was hard to make sense of what he was saying. She had buried thoughts of him so very deep it took a moment to recall the scene. Then she realized that he believed she had gone there to tryst with Marlin and her throat tightened. A bubble of hysterical laughter threatened to erupt, but she fought it down. The anger she was feeling turned white hot.

"You saw us that night? Did you, really? You mean you saw both of us going into the stable—isn't that what you mean? Too bad you couldn't have seen through the walls of the stable as well. Too bad you couldn't have seen what went on inside. If you had, you might have seen me telling him I wanted him to leave me alone. You might also have seen how angry that made him. Mad enough to try to tear off my clothes. Mad enough to try to"—she swallowed past the hard lump building in her throat—"to force himself on me. If it hadn't been for Mr. McCullough, your groom, he might very well have succeeded. Now—if you will excuse me—I have to return to the house. I have work to do."

She tried to walk past, but Justin stepped in front of her. "You're lying."

She lifted her chin. Angry tears burned her eyes. "Am I? You're the liar, Justin. Everything you ever did, everything you ever said, was a lie. I'm glad you threw me out of your house when you did. God only knows how many more of your lies I would have believed." Turning away from him, blinking against the wetness that blinded her vision, Ariel raced back into the house and up the servants' stairs.

Halfway to the top, she paused, listening for the sound of the closing door that would tell her Greville had returned to the soiree. She never heard the sound. She thought that the earl must have left without ever seeing Lord Horwick, but she didn't check to be sure.

She didn't want to think of him. Not now, not ever again.

She didn't want to remember the sight of him standing there in the moonlight, so tall and unbearably handsome. She didn't want to remember the pale cast to his usually swarthy skin when she had told him what had happened that night in the stable.

The coach thundered up the alley behind the house in a swirl of dust and dead leaves, and Justin leaped out before it had come to a shuddering halt. Though the hour was late, he headed straight for the stable.

"Where's McCullough?" Rousing one of the young grooms from his bunk, Justin waited impatiently as the youth named Mickey began a nervous stutter the moment he saw the black look on his employer's face.

"He's . . . he's . . ." Mickey swallowed. "I think he's upstairs in his room." Justin had started in that direction when he heard the Scotsman's voice.

"I'm right here, milord." The brawny man strolled toward him from a lantern-lit stall, wiping his hands on a rag he'd plucked off the saddle he had been oiling. "Ye wished to see me?"

Justin glanced around, saw several of the stable lads peeking out from the door to their quarters. "I need a word with you . . . in private."

The Scotsman jerked his head toward the stairs. "We can go up to my room."

Justin nodded. "Fine." They made their way in that direction, and as soon as the door to McCullough's room was closed, Justin turned to face him. "I want to know what happened the night Miss Summers was out here with Phillip Marlin."

The Scotsman looked suddenly wary. "I'd rather the lassie be the one to say."

"Miss Summers is no longer here, as perhaps you may have heard. Now I'm asking you to tell me what went on."

McCullough scratched the growth of red stubble on his jaw, then gave up a sigh of resignation. " 'Twas late. I was havin' a bit o' trouble fallin' asleep. I heard noises below stairs. I thought 'twould be wise if I had a look."

"And what exactly did you see?"

"I saw the two of 'em, the blond mon—Phillip, she called him—and the lassie, Miss Summers. She was talking to him real nice, tellin' him that she was sorry, tryin' ta make it clear she dinna have feelin's for him, no the sort he was wantin' her to have. She told him it would be best if he left, that you wouldna like it if you found out he had come here."

"What else?"

"She told 'im . . . She said she loved ye."

Justin's mind spun. It was impossible. It couldn't have happened. But one look in the Scotsman's eyes said it was the truth. His heart seemed to stop beating. For a moment, he thought he might be sick. "You're certain that's what she said."

"Aye, sir. 'I love 'im.' That's what the lassie said."

He was sweating. It was cold in the stable and his shirt was wet with sweat. "What happened then?"

"I started to go back upstairs. It weren't my business, ya ken? And I dinna want to eavesdrop on the lassie's conversation. Then I heard the mon say he was gonna have her—whether she wished it or no." He shook his head. "I'm no' a mon who caters to another mon takin' what a lassie's no' willin' to give."

Justin closed his eyes, pain cutting into his chest like shards of glass.

"I pulled him off her," the Scotsman went on. "I hit him and he went down. I sent the lassie back to the house." He grinned. "Then I hit him again."

If he could have, Justin would have smiled. He was certain he would never smile again. "Thank you, Mr. McCullough, for telling me the truth . . . and for taking care of her." He started for the door, stopped, and turned. "One last question."

"Yes, sir?"

"Why didn't you tell anyone?"

"The mon were the son o' an earl. He threatened to have me tossed into gaol for hittin' him. The lassie, she told him he had better no' say a word or she'd tell you what he'd done. She said none o' us was to speak o' it again. 'Tis exactly what I meant to do till ye came here tonight."

Justin just nodded. Ariel had come out here to tell Marlin she was in love with another man. Knowing her as he did, he knew that she would have felt she owed Philip that. For her honesty she had nearly been raped, and instead of protecting her, instead of asking her why she had gone to see Marlin, he had assumed she had betrayed him and tossed her out in the street.

But Ariel had never betrayed him. Not in the beginning. Not that night with Marlin.

It was he, Justin Bedford Ross, who had been the betrayer. It was he who had taken her innocence, who had used her viciously that morning in his study, who had crushed her like a newly opened flower beneath the heel of his boot.

Justin paused on the path leading up to the house. Beads of perspiration broke out on his forehead and his stomach churned with nausea. Turning, he took several long strides off the path, bent his head, and violently retched beneath the branches of a rosebush in the garden.

CHAPTER SEVENTEEN

Ariel mopped perspiration from her forehead and continued scrubbing the bedchamber floor. Lady Horwick had decided to open several more moldy, musty-smelling rooms that hadn't been used in years, and the brunt of the work had fallen to her. As soon as she finished, there was a cupboard full of tarnished silver that needed to be polished, the rugs in the dining room had to be beaten, then there was laundry to fold and put away. After that she would have to—

"I'm sorry to interrupt, my dear, but there's a gentleman downstairs to see ya." Mrs. O'Grady smiled. "One of Lord Horwick's business acquaintances. He's waitin' for ya in the White Drawin' Room. Hurry now, if ya please. Ya don't want to be keepin' him waitin'."

A knot formed in Ariel's stomach. A gentleman? It couldn't be. Surely not. But last night Greville had stumbled upon her and it seemed an impossible coincidence. Her pulse began a dull, thready drumbeat. The earl wouldn't come; he had sent her away. He no longer desired her. He cared nothing for her in the least. But who else could it be? And if it were he, why was he here?

Her hands shook as she set the mop aside and started for the door, shoving stray tendrils of hair back from her cheeks, tucking them up under her mobcap. She made her way down the newly repaired servants' stairs and along the hall to the White Drawing Room. Like most of the downstairs rooms, it was elegantly appointed and showed none of the wear evident in the rest of the house.

Ariel paused outside the ornate white-and-gilt door leading into the salon, took a deep breath, and walked in. Greville turned the moment he heard her, and she sucked in a breath at the sight of him. Instead of the handsome, calmly controlled aristocrat who had appeared in the entry the night before, the man who stood in front of her had a pale cast to his usually dark complexion and smudges beneath eyes that looked hollow and sunken in.

"Thank you for coming," he said. "I was afraid you would refuse to see me."

"I work here. I do as I'm told. Since you are a friend of Lord Horwick's, I had no choice but to come."

He nodded, glanced away. "I've something to say to you. I have no idea what you will think, or if there is the slightest chance that you will believe me."

"Say it then. I have work to do."

"This is difficult for me." He glanced down, then up, nervous in a way she'd never seen him. "Words of this sort do not come easily for a man like me." Ariel said nothing. There was something in his eyes, something so turbulent her heart picked up its pace. "I'm sorry for what I've done to you—more than you will ever know." He rubbed a hand wearily over his face. "You see, I knew you were lying the night I was supposed to meet Clay at the club. I wanted to know why. I never really left the house that night; I merely pretended to."

She wasn't surprised, not now that she knew the extent of his deceit.

"I saw Marlin go into the stable," he continued. "I saw you follow him in. When you came out with your clothes mussed and your hair unbound, I . . . I assumed the worst." He looked away, his expression bleak. "I was wrong."

The words came out hoarse and a little bit gruff. Ariel ignored the way they made her feel.

"I wanted to hurt you," he went on. "I wanted to pay you back for what I believed you had done."

For the first time, everything that had happened began to make sense. Until this very moment, she had refused to think about it, refused to let him into her thoughts again, even for a moment. Her legs started shaking. She was afraid they wouldn't hold her up. Slowly she sank down on the edge of a nearby chair.

"When I sent you away, I believed you would go to

Marlin. I knew he wanted you. It never occurred to me that you would have no place to go, no one to look after you."

"Why would you care?" she asked bitterly. "You got what you wanted. You were tired of me. You said so that morning. You said—" Her voice cracked on this last, and as hard as she willed them not to, tears welled up in her eyes.

Justin was beside her in an instant, down on one knee, reaching out to capture her icy fingers between his hands. They felt even colder than her own.

Ariel pulled away from him and came to her feet, turned, and walked shakily over to the window. She heard his voice coming from behind her, just a few short feet away.

"You were right in what you said. I *was* a liar. I lied to you that morning, but not in the way you think. I lied about the woman. There was no other woman. Worse than that, I lied about not wanting you. I've always wanted you, Ariel. From the first time I saw you, I wanted you. I look at you now and I want you."

Ariel's throat closed up as she whirled to face him. "I don't want to hear it. Not another word." She started for the door, but he stepped in front of her, blocking her way.

"You don't belong here. No matter what you think of me, this isn't a place you should be. Go up and get your things. I'm taking you out of here."

Ariel fought a fresh rush of anger. "You're insane. I'm not going anywhere with you. I wouldn't step one foot outside this house with you."

"I know how you must hate me. You have every reason to feel that way, but—"

"I'm not going with you, Lord Greville. Not now, not in the future."

His posture stiffened, making him look even taller than he usually did. "Ariel, listen to me. You can't possibly continue to live here. Surely by now you know what Horwick is like. He has a reputation for ruining the young women who work for him. Forgodsake—his bloody steward goes out and finds them for him. Come home with me and I'll—"

"You'll what? Allow me to warm your bed again? Make love to me until you find someone else you prefer? Let me make this clear, my lord. I wasn't interested in becoming Phillip's mistress. I am no longer interested in being yours." She looked straight into those piercing gray eyes. "I've learned something since I came to London. Being a lady has nothing to do with money and fashionable clothes. It has to do with pride and self-worth. I'm worth more as a chambermaid than I ever was as your whore."

A muscle tightened in his cheek, and something that might have been regret burned in his eyes. Ignoring the painful squeezing of her heart, Ariel turned away from him and made her way to the door. This time he didn't try to stop her. By the time she reached the back stairs, her heart was hammering wildly and a heavy weight rested on her chest, making it hard to breathe.

Ariel kept on walking. She had suffered enough at the hands of Justin Ross. Whatever fate awaited her, she never wanted to see him again.

For the balance of the day, Ariel worked herself to the point of exhaustion, then, when darkness set in, retired to her third-floor room and dropped into her narrow bed as if her body were tied with lead weights. She didn't want to think of Justin. She didn't want to remember the ravaged look on his face.

All afternoon, work had been her solace, blocking her emotions, keeping the pain away. During the day, her conscious mind had been safe from him, but now it was night and she couldn't block him from her dreams.

They were filled with painful images, visions of the ruthless man he had been the morning he'd made love to her, then tossed her out in the street. The frigid expression on his face, the icy cold that seemed to seep through his very skin. Glacial eyes that bit into her like frozen stones, numbing her to the bone.

"You knew sooner or later it would happen. . . . It would be better if you left today."

"Justin . . ." she whispered into the darkness, her heart breaking, and the sound of her own ragged voice sent the awful dream spinning away.

Through the tiny window above the bed a weak sun rose in the east. Ariel shivered against the cold in the room, shoved her long blond braid over her shoulder, and wearily climbed from beneath the covers. A few minutes later, she was dressed in her black skirt and white blouse and heading downstairs to begin her exhausting day's work.

She skipped breakfast. She couldn't force down a morsel of food. Her head ached and her muscles felt cramped from lack of sleep. She had only been working a couple of hours, the long day stretching endlessly ahead of her, when Mrs. O'Grady came in search of her.

"You've a package, my dear. It arrived by carriage just a few minutes ago. It's waitin' for ya on a table in the entry."

It was a single red rose in an exquisite silver vase. The card read simply: *"Forgive me."* No signature was needed. She knew only too well who it was from.

But she couldn't forgive him. Not for the things he had believed about her. Not for the callous way he had treated her. Not for leaving her heart a broken, battered thing inside her chest.

Another gift arrived the following day, a delicate music box that played a tune from the Bach concerto they had listened to in the park in Tunbridge Wells. This gift had no card, nor did the one that arrived the following day, nor the one that came the day after that. Ariel returned each one. When the next gift arrived, along with a letter, it went back unopened, as did all of those that followed.

None of them mattered. No gift, no matter how expensive, no letter, no matter how beautifully written, could convince her that the unfeeling, brutal man she had known that morning in his study hadn't been the real Justin Ross.

*   *   *

Justin entered a small private dining room at one of Clay's favorite restaurants: Rules, Maiden Lane, Covent Gardens. He wasn't hungry. He hadn't the slightest appetite since he'd seen Ariel dressed in the uniform of a chambermaid and working for that lecher Fletcher Giles.

Justin had never really liked the Earl of Horwick, but the man had a good deal of business acumen and they had wound up as partners in a couple of investment ventures. Justin had liked the man even less when he began hearing rumors that the earl had forced his unwanted attentions on a number of young serving women in his employ over the years.

Now Ariel was among those poor souls who worked for him, and Justin knew exactly why she had been hired.

"You look terrible." Clay's voice broke into his thoughts. "You had better sit down before you fall down." Clay called one of the waiters over and ordered something from the menu for both of them. "You look like you haven't eaten in a week."

Justin gave up a weary sigh. "I haven't had much of an appetite." Seated on a tufted red velvet chair in an ornate, heavily curtained private dining room, for the next half hour he relayed the story of what had happened to Ariel in the stable, how he had brutally used her the following morning and sent her away, and how she had wound up working for Horwick.

Clay softly cursed. "I'll admit, I've made a mess of things a number of times in my life, but I've never nicked it as badly as this."

"She refuses to see me. She won't open my letters. She's sent back every gift I've sent. What am I going to do?"

"Perhaps you should simply tell her how much you care for her. It's obvious that you do."

Justin shook his head. "Not to her, it isn't. She won't listen to anything I have to say, and even if she did, she wouldn't believe me."

"Well, she bloody well can't go on working for Horwick. Sooner or later the old bastard will go after her. Unless of course you've warned him not to."

"I haven't had the chance. He was away on business all last week. Fortunately, his wife is now in residence. He'll be on his best behavior, at least until she leaves."

"From what I gather, she'll be on her way this morning. She gave a birthday ball for her favorite niece two nights ago; now she's headed for the country."

"You were there?"

"I dropped in for a while, since I was fairly certain the lovely young widow I mentioned would also be attending."

"You didn't happen to see Ariel by chance?"

Clay shook his head. "Sorry. As I said, I didn't stay long. The lady and I decided we could spend our time in much more pleasant pursuits than listening to Lady Horwick extol the virtues of her bucktoothed niece."

The meal arrived just then, thick slices of venison wallowing in gravy, oysters, peas, and a crusty pigeon pie.

"Eat up. You're going to need your strength if you're going to figure a way out of this mess you've gotten yourself into."

Justin halfheartedly dug in, knowing he couldn't help Ariel if he allowed himself to fall ill.

Clay took a sip of his wine. "I didn't see Ariel at Horwick's, but I did see your sister."

Justin nodded. "I heard Barbara was in town. She is visiting Lady Cadbury, I gather."

"She was particularly chummy with your good friend Phillip Marlin. I thought they made quite a pair."

Justin glanced up from his meal. "I'm going to call him out."

Clay set his wineglass very carefully down on the table. "That isn't a good idea—not that the bastard doesn't deserve it. But if you kill him, you'll only stir up more trouble. Ariel's name will be dragged through the mud. He simply isn't worth it."

"I can't just ignore what he did to her."

"Yes, you can. At least for the present. You have Ariel

to consider. She has to be your first concern."

Justin said nothing. Clay was right. He had to think of Ariel first; then he would deal with Marlin. He forced himself to eat another bite of meat, but the food tasted like sand in his mouth.

"It could be worse, you know. At least you found out she wasn't swiving Marlin. And she certainly isn't in love with him."

"No, she isn't in love with him," Justin said softly. "She told him that she was in love with me."

The oyster Clay had speared paused halfway to his lips. He set the silver fork back down on his plate. "Christ."

"My sentiments exactly."

"What are you going to do?"

"I don't know. See her again. Try to convince her to leave. I've got to find a place for her to live, somewhere she'll be safe."

"She'll think you want—"

"I know exactly what she'll think, but it isn't the truth. I won't go near her. She doesn't want to see me and I don't blame her."

"Everyone makes mistakes," Clay said gently. "You're a good man, Justin, whether you believe it or not. You have feelings just like anyone else. Sometimes those feelings get in the way. They make you blind to seeing things the way they really are. You try to ignore them, but they're still there inside you. Pretending you don't have them doesn't make it so."

Justin said nothing.

"You never meant to hurt her," Clay went on. "Maybe in time, Ariel will understand that."

Justin didn't answer. After the way he had treated her, Ariel would never understand. It didn't matter. He had to help her. He owed her that much. That and so much more.

Ariel pulled the sheets from the big tester bed. Lady Horwick's last ball had ended two days ago—thank God. Most of the guests had already departed, and the few that remained would be leaving today.

She stretched and yawned and rubbed her aching back, then grabbed the ends of a clean white sheet and snapped it open above the feather mattress. She was busily tucking in the corners when she heard the door open, then softly close again. Expecting to see Mrs. O'Grady or one of the other chambermaids, she straightened at the sight of Lord Horwick's rotund figure standing in front of the door.

"Well, my dear. At last we are alone."

Ariel stiffened. "You mean your wife has departed and *you* are now alone."

His tongue slid out to wet his thick lips, and he grunted. "I mean *we* are alone, my dear. I realize you have not yet resigned yourself to the inevitable, but by the time I leave this room, you will have."

Ariel's lips went tight. She was more angry than frightened, and extremely tired of Lord Horwick's ridiculous assumption that sooner or later she would accept his disgusting advances. "I told you, I am a chambermaid, nothing more. If you can't accept that, then I shall be forced to resign my position." It was a daunting prospect, since she'd had so much trouble finding a job in the first place. Perhaps if she was firm with him, he would finally leave her alone.

Horwick smiled. "Finding employment for a young woman without references can be quite a task." He moved closer, removed his velvet-collared tailcoat, and tossed it onto the half-made bed. "Why go to so much trouble when by simply making yourself available to me on occasion you can have a very pleasant situation here?"

She clamped down on an angry retort and began to circle away from him toward the door. "I have no wish to make myself available to you or anyone else. Now kindly allow me to leave."

He simply shook his head. "I've been more than patient. It's time you discovered which of us is master here and which of us is servant." Horwick lunged toward her and

Ariel skittered away just out of his grasp. She reached the door and shrieked in outrage when she discovered he had locked it. Ariel whirled to face Horwick the same instant his short, bulky frame slammed her up against the door.

"Get away from me!" She tried to twist free, but a beefy hand dragged her head down and thick wet lips slid over her mouth. Anger rose up in a blinding wave and Ariel bit down on his lip. Horwick roared in outrage. He spit a curse but refused to let her go. Instead, she felt his blunt-fingered hand groping her breast and all the fury she'd been feeling toward Horwick—toward men in general—reared up with colossal force.

From the corner of her eye, she spotted a heavy Chinese cloisonné vase. Twisting until she could reach it, she took a firm hold, swung it up, and brought it crashing down on the earl's thick head.

A bellow of fury erupted. Swearing foully, he grabbed his aching skull, which bled from a cut on the top, and sagged to his knees, bracing himself against the dresser.

Praying she hadn't done any permanent damage, Ariel wildly glanced around for the key. Dear God, it had to be in his pocket! His coat was on the bed. She raced toward it and madly dug through the pockets. She found the object easily, but her hands were shaking so much she could barely get it out.

"You little bitch!"

Ariel whirled toward the sound of Horwick's voice. He was on his feet, swaying unsteadily, blood trickling from the gash on his head down the side of his face and dripping off one fat cheek. "You'll pay for this!" he shouted. "By God you'll pay!"

Ariel streaked for the door, jammed the key in the lock with a shaking hand, and wildly turned the handle. She yanked it open and stepped outside just as two of his lordship's footmen came racing down the hall.

"Stop her!" Horwick shouted. "That woman tried to kill me!"

The color drained from her face. *Oh, dear God.* She tried

to dart past the footmen, but one of them caught her around the waist and another grabbed her arm, wrenching it painfully up behind her. Through the open bedchamber door, Lord Horwick staggered out into the hall.

"Call a constable!" he demanded. "I want justice. I want this woman to pay for what she's done!"

Ariel turned stricken eyes to the earl. "Please . . . I didn't mean to hurt you. I was only trying to protect myself."

But already the household was in chaos, the kitchen help scurrying out to discover the source of the excitement, a footman and two linkboys racing out the door. A few minutes later, a group of watchmen thundered up the stairs. Horwick blustered and ranted, inventing a tale of attempted murder and ordering her tossed into gaol.

"He's lying!" Ariel shouted as the men dragged her down the hall toward the stairs. "The earl attacked me! I was only trying to defend myself!"

But no one believed her, not even the other servants. And even if they did, they weren't about to interfere. Jobs were simply too scarce.

As they neared the front door, she glanced frantically around one last time, looking for Mrs. O'Grady, then remembered the housekeeper had taken a few days off to visit relatives out of town.

"Dear God," she whispered as the watchmen hustled her down the front steps and into the their waiting carriage, terrified and not having the faintest idea what she should do. For an instant, she thought of Justin, but she wasn't really certain he would help her even if she found a way to reach him. And if he did, she could too well imagine what he would expect from her in return.

Fighting back tears, Ariel leaned back against the worn leather seat of the carriage, staring at the unforgiving faces of the watchmen, wondering how the beautiful life she had once imagined could have gone so very wrong.

Justin adjusted the knot of his white cravat for the second time and pulled down the cuffs of his fine lawn shirt.

Dressed in a dove gray tailcoat, silver brocade waistcoat, and burgundy breeches, he checked his image in the mirror one last time and started for the door.

He was headed for Lord Horwick's, determined to speak to Ariel, to convince her to move into the town house he had rented for her use. He had sent the earl a message four days ago, determined to see him, wanting to make it clear that Ariel was under his protection and that Horwick should leave her alone, but the earl had apparently left the city.

Justin was more than grateful. Knowing Ariel was safe, he'd spent the next three days working up his courage, trying to decide what to say. In the end, he had simply decided he would remove her by force if she refused to listen to reason. With that goal in mind, he hurriedly descended the stairs and climbed aboard his carriage.

It didn't take long to reach the earl's. He rapped firmly with the brass knocker on the front door and the stout little butler pulled it open.

"Good afternoon, milord. I am sorry to inform you Lord Horwick is not at home."

"I realize that. I am here to see Miss Summers."

"Miss Summers?"

"That's correct." Justin started past the little man into the foyer of the house. "I'm rather in a hurry to see her. If you will kindly tell her I am here—"

"I'm sorry, milord, but Miss Summers isn't . . . Miss Summers is no longer employed by Lord Horwick."

Justin's hard stare bored into the butler, whose face turned a faint shade of green. "Are you telling me she is not in the house?"

"No, milord."

A sinking feeling settled in the pit of his stomach. "Then where has she gone?"

"I'm not . . . not exactly sure, my lord."

There was something furtive in his manner. Justin reached out and gripped the front of the little man's white shirt and dragged him up on his toes. "Then find someone who is sure—and you had better be quick about it."

Justin released his hold and the terrified man scurried away, disappearing into the interior of the house. Awaiting his return, Justin paced the entry, his stomach knotted with fear. Where had she gone? How would he find her? Had something happened? Why hadn't he come sooner?

When the clock in the entry began to chime and the butler had still not returned, Justin started off in the direction he had gone.

He had only taken a couple of steps when the housekeeper, a short, robust gray-haired woman, stepped out into the hall and hurried toward him "Lord Greville, thank heaven you are here. I'm Mrs. O'Grady—Lord Horwick's housekeeper."

Horwick's name made the knot tighten in his stomach.

"I've been beside myself since I heard the news," she rambled on. "I've been away, you see, visitin' my aunt, and only just returned home this mornin'."

"Where is she? Where is Ariel?"

"Oh, my lord, 'tis the most dreadful thing."

Justin caught hold of her arms. "Mrs. O'Grady, please—tell me what's happened."

Her worried eyes fixed on his face. "There was an . . . an altercation of sorts four days past. Lord Horwick accused Ariel of tryin' to murder him. The constable came and took her away. The poor, dear child's locked up in Newgate Prison."

But Justin was already moving, heading for the door and his waiting carriage.

"She was only tryin' to defend herself," Mrs. O'Grady called after him, trailing him down the front porch stairs. "Some of the servants took up a collection and paid the garnish, so the guards wouldn't . . . so no one would hurt her."

His jaw flexed, but he made no comment, just jerked open the carriage door.

Looking more worried than ever, Mrs. O'Grady reached out and caught hold of the tail of his coat. "Please, my lord, there's no one else ta help her."

He turned to her then, saw the distress in her plump, lined face, and summoned a calming smile. "Put your worry to rest, Mrs. O'Grady. Ariel will be safe. I'll take care of everything."

Her shoulders sagged with relief and she smiled, brushed at a tear that crept from the corner of her eye. "I knew it. I saw it in your eyes the day you came to see her. I knew she could count on you."

Justin merely nodded. Of course she could count on him. She just didn't believe it. Damn, why hadn't he gone to her sooner, forced her to leave that bloody damned house? If he had, she wouldn't be locked up in prison.

One more failure.

One more mark against his black soul.

One more deed she would never forgive.

CHAPTER EIGHTEEN

The carriage rumbled at top speed through the streets of London, carrying Justin in all haste to Newgate, the main criminal prison in London. Instructing his coachman to wait out in front, he made his way directly to the warden's office. A few minutes of conversation, a pouch of coins dispersed into grateful hands, and he was shown through the gates into the prison.

"Right this way, milord," said one of the guards, a tall, skeletal man with rotten teeth who led him down a set of stairs lit by flickering rushlights. The smell of unwashed bodies, urine, and vomit rose like acid into his nostrils, worsening with every step he took deeper into the bowels of the prison.

At the bottom of the wooden stairs, long rows of dank, dark cells, holding up to ten prisoners each, stretched out in front of him. He could hear women weeping. One of them shouted vile curses while another laughed maniacally, the eerie sound echoing off the walls. Most of them simply stared out through the bars with glazed, hollow eyes that appeared blank and unseeing.

Justin steeled himself. Ariel had been living in this hell of rancid flesh and rotting offal for four long days. He knew the way the guards often treated the female prisoners and fervently prayed that the money Mrs. O'Grady's friends had paid had kept her safe.

"Not much farther," the guard said, swinging the lantern he carried out in front of him, using it as a pointer. "Just down there."

Justin lengthened his strides, forcing the guard to hurry his pace to keep up. The skinny man stopped in front of a crowded cell and held up the lantern. Through the narrow iron bars, Justin could see there were no cots, just damp, dirty straw on the cold stone floor. Some of the women huddled against the walls; others lay sleeping. Ariel sat with her back against the rough stone, staring straight ahead. Her simple black skirt was torn in several places, her white blouse gray with filth. The hem of her skirt was ruched up, and he could see that her feet were bare. There was dirt on her face, and her long blond braid looked lank and dull and was littered with stems of straw.

Justin's heart turned over. He forced himself to breathe in a lungful of the fetid, foul-smelling air and moved closer. "Ariel?" He spoke to her softly through the bars. "It's Justin. I've come to take you home."

She made no movement, her mind far away from her pitiful surroundings. She didn't even acknowledge he was there.

"Ariel? Can you hear me?" When she still made no move, he turned a hard look on the guard. "Open the door."

The skinny man did as he was told, the rusty lock grating, the iron door yawning as it swung open. Justin stepped inside and began picking his way over the women sprawled on the floor, shouldering his way past those who were standing.

"Eh, 'andsome," one of them called out. "You 'ere for me?" Several others cackled with laughter, but Justin ignored them. When he reached the spot where Ariel sat, he slowly knelt beside her. In the light of the lantern, her skin looked as pale as marble and her eyes were so dull and bleak that a thick lump rose in his throat.

"Ariel, love, it's Justin. Can you hear me?"

Her eyes flickered, slowly moved to his face. "Justin . . . ?"

"I've come to take you home." Bending down, he slid his arms beneath her knees, scooped her up against his chest, and started back toward the door. Ariel pressed her face into his shoulder. He felt her tremble; then she began to weep.

The lump in his throat ached painfully. Justin strode through the heavy iron door, down the long row of cells, and up the stairs. He didn't pause until he was outside the building, feeling the sunlight, breathing clean air. Still, he kept walking, out through the tall front gates, along the paving stones till he reached his carriage. Climbing swiftly inside, he settled Ariel on his lap, an arm wrapped protectively around her. A footman closed the door, and a few seconds later the coach lurched into motion.

"It's all right," he said gently, smoothing strands of silvery hair back from her cheeks. "You're safe now. You've nothing more to be afraid of. Everything is going to be all right." She felt so fragile, so weak. It was obvious she hadn't eaten. The smudges beneath her eyes said she hadn't had any sleep.

Ariel made a soft, whimpering sound, and Justin tightened his hold around her. He whispered soothing words and held her against him until they reached the house; then he lifted her up and swiftly departed the carriage, whisking her safely inside.

Knowles hurried toward them, a frown creasing his usually stoic face. "Good heavens."

"Have a bath prepared and sent up to her bedchamber."

"Yes, my lord."

"She'll need some food as well."

"I'll see to it myself."

Justin nodded his thanks and carried Ariel up to the room she had used before, setting her carefully down on the edge of the four-poster bed. "Are you hurt?" he asked gently.

Her eyes closed for an instant; then she slowly shook her head. She didn't say anything, just sat there staring down at the hands she had limply folded in her lap. Looking into her weary face, Justin hesitated only a moment, then began to unfasten the buttons on her dirty cotton blouse.

"The lads are bringing you a bath," he said softly. "We need to get you out of these filthy clothes."

Ariel's hand caught his. Big blue eyes lifted to his face. "I'm all right now. I can do it myself."

"You're certain you aren't injured? The guards didn't
. . . they didn't hurt you?"

She swallowed. "No."

A pair of linkboys arrived with a steaming tub of water.
Justin waited for the boys to set the tub in the middle of
the room, then rose to leave.

"I'll send Silvie in to help you."

"Thank you."

Turning away, he went to fetch the woman who had
served as her maid, then paced nervously outside the bedchamber door until the dark-haired girl finally opened it and
stepped back out into the hall.

"How is she?" he asked, the moment the door was
closed.

"She's sleeping, milord. She was exhausted. She fell
asleep before she even had a chance to eat."

Justin exhaled a weary breath. "I'll sit with her awhile.
I don't want to leave her alone."

"Aye, milord."

Slipping quietly into the room, careful not to wake her,
he sat down in a chair at the side of the bed. She slept
fitfully and seemed to be suffering unpleasant dreams.
Whenever she began to thrash about, Justin reached over
and took her hand. Each time he did, her movements stilled
and she drifted back into quiet slumber.

She slept through the day, into the evening, and late into
the night. He told himself he would leave before she awakened, before she had time to realize he was there, but just
before dawn he fell asleep. He dreamed of Ariel, and in his
dreams she smiled at him the way she had in Tunbridge
Wells.

Morning sunlight filtered through the curtains, slanting into
Ariel's eyes. She blinked several times against the brightness behind her closed lids, then finally cracked them open.
The smell of lilacs drifted up from her hair. A clean white
pillowcase nestled against her cheek, and a soft cotton night
rail fell lightly down over her knees.

For an instant, she thought she was dreaming, that she was yet in Newgate, that when she awakened she would still be breathing the fetid air, still be tortured by the keening of the women.

Then she remembered Justin. That he had come for her and that she was once again in his house. She started to sit up, saw his tall frame cramped uncomfortably into a chair beside the bed, his eyes closed, his long tapered fingers gently holding onto her hand.

A painful swell of emotion tightened deep in her chest. For an instant, Ariel couldn't breathe. Justin had come for her. He had saved her from a fate she couldn't bear to imagine. How could that be?

Easing her hand from his, she slowly swung her legs to the side of the bed, wincing a little at the stiffness. For a moment she simply sat there watching him. Though his breathing was deep and even, he looked nearly as tired as she, the skin beneath his eyes faintly smudged, thin lines etched into his forehead. And yet in his features, there was a boyishness she had noticed before, a softness that appeared only in sleep. His hair was mussed, a dark lock hanging over his forehead. Thick black lashes formed crescents against his lean cheeks.

He stirred then, slowly opened his eyes, sat up abruptly in his chair. "Ariel . . . I'm sorry. I must have dozed off."

"Yes. . . . Apparently you did."

Those dark gray eyes found hers, and instead of the reserve they usually held there was an unmistakable look of concern. "How are you feeling?"

She thought about the awful days and nights she had spent in prison and felt the sting of tears. "It was terrible. The filth and the foul odors. The way they treated the women." Her throat hurt. "As long as I live I shall never forget it."

"It's my fault. I should have made you leave the house. I wanted to. I—"

"It's Horwick's fault. He is the one who should be locked away." She looked up at him, saw the remorse that still haunted him, and something loosened inside her. "I am much better now that I have rested," she said softly. "How did you know I was there?"

Some of the tension eased from his face. "I went to see you. The butler said you were no longer employed there. When I tried to find out where you had gone, Mrs. O'Grady appeared. She told me what had happened."

Mrs. O'Grady. Such a dear, sweet lady, and the only one with the courage to stand up for her against Lord Horwick. That thought struck an awful chord. "Horwick—oh, my God! When he discovers what you've done, he'll come after me. I'll have to go back to prison. I'll have to—"

"You won't have to go back to prison. Not ever. I promise you that. And I'll take care of Horwick."

"But how did you get me out of there? The earl has accused me of trying to murder him. I wouldn't do something like that. I hit him over the head with a vase, but only to keep him away from me, and he more than had it coming."

His mouth edged up. "I'm sure he did. At any rate, you were released into my custody. As soon as I speak to Horwick, the matter will be ended."

"But how can you be sure? Perhaps he won't agree. Perhaps—"

An icy look came into those steel gray eyes, a look Ariel remembered only too clearly.

"Leave Horwick to me," Justin said with a deadly calm that left no doubt the man would relent or pay the price. Ariel shivered.

Justin rose from his chair, unfolding his tall frame to its very impressive height. "I'll tell Silvie you are awake and in need of her assistance."

"Thank you."

He crossed the room without looking back and Ariel watched him go, her thoughts in turmoil. She was back where she had started—living in Greville's house, indebted to him once more. She had no money, no one to turn to. Even the money she had earned at Lord Horwick's was lost to her, hidden beneath the pillow upstairs in her bedchamber and no way to retrieve it. It wasn't fair. It simply wasn't!

She sighed and got up from the bed, trying to think what to do. She had a very expensive education, yet what good had it done her? She had worked to make her own way and failed miserably. Instead, she had lost her money, been thrown into gaol, and wound up once more under the earl's control.

But she was no longer the naive young girl she had been. She knew the sort of man Justin was. He did nothing that wasn't to his own benefit. What price would he try to extract from her this time?

Ariel suppressed an icy shiver.

Sitting behind the desk in his study, Justin read the column in the *London Chronicle* for the second time that morning and uttered a curse. With the servants having witnessed the incident at Horwick's and Ariel's subsequent arrest, he should have known an article would eventually appear in the papers. Though only their initials were used and Ariel's name was the only one clearly stated, it was fairly obvious which members of the aristocracy were involved and it wouldn't take long for speculation to spread through the *ton*.

Damn, he'd thought he could keep the matter quiet. He should have known better. Except in his business dealings, he was rarely ever lucky. He was rubbing his tired eyes, wishing things could be different, when the door slammed open and Clay walked in, waving a copy of the paper.

"Have you seen this?"

"I've seen it. One of old Horwick's servants must have wanted to earn a little extra money."

"I imagine so. Horwick and Greville, two of London's most notable aristocrats, in a scandal involving sex, attempted murder, and a beautiful, mysterious woman. It was simply more than a man could resist."

"I'm sure it brought him a tidy sum," Justin said sourly.

Clay tapped the paper. "It says here that Ariel was Lord H.'s mistress. It says he caught her trying to steal his money and that was the reason she hit him. Apparently they think you—Lord G.—met her at Horwick's and took a fancy to her. That is the reason you decided to help her." Clay slapped the paper down on the desk. "What're you going to do?"

"I spoke to Horwick yesterday. He's already agreed to drop the charges."

Clay grinned. "I imagine you made it fairly clear what would happen to him if he didn't."

Justin's mouth edged up. "Fairly clear."

"What about Ariel? If she wasn't ruined before, she certainly is now. What do you intend to do about that?"

"Get her out of here. Silvie is packing her things as we speak. We'll be leaving for Greville Hall within the hour."

The door slammed open for the second time in only a very few minutes and this time Ariel stormed in. In the two days since her departure from Newgate, with the bed rest he had decreed and half his staff pampering her, she appeared to be fully recovered. Her skin glowed and her blond hair shone with silver lights. It was hard to believe she was the same dirty urchin he had carried home from the prison.

There was fire in her eyes today. She eyed him angrily, her slender hands clamped on her hips. "I demand to know what is going on. Silvie says you told her to pack my things. She's says you're taking me out of London. I realize I am again in your debt for helping me with . . . with my problems with Lord Horwick, but that doesn't give you the right to make decisions that concern my life. If you wish to leave the city, you may do so, but I am not going with you. I made my own way before; I can certainly do so again. In fact, I would prefer to be on my own."

Justin didn't point out the little success she'd had on her last attempt. He simply reached for the paper Clay had laid on the desk and handed it over. "Fourth column down," he said.

With an uncertain glance, Ariel unfolded the paper and

began to read. She quickly skimmed the article, then read it again more slowly, the rose in her complexion slowly fading to pale. "This isn't true. Not a single word of it."

Justin eased the paper from her trembling fingers. "I want you away from the gossip. At Greville Hall, you'll be safe from wagging tongues. It's quiet there. You'll have time to decide what you wish to do with your future."

"But your sister is in residence. She'll be furious if we intrude."

"I have already sent word of our arrival. Besides, the house is mine, not hers. Barbara lives there because I allow it. If I wish to stay for a week—if I decide to stay for a year—it is none of her concern."

Big blue eyes locked on his face. "I am also living by your charity. What sort of payment do you expect from me?"

Justin glanced away, guilty and uncomfortable at the accusation in her face. What he wanted from her was the warmth of her smile. What he wanted was the sound of her laughter, to hear her softly sighing his name. He expected none of those things.

"You will go there as my guest, nothing more. I want only to be certain of your safety."

"Why? Why are you doing this?"

"Because I care about you, dammit! Is that so terribly hard to believe?"

Ariel looked stunned. Justin stared at her, feeling a mixture of anger and some other, more turbulent emotion he couldn't name.

A few feet away, Clay muttered something, then cleared his throat. "I don't want to keep you from your journey. You've a distance to cover before you reach Greville Hall." To Ariel he said gently, "Sometimes in life we overlook the obvious. Go with him, love. In time, things will all work out."

Ariel said nothing for several long moments; then she nodded.

Justin felt a wave of relief. "I've a few things to finish

before we leave," he said. "I'll meet you in the entry at half past the hour."

Wordlessly turning away, Ariel walked out of the room and quietly closed the door.

"I'll keep an eye on things here," Clay offered. "If there's anything you need, just let me know."

Justin's mouth curved up in a grateful smile. "Thank you, Clay. For everything." He was lucky to have a friend like Clay. Justin watched him leave the study, then turned to finish the paperwork on his desk. Try as he might, he couldn't concentrate, and the lines on the pages seemed to blur. Setting the files away, he pulled open the bottom drawer of his desk. At the very back, a small velvet box lay on its side, tossed away as if it were of no more value than a crumpled piece of paper. He drew the box out and flipped open the lid. Nestled in a bed of white satin, perfectly fashioned sapphires burned brilliantly up at him. Surrounding them, the icy white of the diamonds glinted in cold accusation.

From the moment he had read her first letter he had only meant to help her. Instead, he had done nothing but hurt her. He had taken her innocence, used her, and betrayed her. He scoffed as he stared at the stones glinting at him from their satin-lined box. Marrying her would have been the cruelest betrayal of all.

Justin lifted the beautiful ring from its perch and rested it in his palm, surveying each brightly cut gem, wishing he could have given Ariel the perfect, bright life symbolized by the ring.

But he couldn't give her that. There was no brightness in him, only darkness. Ariel had been the light, the luster, the fire. Somehow he had managed to dim even that.

His fingers tightened around the magnificent sapphires until the stones bit cruelly into his palm. His hand squeezed into a fist and the sapphires cut into his flesh with a burning sting, but he didn't stop, didn't try to lessen the pain.

Not until he felt the sticky wetness of his own blood, running between his fingers.

CHAPTER NINETEEN

Clay caught up with Ariel just as she reached the staircase. "Miss Summers? Ariel . . . ?"

She stopped and turned, her worried gaze flying to his. He couldn't miss the turmoil that darkened the blue of her eyes. "I have to get ready. There isn't much time."

"I know. I just . . . I realize you are upset. I know this has been a terrible experience for you, but it has also been a very bad time for Justin."

The curve of her lips flattened out. "Bad? Bad in what way? Surely you aren't going to stand there and tell me he was lonely? I imagine he had any number of women to keep him company after I was gone. I doubt either one of you has trouble finding willing female companions."

"No, there has never been a shortage of women for either one of us." She turned and started walking, but Clay caught her arm. "Justin isn't interested in other women. He hasn't been since the day he met you. Don't you see? It's you he cares about."

She looked away, glanced down at the floor, studied the swirls in the marble. "It doesn't matter. I'm not interested in a man who doesn't trust me, who believes that I would be unfaithful."

"Perhaps if you knew him better you might understand. Did Justin ever tell you about Margaret?"

"Margaret? Was that his mother's name?"

"Margaret was the young woman Justin had the misfortune of falling in love with. It was a long time ago, of course. When we were away at school and both of us were younger. Margaret was beautiful and headstrong, and she told him that she loved him. For the first time in years, he allowed his emotions to surface. He believed that in time they would marry. Instead he caught her in bed with Phillip Marlin."

Ariel's eyes widened in shock.

"When he saw you that night and believed you'd gone to Phillip, just as Margaret had done, he must have gone a little bit insane."

Her lips trembled, but her chin went up. "He should have asked me about it, at least let me explain. He should have had faith in me. Instead he believed that I was like . . . like her. I am not the least bit like that."

"Justin was wrong, Ariel. He made a mistake. But all people make mistakes. In the past, Justin has been hurt very badly. That makes him more wary, more guarded than most. But he isn't a fool. He's a man who learns from his errors. He won't make the same one again."

Ariel said nothing, but her eyes held an ocean of pain.

"Think about it," Clay said gently. Her troubled gaze followed him as he turned and walked away.

Wearing a gown of amethyst silk that revealed an ample portion of her milk-white breasts, Barbara Ross Townsend floated through the high, gilded double doors of the elegant Rose Salon of Greville Hall. Sunlight streamed in through the tall damask-draped windows in front of the house and glittered on delicate crystal chandeliers.

Barbara smiled at the golden-haired man who awaited her, coming to his feet the moment she slipped through the doors.

"Lady Haywood . . . Barbara. I came as quickly as I could."

"Phillip, darling, it's marvelous to see you." She clasped his waiting hands, and Phillip leaned forward to kiss each of her cheeks.

"You look lovely as always." He smiled. "We didn't have nearly enough time in London. I've thought of you every moment since you left."

She had known Phillip Marlin for years but until lately had paid him little attention. Not until her latest visit to London. She'd been a guest of Lady Cadbury, there to attend the marchioness's annual soiree. Phillip had been in attendance, as well, and they had danced several times to-gether. He was solicitous and attentive, more so once he sensed her interest was returned.

Several times in the past he had let it be known he found her attractive, an appeal perhaps heightened by the enmity that existed between him and her half brother. Until lately, she had ignored his overtures. Now she was glad she had waited.

Barbara knew well her appeal to men. With her black hair, fair skin, and pale gray eyes, she had a sensual, slightly exotic air that men found irresistible, and her one unpleasant experience with childbirth hadn't marred the beauty of her body. Her rose-tipped breasts stood high and her waist remained trim. She had all the feminine attributes a man like Phillip Marlin found enticing, and being Justin's half sister made her even more so.

After their evening at the soiree, Phillip had asked her to dinner. At the end of their third evening together, they had begun a torrid affair.

Barbara smiled as his eyes drifted down for a slow pe-rusal of her breasts. "Your message sounded urgent. You said there was a matter of importance we needed to dis-cuss."

"There is. But now that you are here, we'll have plenty of time for that later." She lightly caressed his jaw, then took his face between her hands and pulled his mouth down to hers for a kiss. Beneath his coat, his heartbeat quickened. She felt the thickening bulge of his arousal and inwardly she smiled. "Why don't we go upstairs for a while? Perhaps . . . afterward . . . we'll both feel more in the mood for a serious conversation."

Phillip's sensuous lips curled up at the corners. "I be-lieve I would like that." He kissed her again, more deeply this time, sliding his tongue into her mouth, pressing her body against the hardness between his legs. "Yes, I believe I would like that very much."

It was two hours later before they had the discussion for which she had summoned him. She was pleased to discover

Phillip was even more agreeable to her proposition than she had hoped he would be.

They left the bedchamber and returned downstairs, Barbara holding onto his hand. She had envisioned a leisurely afternoon, but instead a messenger arrived, and her plans were forced to change.

"I can't believe this! Of all the gall." She handed the note to Phillip. "He is coming here today. No warning, no notice, just arriving as if it were his right." Which of course it was, but that didn't matter to Barbara. "I'm afraid you'll have to leave, darling. I'm sorry you came such a distance for nothing."

"Hardly for nothing." Phillip's mouth curved. His eyes ran over her body in a slow, heated glance that was a pointed reminder of the things they'd done upstairs. "Knowing Greville, he won't stay long. Not when he has so many pressing business matters waiting for him back in London."

Barbara lifted her long black lashes and gave him a seductive smile. "You'll come back once he's gone?"

"Of course, darling." He walked up behind her, slid his arms around her waist, and drew her back against his chest. "We've a number of details to work out, and there are other"—he kissed the side of her neck—"even more enticing reasons for a visit."

Barbara smiled and turned to face him, her fingers gliding over the lapels of his coat. "I'll send word as soon as he leaves. In the meantime, perhaps you will think of a way to implement our plan."

"Indeed, perhaps I shall." A long, lingering kiss, and then he was gone.

Barbara smiled to think how easy he was to manage, how similar their interests and desires, and how, with his help, she had so cleverly set things into motion. Then she thought of the man who would soon be arriving at the house and her satisfied smile slid away.

Justin Bedford Ross was her nemesis, a thorn in her side since the day she had discovered his existence, an interloper who had stolen her son's rightful heritage. Dear God, how she hated him.

Almost as much as she hated the man who had adopted him and made him the Greville heir.

Her father, the man who had ruined her life.

The journey to Greville Hall was made mostly in silence, Justin's mood dark, Ariel's mind whirling with thoughts she couldn't seem to rein in.

Because I care about you! Is that so terribly hard to believe? Justin's words rolled around in her head. A week ago she would have said yes, it was impossible to believe. She would have been convinced that the Earl of Greville cared for no one but himself. That he was cruel and vicious, that he had enjoyed using her and sending her away.

But that had been before he had returned to Lord Horwick's to beg her to forgive him. Before she had been thrown into prison and he had come for her, carried her away from that terrible place, his expression so bleak, so filled with self-loathing that a painful band had tightened around her heart.

Before she had awakened and found him holding her hand.

Now as she looked at him, sitting on the carriage seat across from her, his unseeing gaze fixed out the window, his thoughts even further away, she remembered the story Clay had told her of the girl Justin had loved and how she had so cruelly betrayed him. His father had denied him. His mother had abandoned him. Who had ever loved him?

No one but her.

The thought brought a sharp, unexpected jolt of pain. She had loved him once. That love was dead now, buried so deep she could never find it again. Never wanted to find it again.

Or was it?

From beneath her lashes, she studied the hard set of his jaw and remembered how it softened in slumber, making him look almost boyish. She remembered the fiercely protective gleam in his eyes when he told her she would never have to go back to prison. The tender way he looked at her when he thought she didn't see.

Ariel shook her head. She was fantasizing, imagining things, pretending he was something he would never be. Even if he cared for her, he didn't love her. Justin was a man incapable of love. He simply didn't possess that sort of emotion.

The turbulent thoughts continued, banging around in her head until an ache began to throb at her temples. She closed her eyes and rested her head against the tufted velvet cushions, listening to the rattle of harness, the rumble of carriage wheels rolling along the dirt lane, determined to force her mind in a different direction.

She tried to concentrate on what she would do with her future, once the scandal had died and she was once more on her own. He would help her make a new start, she now believed. At least in that small way she was certain he had told her the truth. Anything more, she refused to consider.

One thing was certain. She couldn't let her guard down, not even for an instant. If she did, those penetrating looks and sultry glances would begin to summon memories she didn't dare recall. Memories of how it had felt when he kissed her, touched her, made love to her. How her blood sang when he was inside her. If she thought of those things, she would want him again, and wanting him might lead to loving him. It was a fate she didn't dare risk. She had survived loving him once. She couldn't do it again.

She couldn't survive another crushed and bleeding heart.

Greville Hall was even more magnificent than Ariel remembered. In the years since she'd been away, she had forgotten the way the huge house nestled in the sheltered green valley like a pearl among the rolling hills, the way the pale yellow stone glinted so softly in the sunlight. Standing three stories tall with majestic gabled roofs, a sea of chimneys, and a lovely gilded dome that reached more than seventy feet into the blue November sky, the house seemed to sparkle like the jewel it was.

The carriage rolled to a stop beneath a white-columned veranda that sheltered guests on their arrival, and a footman opened the door. Wide stone steps stretched across the front of the house, and Ariel felt Justin's hand at her waist as she climbed to the top and went in through one of the massive double doors the butler held open.

"Welcome to Greville Hall, my lord."

"Thank you. Perkins, isn't it?"

The aging butler beamed that the earl, who had only been to the house on one occasion, had been able to remember his name. "Yes, my lord. Harold Perkins." While Justin spoke to the man about matters pertaining to the house, Ariel stared in awe at the magnificent entry. Above their heads, light streamed in through a huge gilded dome brightened by stained-glass windows. Deep ruby reds, emerald greens, and sapphire blues cascaded down on ancient Roman statues and gilt-framed paintings that lined the walls.

"It's incredible," she whispered when Justin joined her and offered his arm. "More beautiful than I ever imagined."

Something softened in those cool gray eyes. "Since you like it so much, we shall have to take a tour. I warn you, though, I have no idea where we might wind up. I've never been through the house myself."

How odd, Ariel thought, to own such a treasure and never explore it. If she were mistress of Greville Hall, she would know every crook and cranny, every painting on the wall, every flower in the garden.

Then she heard the sharp, shrill sound of his sister's angry voice. Barbara Townsend strode into the entry, and Ariel knew exactly the reason Justin had never spent time in the house.

"I see you have arrived—at precisely the time your note advised. Always so prompt, so totally predictable—so utterly and completely boring."

Justin's expression remained bland. "Since that is the

case, we shall make it a point to spare you our company as much as possible."

Barbara arched a brow. Though her lips curled up, there was nothing friendly in the smile she cast in his direction. "Even so, you shan't want for company while you are here, will you? Not with your pretty little whore to keep you entertained. Why bother with propriety? Just because your innocent young nephew happens to reside in the house, why should that prevent you from dragging your mistress along?"

Justin's expression tightened, turned icy hard. His jaw was set, his eyes such a frigid dark gray they looked almost black. One of his hands balled into a fist and a muscle ticked in his cheek.

His piercing gaze sliced like a knife into his sister. "You're mistaken, my dear. Ariel isn't my mistress." His eyes swung to Ariel but only for an instant; then his mouth tightened into a cold warning line. "She is soon to be my wife."

The breath Ariel hadn't known she was holding slipped from her lungs. Justin's gaze returned, locked with hers, and didn't move away. She read its plea more clearly than any words he had ever spoken.

Don't say no. Let me do this for you. Even if marriage hadn't been his intention before they stepped inside the house, there was no doubt he meant every word. He would marry her. He would protect her from cruel, vicious people like his sister. He didn't love her, but he would give her his name, give her a future.

His eyes remained on hers for a split second longer, and in their dark, smoky depths Ariel caught a glimpse of something else, something she hadn't expected, something so potent, so powerful, she had to steady herself on legs that suddenly turned shaky.

There was no mistaking the look in those dark, stormy eyes, no mistaking the need, the terrible yearning, unlike anything she had ever seen in his eyes before. There was no way to miss the silent prayer that willed her to say yes.

It stunned her with the force of an icy wind, and in that moment she knew that the love she had felt for him had never really died. It was there in her heart as it had always been. There reaching out to her, making itself known.

She loved him and watching his face, seeing the terrible longing that hid beneath his cool, emotionless facade, she had no choice but to marry him. She would take any risk, no matter how great, no matter how dangerous, against the chance that one day he might love her in return.

Tears burned her eyes. No words would come and even if they had, she couldn't have said them. Instead she stepped toward him, reached out, and gently took hold of his hand. His fingers laced with hers, tightened almost painfully. He drew her closer, slid an arm possessively around her waist.

He stared his sister straight in the eye. "Ariel is soon to become the next Countess of Greville."

Barbara's expression turned feral, her lips stretching into a tight, ruthless smile. "And just when is this momentous occasion supposed to occur?"

"We'll be married by special license as soon as I can arrange it." He glanced at Ariel, and for the second time in the span of minutes, a look appeared that she had never seen. With a sudden burst of clarity she realized it was hope, the sight so unexpected and so utterly endearing it made a thick lump rise in her throat.

"In the meantime," he said, returning his attention to his sister, "I presume you have our rooms prepared."

She cast a glance up the stairs. "I've had the bedchamber adjoining yours made ready. I didn't realize you would be wanting more proper accommodations."

His jaw tightened, but he made no further comment. Instead, he turned to a footman who stood near the door. "See to the bags, if you please. The lady is undoubtedly tired and in need of a rest. I should like to see my nephew; then I believe I shall also retire for a while before supper."

"Aye, milord." The young blond footman hastened to do the earl's bidding.

Ariel followed the butler up the stairs. The door to the room stood open and a chambermaid busily finished setting the bedchamber in order. As bright and lovely as the rest of the house, it overlooked the lavish formal gardens at the rear. It was done in shades of cream and rose satin, with beautiful silk damask curtains at the windows and an ornately carved rosewood bed on a dais against one wall. Ariel waited for her trunks to arrive, garments she had left at Justin's house the day he sent her away, and they appeared a few moments later.

Silvie arrived with them, having ridden in the second carriage with the footmen and the luggage. She helped Ariel out of her dusty, travel-stained clothes and into her quilted blue wrapper. While Silvie unpacked her clothes, Ariel wearily sat down in a chair before the fire.

Good heavens, what have I done? Though the room was warm, a tremor ran through her. Everything had happened so quickly. Justin had told his sister that they were to marry. Wordlessly—insanely—Ariel had agreed. Dear God, she must have been mad, completely out of her head!

A memory of his face arose, but the image held none of the yearning, the terrible need she had seen. What if it were only her imagination? What if they wed and she discovered he was indeed the cold, heartless man he had seemed?

She needed to talk to him, needed to know what he was thinking. She needed to reassure herself she was doing the right thing.

Crossing the bedchamber, she sat down at the antique French writing desk in the corner and penned a brief message, asking him to meet her at seven o'clock that evening in the garden. Then she handed the note to Silvie and asked her to deliver it to the earl. Bobbing a quick curtsy, Silvie left to find him, and Ariel climbed wearily up on the bed. A little rest and surely she'd be able to think more clearly.

But two hours later, she was still awake, her thoughts just as muddled as they were when she lay down to sleep.

*   *   *

Barbara paced back and forth in front of the marble-manteled hearth in her elegant suite of rooms. The master suite. The lord's bedchamber. The rooms Barbara had usurped since she moved back into the house after her husband died. With their rich royal blue and silver decor, they were the most elegant rooms in the house. Why shouldn't she use them? Justin never came to Greville Hall, and the one time he had, he'd been perfectly content to use the smaller suite of rooms he now occupied down the hall.

Barbara paced to the window and made another turn, her ruby velvet gown flaring out, the muscles in her shoulders aching with tension. *By rights the rooms should belong to Thomas.* Since the boy, not her father's callous bastard son, should have been the heir.

The thought brought an image of that devil-in-the-flesh, her cold, black-hearted brother, and a fresh wave of fury broke over her. How dare he calmly arrive at her house and announce he would marry his latest whore! How dare he! For years, he had sworn he would never wed. He had no use for a wife and children, he'd said. He simply wasn't the sort.

And fool that she was, she had believed him. She'd been certain that in time her son would inherit. She had mistakenly thought she had plenty of time to hasten that outcome along. Now, having seen the way her half brother looked at Ariel Summers, as if she were a glorious banquet on which he intended to feast, she had no doubt he would rut with the wench until he got her with child, and virile as he was, likely it would be a son.

A boy who would inherit the Greville title and fortune that should have belonged to Thomas.

Barbara whirled toward the hearth and her fist slammed down on the mantel. She needed to see Phillip again, to tell him this latest turn of events and discuss what they should do. She would send him a message, set up a meeting at the inn in the village.

For the first time since her brother's arrival, she smiled.

Perhaps having Justin and his whore in the house was a blessing rather than a curse. She would know his plans, his whereabouts, for as long as he remained. And out here in the country, anything could happen. Shooting accidents, an untimely fall from a horse, a deadly bout with tainted food. The possibilities were endless.

Calmer now, Barbara sat down at her desk and scratched out a message. She would see it delivered this very day, get word to Phillip and move up the timetable on their plan. For the first time, it occurred to her that perhaps Justin's little whore was already with child, that perhaps that was the reason he'd decided to marry her. If she was, Barbara would soon find out.

Justin would be dealt with and, if a child was forthcoming, so would his little whore.

Justin strolled along the paths in the garden. It was lovely here, he conceded, even in mid-November. Winding gravel walkways lit by flickering torches. Perfectly manicured hedgerows forming graceful patterns in the lawns. An old-fashioned maze loomed in the distance, topiary sculptures of birds set to guard the entrance.

Making his way to the marble fountain that bubbled in the center of the garden, he sat down on one of the curved marble benches that encircled it. He was early for his meeting with Ariel. He straightened the cuffs on his shirt and fiddled with the knot of his cravat.

He'd hoped to use the extra time to consider what he would say to her when she arrived, but so far nothing had come to him. He wasn't sure why she had sent the message. He wasn't even certain she had actually agreed to the marriage. Perhaps she simply wished to stifle his sister's venomous tongue, if only for a while.

Justin sat there in the darkness and one of her letters came to mind:

There is great excitement at school today. Cynthia Widmark, one of my classmates, is going to be married!

Though she has known the young man for a number of years, until recently her parents believed she was too young to wed. They have relented, it seems, and agreed to a betrothal. Cynthia is gloriously happy. I can only imagine how wonderful it must feel to fall in love, marry, and have a family. I wonder if I shall ever be as fortunate as she.

Justin thought of the letter and wondered if Ariel would ever consider herself fortunate to be married to him. She had once said that she loved him. He wondered if, back then, it was actually true. Or perhaps she had said it merely to dissuade Phillip Marlin. He tried to think what woman had ever loved him. Not Margaret, for certain. Not his mother, at least not enough to keep her from leaving and never coming back. Perhaps his grandmother, but that had been so long ago he couldn't quite recall.

Justin glanced back toward the house, searching the empty walkways for Ariel. It was quiet in the garden, except for the crackle of the burning torches and the patter of the fountain. It was chilly out here in the dark, the night crisp and clear, the stars winking like jewels in the blackness overhead. He hoped she would remember to bring a shawl.

Footsteps crunching lightly on gravel brought him to his feet, nervous now, growing more uncertain. God's blood, what should he say?

"Justin . . . ?"

"I'm here . . . by the fountain." She turned and walked toward him, her expression as uncertain as his own. For a moment, neither of them spoke. Then they both tried to talk at once and again nervously fell silent.

"I'm not exactly certain where to begin," Ariel finally said, looking up at him. "Did you mean what you told your sister?"

"You must know that I did."

"Why? Why would you want to marry me?"

He wasn't sure how to answer, wasn't certain he knew

the answer himself. "It's past time that I married." As good a reason as any he could think of. "I'm in need of a wife. You're in need of a husband, or at least someone to look after you. It would seem the answer to both of our problems."

"You said you weren't the sort for marriage."

"Perhaps that's what I thought . . . at the time. But life goes on; people change. You asked me once if I planned to have children. I hadn't thought to do so, but perhaps I was too hasty. Now, I think I should like to have children very much." *As long as they would be your children, as well.*

"I see."

But she didn't sound overjoyed at the prospect. Maybe he hadn't explained things clearly enough. "I've seen you with Thomas. I know you like children. I believe you would make a very good mother. In return, I can give you what you've always wanted. You'll be a countess, Ariel. Lady Greville. You'll have money, a position in society. No one will ever be able to hurt you again."

Ariel turned away from him, moved off toward the fountain, skimmed a finger across the cold, shadowy surface of the water. "If we are to have children, you must intend to spend time in my bed. If that is the case—"

"I want you, Ariel. I always have. I don't intend for this marriage to be in name only."

Seconds ticked past. "I won't lie to you, Justin. I'm frightened. I trusted you before. I'm terrified to do it again."

Regret settled over him like a damp winter mist. Walking to where she stood, he caught her chin between his fingers and slowly turned her to face him. "I can't undo the past. I can only promise that nothing of the sort will ever happen again."

Her eyes, so blue in the light of the torches, scanned every line of his face. "Do you love me, Justin? Even the tiniest bit?"

A tight band squeezed around his chest. He wished he could say the words she wanted to hear, ached to make her girlish dreams come true, but he didn't know the first thing about loving someone, and he would never lie to her again.

"I care for you, Ariel. More than I ever believed I could. But love . . . ? Love is something I know nothing about. In truth, I don't believe I am capable of such a feeling. I can only tell you that I'll take care of you, provide for our children. And I'll do my very best to make you happy."

She worried her bottom lip. "I don't . . . I don't know."

The words tore through him. The tightness around his chest contracted until it was hard to breathe. "Let me take care of you, provide for you as you deserve. Please, Ariel." *I need you.* "Say you'll be my wife."

She gazed into his face and he wondered what she read there, what secrets the harsh lines and shadows revealed. Whatever it was, tears glittered for an instant in her eyes. "I'll marry you, Justin."

He hadn't meant to kiss her. He simply looked into that beautiful teary gaze and couldn't stop himself. Framing her face in his hands, he captured her trembling lips and kissed her with all the longing he had known since he sent her away. Regret for his betrayal mingled with the knowledge that she would soon be his, and his need for her built. Hunger rose with it, like a fire erupting in his blood.

For an instant he allowed his passion free rein, pulling her into his arms, kissing her deeply, feeling her slim fingers digging into his shoulders. He was hard and aching, his arousal throbbing to be inside her. He kissed her a moment more, then tore himself away, ending the moment before he went too far, before he did something else that he would regret.

A shudder rippled through him as he fought to regain control. His chest rose and fell as if he'd run a winning race. "I think it would be best if you went in," he said softly. "If you don't, I'm afraid I shall be tempted to break the promise I made when we came here."

Ariel looked up at him, her face flushed, her lips still moist from his kiss. He saw the uncertainty in her eyes and he hated himself for it. He lifted a hand to her cheek, touched her feather-lightly.

With a last worried smile, she turned and hurried back toward the house.

Justin watched her go, fighting the desire that still burned in his blood. For the past few days he'd been able to control it. Now that she had agreed to marry him, it tore through his body like the claws of a ravenous beast.

Lust was a familiar emotion.

It was the tenderness he felt as he watched her disappear inside the house that amazed him. For a moment, he didn't even realize what it was.

Wearily he sank down on the bench, rubbing the back of his neck, trying to sort out his thoughts. Earlier he'd sent word to his solicitor, asking him to arrange for a special license. In a few short days, he would be wed.

He stared down at his hand, flexed his fingers, felt the muscles tighten in his forearms. Over the years, he had kept himself physically strong and mentally tough. He'd taught himself to be fearless, then used that fearlessness to earn his fortune and make his own way.

Now as he looked toward a future that included marriage and, in time, perhaps even children, he discovered a rising terror unlike anything he had ever known. In truth, he had never been more frightened than he was at that moment, sitting alone in the shadows of the gardens, thinking about the strange turn of fate that had brought him to this unexpected moment in his life.

CHAPTER TWENTY

A storm set in. The tall cypress in the garden leaned toward the earth, bending to the bitter north wind that howled down through the valley. Rain pelted the ground and spattered against the windowpanes. Eerie branches of lightning lit the murky landscape, and thunder cracked over the hills.

It was nearly dark. The vicar had been late in arriving, but Justin had refused to wait another day. Inside a small but elegant salon done in pale blue and gold, the wedding ceremony was about to begin.

Only a few guests were attending: Barbara and Thomas; Clayton Harcourt, who had, at Justin's request, arrived from London late that morning; Ariel's little maid, Silvie; the housekeeper, Mrs. Wilson; and the butler, Harold Perkins—the last three, being servants, standing a little away from the rest. The vicar, a man named Richard Woods, waited to begin the ceremony, his plump wife, Emily, already teary-eyed, standing next to Clay.

The wedding commenced exactly on time. In a few short minutes Ariel Summers, born a peasant, daughter of an impoverished and illiterate tenant farmer, would become Ariel Ross, Fifth Countess of Greville.

In a high-waisted gown of pale blue velvet trimmed with bands of ecru lace, she stood next to Justin, her hands faintly trembling, her face cold and numb. As the vicar began the service, Justin stared straight ahead, his jaw rigid, his gaze shuttered against whatever he might be thinking.

Ariel tried to keep her own unsettling thoughts at bay and concentrate on the vicar's words.

"Christ said, 'As the father hath loved me, so hath I loved you. This is my commandment—from this time forth—that you love one another.' "

"... *that you love one another.*" It was God's commandment and Ariel knew in her heart that she kept it. She loved Justin Ross. But she wanted him to love her in return. From the corner of her eye, she spotted Clay Harcourt smiling at her, looking as if he read her thoughts. He had challenged her once, instilling the notion that she could actually teach Justin to love. Perhaps if they had never had that conversation, she wouldn't be standing here now.

"Join your right hands," the vicar instructed. She felt Justin's grip, solid and strong. Her own hand trembled. "Do you, Justin Ross, Earl of Greville, take this woman, Ariel Summers, to be your wedded wife? To have and to hold from this day forward, for better, for worse; for richer, for poorer; in sickness and in health; to love and to cherish till death do you part?"

"I do," he said firmly.

The vicar turned to her, repeated the vow, asked for her answer. "I do," she answered softly.

"May I have the ring?"

Justin pulled it from the pocket of his silver brocade waistcoat and handed it over. Beneath the blazing candles, elegant sapphires flashed with blue fire; diamonds sparkled like pure, clear ice. Ariel stared at the ring in surprise, thinking she had never seen anything more stunning.

"This ring is given in token that you will keep this covenant and perform these vows. My lord, do you so promise?"

Again Justin answered, "I do."

"You may place the ring on her finger." The vicar returned it to Justin, and he slid it onto her left hand. It felt cool and slightly heavy, but not unpleasantly so. It was simple yet so exquisitely beautiful a lump of tears rose in her throat.

Where had it come from? Justin hadn't had time to purchase it. Clay must have brought it from London. It was amazing he could choose a ring so perfectly suited to her.

The vicar's voice rang out: "As you, Justin Ross, and you, Ariel Summers, have consented together in wedlock and have pledged your troth to each other in the sight of God and in the presence of this company, in the name of the Father, the Son, and the Holy Ghost, I now pronounce that you are man and wife. Whom God hath joined together, let no man put asunder." He smiled. "You may kiss your bride, my lord."

But Justin was already leaning forward, pressing his mouth to hers. His kiss was softly erotic and amazingly tender, yet it burned with an underlying heat that sent little shivers into her stomach. For weeks, she had blocked the memory of his sensuous kisses, of his lean, muscular body, of his graceful long-fingered hands as they moved so skillfully over her sensitive skin. Now the memories came rushing back with the impact of the storm raging outside the windows.

Uncertainty surfaced, worry about the future, of what might lie ahead. Ariel shoved them away. Instead, she glanced at the clock on the marble-manteled hearth, remembered the pleasure she had once known in his arms, and thought how interminable the hours would be before they retired upstairs and he would make love to her again.

"Congratulations," Clayton Harcourt said, leaning over to kiss her cheek. "I wish you both every happiness."

"Thank you."

He slapped Justin on the back. "So you were smart enough to marry her after all. I had begun to wonder."

"I believe it would be more aptly put, the lady was foolish enough to agree."

Clay chuckled softly. It was obvious he was happy for his friend and that he approved of the woman Justin had chosen. It pleased her to think her husband's dearest friend had accepted her so completely.

Little Thomas came racing toward them just then, grinning from ear to ear, a gaping hole where another small tooth should have been. "Are you married now, Uncle Justin?"

He smiled and hoisted the boy up, propping him against his chest. "It would certainly appear that way. Ariel and I are married, which means she is now Lady Greville. She is also your new aunt."

"My aunt?"

"That's right. From now on you must call her Aunt Ariel."

The child looked over at her shyly, peeping from beneath thick black lashes so like Justin's. "Aunt Ariel?"

She smiled, charmed as always by his sweetness. "I've never had a nephew before. I believe I am going to like being an aunt very much."

Thomas laughed joyfully, one small arm clinging to Justin's neck. "Me, too, Aunt Ariel."

Liking the notion more and more, she watched as Justin set the boy back on his feet.

"Why don't you go into the room next door and get yourself something to eat?" he said. "I believe I saw some apple tarts that looked particularly good." Through the door to the adjoining room, a linen-draped table groaned beneath the weight of endless silver trays laden with food: scallops of succulent goose, roast quarter lamb, lobster curry, pheasant pie, an array of steaming vegetables, and decadent desserts: a scrumptious chocolate cream, a delicate almond pudding, custards, fruit compotes, and of course the apple tarts.

Tall white beeswax candles burned in a beautiful silver centerpiece, and a stack of silver-rimmed porcelain plates had been set out to feed hungry guests.

The little boy dashed away, and from the corner of her eye, she caught an image of someone moving toward them. Her warm smile faltered and slid away, her mouth going dry at the sight of Barbara Townsend bearing down on them. Carrying a glass of champagne, her elegant silk skirts flying out behind her like the wake of an approaching ship, Barbara stopped directly in front of them.

Her lips curled into one of her feline smiles. "I suppose I should congratulate the happy couple. I must admit, I never expected to see the day. I wonder what Father would say if he knew his son had married a—"

"I would watch what I said, if I were you," Justin

warned, no longer willing, it seemed, to play his sister's ruthless games. Unconsciously Ariel moved closer, and his arm went protectively around her.

"I was merely considering what Father would think of the daughter of one of his tenants becoming the Countess of Greville." How she knew that particular bit of information Ariel wasn't sure, but Barbara was ever full of surprises.

"Considering how badly he wished his bloodline to continue, I imagine he would have been more concerned with my getting an heir than whether or not the lady I married came up to his daughter's social standards."

Barbara sipped her champagne, eyeing them darkly. "Perhaps you're right. Father was always more interested in youth and beauty than good breeding."

Ariel blanched. Justin ignored the remark, but a muscle ticked in his cheek. A servant appeared in front of them, carrying a silver tray filled with crystal goblets, and Barbara slipped away, off in search of more interesting quarry, leaving them apart from the rest of the guests.

"Would you care for a glass of champagne?" Justin asked. "I imagine we could both use something to relax our nerves."

Ariel simply nodded. She could indeed use something to ease the tension thrumming through her. "Thank you." She accepted the glass and took a sip, felt the fizz of bubbles on her tongue and his beautiful gray eyes on her, but they carefully shuttered his thoughts.

"It's obvious you're unsettled," he said. "If you are worried about tonight, don't be."

Her stomach instantly knotted. "Tonight?"

"I realize in the past few weeks your feelings toward me have changed considerably. We are married. As your husband, there are certain . . . demands I shall be making upon you. But I don't intend to press you before you're ready."

The glass of champagne trembled in her hand, several drops spilling over the rim. "But I thought . . ." Her heart seemed to slow its beat. "I thought you wanted me, Justin."

In an instant, the shuttered look was gone. Eyes the gray of the sky outside held a hunger that seemed to burn across her skin. "I want you, Ariel. Every time I close my eyes, I remember how beautiful you looked lying naked beside me, what it felt like to kiss your lovely breasts, how hot and tight you were when I was inside you. I want you the way a dying man wants to live. But I won't ask for something that you're not ready to give."

Ariel simply stood there, feeling the fire sparked by his words, the air thick and hot and swirling with a force that was almost tangible.

"You're my husband," she heard herself saying. "Tonight is our wedding night. I'm prepared to fulfill my wifely duties."

The heat in his eyes seemed to dim and slowly fade and they brimmed instead with sadness. "Perhaps in time, you'll be ready to do more than fulfill your duties. Perhaps you will remember the way it was between us in the past. Perhaps the time will come when you want me again."

He turned then and walked away, and Ariel felt suddenly empty. She had lied to him—a lie of omission. She already remembered, already wanted him. Whatever he felt for her, whatever problems lay ahead, her desire for him remained. Just watching him standing across the room in conversation with Clayton Harcourt made her heart beat faster, made the heat tug low in her belly.

Wearing dove gray breeches that clung to his hard-muscled thighs, a dark blue tailcoat stretched over his broad shoulders, he looked powerful and male, and impossibly attractive. He was lean and hard and virile. He was her husband and though he didn't love her, he wanted her.

Ariel wanted him, too.

Tonight was her wedding night. As a child, she had dreamed of it. As a woman, she knew, if the man were the right one, what pleasure the night could bring. She had married Justin, taken the risk of loving him again. Now she longed for him to come to her, to make love to her. Her mind warned her to beware, but her body wanted him as it always did.

Ariel shoved her doubts away. Justin was her husband. She would set aside her pride and tell him the truth. She watched him a moment more, debating, trying to convince herself. *Do it now,* a little voice urged, *before you lose your nerve.*

In the light of the candles, the diamond stickpin in his cravat seemed to wink at her, summoning her forward. Taking a fortifying sip of her champagne, she set the glass down on a nearby table and crossed to where he stood. He turned at her approach, and for an instant she glimpsed the same burning hunger that she had seen before. He banished it as quickly as it appeared.

"Excuse me," Clay said with a discerning smile. "I believe I have suddenly developed an appetite." He winked at her and purposely stepped away, giving them a moment alone.

Ariel took a steadying breath and fixed her attention on her husband. "There is something I wish to say. Something I was embarrassed to say before. I would like to say it now, before I lose my courage."

His slashing black brows drew down. He set aside his barely touched glass of champagne, a wary look setting in. "Then I suppose you had better get on with it."

She moistened her lips, the words more difficult than she had expected. "Earlier . . . when we discussed our wedding night . . . I spoke to you of duty. I was embarrassed, afraid to admit the truth. I should have been speaking of need, not duty. I haven't forgotten the nights we shared. I never will. I've missed you, Justin, these last terrible weeks, and I want you to make love to me. Tonight I would have a true wedding night . . . if that is your wish, too."

Something burned in his eyes, blazed with the same white-hot fire as the lightning outside the window. They turned dark with purpose. Ariel gasped as he set his jaw, bent, and scooped her up in his arms.

"What . . . what are you doing?"

"I'm taking my wife to bed." Long, determined strides carried him toward the door, servants scattering like mice out of his way. "By her own admission, that is where she wishes to be. God knows it is where I wish to be." Ariel clutched his neck and peered over his shoulder, her face turning crimson as he strode out of the drawing room and she caught the knowing smiles of a pair of young blond footmen. Behind them she heard Clay Harcourt's husky laughter, saw Barbara Townsend's face turn an angry mottled red.

Justin simply ignored them.

"What about the vicar and his wife?" Ariel asked in amazement as he strode down the hall toward the stairs in the entry. "And your friend Mr. Harcourt?"

"From the enormous amount of food on their plates, I doubt the vicar or his wife will even know we are gone. And Clay will certainly understand." Taking the sweeping marble stairs two at a time, he strode down the sconce-lined hall to his suite of rooms. He turned the silver knob, shouldered open the door, and carried her into the sitting room. A firm kick closed the door behind them.

"Besides," he finished, striding past the ornate marble-topped tables into his bedchamber, "I don't give a damn what they think. I care about making love to you. And since it is your wish as well, that is exactly what I intend to do."

His words sent a frisson of heat sliding through her. A wave of uncertainty followed, worry that she was making another mistake. Ariel determinedly ignored it. Closing her eyes against her fears, she clung tightly to his neck.

The storm heightened. The wind howled, rattling the windows and making the candles flicker. Justin let go of her, and she slowly slid the length of his body. She could feel his arousal pulsing against her, and an answering pulse started low in her belly. The air in the room seemed to crackle around them, as if they stood on some ancient precipice out in the wind and the rain.

Ariel stared up at him, unable to tear her eyes from his face. She was his wife and she wanted him. Needed him.

Yet fear of the future lurked like a shadow in the corners of her mind. With every gentle touch, every whispered word, she belonged to him more, loved him more. She knew the danger, knew how grave a chance she was taking. Knew that in giving herself to him so completely she risked her very soul.

Justin gently touched her cheek, brushed a finger back and forth along her jaw. "Ariel," he whispered, his voice a soft caress. Looking into her eyes, he bent his head and kissed her, his lips clinging, then pressing deeper. It was a fierce, saturating, penetrating kiss that sent heat flooding into her stomach. Ariel opened to him and his tongue swept in, silky wet, hot as fire. The kiss she gave him in return was even hotter, bolder, more seeking, driving out the fear, locking it away. Today he was her husband, her lover. He belonged to her and she to him. Tomorrow the fear would return, but not now, not tonight.

Sliding her hands inside the vee of his dark blue tailcoat, she urged it off his shoulders. She fumbled with the beautiful diamond stickpin, finally got it free, pulled the knot on his white cravat, and slid the long length of fabric from around his neck. She worked the buttons on the front of his shirt and it fell open, exposing taut muscle and dark skin covered by curly black chest hair.

Justin kissed her again, softly, deeply, pulled the pins, one by one, from her hair. Pale silver-gold waves slid in a long fall around her shoulders. Turning her back to him, he pulled the heavy mass away and kissed the side of her neck, began to remove her blue velvet gown. In minutes he had stripped her naked. Then he started kissing her again.

His hands skimmed over her shoulders, her breasts. He pressed small butterfly kisses into the corners of her mouth, kissed her deeply again. She thought that he would hurry, that his fierce need would drive him to take her swiftly. Instead he paused, circled her waist with his hands, lifted her up, and set her on the side of the bed. Another deep kiss and he eased her back on the bed, settling himself between her parted thighs.

She thought that he would hurry, that he would open his breeches and drive himself inside her, as she so desperately wanted him to do. But when she reached for him, he only shook his head.

"I won't be rushed. Not on my wedding night. You belong to me now and I mean to cherish you, as I should have done before."

It was such a beautiful sentiment that when he kissed her again, so softly, so fiercely, she didn't question what he meant. Not until he began a slow assault on her body, kissing the pulse in the hollow of her throat, trailing his mouth across her shoulders, using his tongue to circle the peaks of her breasts, making them tighten and throb. He took the roundness into his mouth and suckled gently, deeply, making her ache in her most tender places.

Ariel arched her back as his lips moved lower, trailing kisses over her rib cage, circling her navel with his tongue, tasting the flat spot between her hipbones, moving lower, kissing the soft, pale hair at the juncture of her legs.

She gasped when he found the hot, wet dampness at her core, parted the folds with his tongue, and settled his mouth over the tiny swollen bud of her desire.

"Justin!" she cried out, her teeth sinking into her bottom lip, her hands shaking as she reached out to him, her fingers curling into his thick black hair. "Oh, dear God!" She thought to make him stop, for surely this was a sin, but the pleasure was so sweet, the fires so hot, she couldn't bring herself to say the words.

Her hand gripped his shoulder. She felt the softness of his fine lawn shirt, remembered that he was still dressed while she lay naked and exposed. The image was so sensuous, so utterly erotic, a fresh rush of dampness swept into her core. Justin slid his palms beneath her buttocks to hold her in place, exposing her to the wicked assault of his tongue. Her body shook with fierce sensation, and Ariel heard herself moan. His shoulders wedged her thighs even farther apart, and he stroked her deeply, skillfully.

Determinedly.

The pleasure built, became almost unbearable. Slivers of fire slid into her stomach, melted over her skin. Her flesh burned. The breath rushing out of her lungs seemed to scald the inside of her mouth. She was writhing on the bed, arching upward, pleading for the release he was so determined to give.

It came with astonishing force, a wave of pleasure so deliciously sweet, so totally consuming, she sobbed out his name. She was crying, the tears cascading down her cheeks, when he leaned over and softly kissed her lips.

He left her only long enough to remove the rest of his clothes; then he joined her on the bed. For several long moments, he simply held her, wrapping her tightly in his arms, cradling her against his chest. His arousal pressed between them, hard as steel, hot as fire, and she knew what it cost to hold himself in check.

The heat of his body seeped into her skin. His hard, masculine strength made her need for him surface once more. Ariel cupped his cheek, leaned over, and kissed him, sliding her tongue inside his mouth, making the muscles across his chest go iron hard. With a low male groan, Justin took control of the kiss, turning it hot and fierce, sweeping her up in sensation.

Lightning flashed, illuminating the room and the hunger in his eyes. A crack of thunder shook the windows. Then she was beneath him, his long, lean body rising above her. He parted her legs with his knee and took her with a single deep thrust, filling her completely, making the fires burn out of control.

She thought that he would hurry, that his need would be too strong for him to wait. Instead, he set up a slow, driving rhythm that had her arching upward, wrapping her legs around him, opening herself more fully to each of his powerful strokes. Heat and need built to crescendo. Ariel cried out as she reached a shattering release, and Justin followed a few seconds later, his body shuddering, tightening, pulsing deep inside her.

Afterward they lay entwined, hearts pounding, bodies

damp with perspiration. *I love you*, she thought, but didn't say it. The fear had returned more quickly than she had imagined, and it kept the words locked away. Instead, she lay beside him in silence, listening to the echo of thunder and the whistle of the wind, wondering about the future.

She had felt this way before, had believed in him as she wanted to now. She had wound up out in the street with no money and nowhere to go, with a heart that was shattered into a thousand pieces. How easily he had made her forget that. How badly she wished she could pretend it never happened. Instead, she lay in the darkness remembering the pain, the agony of betrayal. Wondering how big a fool she had been to trust him with her heart again.

She felt him stir beside her, come up on an elbow. Eyes as dark as the night outside moved slowly over her face. She knew he read the fear. Had felt it even as they were making love. She could see it in his expression, hear it in the long, pain-filled sigh that escaped his lips.

"We should have waited," he said, drawing a little away, the muscles tense across his shoulders. "You wanted me, but you're afraid to trust me. I can see it in your face."

Ariel moistened her lips, shook her head, tried to keep the tears from collecting in her eyes. "I'm sorry. In time—"

Justin moved suddenly, rising like a panther off the bed, moving to stare out the window. A flash of lightning illuminated his naked body, the long, sleek muscles in his legs, the ridges across his flat stomach. "Time . . . yes. We're married now. We'll have all the time we need."

He stood there for moments that seemed like hours, then turned and padded softly back to the bed. Gathering her close, he gently kissed her, but he didn't try to touch her, and he didn't make love to her again.

CHAPTER TWENTY-ONE

The weather remained inclement, the roads too muddy for travel, though the vicar and his wife made a miserable sojourn back to the parsonage in the village.

Weary and troubled by the events of his wedding night, Justin headed downstairs. In the Oriental Salon, he stumbled upon Clay, who looked far more rested than he.

"Well, I see you survived the night," Clay said with a grin, lounging in a wing-backed chair in front of the fire, a newspaper cast carelessly over the armrest. "How does it feel to be a married man?"

Justin tossed a dark look in his direction. "To tell you the truth, I'm not certain."

Clay arched a coffee brown eyebrow. "Trouble in paradise already?"

"I shouldn't have made love to her. After all that's happened, it was simply too soon."

Clay got up from the chair and strolled toward him, paused beside a carved cinnabar vase. "Perhaps you're right. With everything happening so quickly, Ariel is bound to be a little confused. She's a smart girl. It won't take her long to sort things out." Clay picked up the vase, examined the intricate carvings. "By the way," he said casually, yet Justin thought there was a faint note of tension in his shoulders, "a friend of your wife's arrived at the house this morning. Kassandra Wentworth. Apparently, she is just returned from the Continent. I believe you know her father."

"Lady Kassandra is here?"

Clay nodded. "Arrived just a short while ago."

"I know Lord Stockton. We've had business dealings together." He did indeed know the viscount, Kassandra Wentworth's father. On one occasion, the viscount had voiced his irritation at his wayward daughter while at the

same time extolling her beauty and telling Justin she would
soon be of an age to wed.

Justin hadn't been certain whether the man had been
seeking advice or hoped to spark interest in a match between them.

"I've never met the girl," he said, "but Ariel speaks of
her often. How did she know we were here?"

"According to what she told your sister, she read a notice in the paper that the Earl of Greville was to wed. I
gather she and Ariel had previously discussed your relationship. Miss Wentworth put the pieces together, went to
your house in Brook Street, bullied your butler into divulg-
ing where you'd gone, and traveled here forthwith."

Justin was faintly intrigued. Knowles wasn't a man who
was easily intimidated and certainly not by some chit of a
girl. "Where is she now?"

"Upstairs in the room your sister grudgingly assigned
her. Barbara wasn't any too pleased to have another houseguest, but Kassandra left her no choice." A smile of what
might have been amusement touched his lips. "She is quite
a determined little baggage."

Justin almost smiled. "In that case, I had better summon
my wife. Ariel is extremely fond of the girl. She'll be
pleased to know she is here." But they hadn't always been
friends, he remembered, thinking of a paragraph Ariel had
written in one of her letters:

*A new girl arrived at school today. Her name is Kas-
sandra Wentworth. She is the youngest daughter of a
viscount, rich and terribly spoiled. I swear her nose
sticks so high in the air it is amazing she doesn't catch
flies in it. I don't like her overmuch and she doesn't like
me.*

Those feelings had changed over the years. Ariel had
once told him that Kitt Wentworth was the only true friend
she had in the world, the only person she could trust completely.

The thought bothered him. Ariel might be his wife, but she had lost whatever small amount of faith she had ever had in him. She didn't trust him. He wasn't sure she ever would again.

"I suppose you've already eaten," he said to Clay, thinking he should probably put something in his stomach, though he didn't have much of an appetite.

"I did, but that was hours ago."

Thinking he could use at least a cup of strong black coffee, he slid open the door, and a red-haired whirlwind rushed past him into the room. Kitt Wentworth, he saw, was petite and lovely, with bright green eyes, a fair complexion, and what appeared to be quite a voluptuous figure. She stared at Clay—or rather past him—surveying the room for Ariel. Disappointed at not finding her, she turned her attention to Justin.

"Lord Greville, I presume."

"That's correct, and you are Lady Kassandra Wentworth, I imagine."

"I am." She glared up at him. "Where is she? What have you done with her?"

Justin could have told her he had done the most intimate things imaginable and he ached to do them again. With profound self-control he refrained. "My wife is still abed." He couldn't resist adding, "Last night was, after all, her wedding night."

Spots of color appeared in Kitt's cheeks, but she didn't look away. "I should like to see her. I should like to discover for myself if she is all right."

A thread of irritation filtered through him. "I assure you, my wife is in perfectly good health. Now, if you will rein in that temper of yours, I'll see that she is awakened and you may ascertain the state of her well-being for yourself."

She studied him a moment, then made a brief nod of her head. Justin stepped into the hallway and instructed the butler to summon Silvie and deliver the message that Lady Kassandra had arrived downstairs, then returned to the drawing room.

He walked into a stony silence, Clay standing stiffly, Kitt's chin thrust forward at a belligerent angle.

"I've been remiss in my duties as host," Justin said blandly, taking in the hostile stance of his two fractious guests and wondering at the cause. "Introductions are certainly in order. Lady Kassandra, may I present my good friend—"

"There is no need for introductions," she said coolly. "Mr. Harcourt and I have already met."

Justin arched a brow. "Is that so?" Interesting that Clay hadn't mentioned it.

Kassandra flicked a disapproving glance in his friend's direction. "Mr. Harcourt was invited to supper at our town house last Tuesday night." She granted him a condescending smile. "Later I discovered that my father was actually entertaining the idea of a match between us. I put an end to the ridiculous notion, of course."

"Did you?" Clay drawled, a dangerous look on his face. "That isn't the impression I got. Particularly not when *my* errant sire, His Grace, the Duke of Rathmore, has mentioned on no few occasions how fortunate I would be should I agree to take you off your father's hands."

Kassandra whirled to face him. "What?"

"The duke and the viscount seem to see it as a business merger, since they are in bed together in a number of financial matters."

"You're lying."

"Actually, there are several other advantages as well. Now that he has remarried, your father wishes to be rid of his spoiled, ill-tempered youngest daughter, while mine sees it as an opportunity to redeem his worthless son."

The room went still, except for the sound of Kassandra's rapid breathing. *Worthless*, Clay had called himself. Hardly the word for Clay, Justin thought, though that was the impression his friend was determined to give, especially to his father, who, like Justin's own late sire, refused to legitimize his eldest son's birth. With Justin's help, Clay had turned the duke's substantial allowance and the money he earned gaming into a tidy fortune he refused to tell anyone about.

Justin's gaze settled on the girl. She was angry, her lips pressed into a narrow line, but there was hurt in her eyes as well, as if she recognized the truth of Clay's words.

Neither of them spoke. Clay's jaw was set and Kitt scowled.

Then the door slid open and Ariel burst into the room. She smiled with delight when she spotted her friend, who laughed joyously and rushed toward her with open arms.

The two girls hugged, both of them grinning, wiping away happy tears. "I am so very glad to see you," Ariel said. "However did you know where to find me?"

Kassandra repeated the tale Clay had told him, leaving out the part about bullying poor Knowles, and apparently Barbara, as well.

"I presume you've met my husband," Ariel said, not quite meeting his eyes.

Kassandra nodded a little bit stiffly. "Yes."

"And Mr. Harcourt?"

The girl's dark look returned. "We were previously acquainted."

Ariel caught Clay's fierce glance, and Justin could see her mind begin to turn, assessing the hostility between the pair. Ignoring Clay's scowl and Kitt's disdain, she reached out and caught her friend's hand.

"Gentlemen, if you don't mind, perhaps you'll excuse us. We haven't seen each other for quite some time. We've a good deal of catching up to do."

Both men acquiesced with a polite bow, though Justin noticed Clay's jaw still looked tight.

Ariel gave Justin a hesitant smile, then smiled warmly at Kassandra. "I'm dying to hear all about Italy," she was saying as she led the girl toward the door.

Kitt tossed a last probing glance at Justin. "And I imagine you have a great deal to tell me, as well."

Justin imagined that she did. He wondered what Kassandra Wentworth would think of the man responsible for sending her best friend to prison.

Ariel sat across from Kassandra in a small, sun-warmed drawing room that overlooked the garden, a favorite, Perkins had told her, of the former Lady Greville. Mary Ross had locked herself away in the charming salon, perhaps, Ariel thought, as a refuge from her husband, a man who openly flaunted his affairs with younger women.

Done in soft shades of yellow and cream, the room was less elaborately furnished than the rest of the house and seldom used by the family, yet its cozy elegance made it Ariel's favorite, too.

"Well, the man is certainly handsome enough," Kitt said, making herself comfortable on the sofa in front of the fire. "From what I had heard of him, I imagined the Earl of Greville to be some sort of ogre."

Ariel's hand shook on the porcelain teapot she held, a sudden memory surfacing of Justin the morning he had sent her away. Was he the caring man he often seemed or the heartless man who had used her and cast her aside without the slightest qualm?

She took a firmer grip on the handle of the pot and finished pouring the tea. "Justin has suffered a difficult past. He has taught himself to be hard in order to survive, but I have seen his gentler nature." She set the teapot back down on the serving cart. "He isn't an easy person to understand. Even I am not completely certain the sort of man he truly is."

"Then why on earth did you marry him?"

Ariel shook her head, wondering how she could possibly explain, not completely certain herself. She took a seat next to Kitt and began to tell her all that had happened, watching her best friend's eyes go wider with every word.

"I know the risk I'm taking. But I love him, Kitt, and I don't believe I could ever love the kind of man he sometimes appears to be."

Ariel went on with her story, telling her friend everything that had happened since Kassandra had left for Italy, including her encounter with Horwick, her terrible days in Newgate, and Justin's heroic rescue.

"He came for me, Kitt. I don't know what would have happened to me if he hadn't."

"I only wish I had been here. You could have come to me in the beginning and none of this would have occurred."

"Perhaps. Then again, perhaps it was simply a matter of fate. I'm Justin's wife. I can't say I am sorry." Not sorry. Not yet. Just terribly, dreadfully afraid.

"You say that you're in love with him. Is he also in love with you?"

Ariel stared down at the cup and saucer resting in her lap. "No." She didn't realize the objects tilted at a precarious angle until Kitt reached over and gently righted them, picked them up, and carefully set them down on the table in front of her.

"Perhaps you're wrong," she said softly. "If Greville doesn't love you, why did he marry you? You have no fortune, no title. There is nothing for him to gain."

Ariel looked up. Phillip had said that Justin never did anything unless he had something to gain. "He needed an heir. I suppose that is the reason."

"The man is unbearably handsome—and rich as Croesus, from what my father has said. There are countless women who would be more than happy to marry him and give him a child."

Ariel sighed. "He's attracted to me. Perhaps that is the reason."

"Attracted? You mean he wanted you in his bed," Kassandra said darkly.

A flush crept into Ariel's cheeks. He wanted her, yes. At least he had last night. But he had also sensed her hesitation, her uncertainty, and he hadn't made love to her again. "He's my husband. I desire him, as well. Oh, Kitt, there is no way to describe what it's like when we're together."

Kassandra said nothing, but she looked vaguely disturbed. Ariel wondered, as she had before, if there was something painful in Kitt's past of which she had never spoken.

Kassandra leaned forward and took hold of Ariel's hand. "In time, it will all work out. You must believe that, Ariel."

"I want to. Things are just so confused." But she wondered how it could ever possibly work out. She was in love with a man who didn't love her. As Kitt had said, Justin was an extremely handsome man. Clay had admitted any number of women found him attractive. Without love to bind them, sooner or later he was bound to grow tired of her. Would he take a mistress, as most married men did?

The thought of Justin making love to another woman made her stomach roll with nausea.

Doubts plagued her, and a terrible fear of the future. They were worries she couldn't share even with her very dearest friend.

Mustering a smile, Ariel groped for a change of subject. "So . . . tell me about you and Clayton Harcourt. I gathered, from the hostile look you gave him, he isn't one of your favorite people." Ariel hoped Kitt would deny it. She didn't like the notion that two of her and Justin's dearest friends were so obviously at odds.

"I realize he is a close friend of Lord Greville's, but God's breath, Ariel, the man is one of the most notorious rakes in London. He has slept with half the women in the *ton* and the other half are panting to get into his bed. He is arrogant and ill-tempered. He is rude and condescending and—"

"And gorgeous to look at. Clay is nearly as tall as Justin. He's extremely well built and most of the time quite charming. Are you saying you don't find him the least bit attractive?"

"Attractive? I loathe the very sight of him. I can't imagine how Father could even consider a match between us."

Ariel listened as Kitt described the viscount's efforts to arrange a betrothal and what Clay had said in the Oriental Salon.

"He was cruel and hateful." She glanced up, tears collecting in her eyes. "And every word he said was true."

"Oh, Kitt." Ariel reached over and hugged her. "Surely

your father loves you. Perhaps he believes Clay would make a very good husband."

"He only wants to be rid of me, just as Harcourt said."

"It isn't like Clay to be cruel on purpose. From what you've told me, you made the idea of marrying him sound almost laughable. I think you may have hurt his feelings."

Kitt dashed the tears from her cheeks. "The man has no feelings. He is self-centered and . . . and I can see the wolfish gleam in his eyes whenever he looks at me."

Ariel laughed then. "Well, he has never looked at me that way. Perhaps you should be flattered."

"Well, I'm not. And I'm certainly not interested in marrying him. As a matter of fact, I don't want to marry anyone at all."

Ariel didn't say anything to that. She knew that in time, Kassandra would be forced to wed. It was the way of the aristocracy, the way of women in general. Ariel was a perfect example of what happened to a woman who tried to exist on her own in a world run by men.

The thought was sobering. She was married, her life in the hands of a man she didn't understand. What would happen to her? What would the future bring? She glanced at her friend, who had also turned pensive.

What sort of future lay ahead for either of them?

Kassandra returned to London two days later, Clay Harcourt following the afternoon of that same day. Ariel viewed their departure with mixed emotions. She wanted to spend time with the man who was now her husband, but with Kitt gone, she no longer had a friend to confide in. She thought of Kitt's troubled face and wondered if Lord Stockton would continue his matchmaking efforts on his daughter's behalf and whether Clay Harcourt had any sort of interest in pursuing a marriage between them. Ariel doubted it. The pair could scarcely be alone in the same room without an argument erupting.

She sighed to think of it. Clay knew Kitt's reputation. On the surface, she was spoiled and willful, and there was no doubt she was far too reckless. In most things, she did exactly as she pleased, and no one, not even her father, seemed to care enough to stop her. Kitt had come close to ruination on more than one occasion. It wasn't any wonder her father was so eager to see her safely wed.

Still, under all the bravado, Kassandra Wentworth was lonely and desperately in need of love. Ariel prayed Kitt would find a man who would give her that love.

Even as she prayed for the same thing for herself.

Gazing out the window of the intimate yellow salon, she heard the sound of approaching footsteps and turned to see Justin standing in the doorway.

"I thought I might find you here." His smile was soft, but his gaze was unreadable, carefully disguising his thoughts.

Ariel forced herself to smile. "I was going to do some reading. Kassandra loaned me a book—one of Mrs. Radcliffe's gothic novels. Did you wish to speak to me?"

"I have news. A letter arrived from my grandmother. Knowles gave it to Jonathan, who included it among some business papers that needed my attention."

"Your grandmother? How wonderful."

"I hear from her about this time each year. She always has a dinner party at Christmastide. She says she hopes I'll be able to come. She doesn't know about you, yet. I shall write and tell her, of course, and thank her for the invitation."

Ariel came up off the sofa. "Oh, Justin, we must go. You have so little family and I have none at all. And I would so very much like to meet her."

He looked down at the letter. "For the past several years I've been meaning to go, but something always seems to come up. I don't suppose she really cares all that much. I have several distant cousins who undoubtedly will join her, and Grandmother has always been content to live by herself, she and the few servants she'll allow to attend her in that rambling old stone house of hers."

"How long has it been since you've seen her?"

"Not since I was a boy. I send her money, of course, and we correspond by letter several times a year. I imagine she is getting to be quite old."

"Please say we can go. Family is so important, and your grandmother undoubtedly misses you."

He hesitated so long she was sure he was going to refuse. "All right," he finally conceded. "If that is your wish, then we'll go."

Her smile came more easily, warmed by his effort to please her. He saw it and his eyes swung to hers, darker now, filled with some indefinable emotion.

"I've always loved your smile," he said softly. "It warms me like a fire in winter."

Ariel stared in surprise, amazed he would say such a thing, equally drawn to his harsh, winter-dark beauty, wanting him to kiss her, touch her, knowing it would be a mistake.

As if he read her thoughts, his features closed up, his mask falling back into place. A knock at the door saved them from an uncomfortable moment.

"I'm sorry to disturb you, my lord," the butler said. "But your solicitor, Mr. Whipple, has arrived."

Justin simply nodded. "Show him into the study. Tell him I shall join him there shortly."

"Yes, my lord." Perkins scuttled off to do the earl's bidding, and Justin returned his attention to her, his features once more bland.

"I look forward to seeing you at supper," he said, making her a brief, formal bow. Ariel watched him go, a warmth in the pit of her stomach. Hope was rising again, beckoning her as it always did. She was trusting him more, risking herself more.

She prayed with everything she held dear that she wasn't making a terrible mistake.

Phillip Marlin paced impatiently in front of the fire in a small private bedchamber above the stable at the rear of the Cock's Crow Tavern. It sat on a crossroads not far from the village of Ewhurst, an easy ride from Greville Hall and conveniently located to London. Barbara had chosen the inn for its location but also the discretion of the tavern's owner, a man named Harley Reed.

Phillip had arrived two hours early and now grew impatient. He had traveled with all haste, responding to the urgency in Barbara's message. He was anxious to discuss the plans they had only begun to formulate.

And oddly enough, he was eager to see her.

Light footfalls on the stairs warned him of her arrival. He strode to the door and jerked it open. Barbara slipped past him into the room, shoving back the hood of her fur-lined cloak.

Stunning gray eyes moved over his face, hitting him with the impact of a blow. When she smiled, he remembered the crush of those soft red lips, the taste of her milky skin, and heat speared into his groin.

"Barbara . . ." The word hung suspended as she tugged the cord holding her cloak in place and tossed it over a nearby chair. Then she was in his arms, pressing those full lips to his, consuming him in a way he had never experienced with another woman. "I've missed you," he said, greedily returning the kiss.

"Phillip, my darling." Her mouth clung to his once more. He wanted to tear off her clothes, to drag her beneath him on the narrow bed in the corner and ruthlessly plunge himself inside her. He wanted to feel her nails digging into his flesh, her teeth sinking into the muscles across his shoulder, giving him a little stab of pleasure/pain.

"We need to talk," she whispered, running her tongue along the rim of an ear, tugging on his earlobe, then kissing him again. "I need to know how our plans progress."

But Phillip was already beyond listening. Instead, he urged her backward until her legs hit the edge of the bed and she went down. He came down on top of her, bracing himself on his elbows, shoving up the skirt of her ruby velvet gown and cupping her mound, hearing her sharp intake of breath. Before he could plunge his fingers inside her, Barbara caught his hand.

"Not yet, darling," she purred. "I've got what you want, but you'll have to wait. It will be better that way. . . . You know it will."

Heat flooded into his groin. He had always been the one in control, taking what he wanted, ruthlessly if he chose. Barbara wouldn't allow it. Instead, she took from him, refused to meekly submit. She was beautiful and exotic, and nearly as ruthless as he.

She was more exciting than any other woman he had ever known, and he would do anything to please her.

"Have you made the arrangements?" she asked, coming up off the bed, surveying him down the length of her fine, aristocratic nose.

"I've made inquiries, started things rolling. Once it's done, we'll have everything we want—and the rest of our lives together."

"Yes. . . ." She moved toward him, laced her fingers in his thick gold hair, drew his mouth down to hers in a lingering kiss. "Help me with my clothes," she whispered against his lips.

He obeyed instantly, moving in front of her, kneeling to remove her soft kid slippers. Her feet were high-arched and graceful, pale in the moonlight streaming in through the window. He stroked the inside of an arch, ran his hand up her calf, over the delicate white silk that ended just below her knee.

"Now the garters and stockings."

His groin tightened. He willingly complied, rolling down the creamy silk, nearly prostrating himself as he bent to kiss her toes. Slowly, torturing him with glimpses of her perfect white flesh, Barbara removed each article of her clothing, taking her time, seducing him with her body.

"Why don't you join me?" she said once she was naked, making his arousal throb. He did so hurriedly, removing his shirt and breeches, his smallclothes. He felt those hard gray eyes, moving up and down, assessing the thick ridge quivering against his belly. Then she crossed the room to the bed.

"Come to me, my darling." Barbara smiled as she spread her thighs, and a shudder of anticipation rippled through him. Phillip hurried to join her, desperate to be inside her.

"You're certain you can arrange it," she whispered against his ear as she pulled him down on top of her.

"Trust me, I won't fail you." He pressed his lips to her collarbone, began to kiss his way down her body. "I won't fail either of us."

He felt her fingers, stroking through his hair. "I know you won't, my darling." A hand on his head urged him lower, silently commanding him to please her. Phillip bent to the task, his shaft aching painfully, taking pleasure from the duty even as he prayed she would soon end his suffering.

Thinking of her words and their plans for Greville, Phillip hardened even more, anticipating his enemy's demise.

Wanting it even more than he savored the raging climax he would soon find with Barbara.

CHAPTER TWENTY-TWO

November moved toward an end. Barbara had been surprisingly congenial on discovering Justin's plans to remain at Greville Hall for the upcoming holidays.

"The gossip will resume as soon as we return to the city," he told his sister. "I refuse to subject my wife to the vicious wagging tongues. In a month or two, with Clay reminding them of Horwick's sordid reputation and Kassandra hinting at a love match, the entire affair will eventually be forgotten."

Ariel knew their friends would do just that—make every effort to ease the way for their return to society. They were true and loyal friends. She hoped the day would come when each would learn the value of the other.

In the meantime, life with Justin was becoming more and more strained. It was impossible to mistake the desire he no longer tried to hide; it appeared, white-hot, every time he looked at her. And yet he did not come to her bed.

It was a curse.

And a reprieve.

Just a little more time, she told herself. She needed to understand him, needed to be sure she could trust him. She would protect herself as long as she possibly could.

The days wore on. The holidays were fast approaching, and Ariel set to work on the gift she had in mind for his grandmother. When he returned that night from a ride into the village, he found her with paper and scissors, waiting for him in the library.

"I'm sorry I'm late," he said wearily, stripping off his riding jacket and tossing it over the back of a chair. "I hope you didn't put off supper."

"Actually, I thought we might sup in here . . . after we are finished."

A black brow slanted up. "And what is it we are finishing?"

She gave him an encouraging smile. "We're completing the silhouette you promised I could fashion. It will make the perfect gift for your grandmother."

An odd look appeared on his face. She could have sworn it was embarrassment.

"Come on now," she teased when he still seemed hesitant. "I promise it won't hurt. You agreed to let me do a profile miniature and I am holding you to your word."

He glanced over, saw the candle she had readied, the easel and paper, and gave up a sigh of resignation. "And I imagine I shall have to await any sustenance until after your artistic fervor has been satisfied."

She laughed. "I imagine it would be all right if we dined first, since you seem to be so ravenous."

His eyes turned a little darker gray. "I'm ravenous, Ariel," he said softly. "But not necessarily for food."

Ariel didn't reply, but a little whisper of warmth filtered into her stomach. She pretended to straighten her supplies, infusing a light note into her voice. "Supper or the profile, my lord?"

Neither, his dark look said, but he strode resignedly toward the chair she had set beside the candle and seated himself with such a put-upon expression she fought not to smile.

"We might as well have done with it," he grumbled. " 'Tis obvious you are determined to have your way in this."

"Exactly so, my lord."

Lighting the candle, she set to work, using the shadow it cast to outline his profile. Tomorrow she would cut out his image, creating a master. Then she could transfer it onto a piece of plaster, add gold-painted highlights and a bit of sparkle. There was a craftsman in the village who did a lovely job of framing.

Ariel set to work, ignoring the rustle of his clothes as Justin shifted restlessly in the chair, careful to keep her

mind on her work. When she had finished, she studied the
picture she had drawn, admiring the strong, masculine profile, tracing the lines with the tips of her fingers, wishing
she had the courage to touch those same hard contours on
his face.

She shook her head against the image and forced her
attention back to her work, certain his grandmother would
be pleased.

Ariel fervently hoped the elderly woman would rejoice
in her long-overdue reunion with her grandson. Secretly she
prayed the lady would approve of the wife he had chosen
as well.

November was nearly at an end. Justin had been married
for less than ten days when the letter from Clay arrived. A
financial problem had arisen in regard to the mining en-
deavor they had undertaken together. In the note Justin read
while sitting in his study, Clay apologized for disturbing
him so soon after his wedding, but his presence was needed
in London if their mining venture was to go forward as
they had planned.

Justin cursed. He didn't want to leave, not yet. Though
the nights without Ariel had been pure hell and even the
days often strained, he believed he was making some progress. There were times she actually looked at him without
the uncertain, guarded expression she so frequently wore.

He intended for those occasions to grow. He meant to
win her trust, no matter what it took. But the mining project
was important. Now that he and Clay were the owners, they
were responsible for the safety of the men who worked
there. Justin had made a thorough inspection of the site
before the purchase was completed and returned with a list
of improvements necessary to keep the miners safe. The
work had been started. Justin wanted the task completed in
all haste.

A safer mine meant less chance of a very costly cave-
in. In the long run, the profits would be higher. It had nothing at all to do with the fact that dozens, even hundreds of

men's lives could be lost if the mines were not kept in careful repair. It was simply a matter of money, Justin told himself, just like every other decision he made.

Sensing the urgency in Clay's message, he instructed a footman to have a horse saddled and ready, then headed down the hall to find Ariel. He discovered her in the conservatory, working over the portrait miniature she had fashioned, carefully highlighting his plaster image with faint strokes of gleaming gold paint. He paused in the doorway to watch her, enjoying the look of concentration that pulled her fine, winged brows together, the way she held the tip of her tongue in the corner of her mouth as she worked. Her lips were parted, as pink and moist as her tongue.

His groin tightened. Justin clamped his jaw against the unwanted arousal.

Ariel glanced up just then and gave him an enchanting smile. "I didn't hear you come in."

He shifted, came away from the door, found himself smiling in return. "You were working. It looks as if you're almost finished."

"Almost. I still need to have it framed."

He nodded, his thoughts shifting to the trip he would have to make, already wishing he didn't have to go. "Something's come up. I have to return to London for a couple of days."

"Business?" She set her paintbrush aside and wiped her hands on the apron tied over her gray wool dress.

"The mining project Clay and I are involved in. A banking matter, money we need for improvements."

"How long will you be gone?"

"Not long. A couple of days. I'm leaving as soon as I can pack a valise."

Her expression changed, became more uncertain. "I wish you didn't have to go."

He reached out to her, ran a finger along her jaw. "So do I." But he did have to go, and the sooner he left, the sooner he could return.

"I don't suppose I could go with you?"

He'd thought about taking her along, but wanting her as he constantly did left him edgy and out of sorts, and the roads were muddy, the skies overcast and grim. "I can travel faster if I go alone. Besides, the weather may turn even more unpleasant. I'd rather you stayed here."

Ariel glanced away. "Perhaps you're right. Christmastide approaches. I need to finish the gifts I am making."

"See me out?"

Ariel nodded and accepted his arm, walking with him down the hall to the entry, waiting as he climbed the stairs and went into their suite. When he returned a few minutes later, satchel in hand, she reappeared, his cloak draped over her arm. She held it out for him, settled it around his shoulders, tied it at the base of his throat.

He circled her waist with his hands and drew her closer. "I'm going to miss you."

"Will you?"

Bending his head, he brushed a soft kiss over her lips. "I'll be back as quickly as I can." Turning away, he headed for the door and his waiting horse. Wondering, perhaps for the first time in his existence, if putting business ahead of everything else was really the way he wanted to live.

Ariel sat in the study, her head bent over the paperwork on the gleaming mahogany desk. During the days since their arrival, Justin had commandeered the study as his own personal domain. Not that it mattered. Barbara had little use for the dark, wood-paneled, overly masculine room. She was hardly interested in matters of business.

But Ariel was, and with Justin gone these past few days, she'd grown restless. Stacks of business reports, investment proposals, and ledgers that needed reviewing formed a rising pile on his desk. Ariel had worked with him enough to know what needed to be done with most of them and, lonesome in his absence, had wandered into the study and wound up sitting down to work.

As always, she was quickly immersed, challenged by the columns of numbers, playing mathematical games in her head, rapidly performing tasks that would have taken her husband hours to complete.

Her husband. She was only beginning to think of him that way. And yet she liked the notion. Since their marriage, Justin had been strong and supportive, the kind of husband a woman dreamed of marrying.

If things continued in that vein, perhaps, as Kitt had said, in time it would all work out.

Ariel started on another column of numbers, heard the rustle of silk, and glanced at the door. Barbara Townsend floated toward her in that graceful way of hers, a smug smile on her face.

"Well, apparently he has discovered a use for you after all."

Jabbing the quill pen back in its silver holder, Ariel came to her feet. "And exactly what is that supposed to mean?"

Barbara's smile stretched wider. "Why, dearest sister-in-law, you've been wed for less than two weeks and already your groom hies off to London. It would appear your talents lie in directions other than the bedchamber."

Heat rushed into Ariel's cheeks. "My husband was forced to return to the city on a matter of urgent business. He'll be back in a couple of days."

"Will he?" A sleek black brow arched knowingly. She shrugged her shoulders. "Then again, perhaps he will. A day or two of carousing with Clayton Harcourt should provide him ample opportunity to satisfy his penchant for variety, at least for another few weeks."

The color in Ariel's face drained away. "I don't believe you. You only want to cause trouble for Justin. Why do you hate him so much? What has he ever done to you?"

"What has he done? He was born, that is what he has done. The man is a bastard, the son of my lecherous father and one of his numerous whores. Justin's mere existence is an insult to my mother and to me. On top of that, he has stolen my son's birthright. It is Thomas who should now be Earl of Greville."

"Perhaps one day he will be."

"Are you telling me you do not carry my half brother's child?"

"Not yet. Though I hope one day I will."

Barbara's vicious smile remained firmly in place. "It could happen, I suppose . . . if he doesn't squander his precious seed all over London."

"He is there on business."

Barbara laughed. "Surely you are not that naive. Justin could never be content with only one woman. He has always been the sort to move from bed to bed, taking his pleasure wherever he chooses. Oh, he isn't like Clayton Harcourt. Harcourt would need a dozen different women to satisfy his lusty appetite. My brother prefers them one at a time. Of course, now that he's married, I suppose he's attempting to be a bit more discreet."

"It isn't true."

"You might as well get used to it, my girl. They are all the same. That is simply the way it is."

Ariel made no reply. Her hands were shaking. Her face felt bloodless and numb. Barbara was lying. She only wanted to stir up trouble. But when Ariel looked into those hard Greville gray eyes, she saw that Barbara Townsend believed every word she had spoken. She was convinced that Justin was being unfaithful, and if his sister believed it so strongly, dear God, it might just be true.

A wave of nausea rolled over her. Ariel sank back down in her chair.

"You look as though you could use a cup of tea," Barbara said sweetly. "I shall have Perkins fetch you a good strong cup." With that she departed the study, hips swaying as she moved out the door.

Ariel stared after her, feeling sick to her stomach. She wanted to believe in Justin as she once had, but dear God, it was so hard to do. He had come to her bed only once since their marriage. He seemed to want her, and yet he had left her and gone off to London. She had never forgotten the cruel words he had spoken that morning in his study.

"Last night Clayton and I ... stumbled across some rather entertaining companions."

"You aren't talking about ... about women?"

"I'm sorry, my dear, but you knew sooner or later it would happen. You were quite good, really ... but a man's tastes change."

Ariel shivered. *"A man's tastes change."* It was true, she knew. The late earl was proof enough of that.

And two days later, when Justin had still not returned and she'd had no word from him, she thought that Barbara must be correct.

She couldn't sleep. She couldn't work. Her appetite disappeared completely—along with her hopes and dreams.

When Justin arrived at Greville Hall the following night in a driving rain, his clothes damp and clinging, his cloak dripping water and plastered against his long, booted legs, instead of greeting him in the entry as she had intended, she remained upstairs in her room. She didn't want to see him. She was afraid of what she would read in his face.

She was afraid she had been an even bigger fool than before, and if it were true, this time her heart would not mend.

Justin drew the cloak from his shoulders and handed it to Perkins, who held it away from him, bushy gray eyebrows raised as he carried it dripping down the hall. Hoping Ariel would be waiting, Justin glanced around the entry, but instead of the wife he so eagerly wanted to see, little Thomas came running.

"Uncle Justin!"

The child leaped into the air and Justin caught him, lifted him up, and held him at arm's length. "Good God, you've grown a full stone heavier since I've been away."

Thomas laughed delightedly as Justin set his small feet firmly back down on the floor.

"Did you bring me a present?"

He arched a brow. "Were you a good boy while I was gone?"

The little boy's smile slid away. "Mama said I was bad. She made me go to bed without my supper." He grinned, exposing the hole where his teeth should have been. "Aunt Ariel sneaked me a mutton pasty and an apple tart, but don't tell Mama."

Justin squeezed the boy's shoulder. "Your secret is safe with me." Reaching into his pocket, he pulled out the small wooden ship he had brought the child from London. It was fashioned of fine Oriental teak, with miniature white canvas sails and black-painted string to serve as rigging.

"It's beautiful," Thomas said, touching the ship with awe.

"Not an it, a she. Ships are all thought of as women. This one's the *Mirabelle*. See? Her name's painted in gold on the stern."

"The *Mirabelle*." He traced the name with his finger. "That's a really pretty name." Clutching the little ship to his chest, he grinned. "Thank you, Uncle Justin."

"You're welcome." Justin glanced around again, searching for Ariel. "Where's your aunt? Have you seen her?"

"She's upstairs in her room. I don't think she is feeling very well."

Justin frowned. He ruffled the boy's dark hair and turned toward the stairs, climbing them hurriedly, then striding down the hall. He knocked briefly, opened the door, and went in.

Ariel was sitting in front of the fire, her fingers moving over a piece of stitchery. She turned at his approach.

"Ariel . . . love, are you all right? Thomas said you weren't feeling well." He strode toward her, would have pulled her up off the sofa and into his arms, but something in her eyes held him back.

Ariel carefully laid her stitchery aside. He thought that her face looked pale. "I'm fine. I didn't . . . I didn't hear you come in."

Why did he wonder if that was really true? And if it wasn't, why not?

"I rode like blazes to get here. I hoped to be home sooner, but a meeting came up I had to attend. On top of that, the papers at the bank weren't ready for me to sign. I could have gone back later, but I didn't want to make another trip."

She came up from the sofa and gave him a smile, but it wasn't the sort he had imagined. It was filled with uncertainty, her eyes faintly shadowed.

"Are you sure you're feeling all right?"

"I'm just a little tired is all. I'm afraid I have the headache. I thought I would go to bed early . . . that is, if you don't mind."

He minded. He had hoped, insanely, that while he was gone she might have missed him. That when he returned, she might welcome him—without uncertainty, without hesitation—back into her bed. But it wasn't going to happen, and if she were truly ill, she needed to rest and take care of herself.

He managed to summon a smile. "Get some rest. You'll feel better in the morning."

But she didn't seem her usual self even then, and his worry began to grow. She avoided him most of the day, and that evening at supper she seemed so distant he left her and retired to his study.

He couldn't help wondering what had happened in the days he had been away, what could have made her withdraw from him even more than she had already.

Give her a little more time, he told himself. But deep inside he began to worry that what little she had ever felt for him had finally faded and completely disappeared.

December brought chilling winds and icy rain. Though the weather was inclement, Ariel saw little of her husband. Ever since his trip into the city, she had avoided him. Sadly, he seemed not to care. She was terrified Barbara was right and that he had gone to London to be with another woman.

The trust she had earlier begun to rebuild had all but drained away.

Still, there were occasions when they were thrown together. Like the evening Barbara announced she was giving a party—a Christmas soiree, she called it—to celebrate the official beginning of the season. Nothing extravagant, Barbara promised, just a few of her closest friends.

At first Justin protested, but Barbara was insistent.

"The invitations were sent out weeks ago. It never occurred to me you might disapprove. We hold a Christmas party at Greville Hall every year. It's practically a family tradition." She smiled thinly. "But then you wouldn't know anything about that, would you?"

Justin clenched his jaw but made no reply.

"Perhaps it's just as well," he told Ariel, once Barbara was gone. "We shall be forced to reenter society sooner or later. Perhaps a smaller affair here at the house is a good way to begin."

With the way things stood between them, she was scarcely ready to entertain, but as he had said, the time would have to come, sooner or later. "Perhaps you're right. At any rate, the party is only a few days away. If the invitations have been already been sent, I don't see we have much choice."

"And I shall add a few names of my own to the guest list, people we can count on for support."

The soiree would go forward, it seemed, but it mattered very little to Ariel. Justin still hadn't come to her bed. If he wasn't sleeping with someone else surely he would have sought her out by now.

The night of the ball arrived and the tension between them seemed almost palpable.

Dressing with care, Ariel chose a high-waisted gold silk brocade gown. It was a magnificent creation, with sparkling white brilliants across the front of a low-cut bodice that exposed the tops of her breasts. It was a seductive gown, chosen to help bolster her flagging spirits.

The party was already in progress when she made her

way downstairs, her nerves thrumming, a tight knot in the pit of her stomach. She was surprised to find her husband waiting. When he looked up at her, surveyed the gown and her upswept pale blond hair, one of his rare, charming smiles appeared, and the knot in her stomach loosened a little. She descended the stairs with a bit less trepidation and actually managed to smile.

"You look beautiful," he said, pressing a kiss to the back of her hand. "I'll be the envy of every man here."

A flush rose into her cheeks, though she was certain it was she who would be envied. Tall and elegantly garbed in dark gray and burgundy, the diamond stickpin sparkling in his cravat, he looked dark and forbidding, and unbelievably handsome.

Justin smiled and offered his arm, and they moved across the entry, down the hall, and through the wide double doors of the drawing room.

Barbara's notion of a small soiree turned out to be a sterling affair: an orchestra playing in the long gallery, the furniture removed for dancing, a drawing room set aside for gaming, and a sumptuous late-night buffet. The house was decorated elaborately in cream and silver, with evergreen garlands draped over the mantels and white blooming hellebores scenting the air from silver urns.

Music drifting in from the gallery mingled with voices in the drawing room, and Ariel's nervousness returned. With the scandal Horwick had created and the Earl of Greville's hasty marriage to a woman of scarlet reputation, she knew the kind of reception they would face. As they moved farther into the drawing room, Ariel's fingers trembled against the sleeve of Justin's coat. She could hear the whispered words and see the measuring glances.

Beside her, Justin's features looked bland, but a muscle throbbed in his cheek. Ariel frantically searched the room for a friendly face, wishing Kassandra had come, but her father, worried about his daughter's penchant for trouble, had forbidden her to make an appearance. For once Kitt had obeyed.

Instead, the first to approach them was Clayton Harcourt, who smiled and made an elaborate bow over her hand.

"You're looking radiant tonight, my lady," he said with a charming smile.

"Thank you, Clay. I'm so very glad you could come." That was the truth. It was good to have at least one friend in a room full of enemies.

Clay must have read her thoughts, for he leaned a bit closer. "Your husband thought you might need a little moral support, so I brought along a friend." He turned his attention to the handsome gray-haired man beside him, a man who was as tall as Clay, with the same warm golden brown eyes. "Your Grace, may I present to you the Countess of Greville. My lady, the Duke of Rathmore."

She sank into a curtsy, her heart thundering wildly. Clayton's father. It never occurred to her that Rathmore might stand behind them. "I'm honored, Your Grace."

He gave her a smile of obvious approval. "The pleasure is mine, my lady, I assure you. Your husband and I are well acquainted, of course. I'm pleased to see the rogue has finally had the good sense to wed—and a woman of rare beauty, I might add."

She flushed a bit. "Thank you."

"I shall expect you to save me a dance, young woman. I haven't traveled these damnable muddy roads only to discover your dance card is already filled."

She laughed, the duke's droll humor putting her immediately at ease. "I should never do such a thing. I would be honored to dance with you, Your Grace—anytime you wish."

He grinned and a dimple appeared in his cheek. Clay had one in almost exactly that spot, she recalled. They chatted pleasantly for a while; then an old acquaintance of the duke's appeared and persuaded him away.

Still, Clay's machinations had worked. With the duke's stamp of approval on the earl and his bride, the atmosphere in the room swiftly changed. Several other guests—Lord Foxmoor, whom Ariel had met briefly in Tunbridge Wells,

Lord and Lady Oxnard, and half a dozen others—came over to pay their respects. Even Lady Foxmoor seemed to forgive Ariel her former transgressions. Ariel thought it had a great deal to do with the partnership Lord Foxmoor was involved in with Justin and the substantial profits it continued to earn.

The evening went on, endlessly it seemed to Ariel, but so far nothing had really gone amiss. The dancing continued, and when the orchestra struck up a waltz, Justin led her out to the long gallery and onto the makeshift dance floor.

When he settled a hand at her waist and swept her into a graceful turn, Ariel sighed in sheer pleasure.

"I've dreamt of waltzing with you," Justin said softly, his long, graceful strides carrying them around the dance floor as if they were floating.

"Have you?" She could feel the brush of his thigh, the strength of his hand at her back, and a soft curl of heat sifted into her stomach.

"On more than one occasion." His eyes moved over her face. "Do you know what I usually dream?"

She couldn't look away from those hard, dark features. "What do you usually dream?"

"I dream of our wedding night. Of how sweet you tasted, how your body responded to mine, of what it felt like to be inside you. I dream of being inside you again."

Her stomach contracted. She fought down a fierce rush of longing. For an instant, she lost track of the dance and he pulled her closer, guiding her easily, finding the rhythm of the waltz once more. His eyes were a clear dark gray and his gaze intense. He hadn't missed the way his words had affected her.

How could they not? She remembered that night every bit as clearly as he.

The music stopped before she wanted it to. With a faint bow of his head, he stepped away, his look enigmatic once more.

The duke appeared in the gallery a few minutes later to

claim the dance she had promised, sweeping her once more onto the dance floor. Justin's protective gaze followed. He'd been solicitous all evening, careful to keep her away from Barbara's transparent innuendos and the false, condescending smiles of her friends.

Perhaps she'd been wrong, Ariel thought with yearning. Perhaps Barbara had been wrong.

Then a party of late arrivals made their way through the gallery doors, and Ariel's attention swung to them. One of the group stood out from the others, a tall, olive-skinned woman with prominent cheekbones and high, full breasts. She was beautiful in the extreme, overshadowing the short, gray-haired man who appeared to be her escort. She was lovely and exotic, and the moment she turned her thick-lashed black eyes on Justin, Ariel knew without doubt the woman had once been his lover.

Her chest constricted so hard for a moment it was difficult to breathe. She stumbled and would have fallen if the duke hadn't had a firm grip on her waist.

"Are you all right?"

"Yes . . . yes, I'm fine. Just a bit tired is all."

His eyes followed hers and he frowned. "Lady Eastgate. She's a close friend of your sister-in-law's, but I'm surprised that she is here."

Don't say it, she thought, but couldn't resist. "Because she and my husband were . . . involved?"

The duke's assessing gaze swung to hers. "Your husband is a man, my dear, not a saint. Lady Eastgate is a beautiful woman and a widow. And their . . . involvement . . . was over long before he met you."

She pasted on a smile and prayed it was true. Then, with obvious determination, the woman made her way to Justin's side, and Ariel thought with a knife-sharp pain that the duke might very well be mistaken.

Was Lady Eastgate the woman Justin had gone to see in London? She was elegant and sophisticated, the sort who might not care that he was now a married man. When the dance ended, Ariel excused herself and quietly made her way out onto the terrace. She could slip around the house to the rear, climb the servants' stairs to her room, and no one would be the wiser.

All the way there, she thought of Justin and the beautiful, exotic woman. By the time she reached the sanctity of her bedchamber, it was all she could do to not weep.

CHAPTER TWENTY-THREE

"Lady Eastgate." Justin bowed stiffly over the slender fingers encased in long white gloves, his eyes hard on her face. Roselyn Beresford, widow of the Marquess of Eastgate, half-English daughter of a Spanish count, was beautiful and desirable, and for a very short time the lady had shared his bed. But Roselyn's heart was nearly as empty as his own, he had discovered, and his desire for her had rapidly waned.

"It's good to see you, Justin." She smiled behind the sweep of her hand-painted fan. "I've missed you these past few months."

"Have you?" Well, he certainly hadn't missed her, and it was obvious that his loss of affection—if one could call it that—hadn't set well with her. *"No one treats the Marchioness of Eastgate as if she were some cast-off piece of garbage!"* she had screeched at him the night he had ended the affair. She had threatened retribution—which was exactly the reason she was there.

"Congratulations," she said with a thin, brittle smile. "Your sister relayed the news of your recent nuptials. I wanted to extend my felicitations personally."

"How kind of you," he said dryly.

Her eyebrows lifted as she scanned the room. "Where is the blushing bride?"

Justin looked around but saw no sign of his wife. Ariel had been dancing with Rathmore when Roselyn walked in. Where was she now? "Perhaps she has gone for some refreshment. Since she appears to be missing at present, I shall be happy to convey your best wishes for you."

"Oh, but I do so want to meet this paragon you have wed. As I remember it, you said you had no desire to marry. You were quite adamant about it at the time."

Justin smiled coldly. "I hadn't met Ariel at the time."

Roselyn's smile turned snide. "I see."

"I hope you do indeed." He stepped closer, spoke so that only she could hear. "My wife means a great deal to me, Roselyn. I warn you, should you do anything to distress her in any way, I shall take it very personally. Since I know a substantial amount about your late husband's business affairs—or lack of success in that regard—I'll be happy to let those facts become known in places you might find embarrassing. Do you understand me . . . your ladyship?"

Her demeanor turned icy, her dark eyes narrowing into black-lashed slits. "I understand completely."

"Good. Now if you'll excuse me . . ." He gave her the faintest semblance of a smile. "Have a good evening."

Roselyn said nothing, but her lush mouth flattened to a tight little line. Ignoring the hostile glare that followed him across the room, he went in search of Ariel, damning his sister all the way. Barbara had invited Roselyn simply to cause him trouble. He was very afraid she had succeeded.

He checked the gallery, the gaming room, and the main salon but found no sign of his wife. Spotting Clay in conversation with Lord and Lady Oxnard, he paused to ask if perhaps one of them might have seen her.

"She was dancing with my . . . with Rathmore the last I noticed," Clay said, casting him a speculative glance.

"I believe I caught a glimpse of her slipping outside for a breath of fresh air." Lady Oxnard lifted her lorgnette to peer through the terrace doors. "It's terribly chilly out there. I'm sure she must have returned inside by now."

Surely she had, but Ariel was rarely put off by the cold, and he knew how difficult this night had been for her. He stepped out onto the terrace into a fine, drizzling mist. The flagstones were slick beneath his shoes, the chill in the air quickly seeping into his clothes. He saw no sign of Ariel and started back toward the house, but a trace of movement in the garden caught his eye. He strode in that direction, down the steps and along the gravel path to the gazebo. The bushes moved again, and the housekeeper's yellow tabby jumped out of the shrubbery onto a low stone bench.

Cursing, his worry increasing, Justin headed back inside the house.

Still no sign of Ariel. Certain now that something was wrong, he climbed the sweeping staircase to the room adjoining his and rapped on the door. He hadn't thought she would retire with so many guests in the house. Now, his jaw set grimly, he stepped inside without waiting for permission and spotted her silhouette in the moonlight streaming in through the window.

"I've been looking for you," he said softly, moving toward her. "I didn't think to find you here. You aren't feeling unwell, are you?"

"No, I . . ." She glanced down and he saw that she still held her dance card in one hand. He noticed that it trembled. In the wispy light, her face looked pale, her pretty blue eyes clouded with some painful emotion.

He caught her chin and gently lifted it, forcing her eyes to his face. "Tell me what's wrong."

She shook her head, tried for a smile, and faltered. "Nothing is wrong," she said, but her eyes filled with tears.

He wanted to reach for her, to pull her into his arms, but his clothes were damp with mist, and he forced himself to remain where he was. "We're married now. I'm your husband. Tell me what's wrong."

She turned away from him, walked over to the window, stared down at the winter-barren garden. "I saw you with the woman. She was your lover, wasn't she?"

Silently he cursed. "It was months ago, before we ever met."

She turned to face him, her eyes luminous with tears. "I told myself that I would keep silent . . . that I wouldn't ask. But I can't pretend any longer. I have to know the truth."

He stiffened, bracing himself for the worst, something he had done that he wasn't even aware of. "Go on."

"When you went to London . . . your business . . . was it just an excuse to leave? Did you go there to be with another woman?"

For an instant, his heart seemed to stop. "That is what you believe?"

"I don't know; I . . . Your sister said you could never be content with only one woman. She said that was the reason you left, that you needed variety. Tonight . . . when I saw you with Lady Eastgate . . . I knew she had been your lover. I thought that perhaps she was the woman you went to see."

He covered the distance between them in two long strides and dragged her into his arms. He was soaking her gown, but he no longer cared. He wanted her to know the truth, wanted her to believe in him again. He had to make that happen.

"My sister is a vicious little liar," he said against her hair. "You know that as well as I do. There was no other woman. I don't want any other woman. I haven't since the day I met you." He felt her shiver, cursed himself, and stepped away.

"You must believe that, Ariel. If our marriage is to have the slightest chance of success you must believe I am telling you the truth."

"I want to," she whispered. "I want to believe you more than anything in the world."

His gaze remained steady on her face. "I lied to you once in the past. I won't do it again. Not ever. I went to the city on business. I didn't take you with me because I wanted you here, where you'd be warm and safe." His hand trembled as he cupped her cheek. "Say you believe me."

Long, silent moments passed. Then her eyes slid closed and she stepped back into his arms. "I believe you."

His hold tightened fiercely around her. He rested his cheek on the top of her head. "Trust me, Ariel," he whispered. "I won't fail you again." God, it felt so good just to hold her, to smell the scent of lilac that drifted up from her hair.

"You're shivering," he said. "I've dampened your clothes."

"It doesn't matter." Her arms slid up around his neck.

"Nothing matters except that it's me you want and not someone else."

Justin crushed her against him. "I want you," he said hoarsely. "I'll always want you." And then he was tilting her head back, taking her mouth in a hard, possessive kiss, claiming her as he had wanted to do for so long. When she opened to him, welcoming the sweep of his tongue, the darkness inside him seemed to fade and slowly disappear.

"Justin . . ." she whispered, clinging to him as if she'd never let him go. He kissed her again, softly, deeply, wanting her, certain now that she wanted him, too. His hands shook as he began to unbutton her beautiful golden gown. He would make her his, banish her chill with the heat of his body. The gown fell open and he slid it off her shoulders. It pooled on the floor as he lifted her into his arms and carried her over to the bed.

"God, I've missed you," he whispered. "I've missed you so much." Another hungry kiss, Ariel kissing him as fiercely as he was kissing her.

They made love urgently, wildly, making up for the time they had lost.

Afterward, he curled her against his side and simply held her, his fingers stroking gently over her hair. She was exhausted from the tension of the evening. Eventually her eyes slowly closed and she drifted off to sleep. In slumber, the worry was gone from her face, the uncertainty that had haunted her for so long. He wanted to see it banished forever and vowed he would do whatever it took to make that happen.

He thought of his sister's cruelty, the doubt she had worked so hard to instill, and his jaw hardened. If Barbara persisted in causing trouble, he would see her removed from Greville Hall. If it weren't for Thomas, he would do so now, this very night. But he didn't have the heart to uproot the child and send him away.

He knew only too well what it felt like to be shuffled from one place to the next, with no real family, no place to call home.

Still, Barbara's hostile attitude was going to change. If it didn't and that meant sending her away, so be it. One way or another, his sister's cruelty was coming to an end. Barbara would soon learn the consequences should she ever make trouble for either of them again.

He owed it to Ariel. And, he suddenly realized, he owed it to himself.

In the sitting room of the sumptuous master suite the following day, Barbara stood rigid, waiting for the door to close behind her brother's retreating figure. The moment he disappeared out of sight, her hands balled into fists.

"How dare he!" Anger bubbled like acid in her throat. *How dare he!* She whirled toward the writing desk in the corner and marched in that direction. It took a moment to calm herself enough to remove the quill pen and dip it into the inkwell. Even then, tiny drops trailed across the top of the sheet of paper.

"Dearest Phillip," she began, then frowned and hastily scratched through the words. Wadding up the paper, she tossed it away and drew out a second clean sheet. "My darling Phillip . . ." In the body of the letter, she described her encounter with her brother, how Justin had railed at her, threatened to toss her out of the house—a house that rightfully belonged to her son!—spilling out all of the bile she carried inside, knowing he was the single person in the world who would sympathize.

Telling him it was time to go forward with their plan.

She signed it: "With all my love, Barbara," sealed it with wax, and rang for a footman to see it delivered. Her hands no longer trembled. The anger simmered now, just below the surface. Justin might think he had won, and for the present she would let him believe it. But not for long. Oh, no, not for long.

The stakes were high, the risks great, but the game would soon be over.

Barbara hadn't the slightest doubt that ultimately she would be the winner.

*   *   *

The weather cleared. The first rays of dawn broke over the horizon, the crisp, chill air turning his breath to frosty plumes as Justin made his way to the stable. A young groom named Michael O'Flaharty emerged from the shadows, having quickly adapted to his master's early-morning routine.

Each day at sunup, Justin left the house and set off over the rolling hills of the estate he had only just begun to think of as truly belonging to him. Until his recent arrival with Ariel, shadows of an unpleasant past had kept him away. Greville Hall had been his father's pride and joy, a monument to his money and fine sense of taste. The earl had made it a showplace. With his daughter in residence, the earl had spent most of his time there.

For Justin, the lovely stone mansion nestled in the verdant Surrey countryside had embodied all that his father cherished, all that his son was denied.

Justin's mother, the daughter of a squire named William Bedford, had lived, for a time, in a cottage not far away. As a boy, Justin had spent hours prowling the fields around the house, watching, with an aching sense of loss, the comings and goings of the father who refused to claim him.

Though the house now belonged to him and had for several years, the memories it held had simply been too painful.

He discovered that was no longer true.

Justin filled his lungs with the crisp morning air and set his heels lightly to the sleek bay hunter Michael had saddled for him. The animal was lean and well muscled, and keenly perceptive of his commands. The earl had been a good judge of horses and it showed in the finely bred stock in his stable.

My stable, Justin corrected. The beautiful bay hunter belonged to him now. It shouldn't be so difficult a thing to remember.

He nudged the bay into a canter and rode off down the hill. A small copse of trees marked the path in the distance.

He rode the same way almost every morning, traveling through the forest, then fanning out on the opposite side in different directions, learning the land that belonged to him. Chiding himself for not doing so long before this, admitting that if Barbara hadn't been in residence he would have.

But Barbara's bitterness could no longer hurt him, and little by little the shadows were slipping away, the hurtful memories fading, replaced by new, sweet memories he was only just beginning to create. Memories of his time with Ariel.

In the months since she had come into his life, the shroud of darkness that engulfed him had begun to fade, letting in the light of a promising future.

Just thinking about her made a yearning rise in his chest that was almost painful. It was amazing how important she had become to him, how he looked forward to returning to the house to find her waiting, how sweet it was to simply share a meal with her. A single night of lovemaking with Ariel was more pleasurable than all of the hours combined he had spent in the arms of other women.

It frightened him a little, these feelings she stirred, when he had been so certain no feeling at all existed in the icy cavern he called a heart. He wasn't exactly sure how to deal with them, or even precisely what to call them, and since he remained uncertain, he decided to simply enjoy them for as long as they lasted.

Justin reined the bay down into the trees, the naked branches casting long, thin fingers of shadow across his face. Up ahead, the brambles grew thicker, blocking the watery sunlight and shrouding the trail in darkness, a narrow winding path in search of the light on the opposite side. He ducked beneath the branches of a yew tree, the needles white with frost and rustling against his cloak as he passed.

The trail dropped into a slight depression, and the horse's ears perked up. The muscles in the animal's legs went stiff, and the animal shied a bit off the trail.

"Easy, boy." Justin patted the horse's neck and urged

him forward, but the bay sidestepped and began to dance. "What is it, boy?" The gelding blew nervously, and Justin searched the underbrush, looking for the source of the animal's distress.

He spotted the three rough-looking men in the dense growth of foliage the same instant a shot rang out and a sharp, burning pain slammed into his shoulder.

Footpads—bloody hell! Whirling the horse, he leaned over the gelding's neck, and the animal leaped forward, eyes wild, nostrils flaring at the smell of Justin's blood.

"Get 'im!" one of the men shouted, breaking out of the brush and rushing toward him. "Don't let the blighter get away!" Another took off through the woods, trying to cut off his trail. Justin spotted him through the heavy growth of vines and shrubs, caught the glint of metal as the man aimed his pistol. Justin reined the horse hard to the left, into the cover of the trees. The pistol roared, the ball whizzing by so close he could feel the *whoosh* of the wind past his cheek.

His shoulder throbbed. His shirt and riding coat were soaked with blood. He set his teeth against the pain and urged the horse left again, made a sharp right around a tree, ducked beneath the branches, and cut left again, racing toward the sunlight and the distant hilly fields. The third man appeared out of nowhere, stepping into his path, grabbing the horse's bridle, sending the frightened animal up on its hind legs and nearly unseating him.

Justin cursed. The horse whinnied in fear, his front legs pawing the air, the hooves dangerously sharp and only inches from the brigand's face. He hurled himself out of the way and swung the pistol upward. Justin lashed out with his boot, slammed it into the man's thick wrist, and heard a yelp of pain. The gun fired harmlessly into the air and careened into the trees. Another hard kick sent his assailant flying, landing with a grunt in the dirt, and Justin rode hard for the edge of the forest.

Bright sunlight broke through the branches up ahead. The gelding stumbled and nearly went down, righted himself, and kept on going. They reached the opening to the sound of another gunshot, and Justin urged the horse into a flat-out run. In seconds they had reached the crest of the hill and disappeared out of range down the opposite side.

It was a damned good thing. He had lost so much blood he was beginning to feel dizzy, and he wasn't sure how much longer he could stay conscious. Clamping his jaw, he locked his arms around the gelding's neck, loosened the rein, and gave the horse his head.

The thunder of hooves and the bone-jarring pain in his shoulder were the last things he remembered until he heard Ariel's scream.

She was crying, he saw when he summoned the strength to pry open his eyes, and among his muzzy thoughts came the painful notion that he had somehow hurt her again.

CHAPTER TWENTY-FOUR

Ariel closed the door to Justin's room and followed the physician out into the hall. She was surprised to find Barbara waiting, pacing up and down the corridor, looking— for Barbara—decidedly unkempt.

"How badly is he injured, Dr. Marvin?" Justin's sister asked, hurrying to join them. "Is he going to be all right?"

"Lord Greville was fortunate in the extreme." The doctor, a gray-haired man in his sixties, removed the quizzing glass still fixed in a watery blue eye. "The lead ball passed cleanly through the shoulder. Not much damage was done to muscle or bone, though he's lost a good deal of blood. There is always the chance that the wound will putrefy, but I've had quite good luck with the medicinal powders I used, and barring that occurrence, the earl should be back on his feet in no time."

Ariel sagged with relief. "Thank God."

"What on earth could have happened?" Barbara asked. "Was he able to explain?"

"He said something about footpads," Ariel told her, surprised at Barbara's concern. Perhaps in some small way, Justin's sister actually cared about him. It seemed impossible, but it certainly appeared to be true.

"Footpads?" Barbara's black brows shot up.

"Yes," the doctor said. "I gather there were three of them. Apparently, they were after his purse."

Barbara rolled her eyes. "And I thought we were safe this far away from the city."

"They must have been watching his movements," Ariel suggested. "Justin is a man of habit. It would be easy to learn his daily routine."

"Or they simply may have stumbled upon him and thought a man alone would be easy prey," Barbara put in. "I shall have to keep a closer eye on Thomas. They might take it into their heads to abduct him for ransom."

"You needn't worry about that, dear lady." The doctor patted her shoulder. "I shall stop by the sheriff's office on my way home. If those brigands remain in the neighborhood, the sheriff and his men will make short work of them."

"Thank you," Ariel said. "I shall also send word. I'm certain the authorities will wish to speak to my husband."

Dr. Marvin nodded and Ariel thanked him for his help. While Barbara showed him to the door, Ariel returned to Justin's bedside.

He was sleeping, the draught the doctor had given him providing the rest he needed. Still, she was worried. She had never been more frightened in her life than the moment she had seen him being carried into the entry. With his eyes closed and his chest covered in blood, for an instant she had been certain he was dead. The pain in that moment was nearly unbearable.

She didn't remember screaming, but she must have, for his gray, pain-filled eyes cracked open and slowly fixed on her face. When a brief smile touched his lips, Ariel knew that he lived. Love for him swept over her, welled up in her chest, wrapped tightly around her heart.

Ignoring her worry, she had swiftly taken charge. In minutes, Justin lay abed upstairs, resting peacefully, his wound cleaned and bandaged, the doctor summoned.

Except for her conversation with the doctor, she hadn't left his side for a single moment since.

Morning turned to evening. Night came and went. At sunrise, she awakened in a chair beside his bed, surprised to discover Justin was also awake.

"Ariel . . . ?" His voice sounded thick and groggy. As his mind began to clear, his eyes fixed on her face. "What the devil . . . ? Surely you didn't sit in that chair all night?"

She smiled at him softly. "You've been injured. I wanted to be certain that you were all right."

Grinding his teeth against the pain, he tried to sit up, and she hurried to help him. He flexed his shoulder, clamped hard on his jaw. He moved his arm with a little more success and examined the bandages across his shoulder. "It hurts like blazes, but I don't think the wound is too severe."

"The doctor said the ball went straight through. There wasn't any damage to muscle or bone, thank heaven."

He nodded, relieved. "If that is the case, I'll be as good as new in a couple of days—at least I will if that bird-witted doctor hasn't muddled my brain with whatever it was he made me drink."

She bit back a laugh. "You needed to rest. Dr. Marvin merely wanted to be certain that you did."

He tried to sit up straighter. His jaw clenched and she forced him back down on the bed. "You have been shot, sir. The doctor insists on complete bed rest and you will do as he says—whether you wish it or not."

He cocked a black brow. "Is that so? And who, exactly, is going to enforce the doctor's orders?"

"I am."

The edge of his mouth inched up. "Then perhaps—since you'll have to remain in the room to be certain that I obey—I shall acquiesce to the physician's demands."

She eyed him skeptically. "And you'll agree to remain abed?"

Thick-lashed eyelids drifted down to cover his thoughts. "I can't think of anything I should like better than spending the next few days abed—as long as you are with me."

Ariel flushed but didn't argue. It was obvious her husband's wound was not as grave as she had imagined. And equally obvious he meant to take scandalous advantage.

Things had been different between them since the night of the Christmas soiree. That night she had been forced to make a painful decision—whether to believe in Justin, believe he was the sort of man worthy of her love, or allow her fears, and Barbara Townsend's vengeful machinations, to destroy her life.

That night she had looked into Justin's fierce gray eyes

and believed he was telling her the truth. If he was, then he truly cared about her.

Ariel reached out and smoothed back a lock of thick black hair. He was sleeping again, his features softer than they usually were. If she closed her eyes, she could still see his face the morning he had been shot, his eyes closed, his skin deathly pale, the front of his shirt drenched in blood. Footpads, he had said. But there was no way to know for certain, no way to be sure he was no longer in danger.

An odd, tingling shiver crept down the back of her neck. She tried to tell herself she was being foolish, that it was only by accident that Justin had stumbled upon the men and fallen prey to their attack, but the niggling fear that something terrible was about to happen would not go away.

Sheriff John Wilmot followed the butler into one of the elegant drawing rooms at Greville Hall. Four days had passed since he had last spoken to the earl, who was now up and about, showing little of the effects of the shooting except for the tightening of his jaw against an occasional twinge of pain.

Spotting his lordship just inside the room, Wilmot removed his slouch hat and held it in front of him. "I'm sorry to report, my lord, we've found no trace of the men who attacked you."

The earl's jaw hardened, but he nodded. He led the way to a chair in front of the sofa, and Wilmot sat down across from the man's pretty blond wife. She looked at him with a worried expression.

"Do you think the men have left the area?" she asked.

The sheriff shifted on the expensive brocade fabric he sat on and hoped he wouldn't get it dirty. "They'd be fools if they didn't. My men have been scouring the countryside, and there is that reward you offered."

The earl cocked a brow. "How much is this reward?"

"Why, three hundred guineas, my lord. I thought you knew."

"Three hundred . . . ? Good God—that's a bloody fortune." The earl pinned a hard look on his wife, who sat up a little straighter on the sofa.

"You were hardly in a condition to make that sort of decision, my lord. Besides, your life is worth far more than a mere three hundred guineas."

Instead of being angry, the earl merely smiled. "I'm glad you think so, my love."

She flushed prettily and the sheriff thought what a lucky man Lord Greville was to have married a woman who cared about him so much. "You're certain these men were footpads?" Wilmot asked.

"They weren't men from the village. What else could they be?"

He shrugged his beefy shoulders. He wasn't all that tall, but he was heavily built. A slight paunch hung over the top of his breeches and his hair had begun to thin, but he was smart and hardworking. There was very little crime in Sussex County, and John Wilmot meant to keep it that way.

"I realize the men were brigands," he said, "but they could have been hired by someone else. Do you have any enemies, my lord?"

Greville merely shrugged. "I'm involved in a number of business ventures. A man doesn't make the sort of money I've made and not wind up with a certain amount of enemies. I doubt any of them would go so far as to murder me, however."

"You might think about it. Someone wanted you dead. Or at least they wanted your money bad enough to see you dead."

"The latter is far more likely," the earl said, dismissing the notion, though a look of speculation flickered for a moment in his eyes. "The men who attacked me were obviously ruffians," he went on. "And no one knows better than I what a motive money can be."

The sheriff simply nodded. "We'll keep after them. We'll find them if they're anywhere hereabouts." The conversation finished, the earl got up from his chair, and so did the sheriff. Lady Greville joined in bidding him fare-well.

"Let me know if you come up with anything," Lord Greville said to him as he made his way out into the hall.

"You may count on it." The footman closed the drawing room doors behind him, and the sheriff headed out to his horse. The earl was probably right—brigands after his purse. But years of experience and a nagging suspicion told him Greville could be wrong. He would keep an eye on things, he vowed.

He liked the earl and his wife. He wouldn't want any-thing untoward to happen to either one of them.

"The sheriff hasn't yet found them." Sitting once more on the sofa, Ariel toyed with a fold of her skirt. "I'm worried, Justin."

He could see that she was. Ignoring the ache it caused his shoulder, he sat down beside her and gathered her into his arms. "You've nothing to be worried about. By now those men are a long ways from here." He smiled. "Besides, with the reward you offered, half the county will be looking for them. They won't be able to show their faces anywhere near this place."

"I wanted them caught," she said stubbornly.

"So I gathered." He brushed a light kiss over her lips. "Thank you for caring so much."

Ariel got up from the sofa, began to wander absently about the room. "I was thinking about what the sheriff said about enemies. What if the men weren't footpads, Justin? What if . . . what if someone hired those men to kill you?"

"And this person is . . . ?"

"I don't know."

Neither did he, but the notion had crossed his mind as well. He walked over to join her, stopping beside where she stood idly tracing patterns on the top of the pianoforte. "What I told the sheriff was true—I'm bound to have made some enemies over the years, but none of them would have anything to gain by killing me, and as much as they might dislike me, I am simply not worth that much trouble."

Ariel looked up at him. She started to say something, stopped, and shook her head.

"Go on. If you've something to say, you may as well say it."

"There is someone who would benefit. Your sister would have a great deal to gain by your death."

Justin frowned at the unpleasant thought that had also occurred to him. "I suppose that's true. Though we've had our differences, I prefer to believe my sister wouldn't cold-bloodedly murder her only sibling."

She sighed. "I'm sorry. That was a terrible thing to say." She managed a smile, but it was tight and worried. "At least you're mending well. I was afraid you wouldn't feel up to our visit with your grandmother."

"I feel far better than I should, under the circumstances. In truth, I considered playing on your sympathy, using my injury as an excuse not to go, but I've promised, and so we shall go. How is the silhouette coming along?"

"Nearly finished. I'm picking it up in the village on the morrow."

"I hope my grandmother will know who it is."

She tossed him a disbelieving glance. "Don't be silly. Of course she will know."

But he wasn't so sure. It had been years since he had seen her. He had changed from a boy to a man since then. He wondered if she ever thought of him. He rarely thought of her anymore, though as a lad, he had been closer to her than he was to his own mother. He could still remember the way she always smelled of lilacs and the faintly chalky scent of watercolor paints, the hobby she was so fond of. He remembered the plum tarts she insisted Cook bake especially for him, since she knew they were his favorites. And there were the Christmas decorations they always made together: stringing berries, cutting out paper snow-flakes, hanging yew boughs over the fireplace of the old stone manor house where, for a time, he had lived.

He had loved her so much. She was all he'd had back then.

But time had changed things. His father had sent him away to school, and he'd rarely seen her after that. He wondered if she would be glad to see him and felt a niggling pang of conscience.

He'd taken care of her, he told himself. Sent her money, done the right thing. She probably hadn't thought of him in years.

But he couldn't help wondering if she might have missed him and if perhaps he shouldn't have gone to see her long before this.

Careful to keep the hood of her cloak up to hide her face, Barbara climbed the stairs to the room above the stable at the Cock's Crow Tavern. She had told her brother she was off to visit Lady Oxnard, who had recently fallen ill, and quietly left the house.

During the days since the shooting, she had stifled her anger and bitter disappointment, careful to keep it well hidden. The anger was still there, boiling just below the surface, and with it came renewed determination.

Barbara rapped lightly on the door to the upstairs room they had used before and in seconds it swung open. She was dragged inside and crushed in Phillip's embrace.

"Where have you been? I thought you would get here hours ago. I've been worried sick."

She eased herself out of his arms and stepped away, moving toward the fire in the hearth, rubbing her arms against the chill.

"You should be worried." She stared into the orange-red flames. "If they catch one of those men you hired, we'll all be headed for the gallows." She turned to face him. "Good Lord, Phillip, was that the best you could do? A bunch of ruffians who couldn't kill a man outnumbered three to one?"

He walked toward her, stopped just in front of her. "Benjamin Coolie's a professional, one of the best at what he does. He won't get caught and even if he did, he'd swing at the end of a rope before he'd give the authorities any information. In his line of work, someone else would kill him—if I didn't get to him first."

"What about the others?"

"Coolie hired them. They don't know anything about me, and certainly you aren't in any way connected."

Barbara relaxed a little, somewhat mollified by the news. "That idiot Justin married has offered a small fortune as a reward for the men who attacked him. Someone is likely to turn them in."

"They are long gone by now. And as I said, Coolie makes his living doing other people's dirty work. He'll change his appearance and no one will ever realize he was one of the men involved in the shooting. He doesn't usually make mistakes. The next time—"

"There isn't going to be a next time."

"What?"

"Call them off. Tell them you've changed your mind. Tell them anything you like; just get rid of them."

"But I thought we were agreed. I thought—"

Barbara smiled at the unhappy look on his face, like a child who'd been denied a favorite piece of candy. "We *are* agreed. We are simply going to do this another way." She went over to him, slid her arms around his neck, pressed her breasts into his chest. His hand came up to cup one, and his sex went hard against her thigh. She fondled him through his breeches, and he hardened even more.

Phillip moistened his lips. "Shouldn't we . . . Shouldn't we discuss what it is you have in mind?"

Barbara gently stroked him. "Oh, we will. I thought perhaps there might be something you were more interested in at the moment, but if you prefer to talk business . . ." She squeezed him gently, firmly.

"No, I . . . Later we can talk."

Barbara reached for the buttons at the front of his breeches, opened them one by one. She cradled him tenderly, almost lovingly. Phillip moaned low in his throat.

She looked up at him, smiled wickedly. "When we're finished here, my darling, I'll tell you what I've planned for my dearest brother, the soon-to-be late Lord Greville."

The holiday dinner with Cornelia Mae Bedford, Justin's grandmother, was scheduled to take place three days before Christmas. Since she lived just outside Reading, nearly a day's carriage ride away, they set out early in the morning, bundled in warm woolen clothes, a heavy fur lap robe covering their legs.

Determined not to let his business interfere, Justin ignored the stack of paperwork on his desk, but Ariel merely scooped it under her arm and headed out to the carriage.

"It's a long way to Reading. We'll need something to do along the way. I don't mind a little work. You can review some of the new investment projects you're considering while I go over the numbers on these financial reports Clay sent on the mine. You won't have so much to do when we get home."

Justin smiled at her softly. "Most ladies would be appalled at the idea of doing any sort of actual work for their husbands."

"I enjoy being useful. I'm bored silly when I've nothing productive to do."

Working together made the hours on the rutted, muddy road pass swiftly. They stopped at several inns along the way to warm themselves and rest the horses, then returned to the carriage and their work. When they had finished, Ariel leaned back against the seat with a satisfied smile.

"What did I tell you? We're done with our work and we still have time for me to beat you quite soundly at a game of gin rummy."

His laughter rang out, rich with delight, and she thought what a pleasant, joyous sound it was. Since she had returned to his bed, he seemed different, less guarded than he had ever been before. The hope she had once felt was growing stronger than ever, settling determinedly in her heart. He cared for her, she was now certain. Perhaps, as

Clay Harcourt had said, in time he might even learn to love her.

They finished the card game, Ariel ahead in the beginning, Justin moving into the lead a few hands later, battling back and forth, finishing nearly at a draw. On the very last hand, Justin filled a difficult straight, winning the game by a mere three points, both of them laughing as the final card was turned over.

Ariel leaned back smiling, pleased to see her husband smiling as well. Unconsciously she fingered her beautiful sapphire wedding ring, thinking again what a perfect choice it had been, wondering, as she always did, how Clay Harcourt could have chosen something so exactly right for her.

She examined it in the watery winter sunlight filtering in through the isinglass windows, admiring the rich blue fire of the sapphires, the crystal-clear brilliance of the diamonds.

"You're smiling," he said softly. "Do you really like it so much?"

"It's beautiful, Justin. If I could have chosen any ring in London, it would have been this exact one. I've always wondered how it was Clay Harcourt could have known so well what would please me."

Justin took her hand and looked down at the glittering sapphires and diamonds. "Clay didn't choose the ring. I did."

"You? But there wasn't time. You never left the country before the wedding. When could you possibly—"

"I bought the ring some time back."

She frowned. "Some time back?"

"After our return from Tunbridge Wells. I intended to ask you to wed me then, but . . ."

"You were going to propose?" she asked with utter amazement.

"I planned to . . . yes." His face looked suddenly bleak. "Then I saw you that night, going into the stable with Phillip Marlin."

Ariel's mind spun, reeled beneath the impact of his

words. "Oh, my God." Tears sprang into her eyes. For the first time, she understood the magnitude of what had occurred. Justin glanced away, his beautiful gray eyes dark with the memory. "You wanted to marry me. Instead you thought . . . you thought that I had betrayed you. Oh, Justin." She was in his arms in a heartbeat, clinging to his neck, tears running in rivers down her cheeks.

I love you, she thought. *I love you so much.* But she didn't say it. She was afraid he wouldn't know what to say in return.

He held her tightly, his face pressed to hers. "Don't cry. I didn't mean to make you cry."

She dragged in a shaky breath, willing herself to stop, a lump of tears caught in her throat. She wiped away the wetness with a shaky hand and summoned a watery smile. "They're happy tears, Justin. You would have married me even before all of this happened, even before the scandal."

"If you would have had me. God knows I'm not the best husband you could have had, but I swear to you, Ariel, you won't be sorry. I promise you won't ever be sorry."

But as much as she loved him, Ariel wasn't so sure. She wanted him to love her in return, needed to know that he cared for her as much as she cared for him. She didn't think she could ever be truly happy until that happened.

And in her heart, she wasn't completely convinced it ever would.

CHAPTER TWENTY-FIVE

"We're 'ere, milord." With a weary smile, the footman held open the carriage door. The day had been a long one, the last few hours lengthened when one of the wheels had dropped into a rut and some of the spokes were broken. They finally got it fixed and arrived at Justin's grandmother's house well after dark, all of them shivering with cold.

"Thank you, Timms." Justin leaped to the ground. "The kitchen's round back. There'll be something there for you and the others to eat and a place for you to get warm." He reached up and helped Ariel down, pulled her cloak more tightly around her shoulders. Settling a hand at her waist, he led her up the flagstone walkway toward the arched wood plank door.

The old stone house looked the same as he remembered, the shutters a bit more weathered, the shrubs a little more overgrown. The house stood two stories high, with gabled roofs and half a dozen chimneys. Lamplight illuminated the windows in the dining room, and he could see the faint flicker of firelight in the big stone hearth.

An unexpected sense of homecoming settled around him, odd since he hadn't lived in the house all that many years. He lifted the heavy brass knocker and let it fall several times, the echo a familiar one. The sound of shuffling feet preceded the opening of the heavy front door.

For an instant, he didn't remember the ancient, bone-thin butler who stood there grinning.

" 'Tis Sedgewick, milord. We had given up hope, sir. We thought you had decided not to come."

"A wheel broke on the carriage. Damnable nuisance, but we finally got it fixed." He glanced around as he stepped inside, thinking to hear the sound of voices, his distant cousin Maynard and his wife, Sarah, or Phineas and Gerdie and their growing brood of five, but the house was eerily silent.

"This way, milord . . . milady. 'Tis beyond cold outside. Come, warm yourself before the fire."

He followed the old man's creaking footsteps along the hall and stepped into the parlor, beginning to worry about his grandmother, wondering where she was, hoping she hadn't fallen ill.

Sedgewick seemed to read his thoughts. "She is not so young anymore. It's difficult for her to get round. She's in the dining room. She doesn't yet know you are here."

"Where are my cousins?"

The old man shook his head, his watery blue eyes filled with sadness. "They always mean to come, but the journey is a long one, and the weather this time of year is never good. Your grandmother always holds out hope, but in the end . . ." He shrugged his bony shoulders. They were stooped with age, his cheeks hollow and sunken in. Sorrow lined his face when he spoke of the woman who had employed him for more than forty years.

"Justin?" Ariel's worried expression mirrored his own. "Do you think your grandmother is all right?"

His chest felt tight. "I don't know."

They crossed the room behind the butler, past the same horsehair sofa Justin remembered as a boy, the arms protected by embroidered slipcovers his grandmother had sewn.

He paused at the dining room door. The table was not quite as long as he remembered, but it was polished to a glossy sheen, and pine boughs and holly berries formed a Christmas centerpiece in the middle. Twelve chairs clustered around it, eleven of them empty, though each place was set with his grandmother's precious heirloom silver and china and the delicate cut-crystal goblets his grandfather had given her on their first anniversary. Long white candles in the center of the table ate their way steadily through the slowly disappearing wax.

"It's this way every year," the butler whispered. "She

sets this lovely table and Cook prepares a special meal, but no one ever comes to share it with her."

Justin glanced around the empty room and some long-buried painful emotion swelled inside him. He surveyed the table that had been so lovingly set for the family that wasn't there and the frail little woman who sat hunched over all alone, and regret rose like bile in his throat.

Hearing the butler's familiar voice, the tiny white-haired woman turned. When she spotted Justin, tears began to slide down her sunken, wrinkled cheeks. "Justin . . . ?" She started to rise, trembled, and Justin strode forward to help her, catching her wrist, noticing how fragile the bones felt in his hand.

"I'm here, Grandmother."

She smiled up at him, a tender, loving smile that seemed to melt some barrier inside him. It wrapped around his cold, empty heart, filling it with warmth, carrying him back to the days he had lived in the house, reminding him of the few years of his boyhood he had ever been truly happy.

"I'm so glad to see you," she said. "I didn't think you were going to come."

His heart beat dully, painfully. A crushing weight seemed to settle on his chest. "I should have come sooner."

A veined hand reached up, lovingly caressed his cheek. "It's been so long . . . so many years. A thousand times I tried to picture what you would look like. You're all grown-up now." Her thin lips trembled. "I missed all of that . . . all of those years." They curved into a wistful smile, puckering the skin around her mouth. "My, you are so hand-some."

His throat felt thick and tight. He could hardly swallow. How could he have treated her so badly? How could he have simply ignored her for all of those years? Something was stinging, burning behind his eyes. He felt the wetness clinging to his lashes. He told himself it could not be.

He never cried. He was a cold, emotionless man. He wasn't the sort for tears.

He gruffly cleared his throat. "My wife is here, Grandmother. She's been eager to meet you." The only real reason he had come. If Ariel hadn't persuaded him, he wouldn't be here now. And his grandmother would be eating another Christmas dinner alone.

His chest knotted, squeezed painfully.

His grandmother reached out and took hold of Ariel's hand. "I'm so glad to meet you, my dear."

In the light of the candle, he could see the sheen of wetness in Ariel's eyes. "As I am to meet you. Justin has talked of you often." It wasn't the truth, but it made his grandmother's face light up.

"Has he?" It was a sweet little lie, and he adored Ariel for it. "I was afraid he would forget me."

"Oh, no," Ariel said quickly, discreetly dabbing at a drop of moisture. "He would never do that."

"No, Grandmother," Justin said gruffly, his throat aching, hurting so much it was nearly impossible to speak. "How could I possibly forget?" And suddenly he knew it was the truth. He had loved this little woman, the closest to a mother he had ever really known. He'd loved her then and he loved her still.

For so many years he had hidden his feelings, buried them so deep he thought he had lost them completely. The detached, emotionless man he had become had been certain he had no heart. Now he felt it, beating there inside him, aching with what he realized with complete and utter awe was love.

"My wife has fashioned a present for you, Grandmother."

She smiled with sheer delight. "A present? For me? But I have nothing for you in return. I didn't—"

"You've made us a beautiful supper. You've brought back sweet memories that had all but faded. Those are gifts enough."

Ariel handed her the silhouette she had worked so hard to make, and his grandmother accepted it with a frail, shaking hand.

"Why don't we sit down so you can open it," Justin

suggested, noticing his grandmother was beginning to tire.

He helped her back to her chair, and they sat down one on each side of her. She carefully pulled the red string around the brightly wrapped package, then lovingly touched the plaster silhouette, tracing the shadow of his profile.

"It's beautiful," she said with a fond look at Ariel. "Such a precious gift." She was up again more agilely than the first time. "Come, I've the perfect place to hang it."

Justin took his grandmother's arm and helped her into the drawing room, Ariel beside them.

"See?" She pointed toward a group of portraits hanging on the wall. "I painted them after you were gone. I wanted to remember you exactly as you were."

Half a dozen watercolor images lined the drawing room wall. They weren't exactly perfect, but the likeness was passably good.

And all of the portraits were of him.

If he'd had any doubt left that he still possessed a heart, now he knew for certain, for it broke and crumbled in two, aching fiercely where the pieces lay scattered inside his chest.

"You look like your father, but you have your mother's stubborn chin." The old woman smiled. "I imagine you can be as set in your ways as she was."

"I thought you had forgotten all about me," he said softly, gruffly.

"You were the son I never had. I've thought about you every day since the night they took you away."

He bent down, enfolded the little woman in his arms. He couldn't stop the tears that slid down his cheeks. "From now on, things will be different, I promise you. You can come and live with us. There is plenty of room and—"

She drew a little away. "Poppycock. This house is my home." Her thin, veined hand brushed his cheek. "But I would love to come for a visit . . . if that is all right with you."

He nodded, forced a smile, caught Ariel's trembly smile

above the old woman's head. "Of course it is. We would love to have you."

"And we'll come back here as often as we can," Ariel promised, her eyes glistening again.

In silence, they returned to the dining room, where supper had been reheated and was ready to be served. There was roast goose with cranberry-walnut stuffing, quail eggs in aspic, turbot in cream sauce, peas, and ginger-glazed carrots, and for dessert the warm plum tarts that had always been his favorite.

It was a wonderful meal, filled with happiness and love. Justin felt like laughing and crying at the very same time. It was an incredible day, one of the best of his life. He had learned something about himself today, something that changed everything he had previously believed.

He thought of the feelings inside him that he had discovered, an emotion he knew was love. In truth, he realized, it was a feeling not entirely new to him. He had sensed it lately, whispers of it here, threads of it there. Every time he looked at Ariel. Every time he touched her, kissed her, simply watched her walking toward him across a room.

The feeling was so different, so frightening, he had shoved it away, refusing to examine what it was. Still it had persisted, grown stronger every day.

It was love, he knew with a certainty that reached into his very bones. Today he had discovered he wasn't the cold, heartless man he had believed himself to be. He was a man capable of feeling, a man capable of love.

And he was very much in love with his wife.

He wanted to shout it, wanted to laugh out loud with the sheer joy of it. It made him want to sing. And it made him determined.

Once Ariel had loved him as he loved her. He wanted her to love him again. He wasn't sure exactly how to make that happen, but he would, he vowed.

He wouldn't give up until he did.

* * *

They spent two nights at the manor house in Reading as they had planned, then journeyed the following day back to Greville Hall. Before they left, Justin secured a promise from his grandmother that she would come for a month-long visit as soon as the weather grew warm enough for her to travel.

Ariel looked forward to seeing the dear, sweet lady again, though she wondered if by then they would still be residing at Greville Hall. She hoped so. Even Barbara's bitter tongue couldn't spoil the pleasure of living in the country, away from the noise and soot of the city, in a house that seemed to glow with warmth.

The long ride home was tiring, though the roads were less muddy and the journey not so difficult as before. It was late when the carriage turned down the tree-lined drive leading up to the house. Clouds gathered overhead, forming an opaque ring around a dull full moon. Thomas was already in bed, they discovered. Justin said a terse good night to his sister; then he and Ariel retired upstairs to their rooms.

"I'm glad to be home," Ariel said with a sigh, standing in front of the mirror to pull the last of the pins from her hair. "But I am so very glad we went."

Justin came up behind her, slid his arms around her waist, and kissed the back of her neck. "So am I."

She turned to face him, happy to remain in the circle of his arms. "I loved your grandmother, Justin. I feel as if I have a family again."

"Yes, and soon we'll have a family of our own." His eyes said he wanted that to happen very much, and there was something else, something she had noticed more than once on their way home. Whatever it was, it was sweet and warm, and though she was tired from the journey, it made her want him to make love to her.

Sliding her fingers through his thick black hair, she pulled his head down to hers for a kiss. Beneath his clothes, she could feel his body tighten, feel the bands of muscles across his chest expand. Opening to him, she accepted the possessive sweep of his tongue, relaxed against him as his hands reached down to gently cup her breasts.

"Ariel . . ." he whispered, lifting her into his arms and carrying her over to the bed.

They made sweetly erotic love and afterward lay together, content just to hold each other. Eventually they drifted into an exhausted sleep, legs and arms entwined, her head nestled against his shoulder.

It was the smell of smoke that awakened her, sometime late in the night. Her eyelids felt swollen and heavy as she tried to drag them open, her eyes watering, burning, her mind whirling, refusing to congeal into solid thought. It took superhuman strength to haul herself upright on the bed.

Ariel gasped at the sight of the flaming curtains. The fringe at the edge of the carpet was also on fire, blazing little tongues of fire eating steadily toward them. Her horrified gaze swung to the door, but a wall of red-orange flame blocked the opening. Stifling a cry of pure terror, she reached a shaking hand out to her husband, who sprawled beside her in a deep, unnatural sleep.

"Justin!" She shook him roughly, frantically, her fear escalating, making her heart knock wildly against her ribs. "Justin, wake up! Dear God, the house is on fire!"

He blinked several times, his eyes coming open slowly, heavy-lidded and reddened. "What the devil . . . ?" Groaning, coughing, he fought to clear the smoke-induced grogginess from his mind. He shook his head, saw the terror in her eyes and the flames that lit the room with an eerie red glow. "Sweet Jesus!"

Rolling to the side of the bed, Justin shoved himself unsteadily to his feet. With shaking hands, Ariel jerked her quilted blue wrapper up off the chair beside the bed and dragged it on to cover herself while Justin grabbed his breeches.

"The door is blocked by flames," she said desperately. "There's no way out except the window."

Justin hurriedly fastened the buttons on his breeches as

he urged her in that direction. "Then the window is the way we shall go." Using his body to shield her as best he could, he backed her away from the burgeoning wall of heat.

In the hall outside the room, she heard the servants screaming, racing frantically back and forth, banging on doors.

"Fire!" someone shouted. "The house is on fire!"

Standing in front of the window, Ariel stared out at the narrow ledge that was the only chance they had for escape. "I don't know if I can—"

"You'll make it. We both will. I won't let anything happen to you."

She looked up at him, saw the hard, fiercely determined set of his features, and some of her fear receded. She could trust Justin to protect her. Somehow he would get her out safely.

"Stay here," he said. "I'll be right back."

Ariel bit back a cry of fear as he disappeared into the smoke, then returned a few seconds later, coughing, pressing a handkerchief over his mouth. He was carrying a silver-headed cane she had seen beside his dresser. She had never known him to carry it. She couldn't imagine why he would risk his life to get it now.

Then he pressed a small concealed button on the head of the cane, and the four-inch blade of a knife shot out the bottom. "Stand still," he commanded, which he needn't have done, since she was far too terrified to move. Kneeling, he quickly put the knife to use, slicing off the hem of her quilted wrapper to just below the knees, making it easier for her to move.

"Your feet are going to freeze, but you'll be able to grip the ledge far better than you could wearing shoes." He took hold of her hand. "Let's go."

Ariel stared out the window. "God, it's so far down." Though their rooms were only on the second floor of the house, the ceilings were so high in the drawing rooms it was more like the third.

"We only have to make it as far as that trough in the

roof. From there we can climb down to a lower section. The fire hasn't yet reached that part of the house. We'll get someone to bring us a ladder."

There was no more time to argue and really no other choice. Justin stepped over the sill and out onto the ledge, then reached back to take hold of her hand.

"Come on, love. Time to go." With her fingers firmly clasped in his, Ariel could do nothing but follow, climbing out on the narrow ledge, then inching along behind him. The stone was icy cold, freezing her feet and cutting into the tender soles. For an instant, she glanced away, down at the ground, which appeared to be miles below. A wave of dizziness washed over her, and she swayed a little. Justin slammed her backward against the wall of the house.

"Forgodsake, don't look down."

A shiver of fear slid through her. She dragged in a shaky breath and nodded for him to start moving again. By now, several people on the ground had realized what was going on. She heard several horrified gasps; then the onlookers fell silent, mesmerized by the sight of the lord and lady of the manor, half-naked and freezing, moving one painful inch at a time across the tiny ledge outside their bedchamber window.

The crackle and snap of flames filled the air as the raging fire charred its way through the roof above the room that had been theirs. A loud noise signaled the crash of timbers caving in. One of the bedroom windows they passed suddenly shattered, spewing hot, jagged shards of glass into the air. Justin hissed as one of them cut painfully into his thigh. He carefully pulled out the sliver and tossed it away.

She saw the blood oozing down his leg, and a soft sob came from her throat.

"It's all right," Justin soothed. "We're almost there. Just a little bit farther."

She inhaled a ragged breath, and they started along the ledge again, continuing inch by painful inch. Her feet were so cold she could no longer feel her toes. She prayed she would know if she stepped off the ledge and into thin air.

Justin reached the end of the ledge. "I've got to let go of your hand so that I can jump down. Don't move until I've got you again."

Ariel nodded. Justin released his hold and took a short leap that landed him on a lower portion of the roof, then reached up for her.

"Now it's your turn, love." His fingers closed firmly over hers. She started to jump, missed a step, and screamed as she felt the cold air rushing past her cheeks. Terrified, she squeezed her eyes shut and steeled herself to land on the ground in a bloody heap.

Then she was in his arms, crushed against his powerful chest. "I've got you," he whispered. "I won't let you go." He was shaking. She could feel the tremors moving through his tall, lean frame.

Ariel clung to him, fighting back tears, knowing how close she had come to death and that it was Justin who had saved her. He gave her a quick, hard kiss. "Just a little ways farther. In a few more minutes, we'll be down."

She looked up at him, thought how much she loved him, and summoned a shaky smile. "Let's go."

Justin led her away from the flames, along the roof above the conservatory, taking it slowly, his grip so tight she couldn't have gotten free if she'd tried. The ladder was waiting, propped against the roof, one of the footmen having guessed their intentions, and they made their way safely to the ground.

The moment her feet touched the earth, Justin hauled her into his arms. "Don't ever scare me like that again." He buried his face in her hair and clung to her so tightly she could barely catch her breath.

She laughed shakily, trembling with the aftermath of shock and relief. "I'll do my best."

Several of the servants ran forward, Silvie among them. "We were so worried, my lady."

Her little maid wrapped her in a warm woolen blanket, and another of the other women came up, carrying a pair of slippers that came from God-knew-where.

"They've started a bucket brigade, my lord," one of the footmen told him. "I'm not sure how much good it will do."

Michael O'Flaharty arrived, carrying a pair of black leather riding boots. "These are yours. I brought 'em from the stables."

"Thank you."

Someone handed Justin a shirt, and he pulled it on over his bare chest. "Is everyone out of the house?" He glanced around, studying the faces of the people around him. "Where are my sister and her son?"

"I seen 'er ladyship 'eadin' for the front door, milord." One of the upstairs maids pointed in that direction. "She's probably round front. But I 'aven't seen the boy."

Justin's jaw went hard. "Stay here. I've got to find them."

"I'll find Mrs. Whitelawn, Thomas's nanny," Ariel said, forcing down her fear. "Perhaps they're with her."

Justin nodded and hurried off toward the side of the house, making his way to the front. He paused to speak to Frieda Kimble, his sister's lady's maid. The woman was shaking her head, Ariel saw with rapidly building fear, pointing wildly back toward the house.

Justin didn't hesitate, just turned and started running— back into the flames.

Thick, black, choking smoke swirled around him, burning his eyes, clogging his lungs, making it nearly impossible to breathe.

Justin pressed the sleeve of his shirt over his nose and bent low, trying to move beneath the stifling fog of blackness. Thomas and Barbara were still in the house, his sister's maid believed, trapped perhaps in the boy's third-floor bedchamber next to the nursery.

Justin reached the entry, turned, and looked up the stairs at the second-floor railing. The fire had started in the west wing and hadn't yet reached the main portion of the house. But Thomas's room was in the burning wing. If the boy and his mother were still there . . . Justin prayed Frieda Kimble was wrong.

Steeling himself, he started up the stairs. He had taken only a couple of steps when he heard the sound of footsteps behind him. A man's familiar voice stopped him where he stood.

"You needn't go up there. Your sister is in no danger, and the boy is with his nanny." Justin stared down at Phillip Marlin, saw the pistol pointed at his chest.

"I don't remember inviting you to the party," Justin said dryly as Marlin motioned him back down the stairs.

"We've matters to discuss." Marlin's lips curled. "I think the study would be best."

Returning to the bottom of the stairs, Justin crossed the entry and started down the hall in that direction, the barrel of Marlin's pistol pressing hard against his ribs. The study was on the ground floor of the west wing. He could see flames up ahead, hear the shouts of the servants working frantically outside, emptying buckets of water onto the fire in an effort to save the house.

Phillip motioned to the door of the study. Justin opened it and stepped inside. The fire was just beginning to burn in here. The curtains had just caught flame, and a tiny portion of the rug curled with red-orange tendrils. He could already feel the heat, coughed against the smoke that crept along the walls toward the ceiling.

Marlin smiled thinly. "You can't imagine how much I've been looking forward to this."

Justin's jaw hardened. "Oh, I think I can. Your henchmen failed to kill me. If you want something done right, do it yourself—isn't that about it?"

"Just about." Phillip cocked the hammer on the pistol. "Such a sad tale. The Earl of Greville killed in the terrible fire that destroyed his home while trying to save his poor helpless nephew. Ironically, the child was already safe."

Justin surveyed the gun, a silver-etched dueling pistol, one of a pair he had seen on the mantel in one of the drawing rooms. One shot. If he could just get a little bit

closer he'd have a chance at blocking it. He eased forward.
Phillip didn't seem to notice, so he quietly moved again.
Muscles tensed, he readied himself to leap forward.

Then the door to the study swung open and his sister
walked in.

Justin clamped down on the coiled muscles straining for
release. Barbara smiled at Marlin and his stomach curdled
with nausea.

"Welcome, brother dear. Since you weren't accommodating enough to die upstairs in your room, we've been
waiting for you."

He sadly shook his head. "Damn, but I hoped you
weren't involved."

Barbara gave him her most vicious smile, which was
heavily laced with triumph. "How could I not be? You tried
to steal what should have been mine. I had to do something."

"And the house? I thought this place meant so much to
you."

"With you out of the way, there'll be money enough to
build a dozen Greville Halls." She tossed a glance at Phillip. "I believe we've waited long enough. Enjoy yourself,
darling."

Phillip's smug smile and his unflinching hold on the
pistol sent a chill down Justin's spine. The flames crackled
and popped. Something heavy crashed against the floor
above their heads. Phillip's finger tightened on the trigger
and Justin lunged.

The gun went off the same instant he crashed into Marlin's body, the shot echoing loudly in the confining space
of the room, both men landing in a heap on the floor. Justin
felt a burning pain in his side, and his head cracked hard
against the corner of the desk. He fought the spinning in
his brain, the dark circles closing in. Then the world began
to fade and blackness descended, dragging him into uncon-
sciousness.

* * *

Swearing softly, Phillip extricated himself from beneath the heavy weight of Justin's body and climbed to his feet, brushing off his clothes. Holding a white lace handkerchief delicately over his nose, he coughed against the smoke beginning to grow thick in the room.

"It's done. The Greville fortune is now your son's— yours and mine to control once we are married." Phillip reached for her, but Barbara stepped away.

For the first time he noticed the small ivory-handled pocket pistol concealed in the folds of her skirt. She raised the weapon, pointed it at the middle of his chest.

"What the hell are you doing?"

"Men are such fools. And you, Phillip, are an even bigger one than I thought. Did you actually believe I would marry you?" She laughed, bitterly. "Did you seriously imagine I enjoyed the things I let you do to me? I have no intention of marrying you or any other man—not now or ever."

Phillip looked stunned. "You can't possibly mean what you're saying."

"Can't I? You're just like my father and every other man I've ever met, playing the fool for the favors of a woman, always thinking only of themselves."

Phillip's face turned an angry shade of red. "Why, you lying, deceitful bitch—" He took a step toward her, but Barbara's hand tightened around the handle of the gun, stopping him where he stood.

"I *am* grateful to Father for one thing. Watching him with his whores, I learned how a woman could use her body to get what she wants. Thank you, Phillip, for making all of this so easy—" Phillip snarled and leaped forward, and Barbara pulled the trigger. For a moment he just stood there, his eyes wide with horror and disbelief. Then they rolled back in their sockets and he crumpled to the floor, mouth open, staring sightlessly into space.

Barbara glanced around her, saw tongues of flame burning through the ceiling above her head, stepped out of the way as a section of plaster and burning wood crashed down on the carpet just a few feet from where she stood. Smoke and flames billowed into the room.

Coughing, ducking below the thickening smoke, she took a last look at the two men lying on the floor and smiled. Then she turned and walked away.

Passing in and out of consciousness, Justin groaned at the sound of the slamming door. His head thundered. Blood oozed from the gash on his leg. His side throbbed and burned like the sting of a thousand hornets. Dragging in a breath of smoky air, he coughed against the burning in his lungs and rolled to his knees. Gingerly he touched the bullet wound in his side and felt the stickiness of blood, but the lead ball had glanced off a rib and he didn't think any real damage had been done.

That was twice that his sister had failed to kill him.

Justin swore softly, foully. Clenching his jaw, he shoved to his feet and moved unsteadily toward the door. Barbara wanted him dead. He vowed she had just made her last attempt.

The flames climbed higher into the black night sky. Terrified for Justin, unable to find Thomas, Ariel spotted Barbara hurrying out the front door of the mansion and started running toward her. She grabbed her sister-in-law's arm and whirled her around.

"Where is Justin? Did you see him? He went into the house to find you and Thomas and never came out."

"Thomas is with his nanny."

"No, he isn't. Mrs. Whitelawn is frantic. They got separated in all of the chaos and no one has seen the child since."

Barbara's face paled to the color of ashes. "Dear God, Thomas must still be in the house. We have to find him. God in heaven, we have to save him!" Turning, she started running back the way she had come, Ariel racing along beside her. Barbara jerked open the door and they rushed into the entry. The smoke was so thick it was nearly impossible to breathe. Fire roared out of the west wing. It wouldn't be long before the entire house was engulfed in flames.

"Thomas!" Barbara shouted. "Thomas, where are you?"

"Justin!" Ariel ran toward the stairs. "Justin, can you hear me!"

The women flew up the sweeping staircase, turned down the hall toward the west wing, but a wall of flames and blistering heat blocked their way.

"The servants' stairs!" Ariel whirled in that direction and both of them began to run. "Justin!" she shouted. "Thomas, can you hear me?" But the only reply was the roar of the raging flames and the explosion of shattering glass.

"Come on! We have to hurry!" Barbara reached the back stairs first, Ariel right behind her. Saying a silent prayer for courage, Ariel followed her up the smoky passage. They had almost reached the third floor when it happened. Ariel heard a thunderous crack followed by the loud, grinding sound of breaking wood. On the stairs ahead of her, Barbara screamed. Ariel gaped in horror as a portion of the stairway in front of her dropped away, collapsing beneath a wall of flaming debris, crashing three stories onto the floor below.

A cry lodged in Ariel's throat as more heavy timbers plunged to earth, landing on the body sprawled below. *Dear God. Dear God.* There was no way that Barbara still lived. And any moment the rest of the stairway would cave in.

Fighting to control her trembling legs and the wild, erratic clattering of her heart, Ariel backed carefully down the stairs, step by step until she reached the second floor. Smoke billowed up from the floor below and she coughed, desperate to suck in a breath of clean air.

Pulse thundering, she glanced upward. Barbara was dead, but what about her son? If Thomas was still upstairs, there was no way for her to reach him. *Dear Lord, please, help me find the boy!* But her prayer seemed nearly hopeless. *And dear God, where is Justin?* Was he trapped upstairs as well? Ariel's heart clenched at the thought, though she staunchly refused to believe it. Perhaps he had found the child and both of them were safe outside the house.

Praying it was true, she started down the second-floor hallway toward the entry. Since the fire had yet to reach the central portion of the house, it seemed the safest route. Blotting out a lingering image of Barbara's lifeless body pinned beneath the stack of heavy, burning timbers, Ariel raced toward the stairs. She had almost reached them when she heard the sound of crying—soft muffled sobs laced with choking fear.

Dear Lord, someone was still in the house! Coughing, ignoring the choking smoke that seared her lungs and the stinging in her eyes, Ariel started back the way she had come. "Thomas, is that you?" she cried. "Where are you! Please, you have to let me know where you are!" She tried one door, opened it to a barrage of flame, and quickly slammed it closed. Another door was so hot she couldn't turn the knob. "Please, whoever you are, we have to get out of the house!"

Behind her, the door to a linen closet rattled. Ariel whirled toward the sound, saw it slowly open. A child's tear-streaked face, black with soot, poked through the crack in the door.

"Thomas!"

The boy crawled toward her, his body shaking with terror. He stumbled to his feet, reached out, and wrapped his small arms around her, clinging like a small wounded animal.

"I'm . . . scared, Aunt Ariel. I'm so scared." He started coughing, the spasms wracking his small body, making his voice sound hoarse.

"It's all right, Thomas." Ariel started coughing, too. "We're getting . . . out of here." She slid her fingers through the boy's dark hair, gave him a quick, reassuring hug, then gripped his hand, and they started forward.

The smoke was thicker now, making it even harder to breathe. She was covered with soot from head to foot and rapidly growing dizzy. Bending low, trying to avoid the choking smoke, they made it to the sweeping staircase just in time to see Justin staggering out of the hall leading from the west wing.

"Justin!" she shouted, her voice no more than a high-pitched croak.

"Ariel! God in heaven!"

Tugging Thomas along beside her, she made it to the bottom of the sweeping marble stairs, tried to suck in a breath, then pitched forward. The last thing she remembered was Thomas's small voice worriedly shouting her name.

Eyes watering, blood soaking his shirt and breeches, Justin staggered toward where Ariel lay in a crumpled heap at the bottom of the stairs. Thomas raced toward him.

"It's Aunt Ariel! She's hurt!" he cried, making the knot in Justin's stomach tighten into a knot of terror.

Was she injured? Badly burned? Was she even still alive? His mouth dry with fear, he knelt beside her. When he heard her raspy breathing, he knew that she yet lived. Wincing at the pain that shot into his side, he lifted her up in his arms and cradled her against his chest, praying that she was all right. Together, they staggered for the door.

He and Thomas shoved it open, bursting out into the night and the cold, cleansing air.

Justin dragged in a lungful, coughed out smoke, and breathed the fresh air in once more. As he knelt again, his heart hammering with fear, he carefully lowered Ariel onto the grass a safe distance from the house.

A woman ran toward them. "Thomas!" Sobbing with relief at the sight of her young charge, the boy's nanny rushed up and swept the child into her arms. "Oh, thank God."

"He's frightened, but other than that, he's all right."

She nodded, stroking the boy's dark head. Then she saw Ariel's limp form lying on the grass, and her plump face drained of color.

"Is she . . . Is her ladyship . . . ?"

His jaw clenched. "She's still breathing. Tell one of the footmen to go for the doctor. Tell him to hurry!" With hands that shook, he continued checking for burns as Mrs. Whitelawn raced off with her precious burden, heading for the stable, where the rest of the servants had gathered.

Justin's side throbbed and his leg ached, but he barely felt it. His worry for Ariel overrode any feeling of pain. He found no sign of injury and yet she did not awaken. He shook her gently, spoke to her softly time and again.

"Ariel . . . my love, please. . . ." A thick lump formed in his throat. Perhaps she was injured inside. Perhaps even now she lingered on the brink of death. "Ariel, please wake up. I need you," he whispered. "Please don't leave me." He took hold of her icy hand, cradling the soft slim fingers, pressing his mouth against them. "I love you. I love you so much."

He sat with his head bowed, his eyes stinging, silently praying, wishing he had told her how he felt long before this.

"Justin . . . ?" Her voice floated toward him, deeper than usual, tinged with the rough edge of smoke. When he opened his eyes, he saw her reaching toward him. Gently she laid a hand on his cheek. "I was so frightened . . . so afraid you'd been killed."

"Are you injured? Where are you hurt?"

She shook her head. "I'm all right. It was the smoke. . . . I just got so dizzy. . . ."

Relief washed over him. She was safe and well and she was his. He bent over her, pressed a soft kiss on her lips, gently kissed the side of her neck. "I love you, Ariel," he said. "I love you so much."

He felt her tremble. A tear slipped down her cheek. "I heard you before. I was afraid to believe it. I was afraid you didn't really mean it."

He ran a finger along her jaw. "I mean it. I've never meant anything more. I love you. I have for a very long time."

"Oh, Justin. I love you so much. I never stopped loving

you. I tried to, but I couldn't. I know I never will."

A shudder rippled through him, ran the length of his long frame. Joy and relief all mingled together. Wonder that a man like him should be so fortunate.

Wordlessly he helped her stand, and she swayed a little on her feet. Justin's arms went protectively around her. "All right?"

She framed his face between her hands. "I'm all right. As long as I know you love me, everything is more than all right."

Justin bent his head and kissed her. Bloody and hurting, with Ariel in his arms, he knew she was right. Nothing else mattered. Everything was perfect.

CHAPTER TWENTY-SIX

Something wet and cold pelted his face and neck, began to run down the inside of his collar. With a glance toward the heavens, Justin realized it was raining.

"Thank God," Ariel whispered, tilting her head back, letting the saving rain fall over her soot-smudged face. They stood there for a moment, letting it refresh their weary spirits, saying a silent prayer. Then Ariel glanced back toward the house and her expression subtly shifted, seemed to darken with pain. He caught the sheen of tears in her eyes.

"What is it?" he asked softly, turning her chin with his hand.

"It's Barbara. Your sister thought Thomas was with his nanny, but he wasn't. You hadn't come out of the house. We went back inside to find the two of you. The fire was blocking the third-floor hall, so we tried to get round it by going up the servants' stairs. We were almost to the top . . ." Her voice cracked on the last and the tears in her eyes began to roll down her cheeks. "We were almost there when the top of the stairs fell in. Barbara was ahead of me. She fell nearly three stories and some of the ceiling beams caved in on top of her. Oh, God, Justin, I'm so sorry."

He held her close, cradling her head against his shoulder, gently stroking her hair. "It's all right, love. Sometimes things happen for the best. They say vengeance belongs to God. Perhaps that is the way He chose to extract punishment for her sins."

"I don't . . . understand."

Instead of answering, he urged her across the grass toward the stable, out of the cold and the driving rain. For the first time she saw the bloodstains soaking his shirt.

"Oh, my God, you're hurt!"

He stopped beneath the overhanging eaves of the stonewalled stable. "Phillip Marlin and my sister started the fire. They were the ones who tried to kill me."

"Oh, Justin, no." Her fingers closed over his hand. "How badly are you injured?"

"Fortunately, Marlin is not the best shot. The ball glanced off a rib. Hurts like the bloody devil, but it isn't all that serious. Phillip's dead. Barbara killed him."

"But if they were working together, why would she do that?"

"Greed, more than anything, I suppose." He told her all he could remember from the muddled conversation he had heard while he had been drifting in and out of consciousness. It was enough to know the terrible part his sister had played in the tragedy that had nearly cost them their lives.

Ariel stared up at him. "We mustn't tell Thomas. Not ever."

"No. He'll never have to know the truth."

"In time, the pain will fade. And we'll be there to help him."

Justin bent his head and kissed her, thinking how much he loved her, glad he had finally been able to tell her. They continued on into the stable, where Silvie and Perkins draped warm woolen blankets around them.

"It appears God has decided to look kindly upon us, my lord," the aging butler said. "The rain is putting out the fire. Most of the house will be saved."

"Yes. Perhaps in a couple of hours, if the rain continues, we'll feel safe enough to take shelter in the east wing. It'll be smoky, but at least there are beds there and we can get warm and dry."

Perkins glanced around. "Where is Lady Haywood, my lord?"

Justin simply shook his head.

"Oh, dear Lord." The old man scurried off to tell the others the terrible news, while Silvie arrived with strips of cloth torn into makeshift bandages. They sat down in a pile of straw and Ariel cleansed Justin's wounds with water someone brought from the stream. She bound his injured leg and tied a crude bandage around his ribs.

Alone at last in one of the empty stalls, their clothes wet and torn and black with dirt and soot, they leaned back wearily against the rough stone wall.

Justin reached for her hand, brought it to his lips. He looked into his wife's exhausted, dirt-smudged face and thought how much he loved her. "I was terrified when I saw you lying at the bottom of the stairs. If anything had happened to you . . ."

"Justin . . ."

He reached out and touched her cheek, gently brushed a finger over her lips. "I didn't think I could ever love anyone. I didn't think I knew how. The day we went to my grandmother's . . . that was the day I knew—the day I realized that I loved you, that I had for a very long time."

Fresh tears appeared in her eyes. "I love you so much."

He pulled her close, happiness and gratitude pouring through him. She loved him, as he had prayed she would. They clung to each other, there in the straw on the floor of the stable, listening to the pouring rain, watching the orange flames sputter and slowly die, turning to wispy columns of smoke that rose up from the rubble of the west wing.

"We'll rebuild," he said. "We'll make this our home, the place we raise our children."

Ariel gave him the soft, warm smile he had missed for so long. "I'd like that."

Bending his head, he kissed her again. "I love you, Lady Greville." The words came more easily this time, felt so right, so good. "I love you."

His days of isolation were over. He had a family now: the grandmother who had raised him and never forgotten him, a child who needed him, and a wife who loved him. The heart he hadn't known he had seemed to swell inside his chest.

Wet, dirty, and cold, a third of his house a pile of smoking ruins, for the first time in his life, Justin understood what it meant to be truly complete.

AUTHOR'S NOTE

Hope you enjoyed Justin and Ariel's story, which was loads of fun to write. So much so that during the course of the novel, I discovered I wasn't ready to leave the two characters behind. Their tale didn't seem quite finished until I had told Clayton and Kassandra's story. I hope you'll watch for *Reckless*, and that you enjoy it as well. Till then, happy reading and all best wishes,

Kat